F^S_E_X_Yootball

Sexy Football

PETER GILMOUR

ROBSON BOOKS

This paperback edition published in Great Britain in 2004 by Robson Books, The Chrysalis Building, Bramley Road, London W10 6SP

An imprint of Chrysalis Books Group

Copyright © 2004 Peter Gilmour

The right of Peter Gilmour to be identified as the author of this work has been asserted by him in accordance with the Copyright, Designs and Patents Act 1988.

The author has made very reasonable effort to contact all copyright holders. Any errors that may have occurred are inadvertent and anyone who for any reason has not been contacted is invited to write to the publishers so that a full acknowledgement may be made in subsequent editons of this work.

This is a work of fiction. All characters and events are the product of the author's imagination and any resemblance to actual events, locales or persons, living or dead, is entirely coincidental.

British Library Cataloguing in Publication Data
A catalogue record for this title is available from the British Library

ISBN 1 86105 794 6

All rights reserved. No part of this publication may be reproduced, stored in a retrieval system, or transmitted in any form or by any means electronic, mechanical, photocopying, recording or otherwise, without the prior permission in writing of the publishers.

Original design by Mark Finning
Printed by Creative Print and Design (Wales), Ebbw Vale

For Lesley, Shelley and Josh.

We are all poor men struggling to be free.

PART ONE

Trial

1
Blue Dream Babe

The Technicolor cinema of Ralph Goldstein's imagination had been screening hard-core erotica ever since that fateful moment when the balls dropped in his trousers and the sap started rising in his blood. Until that bright and sunny day, football had been the main feature of the movies in his mind, usually starring himself as the scorer of brilliant goals in FA Cup Finals.

Now though, driven by a self-indulgence that knew no boundaries, Ralph found he was able to conjure up horny, rip-roaring double bills that sent shivers down his spine.

He made no excuses. After all, imagination was all that separated us from the animals and football was the best game ever invented. Everyone knew that. As for sex, well, delicious, gratifying, pleasurable, dirty, wicked, immoral – you feel guilty if you want to but who doesn't like it more than anything else?

This particular vision didn't half make his nipples hard. Glorious and delightful yet sleazy and depraved, it almost knocked his fucking socks off.

Somehow Ralph finds himself languishing naked in a luxurious armchair pleasuring Kylie Minogue with his amazing sexual technique. How it came about is a complete mystery but Ralph isn't complaining. Employing his expert knowledge of foreplay gleaned from a Mongolian sex guru in East Penge, he tickles her erogenous zones with enormous feathers as she wriggles and giggles and writhes and moans on the floor at his feet. What a babe! But has he overdone it? The poor girl is soaring to such frightening heights of almost unbearable ecstasy that she's practically weeping with joy. She shivers gently into orgasm three or four times. But who's counting? The part of Ralph's brain that might have made such a calculation is concentrating on a wall-sized television broadcasting live football. It is extra time and the score is one all. Will there be a goal or will it go to penalties? Nails are being bitten, teeth gnashed and prayers offered up.

The outcome of this game is of paramount importance to Ralph and thousands of other blue-blooded fans but Kylie, having abandoned herself so completely to the pulsating emotion surging in her loins, is oblivious to the momentous events simultaneously unfolding many miles away on some foreign field. Suddenly she bursts into song.

'I should be so lucky, lucky, lucky, lucky' and begins caressing her own body, running her hands over warm breasts, erect nipples, taught thighs and freshly shaved mound of Venus. She parts her legs a little wider to heighten the stimulation.

Aah! She's moist and ready. Feverishly craving that inner fulfilment for which there is no substitute. But to achieve it she needs Ralph's own aroused body.

'Now, please, now,' she begs.

His eyes are fixed on the screen.

'Wait.'

'Can't.'

'Not yet.'

'Please.'

'No.'

But the diva from down under can't take no for an answer. She stands and approaches him with salacious intent, impatiently sliding away her flimsy, perfumed thong as she prepares to mount. He watches her tug the delicate string of fabric from the crack in her arse.

Ralph braces, unable to resist but still with an eye on the game. She grips his member with trembling fingers and manoeuvres her own throbbing organ towards it until a sharp intake of breath confirms a successful coupling.

Now she is astride him with her knees pushing down on the arms of the chair for leverage. He grabs her firm young buttocks to guide her movements and feels her clenched muscles thrusting gently in his hands. Not so fast young lady. Nice and easy does it.

But she can't help herself. She's riding him like a horse. Straining every sinew to enhance the physical sensation growing inside until sweat oozes from every pore and her face is flushed with delight.

'Never knew it could be this good,' she utters breathlessly as her body is engulfed by wave after wave of pleasure.

The referee awards a free kick just outside the penalty area. Tension is mounting inside the stadium. A tidal wave is building inside Kylie.

It is direct.

A wild expression crosses her face as now she desperately tries to delay the ultimate, thrilling flood of joy. Slow down girl. The longer she can hold it back the better it will be. She stops moving altogether and clings tightly to Ralph, the two now locked together in silent congress.

The ball is placed, the wall in position, a player prepares to take the kick. All is perfectly still. Bodies tense with anticipation. Past the point of no return. Waiting for the explosion that neither can now do anything to prevent.

That's it! Ralph spurts long and hard causing Kylie to emit a deep moan of satisfaction as she gushes into the most earth-moving orgasm she has ever experienced. Yes!

At that very same moment Gianfranco Zola curls a thirty yard free-kick out of the reach of the Bayern Munich goalie into the top corner of the goal to win the European Cup for Chelsea.

Yes! Oh yes, yes!

And then Ralph wakes up.

2
Coining a Phrase

Nobody's perfect. It's the human condition. But as we lurch around awkwardly in our imperfection, every now and again an outstanding personality produces a sparkling concept that enhances our perception and lifts our spirit.

Ruud Gullit said it and we all heard him. 'What we need is some sexy football.'

But what on earth did he mean? Centre forwards in suspenders? High jinks in the showers? Orgies on the pitch? Ralph Goldstein didn't think so. This was his language and he knew exactly what Ruud meant.

Swilling the remnants of rice and king prawn tikka massala from his teeth with a few hefty gulps of chilled lager, Ralph switched on the telly for the build-up to the opening game of Euro '96. He was expecting the usual, boring experts to utter the usual, boring statements that most football fans could quite easily work out for themselves but as the set spluttered into life, the exotic, dreadlocked features that came into focus didn't belong to any of the regular team. No, much to his great rapture he had tuned in just in time to hear Ruud Gullit coining the immortal phrase that has since become officially accepted in the lexicon of modern soccer parlance. A great moment indeed. Ralph was enthralled and wondered how the tinny speaker of his weary old TV could emit such a lofty aspiration without bursting into flames. His heart leapt as the former Dutch International, one of the finest players ever to dribble a ball across a field, went on to explain his visionary theme to the puzzled football fans of Great Britain who had previously been deprived of such inventive concepts.

In doing so, he touched a raw nerve which, over the years, had caused pain and anguish to The Football Association of England and all English football supporters. The simple fact was that Gullit together with his Dutch compatriots and Italian friends had long ago discovered how to play football better than the English. Superior ball skills and high levels of fitness combined with an innovative approach to tactics had produced a perceptive standard of play that the game's Anglo inventors now struggled to match let alone surpass. Indeed, even coping with such sophisticated continental expertise was fast becoming just a forlorn dream.

Did it matter? Not to a starving child in Africa, but we could only hope to liberate others if we were liberated ourselves.

When Gullit coined the phrase 'Sexy Football' he gave Ralph and all true football fans a certain degree of hope. Maybe there was a vision afoot in the upper reaches of the game that might help us to be liberated. After all, we were all looking for a route to our souls weren't we? Something that touched us inside and offered a clue to the purpose of existence. Yes, football was a microcosm of life that could help us unravel some of its more puzzling dilemmas.

Listening to Ruud waxing lyrical, Ralph's mind drifted back and he found himself re-living some of the major experiences of his life. Visions of sparkling enjoyment, mind-numbing revelation, cringing embarrassment, desperate disappointment and quite a fair dollop of woeful depravity all came back to him through the years each evoking the intense emotions of the time.

His nostrils filled with the aroma of dubbin, the whiff of female body odour and the stench of urinals at football grounds. He felt the chapped thighs of his boyhood, the crunch of autumn leaves underfoot on a frosty morning and the thud of a sodden, leather football against his forehead. He sensed his first taste of girls and heard gentle gasps of virginal sensitivity as the guilty flush of puberty raced back through his veins.

He remembered how he was supposedly taught the game of football and how it was supposedly taught now. Supposedly was the operative word. Of course, nobody taught you about sex. In those dark days long ago it was never even mentioned. You had to work it out for yourself. And as Ralph's consciousness flooded with vivid memories he realised how his own love of football had developed along a parallel stream to his sexual education. In both cases the process had been one of trial and error as there had been precious little guidance or advice available. Then it occurred to him with startling clarity that this simple yet wonderful phrase 'Sexy Football' almost entirely summed up his principle ambition. Ralph had long felt that football could be a beautiful, fulfilling, artistic expression of love if we went about it in a positive manner. And by the way, if it was possible to play football in that way, why not live like that too?

Who was Ralph Goldstein? Just an ordinary sort of bloke. Albeit, after fifty odd years of being buffeted about on the stormy waters of life with little respite in calmer lagoons, perhaps more sensitive than most.

3
The Adelphi

They used to meet at the Adelphi coffee bar in the High Street.

Usually it was Ralph, Chalky White, Darryl Bingham and Wilkie Wilkes.

Cheesy Chiesman would sometimes be there if he could make it although being that bit older than the others he often had more important things to do.

They were completely different characters but the grist that bound them together was football which was almost always the main subject. And girls of course.

They had all left school at an early age without a qualification between them and got themselves jobs which was a much easier prospect then than it would be today. With a few quid in their pockets and no homework to do, they felt as free as larks.

None of them had a single care in the world except for the thorny dilemma of sex which occupied their thoughts and minds during every waking moment and, in Ralph's case at least, when he was asleep too.

Wilkie worked in the same plastics factory as his Dad. Cheesy was an apprenticed accountant, Darryl was an assistant in a menswear shop in Croydon and Chalky worked in a bank. Silly cunt.

Ralph's Dad had managed to get him a job with one of his friends who owned a fancy gift shop in the West End where he quickly learned that there was a huge market for rubbish. Ornate letter racks, leatherette book covers, Eiffel Tower bookends, fluffy tea cosies. The sort of thing that no one really wanted and only bought in order to give to some other poor sod on a special anniversary.

To get to work, he had to commute to London and back from Surrey every day. What a fucking slog that was. It involved catching the seven thirty train, when he didn't miss it, and the bastard was always overflowing with passengers by the time it pulled in even though the terminal from where it started was only two stations down the line. Getting a seat was almost impossible. It was a stopping train so even more people crammed in at every station on the way. By the time it arrived at Victoria about forty minutes later they were all practically bursting out of the doors and windows. Ralph couldn't help noticing how glum everyone looked as, squeezed up tight, day after day, they tried to read their newspapers in the restricted space available. Some had developed a method of folding their unwieldy periodicals in such a way that they could turn the pages over without actually extending the paper out to its full width. During Ralph's period of commuting he never managed to master this particular craft and always arrived in London with a crumpled mass of papier-mâché that wasn't even fit to wrap fish and chips in.

But Victoria was not the end of the journey. He then had to get the tube which meant dodging his way off the crowded platform, into the tube station, down the escalator and onto the underground train which was also bulging to the limit with miserable commuters. Sometimes he was pressed up so close to complete strangers that they were practically fornicating.

After just a few stops it was out again and after another jostling match with the crowd on the platform he would barge his way up the escalator and out through the exit. Fresh air at last! Well, not that fresh. Then it was a brisk ten minutes walk, or run if he was late, (he was usually late) to the place where he worked just off Baker Street. By the time he arrived he was absolutely knackered and that was before he'd even done a single stroke of work. There was no way he was going to keep this up for long. Not if he was to stay in contention for the Olympic wanking title.

Why the fuck did people do this? Ralph always asked. And he promised to liberate himself from the insane drudgery of it all as soon as possible.

Every morning, the highlight of Ralph's exhausting journey was during that final walk when he passed by the end of Bryanston

Mews, the most notorious address in London at the time. It was 1963 and the Profumo scandal was on.

Profumo was the cabinet minister who was forced to resign after lying to parliament about his affair with the call girl Christine Keeler who also happened to be porking a Russian spy at the same time. Silly girl. According to the press, Christine lived with another prostitute called Mandy Rice-Davies in a house in Bryanston Mews where the whole episode was played out. Women of easy virtue they were referred to in the papers. How Ralph loved that phrase. Naturally, call-girls were of the most immense interest to him as an inexperienced young male. Almost as much as football in fact although beer had also begun to establish a strong foothold on the upper reaches of his growing mountain of active vices.

Each time he passed the end of that mews, Ralph couldn't help but cast a prurient, furtive glance at the perfectly ordinary terrace of neat little houses and try to guess in which one the seedy, sexy story all took place. Maybe it was taking place right now! How he hoped for a glimpse of those two horny sirens. But what on earth would he do if one actually appeared? Would she invite him in for a quick one? Just thinking about it would usually give him a hard on. Of course, in those days Ralph didn't even know what a quick one was but the experience did at least teach him how to walk around in public with a full erection without it being too noticeable. After a while, he was a master at it.

In the evenings, after the gruelling journey home, he would grab a quick bite and then make for the Adelphi. Usually he was the last to arrive because of the distance he had to travel to work but, once there, he would chat endlessly with his mates over cups of 'froffy coffee' which was the trendy drink of the time just as designer lager might be today.

'Froffee coffee' was made from brown powder and hot water with a pile of milk suds heaped on top that tended to spill over and dribble down the side of the glass cup it was served in. Ralph loved it. It was supposed to be authentic Italian coffee but it was about as authentic as spaghetti bolognese out of a tin.

He loved that too.

They drank the coffee through the 'froff' and then poured copious amounts of sugar into the suds that were left at the bottom of the cup, mixed it all up together and spooned the resultant sloppy mixture into their mouths.

Coffee bars were the places to be then and froffee coffee was the thing to drink and glass cups were the thing to drink it out of. It was the modern way and Ralph felt that he and his mates were fashionable, cosmopolitan and living life to the full.

Furthermore, he was convinced that the beautiful folk of Europe were doing exactly the same thing in the glittering eateries of downtown Paris and Rome although it was to be some years before he would actually tuck into a plate of spaghetti at a pavement café on the Via Veneto himself. Perverse as it may seem, as Roman glitterati milled around the table and pasta sauce dripped down his chin, he found himself reminiscing about the Adelphi.

Even in those early days Ralph was the odd one out and, not for last time, it wasn't long before he became disillusioned.

If there was one thing he had in common not only with the boys around the table but probably every other teenage lad in the entire world it was the avid determination to find out exactly what kind of seamy pleasures girls were hiding in their knickers. Sex was his absolute top, number one, most urgent, pressing and important priority even though, like all the others, he had no idea what it was like because he'd never physically done it. Only mentally. But while his mates kept a constant lookout for compliant female bodies in order to get their ends away, Ralph sought companionship and love, an attitude considered most curious by the others. Sensitive bastard.

They could never seem to agree about football either. Ralph preferred the Italian and South American way of playing with a slower build up and more skill. But, apart from Cheesy who was not always there to back him up, the others could only relate to the kick and rush approach. The route one – get it down the wings and cross it in – all charge into the penalty box and try to force it into the goal type of tactic. As far as they were concerned, foreigners didn't know how to play the game properly. Only we did. Even at this relatively early age, Ralph began to realise that this very basic, rudimentary and simple approach to football was a result of the xenophobic attitudes passed down through generations and now deeply entrenched in society. It also had a marked similarity with the kind of tactics his mates applied in their pursuit of girls. Certainly it highlighted the fundamental nature of the differences between them.

They'd all be in the Shed at Stamford Bridge with a soggy meat pie in one hand and a cup of luke-warm Bovril in the other shouting their heads off in support of their beloved Chelsea.

'Get it in the fucking box!' Chalky would yell at the top of his squeaky voice.

'Square ball,' Ralph.

'Kick it up the fucking field!' Wilkie.

'Lay it back,' Ralph.

'Shift your arse!' Darryl.

'Play it easy,' Ralph.

'Fucking get on with it.' Chalky.

'Take your time,' Ralph.

'We need to get stuck in to 'em,' someone would say. 'Never mind all this continental, arty-farty bollocks.'

'No we fucking don't,' Ralph would reply. 'We want elegant, beautiful, skilful football. Anyway, it's not continental.'

'What the fuck is it then?'

'Common fucking sense you berk.'

It used to drive him mad. Uncouth louts. Wouldn't they ever learn? At one match Ralph was so incensed by their attitudes that he decided if he couldn't get through to them he'd have to write it all down. That's it. He'd write a book about it. How to play beautiful football and how to teach it to kids so at least the next crop of players would benefit from his superior knowledge of the game. Maybe they'd all listen to him when the book was published. But what should he call it? How to play beautiful football? A better way to play football? The beautiful way to play football?

The beautiful way? The beautiful game? That's it. The beautiful game. Says it all. By the end of the first half he'd written the first chapter and designed the cover.

'Coming to the pub?' Darryl asked Ralph after the match as they squeezed their way out of the ground towards Fulham Broadway tube station.

'No thanks.'

He knew it wasn't the answer they'd be expecting. He was usually first up to the bar.

'What you up to then?' inquired Chalky.

'Going home to write a book.'

'What?'

'I'm going home to write a fucking book, all right?'

No one argued. They knew it wasn't worth talking to him in this sort of mood.

THE BEAUTIFUL GAME

Options

Football is a game of options but before you can begin to explore all the possibilities you must have possession of the ball. This may seem like a pretty obvious statement but I assure you it isn't and we will deal with it a bit more fully later on. Let's assume for the moment that we have got the ball.

The first thing to recognise is that you are not alone. Football is a team game. You've got ten of your mates around you and the main object is to co-operate and achieve something together.

It can't be said often enough, if you've got the ball you're in control of the game. And, of course, if you're in control of the game you can start creating the options that will help you to win it.

Be patient, be smart. Hoofing the ball into your opponents' box and hoping someone will force it into the net is a mug's game.

Let's be creative. Let's try and be sure of what we are doing.

Remember, the possibilities created by people working together are far greater than the sum of possibilities created by those same people working independently. And that's in life, by the way, not just football.

4
Bohemian Sojourns

Looking back, Ralph viewed his life as a constant dilemma during which he had entered various rooms looking for something but didn't know what. He would know when he found it. In his fervent search he had emptied every drawer and cupboard, flinging the contents out onto the floor and leaving a huge mess behind him. But having failed to find what he wanted he moved on to another room and repeated his actions leaving more chaos in his wake. And so it went on.

Over the years, a plethora of undemanding jobs had just about kept body and soul together but almost destroyed his faith in humanity in the process. The only way he had managed to maintain a level of sanity throughout it all was by merrily embarking with manic frequency on extensive sojourns to far-flung places around the globe.

However, although this had enabled him to visit many breathtaking places, meet scores of great people and learn much about the vagaries of human existence, it was a lifestyle that had filled him with an extreme world-weariness. So much so that he now had a problem with life's ordinary matters. He just couldn't be bothered with them.

Items that were generally considered important features of modern life such as mortgages, pensions, careers, cars, shopping, clothes and mobile phones meant little to him and he was simply astounded by the way they were afforded so much reverence by almost everyone else. Although these things seemed to dominate most discussions wherever he went they were a complete bloody waste of time as far as he was concerned. Minor tittle-tattle.

The fact that few seemed bothered by the weightier problems of pestilence and famine in Africa, genocide in the Balkans, global warming or the threat of nuclear war made him intensely hot under the collar. These were just peripheral items on the television news to most people. The boring stuff before shots of motorway pile-ups or celebrities attending award ceremonies or the weather forecast. Things that were happening somewhere else. They preferred to close their minds to it. Cut it off. It was much easier that way. Anything that held out the slightest chance of threatening their cosy existence was stringently avoided even if it meant bequeathing a legacy of desperation to their descendants, poor buggers, who would probably end up in some future age gasping for breath in a hostile wasteland.

Ralph was quite aware that he annoyed people with his dismissive attitude to subjects they considered of great consequence but he meant no disrespect. Well, not much. Anyway, most of them dismissed his ideas too. Usually with statements like 'That's all very well but it's not very practical is it?' Ralph hated this approach. After all, there were lives at stake here. Hardly a day would pass without him boiling with anger at some aspect of the world around him. A prejudiced editorial in a tabloid. A problem at the bank. Hanging on the phone for half an hour to query a bill and finally getting through to some teenage moron in a call-centre in Hartlepool who couldn't care less. Watching the queue he could have joined at the supermarket cash-out disappearing fast while the queue he had joined was held up by a faulty till. A traffic jam.

It was all such a waste of time. Hadn't anyone noticed that the world was hurtling madly towards destruction? Wasn't anyone prepared to be accountable for it? Didn't anyone give a stuff?

The way Ralph saw it, we were creating an environment that was hostile to ourselves. Impossible to live in. Stress, noise, pollution, violence and war had all contributed to a widespread unhappiness that was increasing by the second. The ozone layer had been damaged beyond repair, greenhouse gasses threatened to choke us all and rivers had turned into toxic treacle. We couldn't swim in the sea, go out in the sun or be sure that what we were eating was safe. Christ knows, we could hardly even breath the fucking air any more. Yet despite all this, no bugger seemed at all inclined to try and reverse the process and save the planet. Bad for business, Ralph supposed. The maniacs in charge certainly didn't give a toss. Smug in the knowledge they would all die rich, the gits seemed oblivious to the harm they were wreaking and unmoved by the prospect that their grandchildren would all have three heads, five legs and a life expectancy of eight. It was fucking barmy. Ralph was enraged. Some had road rage or telephone rage or queuing rage. Ralph had them all. He had life rage.

Sometimes he wished he could have presented a friendlier face to the world but the injustice and insanity of it all were constantly in the front of his mind.

How could he be happy and cheerful if children were starving to death in their mother's arms somewhere else on the globe?

He was sure it didn't have to be like this. In quiet moments he glimpsed other possibilities. A sweeter life. A different way to organise things. A better way. One that cut out the sadness and drudgery of modern living. He imagined a world of love and beauty in which all men were brothers. He wanted to live in it. And he was desperate to tell everyone about it. The problem was that few wanted to listen.

Ralph often felt like grabbing hold of people and shaking them out of their lethargy. 'Wake up fat arse! How the fuck can we carry on like this?' But most of them wouldn't admit there was a serious problem until the day they turned on the tap and a lump of shit fell out.

But here at last was something to savour. Was it even perhaps the key to our salvation? Yes, Sexy Football might save us all yet.

5
Willie's Whistle

When Ralph was a kid, the game at junior level was played in what could best be described as strip zones in which players ran up and down in their designated, ten-yard wide bands of the pitch as if somehow prevented from straying to either side by invisible fences. This was supposed to teach you about 'positional' play. Wingers patrolled the side strips, centre forwards lumbered about in the central strip running into the opponents' penalty area and inside forwards occupied the strips roughly in between the two. Very occasionally, in expressions of the most bold and revolutionary daring, certain players strayed slightly out of their unmarked boundaries. These were the creative masterminds. Centre-halves marked centre-forwards, half-backs marked inside forwards and full-backs marked wingers. That was it. Wing-backs, sweepers and zonal defence hadn't been invented. Neither was there yet such a manoeuvre as diagonal running off the ball which would have been regarded as a most bohemian activity. Quite clearly, all this reflected the way everyone was obliged to adhere to the regulations and pre-set ideas of a society that, in those days, was much more restrictive and didn't encourage the expression of individual creativity. Ralph hated it.

He remembered playing football once in a so-called sports class at school and crossing just over his pre-determined line in an effort to beat an opponent to the ball.

'You're out of position idiot!' screamed the young and obviously inexperienced sports master but Ralph took no notice. He was far too involved in the game.

Actually, sir, whose name was John Williams, was a recently graduated geography teacher who had probably been coerced into taking sports to get the job. Ralph certainly couldn't think of any other good reason for him conducting a football session.

In the young teacher's manic fervour to haul Ralph back onto the straight and narrow he bellowed instructions whilst trying to blow his whistle at the same time.

The dickhead always used to run about with his whistle in his mouth. Looking back, Ralph supposed it must have been a sort of nipple substitute. But he continued to ignore the instructions and after a short while the master was practically hysterical. Furiously blowing on the little instrument, he made his way over towards Ralph, took his ear between thumb and forefinger and dragged him painfully across the field.

'This is your area, dimwit,' he shouted as he described a radius of about twenty yards around where they were now standing. 'Don't move out of it,' he ordered. 'And in future, do as you're told or you'll never learn how to play this game properly.'

Carried out in front his sniggering peers, it was a humiliating experience that Ralph never forgot. Unfortunately though, it was only a few minutes before he repeated his transgression and, in an effort to intercept a pass, again strayed out of his designated patch. The master, now visibly incandescent with anger, started blowing his whistle even louder than before. But as he drew breath for another vocal onslaught in Ralph's direction he somehow managed to suck the pea out of the noisy bloody thing and the tiny vegetable flew straight through to the back of his mouth and lodged in his gullet. All of a sudden, Willie as the boys used to call him, collapsed to the ground, clutching his throat and croaking eerily like a sea lion with whooping cough. He was almost apoplectic. Christ, thought Ralph, sorry mate.

The game came to a halt, not because of the hapless state of the master but because the boys were practically peeing their pants with laughter. The silly prat cut such a pathetic figure that most of them thought he was just arsing around for their amusement. But, as they laughed, Willie was turning a rather gruesome shade of purple and it slowly it began to sink in that the situation was a bit more serious than they had thought. Quite naturally, they all gathered round and started furiously slapping the nitwit on his back thereby unwittingly placing him in double jeopardy.

If he didn't choke first he'd be battered to death by crazy teenagers.

The Heimlich manoeuvre wasn't known in those days. Not by them anyway.

Suddenly, sir choked and the pea shot out with surprising velocity hitting Steve (Chalky) White right in the eye and sending him down with a blood-curdling howl like a soldier being shot in a war film. It was turning into a farce. But eventually order was restored and although he seemed perfectly all right again, Willie instructed the whole contingent to do ten laps of the pitch while he went off to find nurse which didn't surprise anyone. He was always off to see nurse at the slightest excuse and they knew why. The filthy swine.

THE BEAUTIFUL GAME

The main barrier to success in any competitive sport is the fear of losing.

If we were able to remove this all-pervading phobia it would leave us free to express ourselves to the limits of our skill and ability and concentrate on the beauty of the sporting contest rather than being frightened to death about making a mistake.

Great players like Pelé, Maradona, Cruyff, Best, Gascoigne and Charlie Cooke all had such an unshakeable belief in their own abilities that they weren't afraid of anybody or anything. That was the single element that set them above others and it is the element we must now encourage amongst all our sports people if we are to be successful.

We must learn to play without fear.

And that's in life by the way, not just football.

6
Gina Lollobrigida and the Peeping Nipple

All the boys were in love with the school nurse, or Eleanor Partridge as she was called. A petite redhead with freckles and pert little breasts, she wore a starched, white, medical overall with buttons all the way down the front. How Ralph dreamed about unbuttoning that inviting garment and fondling whatever was underneath. Of course, being in her thirties, she represented a mysterious apparition of mature womanhood to those dirty-minded adolescents and, as such, was strictly untouchable. Nevertheless, it didn't prevent her being the subject of wild and very rude fantasies as far as Ralph was concerned. That was one thing they couldn't take away from you. She always left her top button open and he was sure she did so on purpose. Ralph and his classmates were about fifteen at the time and horny as rabbits. Whenever any of them happened to be in the vicinity of the fragrant nurse Eleanor they would gaze moronically at that aperture of promise below her neck in the forlorn hope of sighting just the slightest glimpse of brassiere that would send them half crazy with red-hot desire.

One day, Darryl Bingham, one of Ralph's classmates, returned from the surgery in a state of high excitement. He had sought treatment for a headache and waltzed into the surgery without bothering to knock to find Nurse Eleanor, so he said, sitting on sir's lap with one leg up on the desk and sir's hand up her skirt. Having been taken by surprise, sir suddenly tried to stand up and pretend nothing was going on. But in doing so Eleanor was pushed off and unceremoniously dumped on the floor with her legs up in the air and her knickers still half way down her thighs. Darryl insisted that he saw Eleanor's suspenders but Ralph for one didn't believe him at the time. That would have been just too much. In hindsight though, he wondered if Darryl hadn't been telling the truth. Naturally, the lads laughed themselves silly at all this, but although it was a great story, it wasn't a patch on what happened to Ralph.

He had gashed his leg quite badly playing football in a house match when he was ruthlessly tackled by 'Bully' Bullock.

Attacked would have been a better way of describing it in Ralph's opinion.

Bully was a huge individual for his age and almost twice Ralph's size. His pockmarked, ruddy face was always creased with an aggressive snarl as he stalked around looking for someone to terrorise. Needless to say, everyone avoided him like the plague. They could never tell when he might snap. One minute he was their friend and the next he'd have them pinned to the ground with a rusty penknife at their throat. Those he turned against would quite literally fear for their lives but there was nothing any of the boys could do about it because the teachers were just as frightened of the big bastard as they were. Everyone knew Bully was a raging psychopath who was likely to exact his own brand of physical revenge if they displeased him in even the slightest way so it wasn't worth upsetting him for any reason at all. On this occasion he had deliberately gone over the top with his lethal, jagged studs showing and tackled Ralph high up near the groin. The human skin scraped off in the process now hung in strands from underneath Bully's boots. It was Ralph's own fault really. He should have known better than to try and skip round the fat thug with the ball but he was just trying to be clever and now he was paying for it with quite a large hole in his leg. Sir came rushing over to have a look and, in a voice interspersed with little peeps from the whistle clenched in his jaw, dismissed the event as nothing much and judged the tackle as perfectly fair.

'You must be bloody joking.' Ralph croaked.

The master proceeded to issue a stern reprimand to Ralph for his language when he really should have been hauling Bully over the coals for attempted murder but he was obviously as scared of the daft lunatic as everyone else.

The last person who had been foolhardy enough to take Bully to task was Jim Smith, the English master and how could anyone forget it. He was still having treatment for the psychological damage caused as a result.

It was during a cricket net he had been supervising the previous summer during which a promising young bowler almost two years Bully's junior had had the temerity to bowl Bully clean out. Very unwise if you asked Ralph. But instead of taking it in good spirits, after all it was only a practice, Bully marched straight down the wicket and proceeded to pummel the young lad with his bat as if driving a stump into the ground.

As Mr Smith dragged Bully, foaming crazily at the mouth, away from his unconscious victim, all he said was 'I don't think that's really fair do you Bullock?'

That evening, Jim Smith returned home to find his house burned to the ground.

His wife and two young daughters were sitting in the front garden staring with blank, desolate expressions at the burnt embers of their wrecked home. The fire brigade, police and ambulance services had all come and gone leaving the Smith girls to fend for themselves in a state of severe shock. They didn't know what to do or where to go.

The only item anyone had managed to salvage was the television and Mrs Smith was sitting on it holding the lead as if looking for somewhere to plug it in. For some reason, nobody had thought of phoning Jim Smith at the school. They probably each thought someone else would do it. What a shock it must have been as he finally stepped out of his car, ashen faced and trembling, having driven round the block for almost an hour. All the neighbours had been out in their front gardens looking on with varying degrees of pity as he circled by time and again, laughing hysterically and obviously in denial as he pretended to search for his own house which he kept passing without stopping.

In the end, the car simply ran out of petrol and, by an extreme coincidence that some found quite eerie, came to a halt all by itself just by his own gate, a modest wooden structure emblazoned with the name 'Hope Cottage'. It was the only thing left and even that fell off its hinges as he pushed it open. It used to open onto the path that led to his little haven of peace including the extensive library that had taken him almost a lifetime to compile. Now, suddenly and tragically, it had become an entrance to nowhere.

It was a while before this affable and most erudite man was able to accept what had happened and, when he did, it destroyed him as an ordinary human being.

They didn't have counselling in those days.

Although Bully and his vicious father had been spotted lurking in the vicinity earlier that day and no one was in any doubt as to who the arsonists were, the authorities never managed to bring any charges. So, to all intents and purposes, things just continued as normal except that Jim Smith declined to take a cricket session ever again. In fact, the poor chap was never really the same again at all. The experience had drained the life out of him and he went around with an empty expression as if his eyes had been set in cold lard.

Bully's tackle on Ralph was a perfect example of the sort of mad, gratuitous violence that he was well known for and if it had happened off the field any judge would have given him ten years for it. Ralph was absolutely furious with the lily-livered sports master for not taking any disciplinary action because sooner or later you had to take a stand against mindless violence. Preferably sooner.

It was the only way to stop the insane cycle of aggression caused by malicious louts whose main idea of having a laugh was to frighten people to death. Apparently, they just shrunk away if you stood up to them although he hadn't actually got around to trying it himself. Mind you, they also said a shark would just go away if you punched it on the nose but he hadn't got around to trying that either. Anyway, there was no time to dwell on the injustice of it all because blood was dripping down his leg, soaking into his torn shorts and all over the ripped remnants of his right sock. It hurt like hell.

Reluctantly, Sir eventually agreed that it warranted attention and sent Ralph off to the surgery. His spirits lightened. He was off to see nurse, the woman he loved. And off he trudged with gleeful anticipation.

As soon as he entered the surgery, the warm atmosphere, in stark contrast to the cutting east wind of the playing field, made him feel light-headed. Of course, the moment he caught sight of Eleanor the pain disappeared almost immediately and he was transfixed as usual on her breasts.

'What a mess,' she said. 'You'd better take off those muddy boots and the shorts and lie down over here so I can take a proper look.' Ralph stifled a yawn. Muggy heat wafting from the radiator combined with the comforting odours of chloroform and antiseptic to form a heady mixture that filled the room. It seeped into his being and made him decidedly weary. Nurse went to get some warm water, soap and a towel whilst he dutifully obeyed feeling dizzier by the second. He could hardly keep his eyes open. When Eleanor returned she seemed to glide towards him shimmering like a mirage in the desert.

She bent over to inspect the damage, which was on the tender part of his inner thigh, and began to wipe the mud and the blood away. As she leaned over to survey the damage with that button undone as usual Ralph actually caught sight of a nipple just peeping over the cup of her bra. What joy! That, together with the movement of her hands on his upper leg, began stirrings inside him that, try as he might, he could not prevent. He'd never been touched in such a sensitive place even by a girl of his own age, never mind a fully-grown woman.

'Open your legs a bit more,' she commanded. And, as he did so, his willie stiffened and popped out proudly through the hole in his y-fronts. Bloody thing. Got a mind of its own. He could feel it tingling away. This was embarrassing.

'Naughty boy,' said Eleanor but without a great deal of conviction and only half admonishingly. Then she slapped him, playfully but quite hard on his other thigh in mock punishment.

That was it. His buttocks jerked uncontrollably a couple of times and he spurted all over her white uniform with just a tiny blob landing on the bare flesh where her button was open.

It took a little while before Ralph's body stopped convulsing during which time his mind was a total blank. But when his brain finally re-engaged he felt embarrassed and awkward and felt sure she'd be absolutely furious. Bloody hell, I'm really for it now, he thought. Strangely though and much to his surprise, she seemed more sympathetic than angry and he noticed that her face was a little flushed. Was this really happening?

It felt real except that everything now appeared to be surrounded by the blurry edges of a romantic painting.

'Oh dear,' she said softly. But she didn't seem to mind at all.

'Er, sorry,' said Ralph, desperately trying to think up some kind of an excuse for the aberration. 'Didn't mean to.'

But Eleanor's mood seemed to have changed. Now she spoke in a softer, slightly faltering voice and seemed a bit flustered. Sort of hot and bothered.

'Never mind,' she said. 'We'd better clean you off.' And to his utter surprise she slid her soapy, wet hand along his thigh, under his pants and up and down his tender young dick which was still as hard as ever and continuing to poke out through his slightly soiled undergarment. It was the most gorgeous, thrilling feeling he had ever known.

'What a naughty boy,' she said in a dreamy sort of way with her eyes half closed.

'Oooh,' said Ralph, totally dumb-struck as she massaged his throbbing cock with increasing tempo. This was much better than doing it himself. He was even more astonished when she took his hand and slowly guided it underneath her skirt.

But the fabric of her undergarment was sopping moist and he immediately withdrew his hand thinking she had wet herself. Well how was he to know?

'It's all right,' she said and put it back again.

It felt a bit gooey but Ralph wasn't bothered. His rock hard member and Eleanor's hand were the only things that really seemed to matter at that particular moment. It felt good. It felt bloody good. As good as anything could. Then, as if guided by supernatural forces, Ralph's other hand automatically reached up, slipped inside the open button of Eleanor's uniform and actually felt one of those gorgeous little breasts that he had long admired from afar. It was soft and warm to the touch. He watched her gasp as he teased her nipple with his finger. She wasn't complaining and he just hoped he was doing the right thing. Actually, he didn't know what the fuck he was doing. With one hand raised to her breast and the other out sideways fondling her private parts, he felt bizarrely like a sailor sending signals in semaphore. But this was no SOS. His message was more along the lines of 'Stay away please, don't save me, I'll die here thank you'. Encouraged by Eleanor's compliance, he began to rub his hand between her legs and then, purely by instinct, tried to poke a finger through her thick flannelette knickers. Suddenly, her fist was clutching his willy so tightly he began to worry that the fucking thing might come right off in her hand. Her mouth was open, her eyes closed and she seemed to be concentrating very hard on something or another. In fact, she was becoming more intense by the second. Then she pushed Ralph's hand from her breast and began to massage her own nipple which, for some inexplicable reason, seemed to be much larger than when they had started.

A second or two later and without any further warning, she gasped as if belted in the stomach by a heavyweight boxer, her groin jerked forwards and she let out a stifled moan. Just at the same moment Ralph spurted all over her again. He couldn't help it. He didn't want to help it. It didn't need any help. That was it. Well he assumed it was anyway. The whole glorious episode couldn't have lasted more than a couple of minutes altogether.

For a short while afterwards they were both in a soft pant and a bit sweaty. Ralph's brain was in a fog in which a myriad of tiny, multi-coloured shooting stars whizzed around in all directions. He was still gagging for breath and wondering if it was real or just a dream when Eleanor started to readjust her clothing which had become crumpled and skew-whiff during the fray. She seemed quite compos-mentis compared to the state of delirium he was in. Ralph wondered if he should say something. Some little expression of affection or perhaps gratitude but although a few words came to mind he couldn't work out in which order they should go. Anyway, Eleanor was the first to speak.

'Get dressed please,' she commanded in such a matter-of-fact fashion that he was quite taken aback and led to believe that perhaps she wasn't entirely unfamiliar with this kind of situation. Ralph couldn't quite focus properly and his head felt muzzy. Was this really happening or was he just imagining it? Was he awake or asleep?

Then she disappeared into an anteroom where he could hear her running water into a basin. Ralph lay back on the couch feeling relaxed and happy. Within a minute or two he was snoozing soundly. He was in heaven. He had found a new career. He wanted to do it for a living.

The sound of a loud bell brought Ralph to his senses with a jolt. What the fuck was that? Where the fuck am I? What the fuck is going on? It was the surgery doorbell and a second later the door was flung open to admit the imposing figure of the headmaster who strode briskly through it at the same time as nurse Eleanor emerged from the ante-room smelling of carbolic and with a fresh uniform on.

Mr Barton was a tall, no-nonsense type of person. Always immaculately dressed in a dark, three piece suit, stiff, white shirt, paisley tie and jet black brogues that were so shiny you almost needed sun-glasses to look directly at them.

A watch chain hung in two loops across his belly from one waistcoat pocket to another. It was his trademark. Whenever a pupil passed by he'd swing out the timepiece, screw up his eyes and peer back and forth from pupil to watch to ascertain whether the boy was in the wrong place at the wrong time. It was typical of his guilty until proved innocent approach. Talk about a control freak. Barking Barton they called him. He was a right bastard and they all hated him. Pupils and teachers alike. His demeanour was that of a Nazi general and Ralph always had the uncomfortable feeling that the barmy old sod would have marched him off to the gas chamber at the slightest excuse. All he needed was the fucking moustache.

Barton stared down at Ralph in his usual disapproving way and extracted his watch.

'Ah, carbolic!' Announced the pompous academic sniffing the air. 'Just the job.'

He seemed proud of the silly statement.

Daft git, thought Ralph, bet you can't guess what I've been up to. 'Yes sir,' he burbled.

'Boy seems a bit groggy.' The head observed in his deep, booming voice. 'Must be in shock.' He was fucking well right about that.

Eleanor approached the couch briskly and wrapped a bandage around Ralph's injured leg. She took hold of his wrist and glanced at the upside down watch hanging on her uniform roughly, he estimated, over the breast he'd been mauling just a few minutes earlier. Just thinking about it made it essential to grit his teeth and concentrate like a bastard to prevent the old chap from bursting into life again.

'Stop it,' he ordered. 'Down boy!' and much to his relief on this occasion his under-developed little teenaged member obeyed.

He didn't really give a stuff about Barton anymore because he had decided that he and Eleanor would leave all this behind them and run away together. He had it all worked out. After school on Friday was the best time because then it would be the whole weekend before anyone would notice they were gone. Now all he had to organise was where to go, where they would live and how they would make a living. Oh, and how he was going to inform his parents. He was sure they wouldn't mind as long as he was happy. It would all fall into place. Eleanor would be really chuffed when he told her.

'How do you feel now?' Eleanor asked in her 'business as usual' efficient sort of way.

'Much better thanks.'

'Well you run along now boy,' boomed the headmaster. 'I'm sure nurse has much more important duties than to mollycoddle you.'

He seemed to put an unnecessary emphasis on the word 'duties' and was peering with a strange, half-smiling expression at Eleanor. Closing the door behind him, Ralph was sure he heard nurse Eleanor giggle softly and then gasp. What? Surely not. Surely she doesn't let that smelly old bastard touch her up. He was jealous as hell.

Ralph was hardly out of the room before having second thoughts about the running away business but still curiously happy as he made his way back, with a dampness in his groin, to join his classmates.

Naturally, he couldn't wait to tell everyone all about it but it was a while before he found the guts to do so and even then none of the bastards really believed him despite making him swear on the sacred tits of Gina Lollobrigida that it was true. He put this down to sheer jealousy. But he wasn't altogether surprised at their reaction. After all, it was hardly an everyday occurrence and he couldn't be entirely certain whether it had really happened or not. But he wasn't going to let such a minor detail spoil a good story.

THE BEAUTIFUL GAME

The Art of Football

In reflective moments when we are clearly focused and real truth flows easily in the mind, it is easy to understand how football is a form of art.

But anyone foolhardy enough as to actually say so in public can expect to be ridiculed by all those who believe that the game is merely twenty-two prats chasing mindlessly around after a ball. Philistines! What do they know? Football is definitely art.

Intellectuals and other anal-retentive types with no interest in sport will no doubt regard this as an extremely dodgy statement and of course they are perfectly entitled to their point of view. However, people with bricks in their heads should try and understand that, in common with most things in life, it all depends on the angle you view it from.

So then, what is art? (All right, I know, this is not a question you would normally expect to find in a book about football but life is full of surprises and perhaps this is not just a book about football. Not a normal one anyway.) If I was forced to attempt an answer my reply would be, and I am aware I am not the first to say it, that art is what artists do. Whatever you get from it, whether it makes you laugh or cry, that is its meaning.

The Brazilian football teams of the seventies accomplished the best standard that we have yet to believe is possible but, given how the game is now developing, that wonderful celebration of footballing skill is never likely to be repeated. A thousand sighs. The way those shanty town boys played was truly a free expression of the human spirit lovingly staged by world class performers who had reached the highest level of achievement in their field. As such, they were most certainly artists doing art and their performances ranked alongside the music of Santana, the paintings of Gauguin and the writings of Henry Miller in their excellence. Incidentally, these are just some of my particular favourites but you can insert whichever names you like here. For instance, you could just as easily say Ray Charles, Gustav Klimt and Dostoevsky if you wanted. Well I could.

As art, the Brazilian football of the seventies was completely unintellec-

tual, utterly beautiful and gloriously free. The teams that comprised amongst others Pelé, Jairzinho, Garrincha, Rivelino, Gerson, Socrates and Zico won everyone's admiration wherever they played along with most of their matches which were always joyful occasions for everyone who experienced them. It was as if the entire Rio carnival, complete with singing, dancing and strong, rich wine had followed the team to wherever in the world it happened to be playing. What a privilege it must have been to play against them and perhaps even a privilege to lose. Through them we were inspired by the simple joys of life. Love, peace, beauty and playing football without fear. A free expression of the human spirit. If life had any meaning then this was it. It was the reason we were born. But the world has changed and huge commercial entities have taken over.

It's the same old story. Whenever money comes in, all common sense flies out of the window. As a result, the meaning and beauty of the game for both players and fans has now become far less important than profits for shareholders.

7
The Imp and the Devil's Children

About a year into his working life and whilst on his fourth job in a sports shop, Ralph reached the required age to put a cherished ambition within reach. To qualify for the driving license that he was sure would take him one step closer to freedom. He'd concluded that until he left home, having a car was the only way to be free and he had decided to get one as soon as possible. Not only would it immediately enable him to get much further afield without the hassle of having to catch the last train home but, more important than that, it would impress the girls. Not many blokes had cars in those days and none of Ralph's mates did. It would put him ahead of the game for sure.

The others all saw their jobs as the first rung on the ladder of some sort of career. For the first time in their lives they didn't have to go begging their parents for pocket money and, consequently, they felt opulent in the extreme. Their ambitions were to drive fast cars, drink as much alcohol as they could get down their necks and screw as many girls as humanly possible. Of course, none of them had even come close to achieving this last burning desire yet but somehow they knew it was what they wanted. They were also quite certain that the route to the Shangri La of which they all dreamed was money. They were hooked on it like a drug. As soon as they'd had their first taste of an independent means they wanted more of it. And the way to get more was to get themselves promoted or find better jobs or, at the very least, hang on to the ones they already had. Whether those jobs represented vocational satisfaction or brought any real fulfilment didn't come into it. They would have sold their souls for three and thruppence ha'penny each in those days. It was a slippery slope. They were the devil's children and no mistake.

But Ralph had other ideas. He sensed there was a missing element to the equation and although he couldn't quite put his finger on it he strongly suspected the answer lay at least partly in his desire to travel and see the world. But, to know for sure, he'd have to get out there and explore.

Ralph didn't give a flying fuck about his job. For him it was just a means to an end. A way to make ends meet while he figured out how to escape.

On the magical day Ralph passed his driving test he couldn't contain the urge for motorised liberation any longer. But, never having been one to save, his only option was to buy a car on tick. He had worked out that on his wages he could just about afford the repayments on a modest vehicle although he hadn't bothered to take into account the cost of filling it up regularly with fuel. It wouldn't have mattered if he had. In all his deliberations he found every way possible to justify the purchase and was intent on going through with the deal whether he could afford it or not.

As the day grew nearer, Ralph became increasingly excited by the prospect. But as he sat in the car showroom with pen poised to sign the agreement and a sharp-suited, smiling salesman hovering over his shoulder rubbing his hands with glee, he somehow knew it was a big mistake. However, Ralph had made his decision and there was no going back on it now. A short while later he proudly drove his first car out onto the streets feeling like a king.

It was a Hillman Imp.

That was it. He was free! All of a sudden the theatres, galleries, concert halls and fancy restaurants of the West End were there to take advantage of without having to rush back to Victoria Station for 10.55. What girl could possibly fail to be beguiled by his sophisticated taste, his charming, witty conversation and the exotic delights he was now able to offer on the back seat of a Hillman Imp? They'd all be queuing up to offer their bodies to him for sure. What bliss lay ahead.

8
Oysters and Shikses

There was one in every family, and he was it.

Ralph used to joke that he'd had a difficult birth.

Screaming, howling, swearing, kicking, scratching, squealing, blood, gore – the lot. And that was just during conception.

Then he'd wait for the laughter that invariably never came. They'd all heard it before. But that was the usual response to most of Ralph's jokes. Not that he told many. In fact, it was only after a few drinks that he felt like telling one at all. Any other time he wouldn't have dreamed of it. He much preferred the natural humour of life with its spontaneous laughter to the contrived kind with clever punch-lines that provided pre-ordained spaces in which you were almost obliged to laugh whether it was funny or not.

He had never understood why alcohol was associated with violent behaviour because the effect it had on him was quite the opposite. Even when he'd been blind drunk he'd never felt the slightest inclination to attack anyone or lob a brick through a shop window. Indeed, on those occasions when he accidentally found himself three sheets to the wind after finding his way to the bottom of a bottle of claret he became effusive, passionate and philosophical. Lovey-dovey you might even say. The more he drank the greater would be his desire to embrace the whole world and everyone in it. Even the most arrogant, nasty, aggressive types who always seemed to be lurking around whenever he'd lapsed into this wobbly state of mind. Funnily enough, it was particularly that kind of moronic ruffian with whom he invariably ended up in highly charged discussion long after everyone else had gone home. As if he was on some kind of wine-fuelled campaign to educate the world. Actually, most people who knew him thought his mind was a bit wobbly anyway. The consensus was that his crazy ideas were akin to wild fantasy and had no connection to ordinary logic in the generally accepted sense. He took it as a compliment. He'd never been the slightest bit interested in being ordinary. Not in the generally accepted sense. Not in any way at all really. If Ralph joked that he'd had a difficult birth it was probably a psychological reaction to cover the fact that he'd had a difficult life. Or at least more difficult than necessary. Perhaps problematic would be a better way to describe it.

Like all the other Jewish lads, Ralph had his Bar Mitzvah at thirteen but, as far as he was concerned, the moment it was over so were any further obligations to normal, structured society. Freed from the chore of attending Hebrew classes three times a week, he avidly set about utilising his newly gained time for the much more important activities of playing football and chasing girls. He was a man now. That's what they said. A Bar Mitzvah was the ceremony marking the stage in life when a boy became a man and men could do what they wanted.

Fuelled by the desire for freedom, Ralph's rebellion eventually grew to the point when, with a true sense of adolescent drama, he announced to the family that he was no longer Jewish. But his Dad's response was unequivocal, dismissive and stern.

'You can't just give it up.'

'Only the religion side of it.'

'Being Jewish means being religious.'

'But I don't believe in it'

'There's no choice.'

'No choice what to believe in?'

'Not for a Jew.'

'Why should I go along with something I don't believe in?'

At this point his Father sighed as if giving expression to the pain of all Jews throughout the generations. It was his trump card. Designed to give the impression he was about to deliver an utterance that would, once and for all, explain the meaning of existence. Finally he pronounced.

'It's like an elephant.'

'It's what?'
'It's a huge grey thing with a big tube on the front.'
'What?'
'You can't see an elephant in the zoo and say you don't believe in it.'
'What?'
'Particularly if it trod on your foot.'
'But I . . .'
'Ignore it at your peril.'
Pause for thought.
'What about Marx?'
'Meshugenner. What about him?'
'He gave up Judaism but it didn't stop him being Jewish.'
'You call him a Jew?'
'Or Trotski.'
'Oy vey.'
'All right, Jesus then.'
'Oy vey.'

In his new-found liberation, Ralph soon confirmed what he had long suspected. That the ancient lessons crammed into his head by bearded old gits in preparation for his coming of age were completely irrelevant to actually living in the modern world. Furthermore they expected you to continue with this nonsense into adulthood. Well stuff that.

According to Orthodox Jewish ways, those seeking piety were obliged to carry out loads of curious rituals every day. Hundreds of them. It was almost a full-time job. Apparently, these strange duties, which included saying prayers before every activity, however mundane, kissing fringed shawls, adhering strictly to the dietary laws and wrapping leather straps around your arms several times a day, were supposed to make you a better person. But not Ralph. To him it was just a bunch of superstitious old guff carried over from the Middle Ages. You know the sort of thing. It's the same with all religions. What'll happen to me if, one dark day, I fail to carry out this ritual that I've carried out for years even though it has no meaning or purpose? Will I be struck down by a thunderbolt? So they carried on with it just in case and looked critically down upon anyone who didn't. Ralph wasn't going to let this kind of religious bollocks hinder his search for freedom or beautiful football. Maybe they were one and the same. Anyway, how could forbidding you to eat seafood or canoodle with shikses or play football on Saturdays help you lead a better life? Seafood was Ralph's favourite. Indeed, oysters were top of his league of slippery things the world had to offer. And shikses.

He was mystified why the mere idea of leaving the Jewish faith was such anathema to the older generation. Anyone who 'married out' or simply stopped being observant was banished from the community as an unacceptable heretic. Treated as if they were dead. Naturally, like all Jewish people he was quite aware of the horror and tragedy of the past. He had been hearing all the stories since he was a small child and seen older people tremble as they told them so he was in no doubt they were true. But he still had a problem identifying with those who had suffered from Soviet persecution or the terrors of the Warsaw Ghetto or German death camps. Ralph had been born and brought up in the leafy suburbs of Surrey where the most violence you were likely to encounter was a fist-fight between drunks outside the pub on a Saturday night.

Why was being Jewish still so precious to them? Why did they insist on continuing with it when it had caused them so much suffering? Why had Jews throughout the world spent two thousand years praying for rain to fall on a country they'd never seen?

Surely it would have been better to assimilate into the various communities where they ended up and just be anonymous rather than standing out like a sore thumb. Anyway, it all happened a very long time ago. Before he was even born. It was nothing to do with him. The more they thrust it down his throat, the more he rejected it. But that was Ralph – a rebel. He was determined not to be caged up or hemmed in or tied down or restricted in any way whatever; let alone by all this religious gobbledegook. He wanted to be free to live life to the full. To express himself. To liberate his spirit. To feel the earth on his feet and the wind in his hair.

Of course, this was more than a little difficult when you had to go to school every day.

Ralph had spent half his classroom days gazing wistfully out over the sports field wishing he was playing football and the other half gazing wistfully out in the other direction at girls playing netball in the playground. But much as it thrilled him to watch those nubile, young females leaping around in the throes of the sporting contest with their skimpy little skirts flying in the breeze he was remarkably unimpressed with any other aspect of the learning establishment. He just couldn't abide the uninspired ramblings of tired teachers who seemed more bored than he was. It was a complete waste of time. He had no idea what an isosceles triangle was and didn't care. How would it help him if he did? As for the pluperfect. Who gave a toss? What use was it to anybody? School was like a prison to him and he had already begun plotting his escape route.

Little wonder then that after a seemingly aimless childhood of unremarkable academic achievement Ralph's disenchantment finally got the better of him and at the tender age of fifteen he left to make his way in the big, wide world. As he walked out through the gates for the last time he could almost hear the communal sigh of relief that went up from the frustrated body of teaching staff whose combined efforts had failed to exert any influence over this curious, irreverent, friendly, passionate, loquacious, under-achieving, impatient adolescent.

His subsequent career, if you could call it that, had been more chequered than the finishing flag at a grand prix.

The Beautiful Game

Telly Footy

British football is afflicted by a debilitating malaise. Akin to a witch doctor's hex, this apparently incurable sickness holds players under a curious spell that somehow prevents them from:

1. Passing the ball.

2. Carrying the ball in any other direction than forwards.

These fundamental flaws in the way the game is generally played in Britain can be attributed to various causes. One of them is clearly the way that style and skill have been neglected in favour of speed and athleticism but another is the way the game is presented on television. In particular, the 'goal of the month' or 'goal of the season' type of feature gives a wholly inaccurate view of the game and sends entirely the wrong signals to kids who are supposed to be learning how to play it. The way things are going, it won't be long before those silly-arse TV producers will probably be offering us all the chance to vote in other daft competitions like 'goal of the century' or 'goal of the millennium' or perhaps even 'goal of all goals'.

Because of the highly commercial, tabloid approach of terrestrial TV which is the only medium most people have access to, the goals are mainly all they show by way of football highlights. Except perhaps, if we are very lucky, a violent tackle leading to a sending off. But this doesn't give us any real indication of the way a particular game has developed or even the slightest clue as to the tactics employed by either side.

As for the competitions, you can't compare one goal with another any more than you can compare a Monet with a Warhol or Beethoven's Fifth Symphony with the Spice Girls. (Or the corporate fuck dolls as someone once described them.)

It's like trying to read a newspaper with only headlines.

You are attracted by bold, spectacular statements but the substance you need to understand the whole picture is missing.

9
Muffin the Mule and the Electronic Anorak

How the bittersweet memories of childhood come tumbling into your head.

One of the thoughts that confronted Ralph from his past had somehow managed to wriggle its way out of the murkiest depths of his unconscious. It belonged to a period long ago in his childhood and must have preserved itself in a sort of deep hibernation. But now, stirred from its lengthy slumber, it forced its way through to the front of his mind to remind him quite vividly of that melancholy, poignant moment when it was first conceived over forty years earlier. Then, in a blinding flash of inspiration, he made a decision that was to have a most profound effect on his future.

Such moments of clarity had punctuated Ralph's life usually at times when he was least expecting them. Suddenly, a shiver of perception made him gasp in shock as if a bucket of ice cold water had been poured down his trousers when he wasn't looking. But just as he was about to examine matters further, poof! It was gone. Of course, the trick was to recognise the significance of these moments when they happened and to hang on to a bit of them after they disappeared. Easier said than done.

As the years drifted by, his early memories melted into the past like the fading images on an ancient television set with a clapped-out valve. But, as if a hefty clout had stimulated the knackered valve in Ralph's memory back into full working order, the recollection that now flooded his consciousness was one that he clearly and nostalgically remembered as the first of such flashes of enlightenment. He was only ten at the time but the great event appeared as sharp in his mind as if it had happened only yesterday.

It was during the summer holidays and he had been kicking a ball about in the garden as usual. Ralph was always kicking a ball around in those days and if not kicking then throwing, catching or bouncing. His own kid, Joe, was always at it now and he was also ten. It often occurred to Ralph that he was turning into his Dad just like Joe was turning into him.

'The world's gone mad,' his Dad always used to say to him and now he always found himself saying it to Joe. It was true then and even more so now.

Having revelled for a week or two in the glorious annual freedom from academia, Ralph was bored out of his mind. The novelty of doing whatever he wanted instead of having to get up and go to school had completely worn off. Of course, there wasn't much to keep kids occupied in those days apart from climbing trees, playing football or riding your bike if you had one. There was nothing even closely resembling theme-parks or splash pools or multi-media computers or multi-screen, surround-sound cinemas, or bowling alleys or skate parks or gigantic soft-play areas or zap-zones. As for the Internet, or the electronic anorak as Ralph had heard it described, no one would have believed it possible for a moment. It would have come into a category together with other impossible notions such as man walking on the moon or the collapse of the Soviet Union or Wimbledon reaching the Premier League.

It was even a half-hour bus ride to the nearest swimming pool and that was a pretty Spartan affair he could tell you. The water was so cold it would freeze your dick off.

It was the same for all the kids. They were left to their own devices and had to entertain themselves but as long as they arrived home at mealtimes no one was particularly bothered what they got up to. The environment was much safer then with fewer cars on the roads, less pollution, no mobile phones and no chemical additives in food which made it more wholesome. Youngsters were all much more active, walking, running and cycling rather than getting lifts everywhere and there were fewer nefarious influences to corrupt them.

For a start, there weren't any drugs around apart from aspirin – the wonder drug they called it. Oh, and Milk of Magnesia. Hardly class A.

BBC was the only TV channel. Only in black and white and only later on. Programmes didn't start until late in the afternoon when privileged kids would gather round for high tea with Andy Pandy, the Flowerpot Men and Muffin the Mule. The idea of colour telly was far too incredible to take in and it would be sometime yet before even a second channel, ITV, was to burst on to the screen. What a luxury! Two channels. How on earth would they decide what to watch? Of course, they had to get used to programmes being interrupted by commercials which Ralph found an extraordinary concept to deal with. Almost unbelievable. But then, everything was more exciting at that age. Before you found out what the world was really like.

Package holidays didn't exist and hardly anyone except the very wealthy travelled abroad. For the Goldsteins it was the odd day trip to Brighton, a visit to Chessington Zoo or a picnic on Box Hill. The rest of the time Ralph was kicking his heels and complaining there was nothing to do. Read a book? Fuck off, he was far too busy.

Whenever he was bored like this Ralph tended to gravitate to the garden and, like millions of boys before and after him, repeatedly slam a football against the side wall of the house imagining with each kick that he was scoring the winning goal in the cup final. It made him feel at peace with the world and, looking back, he didn't really need anything else. But the house vibrated with each impact and although he meant no harm it drove his mother mad.

'Stop kicking that ball against that wall!' she screamed. 'You're driving me mad!'

And then, 'Why don't you get a hobby?'

Now, as it happened, Ralph had been trying to find a hobby for some time but in those days it usually meant one of two things, stamp collecting or model-aeroplane making, both of which were very popular at the time. But philately had about as much appeal to Ralph as walking barefoot over hot coals. As for making model aeroplanes, he was completely useless at it. Talk about all thumbs! Furthermore, he had followed this trend through into adult life by being completely useless at DIY as well. It wasn't his fault. He just couldn't help it. The mere thought of putting up shelves or mixing cement simply terrified him. He even became distinctly nervous driving past a DIY centre. Whilst he harboured the greatest admiration for those who were good at building and fixing things, it just wasn't for him. He needed to be outside, gallivanting about in the fresh air.

Then, one bright and sunny day, having wrestled with this hobby dilemma for what seemed like a lifetime, the most fantastic notion suddenly occurred to him in a moment of the clearest perception that unexpectedly flooded his mind when he wasn't even thinking about it.

Football was his favourite thing so football could be his hobby!

It was like a light going ping! in his head.

The best ideas are invariably the simplest and you don't always see them for looking as they say. But Ralph saw this one all right. It was the first example of a fact that would be confirmed many times later in his life. That inspirational thoughts always struck you like a bolt out of the blue when you weren't even bothering.

Later, he recognised that this great revelation had been a religious experience roughly equivalent to Moses receiving the ten commandments except just somewhat more significant.

It was certainly a defining moment in Ralph's life and he had never looked back from that day to this. Indeed, forty years later, that was the thought that re-emerged from the dark recesses of his mind, well past its sell-by date but still as fresh as ever, and he continued to daydream.

His second favourite occupation.

10
Midfield General

Having decided to be a footballer, Ralph started looking for a team to play in but in the fifties in the Home Counties it was hard to find anything organised for lads of his age.

Following up one particular lead, he turned up feeling rather nervous on a bitterly cold January day at a draughty, muddy old recreation ground with no facilities for changing. One of the goals was leaning in a precariously crooked fashion having probably been swung on by every drunken lout in the district and you could hardly make out any of the pitch markings. Icy puddles were dotted all over the playing area. If you were unlucky enough to tread in one your foot sank right down into the mud with a squelching sound and freezing water poured over the top of your boots soaking your feet and numbing them to the point where all feeling was lost.

From the moment Ralph arrived, a chill wind whistled mercilessly around his chapped, raw legs, through every orifice he possessed and gnawed at his young bones until he almost shivered his ten-year old little whatsits off. This self-induced torture continued all afternoon with scant protection from his school PT kit which consisted of a thin white t-shirt, flimsy black shorts, short white socks and a pair of football boots such as they were then. Not the ultra comfy, sleek, soft-leather, designer style footwear of today which you can almost wear with your best suit on an evening out at the disco.

No, these were tough, heavy clod-hoppers made from rigid, ungiving leather with enormous, bulbous, rock-hard, steel toe caps and leather studs hammered on underneath with vicious spikes that often poked through and hurt your feet. Boots like that didn't help you play football. They hindered you. They soaked up water at such a rate that you could hardly get your feet up off the fucking ground.

Ralph's first match with his very first team consisted of boys of all ages, abilities, shapes, sizes and levels of intelligence. Despite the obvious disparities, they were somehow united by a passionate, illogical desire to play the fabulous game of football which, to the uninterested passer-by on that day, probably resembled some sort of deranged, avant-garde ballet in thick mud.

The self-appointed manager was a podgy, short, balding, middle aged, red-faced, pipe-smoking person called Charlie whose credentials for the task were hard to define although the rumour going round was that he loved to see young boys in flimsy shorts running, jumping, sweating and generally gasping for breath.

Charlie couldn't pick the team until just before kickoff, partly because he hadn't any idea who would actually turn up and partly because nearly everyone claimed to be a forward. (The perception then was that forwards were the better players and you only got picked in defence if you weren't that good.) His task however was pretty stereotyped. Years ago nobody knew about different systems such as 4-4-2 or 4-3-3 or sweepers or wing backs. It was quite simple. The centre-half was the biggest, toughest bloke you had and it was his task to mark the opposing centre forward who was also very large and supposed to score the goals mostly with his head from high crosses or corners. That was why they generally had flat foreheads and spoke with a lisp.

In those days, centre halves and centre forwards used to stalk the world with a mean expression not unlike the snarl of Clint Eastwood in 'The Good, the Bad and the Ugly'. They felt they had to throw their weight around to keep up a sort of tough image and used their size to frighten the daylights out of you whenever they got the chance. Usually this was by making an issue out of something trivial with the smallest bloke in the changing room. 'That's my place – shift!' But so-called hard blokes usually have soft centres and Ralph soon realised it was only fake bravado. Much as they tried to appear hard, most of these big bastards were closet pussy-cats with a deep-seated vulnerability about something or another.

Then you had the full-backs, who were small and stocky. They marked the wingers who were skinny as skeletons but could run like the clappers. They were supposed to carry the ball down the flanks and cross it in to the centre forward.

There was no such position as a midfielder in those days. The word midfield referred only to the playing area in which inside forwards operated. That's where Ralph eventually played. Midfield general.

You had two inside forwards, one either side of the centre forward and two wing halves, one either side of the centre half. Wing-halves always took the throw-ins. They regarded it as a kind of sacred duty bestowed upon them by the omnipotent deity. Their other job was to mark the inside forwards who were often referred to as schemers and thought of as creative players collecting the ball from defenders and getting it through to the centre forward or out to the wingers. All teams lined up the same way with a goalkeeper behind two fullbacks behind three half backs behind five forwards. Players were only numbered from two to eleven. 'Keepers had so far been denied the honour of wearing number one but as they only ever wore green tops you always knew who they were. Their main aim was to try and keep warm and hope most fervently that the ball kept well away from them. There weren't any subs, the idea of which was generally considered as a continental type of cheating. Other formations were unknown. It was long before continental methods and style had been discovered and it was inconceivable that anyone would know better than us, the inventors of the game, how to play it. No, winning had much more to do with relative levels of skill and effort than the way tactics can and do influence games today.

Naturally then, the biggest, fattest kid who turned up on the great occasion of Ralph's competitive football debut got the job of centre half. Sean was a huge lad with a shock of curly, ginger hair, massive spots, a wobbling belly and thighs like tree trunks that were at least twice the width of Ralph's. He must have shifted a few fish suppers in his time. Nobody was properly kitted out but his shorts were ridiculously small and Ralph prayed for him every time he stretched for the ball. He couldn't help thinking,

'One more meat pie, son and you'll be right out of those.' You called everyone son. Even players twice your age.

'Can't I play centre forward?' Sean asked Charlie.

'No son,' answered the strange little poof. 'I need you to organise the defence.'

Sean seemed happy with that. Not that he had any idea how to organise a defence. Ralph soon found out that he could hardly organise getting himself dressed in the mornings. But it bestowed a semblance of responsibility on him which he gladly accepted.

What Charlie really meant of course was, 'Watch their centre forward and if he shows any sign of breaking through, kick his fucking legs off.'

The more experienced players were easily spotted because they had shin-pads which seemed like items of the greatest luxury to Ralph. As he hobbled around on black and blue legs rapidly stiffening to the point of seizure, he realised that some form of protection was going to be absolutely essential although he had to make do with cardboard until he could afford the real thing.

The match itself developed into a bit of a farce mainly because the other team, which was about as well organised as Ralph's (not at all in other words) also turned up in white t-shirts and black shorts which was the standard uniform for any sort of sporting activity then. This led to problems for the players because, as they were all wearing identical outfits and hardly knew each other, they couldn't always work out who was on whose side. Not that it mattered much as it turned out.

There was one tiny blonde kid, he couldn't have been more than about eight, who had enormous, baggy shorts that flapped around his ankles. Apparently, he'd borrowed them from his fifteen-year old brother. Ralph thought they were supposed to be on the same side but it was impossible to be sure because all the little fellow did whenever he got near the ball was attempt to kick it as hard as he could in whichever direction he happened to be facing at the time. Unfortunately, his aim and timing were not that good and he quite often ended up missing the ball entirely and kicking any player who was unlucky enough to get in the way. Before long, three or four players from both sides were hopping around, howling in pain.

Titch's name was Adam but his behaviour was such that, looking back, Saddam would have been much more suitable. For all anyone knows, he might easily have grown up to be a mad dictator with a ruthless army that roamed around chopping innocent people to bits for no particular reason other than that it was just jolly good fun.

Although the little lad had appeared rather shy when he first turned up, Ralph began to wonder if this hadn't been some sort of a trick because, as the game progressed, he seemed to warm to the occasion and was eventually charging around like a maniac frightening the life out of everyone. By half time, the vicious little git was just kicking out wildly at anything and anyone in front of him including, at one point, a small Terrier that had strayed onto the pitch to chase the ball.

The poor animal received the full force of little Hitler's boot right up its arse and was lifted about six feet up in the air with a blood-curdling yelp. Its owner, a rather glamorous, middle-aged lady who had merely been out for a walk in the park, was furious as she came running on to rescue her little pet which was now lying on its back in the middle of the pitch making a peculiar gurgling sound.

'Hooligans!' she screamed as she approached the group of players gathered round to observe the rather pathetic and obviously pissed-off little creature choking in the mud. Catching sight of young Adolf she lurched crazily at him brandishing a shooting stick above her head and then attempting to poke him with it as if it were a sword.

She was eventually restrained by the referee, George Backhouse, who had to promise her a full FA inquiry into the incident before she would agree to leave the field. George said he would take her details down in the pub after the match but his cheeky wink and affectionate little pat on her bum as she walked away were an indication that it wasn't only her details he'd be trying to take down later. Ralph didn't realise it at the time but George was apparently known for this type of thing. Actually, being only ten, Ralph didn't even know what this type of thing was. But he was eventually to learn that there were many horny bastards in football and, being reasonably quick on the uptake, it wasn't too long before he became one himself. Maybe the worst of the lot.

When everything had calmed down, the referee decided that a dropped ball would be the appropriate way to re-start the game and little Saddam impatiently hopped from one foot to the other eagerly determined to be a participant in this procedure.

Of course, no other player on the pitch wanted to be involved in anything that would put them anywhere within the little thug's striking range. They'd seen enough.

So when it transpired that the trainee terrorist was on the other side and that one of Ralph's team would have to challenge him for the ball, they all started to sidle away from the action. Some of them were whistling nonchalantly or turning their backs whilst trying to give the impression that they were far too busy to get involved.

Much to Ralph's relief, Charlie shouted an instruction to Sean, the chunky centre-half, to get on with the ball dropping and as the big sissy reluctantly approached the referee he seemed to be almost wetting himself at the prospect. But Ginger had obviously developed a game plan as he was walking over. At the very second the ref dropped the ball between him and Saddam, he leaped backwards to safety as if diving out of the path of a runaway bus leaving the area free for the dog murderer to fulfil his heart's desire and kick out as hard as he wanted.

Now, as it happened, little Stalin had quite a strong kick and he took an almighty heave which on this occasion caught the ball perfectly on the half volley sending it straight up in the air, over the trees and out of the park.

Charlie scuttled off to retrieve it which took some time because it had ended up in a hamburger van on the A23 London to Brighton road. The fat old git couldn't resist the opportunity to scoff a cheeseburger with onions before returning with the ball by which time all the players were frozen stiff, completely fed up and praying the game would end very soon.

The match, if you could call it that, had hitherto been played in a style not far removed from a rugby scrum with all the players in one solid group chasing the ball to wherever it happened to be and kicking wildly at it. There was no real, what you might call open play. Ralph had given up on this and taken to standing a few yards away from the bunch shouting things like 'Here, here!' or 'Pass, pass!' all to completely no avail. Charlie was lurching about on the sideline in a comical fashion not unlike a sort of dumpy Jacques Tatti shouting 'Spread out lads', which seemed to be the total sum of his tactical knowledge. To be fair though, it probably was the most appropriate instruction as all the players except Ralph and the two 'keepers were in a huddled mass that moved slowly and painfully from one part of the field to another.

Towards the end of the game and much to Ralph's surprise, the ball squirted out of the mêlée in his direction. He latched on to it with great glee and began carrying it goalwards with the entire squad of both teams in hot pursuit. He could hear the padding of tiny boots on the mud just behind him. It was like being chased by a herd of baby elephants. But no one was close enough to tackle him and no one called for the ball so he naturally assumed he was on to a good thing and hared off as fast as his legs would carry him, dribbling for glory. The match was almost over, it was nil-nil and so far the ball hadn't been within twenty yards of either goal.

The dozen or so spectators assembled on the touch-line shouted louder as Ralph ran on and this gave him great encouragement. He imagined he was about to score for England at Wembley. But the full-size pitch stretching out before him started to seem enormous and it occurred to him that it was ridiculous to make such tiny human beings play football on such a gigantic field. To add to his problems, huge clods of mud from the boggy playing surface had stuck to his boots making his feet so heavy that he could hardly lift them off the ground. Yet despite all the difficulties Ralph had somehow managed to cover over half the length of the pitch and manoeuvre himself into a position where he only had the goalkeeper to beat. He was already anticipating the congratulations of his new team-mates and decided that a nonchalant hand shake would convey the idea that he was used to scoring the winning goal every week. But, although spurred on by the cheers of the crowd, he would have been a lot more confident if his legs hadn't felt as if they were about to fall off at any minute.

Of course, unknown to any of those watching, he was in possession of a highly significant piece of information regarding the matter at hand – that he didn't have the foggiest idea about how to score this goal. After all, he'd never had any proper coaching or been in this kind of situation before.

As he closed in on the target he thought he'd just look up to check how much further he still had to go. It was then that he had the most terrible shock. Standing in front of him shaking like a leaf was his own team's goalkeeper. Only then did it begin to dawn on Ralph that the crowd had actually been shouting at him to turn round because he had been busting a gut going the wrong way. What a complete fucking prat he felt. He prayed for the ground to open up and swallow him whole. Until that moment the poor goalkeeper hadn't touched the ball once during the course of the game. But there he now stood, shivering uncontrollably and glaring with what seemed like a mixture of fear and hate at the idiotic team-mate who was now bearing down on him with all the energy he could muster and threatening to ruin his afternoon. Fuck it, thought Ralph when he realised what was happening. This is fucking silly. But he couldn't just turn round and start running all the way back. That would have been even sillier. Anyway, he was knackered. There was only one thing for it. He stopped dead in his tracks and calmly passed the ball to the 'keeper (there was no pass back rule then).

'Here you are mate,' he said as if he had deliberately run half the length of the pitch in the wrong direction just in order to get the ball to his own goalkeeper. Good move.

The Beautiful Game
Panic Slowly

Once you have created options and found yourself with space and time, the important thing is not to waste them.

You must be ready, bright, alert, alive.

Make decisions quickly and act on them. It's no good using up all your spare time working out what to do because then the opposition will have closed off avenues and you'll have thrown away your advantage.

Don't dither but don't panic. Do something positive. Keep the ball moving even if it is a short square ball.

It's a team game. If you haven't spotted a defence splitting opportunity maybe the team-mate standing next to you has.

When you have an advantage you must capitalise on it.

And that's in life by the way. Not just football.

11
Michaelangelo and the Chelsea Supporter

Ralph had worked in a bakery, sports shop, quarry, airport, sports centre, a number of offices, a number of factories, a number of small businesses and also been a driver of taxis, vans, lorries and tractors. In between jobs and relationships he had travelled through every country in Europe, been all over North and South America, hung out in the Caribbean, visited Israel numerous times and lived on a kibbutz. Consequently, although he had a limited knowledge of many things, he couldn't really pronounce himself an expert in any of them.

Once in Rome Ralph had undergone what he now realised was a spiritual experience. On a visit to the Vatican he was immediately struck by the breathtaking beauty of the Cistine Chapel and stood there agog. Rooted to the spot. Unable to remove his gaze from the beautifully painted scenes that almost seemed to describe the meaning of life. He was inspired. It was one of the most fantastic things he had ever seen.

On his return to London a few weeks later, he set about trying to develop a new kind of Artex that would spray walls and ceilings in the same, multi-coloured, pictorial form. He wanted to bring the great beauty of Michaelangelo's masterpiece to every housing estate in the country. His theory was that if all homes were decorated in this way it would raise the spirit of the nation and the consciousness of society.

But it never came to anything. Ralph always had loads of great ideas that never came to anything. Then, years later, he'd notice that some other bright spark had made an absolute fortune out of an idea that he hadn't bothered to follow through. In fact, 'Should have done it when I had the chance,' could easily have been his epitaph.

Thirty-five torrid years after setting out on life's great journey, most people would have summed Ralph up as a cynic, black sheep and Chelsea supporter but not necessarily in that order. Of course, if you were to have asked him directly, he would have had more to add on the subject. He always did. Although he hadn't attained any formal qualifications Ralph saw himself at the same time as a poet, writer, thinker, muse, philosopher, traveller, sportsman, bohemian and raconteur. Any description of himself by himself would be bound to contain words like that and probably all of them. Certainly, by all means, a man of the world. But others never saw you as you saw yourself, so they said. How the fuck did they know that? Whoever they were.

Even now with family responsibilities and a living to earn, his life-long wanderlust had yet to subside. On his travels he had enjoyed many memorable experiences from which he had gained what might be described as an exotic perspective on life but this had made it difficult for him to settle down in one place and just accept being part of a community. He wasn't content. Nothing ever seemed permanent to him except, of course, for the one permanent thought that binds all mankind – that as soon as you're born you start dying.

Yet despite his relatively meagre means and a rather sketchy education Ralph had managed to acquire an avid taste, not to say a voracious appetite, for the finer things in life. Art, music, literature, travel, fine wines and exotic foods all vied for the prime position on his rota of favourite amusements even though there had only been a few periods during his troubled existence when he could afford to indulge in any of them to the extent he would have liked. But although these elaborate pastimes had contributed substantially to his spiritual ambitions, there were two other activities in which Ralph had participated so enthusiastically, studiously and wholeheartedly throughout all his life that they had had taken on a significance of almost religious proportions.

A difficult thing for an atheist to admit.

Because he was so passionate and, in his opinion, eminently knowledgeable in respect of these two sacred subjects, he began to wonder if he wasn't entitled to declare himself an expert. After all, had he not consistently performed them with the utmost poise and proficiency? Perhaps he was even justified in putting himself forward as the foremost authority in these areas.

It wasn't as if they were merely optional extras or frivolous luxuries that could be easily discarded when not required. To Ralph, the two blessed functions were vital elements without which life had no meaning. Indeed, they embodied the entire purpose and substance of human fulfilment and could not actually be separated from life itself.

They were of course, sex and football.

The Beautiful Game
All for One and One for All

Running forward with the ball and trying to beat anyone who tries to tackle you is many people's sole perception about how to play football. But if you do it all the time you won't get far in the game. Apart from anything else it won't be long before your team-mates get thoroughly pissed off and who could blame them? What is the matter with you? Don't you need them? Do you think you can win the game all on your own? Football is a team game and if you insist on going for glory by yourself you'll run out of friends mighty fast. Serves you right.

That's not to say that solo efforts aren't okay sometimes. Just not always.

Eddie McCreadie's goal for Chelsea against Milan in the Cup Winners' Cup in 1971 at Stamford Bridge is a case in point. McCreadie was an athletic, acrobatic, Scottish international left back and one of the best in the game at the time.

He gathered the ball in his own half and moved forward beating player after player and, after running almost the entire length of the pitch, finally slid the ball past the Italian keeper and into the goal behind which I was standing. He then promptly collapsed in a heap in the penalty area. It was a huge effort and he was exhausted. What a goal! It was most certainly a great sporting moment. One that will undoubtedly have lingered with great affection in the memory of anyone who witnessed it. But you couldn't do it all the time and it's very unlikely that Eddie McCreadie ever did anything like it again. Of course, when the blood's up there's nothing wrong in taking the ball on and acting according to your passionate instincts. Good players, or any players for that matter, will often feel the urge to go for glory and good luck to them. You must follow your heart when the moment is right. Recognising that moment is part of the basic requirement needed to derive the maximum enjoyment from the game. But it can't really be coached. It's an instinct. You either know it or you don't.

And that's in life, by the way, not just football.

12
Swearing and the Scissor Kick

From then on, Ralph's love of football became a virtual obsession. He'd spend every spare minute at the local rec playing with whoever turned up for a kick about and if no one else came he'd practise shooting against the fence surrounding the playground.

Often he would stay until it was too dark to see the ball. At weekends he'd usually get a game in one of the many local sides even though most of the players were a lot older than him. On Saturday afternoons and Wednesday evenings he'd find his way to Stamford Bridge or Craven Cottage and if neither Chelsea nor Fulham were at home he'd go anywhere else he could watch a football match even if it was an amateur game at Sutton United, Wimbledon or Kingstonian. In those days there was a strict separation between the amateur and professional games. Amateur players weren't supposed to get paid for playing but, of course, they did. The good ones anyway.

If Ralph wasn't out playing or watching he'd often be found up in his bedroom honing his bicycle kicking technique. He had seen a South American player on telly scoring a goal with this acrobatic method and was so impressed that he decided to master the art and introduce it into the English game. Time after time he would throw the ball in the air and fling his legs up over his head so that he was airborne and spinning backwards like a tumbler in a circus. He had to time it just right so that his foot made contact with the ball on it's way down in order to belt it against the wall whilst he landed harmlessly on the bed. One day, after a particularly vigorous effort, he landed awkwardly and the bed collapsed underneath him with an almighty crash that shook the house so violently his parents came rushing to the bottom of the stairs.

'What the hell are you doing up there!' his Dad demanded in his seriously pissed off voice.

'Brushing my teeth!' Ralph garbled whilst extricating himself from the debris and desperately trying to invent a plausible excuse for the destruction.

But all the practice paid off one magnificent Saturday morning when, to his absolute delight, he actually managed to score in a match with an overhead kick. Looking back, it was probably his most glorious moment in the game and whenever he found himself reminiscing about his playing days it was the first thing he thought about. The ball came over from a corner at exactly the right height and speed for him to carry out what he had always dreamed of and rehearsed hundreds of times in preparation for that special moment. In the end it was a purely instinctive reaction. He flung himself backwards as the ball arrived under his left leg, which had scissored upwards, and on to his right boot which propelled it with beautiful strength and accuracy straight into the top corner of the net. It was an occasion of sheer magic and everyone applauded. Just perfect. Ralph was elated and wondered if a Real Madrid scout was around to witness it. He would have been signed up on the spot for sure. But as his mind swam in glory, the opposing centre-half ran over and started jostling him.

'Who the fuck do you think you are? Fucking Pelé? Fucking try that again and I'll fucking break your fucking leg,' he said. And just for good measure, 'You fucking cunt.'

It was the worst possible thing you could say so Ralph knew he meant it and was deeply stung. He'd never been on the receiving end of such personalised vitriol before and wasn't quick-witted enough to formulate an immediate response. By the time he'd worked out that 'Fuck off you fucking cunt' would have been the most appropriate riposte his opponent had run off leaving Ralph mouthing a silent curse like a goldfish coming up for air.

Reviewing the event after all these years, it occurred to Ralph that there were only two words left in the English language that were still socially forbidden to any extent. One was 'fuck' and the other was 'cunt'. Together they comprised the worst possible insult although Ralph was at a loss to understand why. One was a synonym for the sexual act and the other a term for the most private part of the female anatomy. Both nice things. Why on earth should they cause people to gasp in such horror?

When Ralph was growing up there were loads of other words you couldn't say in public like bastard, bugger, bloody, shit, crap, bollocks, wank, wanker, tits, fanny, prick, dick, cock, arse, sod, fart, piss, pissed, spunk, erection, French letter and rubber Johnny. (The word condom wasn't even invented then or at least Ralph couldn't remember it being in use until AIDS became an issue). Even bottom, bosom, bowel, breast, belch, burp, bum and knickers were a bit iffy. But these were pretty much accepted nowadays unless you happened to be the Chief Rabbi.

There were also a number of other terms that were considered too taboo to be mentioned on TV or radio even in a strictly scientific context such as period, Tampax, menstruation, masturbation, copulation, ejaculation, sperm, pubic hair, sex, sexy, semen, faeces, penis, prostitute, rape, orgasm, virgin, uterus, homosexual and nipple.

Although these words were all found in the Oxford English Dictionary which was generally regarded as a fairly respectable tome, you never dared use any of them in polite company unless you were prepared to be thought of in roughly the same way as an escaped convict, child molester, sheep-worrier or Communist. Clearly, this was because the words in question all shared a connection with natural bodily functions, the mere thought of which caused most people to rush off into dark corners and hide their faces. Indeed, they insisted on the very strictest privacy when actually carrying out these activities despite the fact that we all performed them in pretty much the same way. (Actually, Ralph had heard of some notable exceptions to this last statement, the truth of which he was still avidly investigating).

The embarrassment people felt could have been for a number of reasons or perhaps a combination of them all. Ralph enumerated them thus:

1. We could not prevent ourselves carrying out these bodily functions.

2. We lost control when we're doing them and once we got

going there was a moment after which we could not prevent the conclusion of the activity.

3. They involved the emission of smelly substances from our bodies.

4. They involved the emission of grunting and slurping noises.

5. They involved the removal of clothing from the private area below the waist.

6. They were much more enjoyable than anything else even though we felt guilty about actually doing them because of all of the above.

But despite the various taboos, Ralph tended to use these words a lot more than most and had already garnered quite a reputation for being outspoken. Not that he wanted to deliberately upset anyone you understand, but he had long felt that colourful language was an accurate and enjoyable way of expression despite the fact that most people did seem to get remarkably angry and indignant about it. He put this down to a lack of sex which was by far the most common cause of general grumpiness. Nevertheless, Ralph was sometimes made acutely aware that he should have been more careful what he said in the changing room. Not everyone understood his crazy ideas. Even his closest mates sometimes wondered if he wasn't slightly touched.

Once, in the victorious after glow of a Sunday league match that his side had won quite comfortably, the lads were in high spirits laughing, joking, slapping each other heartily on the back and generally congratulating themselves. A lively debate was soon underway concerning the main issue at hand which was deciding which pub to go and get drunk in. But during those moments of happy communal abandon, Ralph couldn't prevent himself from spontaneously blurting out, 'You know, football is about as close to sex as you can get.'

Suddenly there was a hush and you could have cut the atmosphere with a knife. The smile dropped from Ralph's face as a feeling of insecurity swept across him. As usual he'd gone too far. His team-mates cast him angry, worried looks and passed critical comments behind his back in quietly muttered tones.

'What the fuck's he on about?'
'Fucking shirt-lifter.'
'Don't bend over in the fucking shower.'
'Always thought there was something queer about him.'
'Backs to the wall lads!'
'Public school pervert!'

And they all got dressed a bit quicker. Ralph was annoyed. He could understand why some people might think he was a pervert but a public schoolboy? How could anyone make such a mistake? It was an insult. He vowed never to say anything like that again. Not in that company anyway. But he was never one to hide his light under a bushel and couldn't always prevent himself from letting lose on the prejudiced attitudes of his mates who seemed incapable of opening their minds to new ideas. Ralph was sure that if they would just fucking well take the trouble to listen they would probably end up agreeing with him. But if they were going to get so upset about the way he expressed himself then they would just have to sort it out for themselves.

Little did he realise the trouble this attitude would eventually cause him in later life.

THE BEAUTIFUL GAME
Rules, Who Needs 'Em?

Of course, you can't expect referees to get everything right and you never could. It's an inherent element of the game. Nobody's perfect and we don't live in a perfect world.

Certainly it would be a much poorer place if we couldn't get upset about a referee's decision from time to time. But that doesn't mean we have to make life harder by invoking rules that spoil the game. Take the offside rule for instance. With the speed of the modern game, it's virtually impossible to enforce it properly.

How on earth can a linesman, (sorry, referee's assistant) judge whether a player twenty yards to his right is offside if the last player to kick the ball is twenty yards to his left? How is he supposed to see them both at exactly the same time if they are forty yards apart in different directions? No wonder they make mistakes.

There is nothing more infuriating than a flowing move being pulled up in its prime because a highly organised back four have all stepped up together in carefully rehearsed unison, flourishing their arms aloft like a formation team in 'Come Dancing'. But this isn't the fandango. They are appealing to the linesman for offside and if they're big enough and shout loud enough they know they'll get the decision they want whether it's justified or not. Particularly if they're playing at home.

Particularly if they're Manchester United playing at home.

And so a promising move comes to an end and possession switches to the fandangos all because of a borderline decision that is often subsequently proved wrong.

It's unfair and silly.

How many times do television replays show that mistakes have been made by linesmen (sorry, referee's assistants) who are not up with the game or perhaps influenced by the aggressive baying of heavily partisan crowds rattling chains and holding nooses aloft just a few feet behind them? It's practically every match.

I'll just say that again just a bit louder. IT'S EVERY FUCKING MATCH!

Of course, it isn't just offside where mistakes are made but this is where the most blatant errors occur and it makes an absolute mockery of events.

The other problem with the offside rule is the very curious subsection which states that a player in an offside position is not deemed to be offside if he is 'Not interfering with play.' Well now. There is really nothing you can say about this except to repeat the view of the great Brian Clough which is that if you are not interfering with play you shouldn't be on the fucking pitch. No one has expressed it better.

A single faux pas by a puzzled official struggling to interpret unclear regulations can lead to disastrous consequences for a club and its fans such as missing out on promotion or being relegated or getting unfairly knocked out of a cup, perhaps even in the final. Just stopping the natural flow of the game is bad enough in itself. It isn't fair on the players, the clubs or, most important of all, the supporters who pay good money to attend matches and, at the end of the day, are the very lifeblood of the game. Who the fuck else is it being played for?

Why people stand for this nonsense on the very regular basis that it happens is a complete mystery. Never mind the fans for a moment. What about the directors of clubs who are responsible to shareholders for profits? Supposing a club failed to gain entry to the money-spinning merry-go-round of Europe because of a stupid decision by a linesman (sorry, referee's assistant), who missed something crucial on a particular day. Whose fault is that?

It is a huge problem which is affecting the game adversely but just like many problems in this world there is a simple solution that would solve it immediately.

Abolish the rule. That's right. Abolish the offside rule and you abolish the problems. With the advance in tactical knowledge, there is every possibility this would lead to a new free-flowing element entering the game that might easily result in an attacking, expressive style of play with more natural movement and certainly more goals.

Just like the Brazil of old.

13
Randy Rebecca and the Hideous Hybrid

She was Ralph's little secret. They'd all give him a hard time if they found out he lusted after her like a tomcat on heat. Rebecca was her name, a vivacious, curvy brunette with aquiline features and, by all accounts, a high intellect. Smart but sexy – a dangerous combination. Rumour had it that she was quite experienced. A goer in fact.

Randy Rebecca they called her. She was a year or two older than Ralph and well-known in the district. You could say that her reputation went before her. Certainly the free and easy manner she adopted with boys and her slinky apparel which comprised the tightest of tops and the shortest of mini-skirts seemed to confirm that there must have been some truth in the rumours. It did to Ralph anyway. She didn't half make his nipples hard and he often wondered when his turn might come round. But even though she only lived just up the road and was always walking past his house he couldn't fathom out how to make contact with her. Talk about nervous. She only had to be within twenty yards of him and his stomach would start churning like a concrete mixer. From time to time he kept a vigil from the landing window and on the glorious occasions when he spotted her coming he'd leap out of the front door and pretend to be polishing up the Imp that was always parked on the drive just in case. But Ralph's tactics never worked because he was always at a loss for anything to say even though he had copiously rehearsed many opening gambits. What a ninny. Why couldn't he just say hello for fuck's sake?

Maybe the Imp was to blame for making him so self-conscious. Sometimes he wished it was a Jaguar e-type or an Aston Martin or a Bond Equipe like his mate, Matty Jacobs who played for Wingate, had been given by his dad. Anyway, at least he had a car.

Not much of a cause for penis envy maybe. But it got him around for the time being.

The longer it went on the worse it got. Eventually he became so besotted with Rebecca that he started going out of his way to create situations in which he could ogle her luscious body whenever he thought she wasn't watching. At night he took to walking past her house hoping to catch a glimpse of her half-dressed at the window and madly fantasising she would invite him up to her bedroom while her parents were out and allow him to ravish her. Whatever that meant.

'Just popping out for a walk,' he would shout to his parents after dinner when already half way out of the front door. 'Need some fresh air.'

Whenever he had the chance, he followed Rebecca around at what he thought was a discreet distance hoping to contrive some way of having a quiet word with her alone whilst naïvely thinking she hadn't noticed him.

He knew the approach was futile and sometimes felt like Inspector Clouseau chasing the Pink Panther. But how else could he get close to her?

Little did he realise that the knowing smile he couldn't see from behind indicated that she was, in fact, quite aware of his presence. He wouldn't have made much of a detective. It was all far too obvious. Anyone witnessing any part of this excruciating saga would have probably construed that he was a right pervert and, indeed, he had begun to wonder about it himself.

It wasn't as if Ralph was in love with Rebecca. Just that as an inexperienced young lad with a heavy aching in his loins he was convinced she would be the ideal person to have a bit of practice on. He was sure she wouldn't mind but to find out he would have to establish communications in some way. The question was how? Months later he was still asking it. By this time he had actually managed to say hello once or twice but hadn't quite plucked up the courage to attempt a conversation. As for asking her out, she wouldn't be interested. She was older and much more experienced. She probably had a whole bunch of far more eligible blokes in tow. That Michael Watkins said he'd done it with her and he was even older than her. What possible chance could Ralph have?

But one Saturday evening, whilst queuing at the fish and chip shop on his way home from Stamford Bridge, Ralph was startled to hear a female voice addressing him from behind.

'Saw you playing football in the rec yesterday.'

Turning round, his eyes lit up like neon signs in Piccadilly Circus. It was her.

'Oh yeah,' he replied feigning nonchalance although his stomach was in knots.

For some reason he acted as if her statement meant nothing to him but he'd seen her in the rec too. Not half! He'd been having a kick about with some of the lads from his Sunday league side and noticed Rebecca in the playground with a couple of her own mates. A single glance and his legs had turned to jelly! Fuck me, look at that. He tried not to stare but he couldn't help it. As she pushed herself back and forth on a swing her skirt rode right up over those gorgeous thighs to reveal the tantalising flash of white knicker peeping out from underneath. What's more, he was pretty sure she was doing it on purpose.

The sight sent his libido into overdrive and his hormones into a frenzy.

It was fucking difficult trying to play football with a hard on.

'We're coming to watch the game tomorrow,' she announced.

There was a cup match next day between Ralph's side, Bartley Colts and their arch rivals AFC Minton. It was the local equivalent of a European Cup semi-final and everyone was talking about it. In fact, it was the reason they'd been putting in a bit of extra training, if you could call it that. In Ralph's case, intensive underwear spotting might have been a better way to describe it.

'Oh yeah.'

'Yeah. That all right?'

'Yeah.'

Go on, for fuck's sake, ask her. I can't. Yes you can. What if she says no? So what? I can't. Yes you can.

There was only one thing for it. He laid her gently down, slid off those white knickers, parted her legs and took her gleefully on the grease and slime of the chip shop floor in full view the crowds of families anxiously queuing up for their Saturday night supper. No one took a blind bit of notice as she squealed and squirmed with delight right in front of them. Never even batted an eyelid. But why should they? It was only happening in Ralph's mind of course. Saveloy madam? Certainly.

He had been having these fantasies for some time. They'd happen everywhere. On the train into work he'd roger every female of any age in the carriage before they got to Clapham Junction. He'd have barmaids in the pub, women walking their dogs in the park and all the young fillies from the school netball team in their skimpy, black skirts and regulation undies without any of them having the slightest idea what he was up to.

He'd have the woman in the dry cleaners on a pile of dirty laundry in the back office, the waitress at the Adelphi, with her warm, bare arse sliding around on the cold, stainless-steel work surface in the kitchen, and the horny, middle-aged female from next door in her own bed while her husband was at work. He was sure she wanted it. They all did. So far, though, it was all in his mind.

Just once, he thought. I want to do it just once. So I know what it's really like.

'Fancy a drink after the match?' Ralph suddenly blurted. What was that? Fucking hell, Who said that? By this time everyone in the whole chippy was listening to their conversation. What if she said no?

'We can go in my car,' he added quickly. It was the first chance to play his trump card and it worked.

'Okay, I don't mind. But you'll have to buy me some lunch after, I'll be hungry by then.'

Ralph didn't really know why he had worried so much about trying to talk to Rebecca. She was actually quite nice and friendly. And warm. So warm that he wanted to cuddle up close, rest his head on those large, soft breasts and just go to sleep.

'Great, see you tomorrow then.'

He left the shop in a befuddled daze, his heart singing as he floated back home about a foot off the ground having completely forgotten to take his packet of fish and chips with him. He'd left it on the counter together with the change from a fiver. But he couldn't have cared less. He wasn't hungry any more.

Was this it, the chance he'd been waiting for?

By the time the match kicked off, there was no sign of her. Although it was a cup match with a great deal of intense local rivalry Ralph's mind was somewhere else. He could only think of Rebecca and what they might get up to after lunch. He kept scanning the horizon but she didn't appear and panic started to set in. She was having a laugh. She never really intended to come.

Chalky White sent a high ball over towards Ralph in the penalty area and he went up to head it. Suddenly, there she was! Behind the goal.

'Hi,' she greeted.

'Hello,' said Ralph. He was in mid air at the time, looking down at those gorgeous tits and trying to make out the outline of her nipples through her ever-so-tight sweater when the ball suddenly whacked him on the side of the head and he crumpled to the ground in an untidy heap. What a fucking prat. For a second or two the world went away and pictures started forming in his mind.

Ralph dreamed he was in Norway surrounded by a snowy landscape and as he lay in the shadow of the icy Fjord, a fat penguin wearing Newcastle United kit waddled over towards him. It had a human head with an unshaven face and ugly hairs protruded from its bulbous nose. He could smell the foul stench of garlic and stale beer on the hideous hybrid's breath as it drew close and peered into his watery gaze.

The weird creature breathed in deeply causing its stomach to distend obscenely to an enormous size and then an icy stream of putrid water spurted from its mouth all over Ralph's head and down his body.

His eyes flickered open and he found himself staring into the quizzical face of Barry, the team's overweight, drunken Geordie of a so-called trainer who had come on to attend to him. Barry was employing the only treatment available for any injury at the time. The bucket and sponge method. It was all he knew. It involved sploshing cold water all over the injured player until he begged you to stop. Ralph was completely soaked and shivering wildly, after all, it was half way through a typical early spring cold snap. This wasn't in the script.

'Where are you, son?' Barry enquired.

'Dancing with the ice maidens of Oslo,' replied Ralph dreamily.

'He doesn't even know who the fuck he is,' said Barry.

'Well get him up and tell him he's Pelé,' suggested Chalky White to the great amusement of the ensemble now gathered round to witness the last rites.

Barry turned to the ref. 'We'd better get him off,' he said.

With the help of the opposing trainer he carried the wounded soldier from battlefield to the Spartan changing room about fifty yards away. Actually it was no more than a wooden hut. They deposited him on a bench and turned to leave.

'It's about twenty minutes to half time,' said Barry. 'I'll check with you then.' And off he went closing the door behind him. Ralph lay in the gloom feeling utterly despondent and in despair about the effect this was bound to have on Rebecca. She probably thought he was a right puny little bastard. She'd never go out with him now.

A few moments later, he was half dozing when the door opened. Surely it wasn't half-time already? Had he lost all sense of time? But it was Rebecca. She slipped in and closed the door behind her.

'You all right?' she asked without seeming at all phased by the fact that she had entered a blokes' football changing room. About the most male domain possible apart from the members' enclosure at Lords. She was so at ease that Ralph found himself wondering how she might have become familiar with that kind of surrounding.

'I'll survive,' he answered in the most macho way he could possibly summon without exacerbating the maelstrom in his head. He felt pathetic. Like an invalid. He assumed she'd come to call off their date but she seemed very sympathetic.

'Poor thing,' she said.

She'd been standing by the door but now walked the few steps across the tiny, cold room towards the bench on which Ralph lay prostrate just as Barry had left him. Waves of heat seemed to emanate from her body as she approached him. Her nipples were certainly visible now, bulging, large and erect through that sexy sweater. Must have been the cool air reacting with the fire in her breast. Despite his sorry state Ralph started to become aroused by her presence.

Rebecca slid a small, rickety old stool over towards Ralph's bench and lowered herself onto it. Her movements were quite deliberate as she fixed his eyes with a friendly, unflinching gaze. As if she knew something he didn't. The stool was about the same height as the bench on which Ralph lay so her knees were practically touching his face and he could almost see right up her short skirt. He didn't want it to seem obvious but he just couldn't stop looking. Was she doing it on purpose?

Mingling with the surrounding odours of liniment and damp wood Ralph could just detect the faint hint of a sweetish scent whose scource, he sensed, lay in that mysterious place between her legs. The more he sensed it, the more stimulated he became.

'You're soaking,' she said, placing her hand on the sopping fabric that covered Ralph's stomach. But he didn't care if it was the onset of double pneumonia. That one, slight contact sent a message directly to his old chap which immediately sprung fully to attention in his jock strap. He tried to hide it by crossing his legs but it was no good.

'At least something's still working okay,' Rebecca announced.

'Sorry.'

'I'll take it as a compliment. Anyway, I should be apologising to you. Shouldn't have said anything while you were playing.'

Ralph started to feel light-headed. Just like at closing time at the Crown and Sceptre after three pints of shandy. Was it the bump on his head? No it was her. Bloody tasty. Sophia Loren, Sabrina and Connie Francis all rolled into one.

Tell her for fuck's sake. I Can't. Yes you can. Go on, tell her. I Can't. Yes you can. If you don't tell her now you never will. I Can't. Yes you can.

Mustering all his courage he took his life in his hands.

'Don't half fancy you.'

'Think I don't know that?'

'Really? How?'

'When a bloke follows you around for months with a huge bulge in his trousers it gives you some idea what's on his mind.'

Ralph was embarrassed.

'Didn't think you noticed me.'

'Not notice a thing like that?'

'Why didn't you say anything?'

'Why didn't you?'

'You hardly even acknowledged my existence.'

'Just part of the game. I was waiting for you to invite me for a ride in that cute little car of yours. If you'd have left it any longer I would have asked you.'

'I was going to but . . . dunno really . . . never seemed like the right time.'

'Never understood why blokes find it so hard to say what they feel.'

'Oh, that's easy. Worked that one out a long time ago. Fear of rejection.'

'Think I'd rather be rejected than miss out on a relationship because I was too shy.'

'Bet you don't get rejected much.'

'That's what you think.'

'No bloke I know would reject you.'

'Those perverts you go round with wouldn't reject a diseased warthog.'

'That's true.'

'Blokes like that think they've only got to buy you a drink and you'll have it off with them but when you won't they go round telling everyone you're a slag.'

'But you've got loads of boyfriends.'

'Have I?'

'Haven't you?'

'Who says?'

'Everybody.'

'Oh yeah. What else do they say? Cheapest ride in town? Gets her kit off for three and thruppence ha'penny? Does it with anybody with a posh enough car?'

'They say you do it, yeah.'

'Anything wrong with that?'

'Er, no, course not.'

'That's all right then.'

'But do you though?'

'Wouldn't you like to know.'

Ralph was warming to the conversation. His earlier nervousness had disappeared and he felt calm and collected. Like he could say anything. Ask her anything.

'Yes I would actually.'

'Do you think I'm a slag then?'

'God, no. I'd never say that.'

'You sure?'

'Course.'

'Good.'

'What about Michael Watkins though?'

'That creep, what about him?'

'He says you did with him and he's got a Triumph Spitfire.'

'Well you can tell him from me he's a liar. The car's all right but he's a dickhead.'

'So you didn't then?'

'You must be joking. Hasn't got the brains he was born with. If he ever tried it on I think I'd break his arms. Or let his tyres down maybe. Probably upset him more.'

'So none of it's true then?'

'What if it is?'

'No problem. I'm just trying to put the record straight.'

'You a reporter from *The Times* or something.'

'No, just interested.'

'I can see how interested you are.' She nodded towards his crotch.

'Sorry.'

'Don't worry, I'm used to it.'

'So you have done it then?'

'Haven't you?'

'Er yeah, course.'

'Well you know all about it then don't you?'

'Course I do but, well I . . .'

'It's all rumours.'

'Is it?' Ralph couldn't help feeling slightly disappointed.

'Well, mostly. I may have been out with a few blokes but I don't do it with anybody, I don't charge for it and I didn't do it with Michael Watkins even if he thinks I did. Do you think I'd do it with a bloke just because he's got a nice car?'

'Well no, it's just that he said . . .'

'I might do it with a bloke if liked him enough but I don't see why I should make a secret of that like everyone else does. It's a perfectly natural thing you know. Everybody wants it even if they pretend they don't.'

'Even girls?'

'Yes Ralph, even girls.'

'Blimey.'

Then the bombshell. 'And since we're being so honest about all this then I suppose I might as well tell you that I didn't come here to watch a silly football match.'

'What then?'

'Can't you guess?'

'Is this part of the game too?'

'No but this is.'

So saying, Rebecca grabbed the waist-band of his shorts and yanked it over what had now become a Nelson's column of an erection exposing the fleshy, hard log in all its glory. Whoah there!

What the fuck was she doing? It was the first time a female had seen Ralph's cock since his Mother had last bathed him at the age of four.

'Mmm, you Jewish then?'

'Er, yes. Do you mind?'

'Not me. I can do without the flabby bits thank you very much.'

Such audacity. They might have been discussing the weather.

Ralph's thumping headache had almost gone but he still felt a bit shaky and began to wonder if any of this was really happening or just a figment of his imagination. But the doubts began to disappear when Rebecca twiddled her index finger around the helmet of his willie. Little teaser, he thought. He was wrong.

Then, much to his joy and amazement, she leaned forward and began licking the tip of his swollen organ. Such sweet caress as he had never before experienced. Blimey, what the fuck is she up to? This is good. This is fucking good. She sat up to re-position herself more comfortably. No, please don't stop. Not now, please. He felt a sudden urge to get hold of those tits and started to raise himself but she pushed him back.

'No you don't,' she ordered. 'You're injured.' Thought so. Wrong again.

She gripped the base of Ralph's throbbing member steady in her hand and moistened her lips with her tongue. Then she slipped them right over the bulging item and proceeded to slide her mouth up and down it as if she was sucking an iced lolly.

This must be oral sex, he thought. This is very good. Very fucking good indeed.

If Rebecca had a reputation then she was certainly living up to it. Not in the depraved way her detractors might have suggested but with a meaningful, touching affection. There was a great deal of slurping, moaning, heaving and grunting. Ralph just lay back with his eyes closed and let her get on with it. He was in heaven. Should he do something? Better not. She'd told him not to. Was it all just a dream? No, it was happening. This was definitely happening.

After a short while he ventured a glance. What was that other hand doing inside her pants? Cor crikey! At the same moment she looked up and met Ralph's gaze with a smiling, painful, guilty expression of lascivious abandon that he found exceptionally beautiful. She was enjoying it as much as he was for sure. That was it. He couldn't hold it any longer and neither could she.

Rebecca closed her eyes, moaned and gulped hard.

When it was over and after a short interval of recovery during which they both panted softly in unison, Rebecca pushed Ralph's wilting member back into his shorts and adjusted her own underwear before standing up to leave.

'Won't need my lunch now,' she announced before wiggling her ass and slipping out of the door before he even had time to ask 'Can we do this again sometime?'

A moment later she put her head back round the door.

'By the way,' she announced cheerily, 'I've only done it once. Some bloke forced me and if I ever see him again I'll cut his dick off. Bye.' And she was gone.

Ralph had hardly moved an inch from the time Rebecca entered until she left but he felt like he'd travelled round the world. Where the fuck did she learn to do that?

Had it really happened? Yes, it had really happened. He was sure about that.

The door opened again. Was she coming back for more? But it was Barry.

'I've come to check on you.' He said 'How are you feeling?'

'Fine,' said Ralph cheerfully, 'I've just had a great blow job from a beautiful, sexy bird and I feel really good.'

'Daft cunt,' said Barry, 'Fucking head's gone. Must be fucking concussion. Better drop you off at the hospital on the way to the fucking boozer.' He paused. 'The bastards'll have to check if you've still got a fucking brain left. Ha, ha ha.'

'No, really,' Ralph pleaded, 'Didn't you see her? She's a cracker.' He felt he deserved a bit of recognition for this.

'I think I'll fucking take you now,' said Barry.

The Beautiful Game
The Passing Game

Don't think that passing is a last resort or that passing back or square is some sort of disgrace or that you are letting someone down by doing it.

There is absolutely nothing wrong with laying the ball square or back.

Indeed, it is an absolutely essential part of the creative way of playing football.

You can gain great advantage from doing so particularly if you are in a position where you have collected the ball with your back to the goal you are attacking.

You can switch the play from side to side and put the opposing defence on the wrong foot or even completely out of shape if you know what you are doing.

What are you doing?

Sometimes, if you don't know by instinct it can't be taught.

Don't do what so many inexperienced players do and turn into trouble.

Play the way you are facing to your team-mate who can see what is happening up ahead.

Sensible?

I should fucking say so.

14
The Cosh 'n' Helmet

As they'd approached the age of eighteen, the lads had shifted venues and started meeting in the Crown and Sceptre, or the Cosh 'n' Helmet as they affectionately called it, in Station Road. For Ralph it was a significant change. It signalled his entry into manhood much more than his Bar Mitzvah or even his new car had ever done. To walk into the public bar (not the lounge – that was mainly for respectable folk like ladies and older, married couples) even if it was only to order half a pint of shandy made him feel like a man, a working man, part of the culture, fulfilled. It was only when certain people opened their mouths to speak that the illusion was shattered and he started to feel like a stranger. Unfortunately, most of those who made Ralph depressed and frustrated in this way were usually sitting at his table. His own friends in other words.

Ralph wasn't detained at the hospital for long and when he was discharged he made straight for the Cosh 'n' Helmet. He had some drinking time to catch up on. Almost as soon as he got there the interrogation began.

'What, in the shed while the fucking game was going on?' asked Chalky incredulously.

'Yep.'

'I don't fucking believe it,' said Wilkie.

'Don't then.'

'Prove it.'

'I don't have to prove it.'

'Why should we believe it?'

'Don't fucking believe it then.'

'You've made it up. Just like Eleanor.' Darryl had never forgiven Ralph for upstaging him over the school nurse incident. It made his own story seem puny by comparison.

'No I didn't.'
'Why you though?' Wilkie.
'Dunno. Didn't ask.'
'What was it like then?' Chalky.
'Great.'
'But she didn't let you . . .' Chalky paused.
'Let me what?'
'You know.'
'Know what?'
'Oh come on Ralph, you know. Do it. You know.'
'Not exactly.'
'So it was just a blow job then?' Wilkie.
'Sort of.'
'What do you mean sort of?' Darryl.
'Well it was more of a suck job really.'
'But she didn't get her knickers off?' Chalky.
'No.'
'She's a cock teaser then.' Darryl.
'No she isn't.'
'Must be a dirty little whore,' said Wilkie with a touch of venom.
'No she isn't.'
'Must be.'
'How the fuck do you know?' asked Ralph.
'From what you just told us, you bastard.'
'I never said she was a dirty whore,' Ralph insisted.
'Well she must be a horny bitch if she really did what you said.'
'She may be a horny bitch but she's not a dirty whore.'
'What's the fucking difference?'
'Enormous. As big as the empty space between your fucking ears.'
'How can you say she's not a dirty whore if she's a horny bitch?'

They all leaned forward. They wanted to know what possible explanation Ralph could offer in defence of his extraordinary statement.

'Look you dimwits, first of all she smells sweeter than a rose and I can assure you she's as clean as our own mothers. Secondly, whores get paid for it.'

'I bet she's got her price,' said Wilkie.

'I bet she fucking hasn't,' Ralph retorted.

'Fifty pence and a current bun I reckon,' added Chalky helpfully.

'Well I don't reckon she'd touch you with a barge-pole for a million fucking quid.'

'Oh no. Why not?' Chalky.

'Cos you're an ugly plonker.'

'Can't argue with that,' commented Darryl.

'She's a horny bitch then,' Chalky.

'What's wrong with that?'

'Well, you know, it's a bit common.'

'How come?'

'Well just to do it with anybody like that.'

'I'm not just anybody.'

'Well someone she doesn't really know then.'

'You hardly know her but I bet you'd do it with her if you got half a chance.'

'I might.'

'He'd do it with the cat's arse if he got half a chance,' Darryl.

'That's true,' Wilkie.

'Wouldn't kick her out of bed,' Chalky.

'Very charitable,' said Ralph. 'And that's okay is it?'

'What do you mean?'

'It's okay if you want to shag her but if she wants to shag you she's a whore.'

'Well you've got to be careful haven't you?'

'Careful of what?'

'Might catch something.'

'Oh I see, she's diseased now is she? You'll be telling me she's a fucking Spurs Supporter next. Anything to sully her reputation.'

They all made the sign of the cross as if warding off the evil eye.

'But she might have something.'

'You might have something.'

'No I fucking haven't.'

'Yes you fucking have.'

'What?'

'A disease of the fucking mind if you ask me.'

'She does it. You can see that just by looking at her,' Chalky.

'Well if she didn't you'd be complaining she was fucking frigid.'

'Most of 'em are,' Wilkie.

'No they're not.'

'Or lesbians,' Darryl.

Ralph was becoming impatient. He'd had enough of this. All right, one more try.

'Look guys,' he said, 'I think I speak for all of us when I say that getting a leg over is our main aim in life apart from playing centre forward for Real Madrid.'

'Correct,' Chalkie was happy to confirm the position.

'However,' Ralph continued in Perry Mason, courtroom style, 'Any girl who won't let us do it must be frigid.'

'Must be,' Wilkie.

'Or a lesbian,' Darryl.

'Or both,' Chalkie.

'Right, so let's see if I've got this right. Any bird who's good enough to give us a bit of a sniff is either a dirty whore, a horny bitch, diseased or common?'

'A bit rough, yeah,' Wilkie.

'And any one who won't is either frigid or a lesbian or both.'

'That's about it,' Darryl.

'For fuck's sake.' Exit Perry Mason. Enter Alf Garnet. 'You can't slag off a girl for liking the same fucking thing as you do.'

'So you reckon Rebecca enjoyed sucking your mangy cock then? If she really did,' Chalky.

'She did.'

'What enjoy it or suck it?' Darryl.

'Both.'

'Why didn't she let you do it to her then?' Wilkie.

'Cos she's not a slapper.'

'What? Rebecca? You must be joking mate. She's a horny bitch,' Chalky.

Christ, not again.

'How the fuck do you know?' Ralph.

'Everyone knows,' Wilkie.

'Well you're a horny bloke.'

'So?'

'Everyone knows that too.'

'But she's a bird,' Chalky.

'So what?'

'She puts it about.'

'So would you if you had the chance.'

'Well I wouldn't mind giving it one but I wouldn't want to marry her,' Wilkie.

'But that's daft. It's like what Groucho Marx said. I wouldn't want to join any club that would have me as a member.' They all laughed.

'What's communism got to do with it?' It was Chalkie.

Ralph sighed.

'Well I think she's really nice. To me she's an angel.'

'Don't tell us you're fucking in love with her,' Darryl.

'It's nothing like that you daft sod. It's just I've realised they like it too and there's nothing wrong with that.'

'Except it makes her a bit of a dirty whore,' Wilkie.

'Not to me you ignorant pillock. I'm grateful to her even if it wasn't the full frontal.'

'There you are then,' said Darryl with an arrogant haughtiness.

'What the fuck do you mean by that?' Ralph asked impatiently.

'She's a fucking cock teaser. Told you so.'

There were nods of agreement and sounds of disapproval around the table.

It was no good. He just had to get out and explore the world. He'd suffocate here.

The Beautiful Game

Your Best, At All Times

Every pass, tackle or shot must be a good one.

Never relax back with a 'That'll do' attitude. Concentrate on what you are doing for every second of the match. Make sure that everything you do is done to the very best of your ability at all times.

Even if you have a bad game, if you can honestly say you did your best, no one will have any reason to slag you off. And if they do, fuck them. Your conscience is clear.

'That'll do' never won anything.

In football or in life.

15
Collision Decision

Then, out of the blue, an incident occurred that brought Ralph's plans to fruition a lot quicker than he'd expected. Car ownership had most certainly turned out to be watershed in his life and for a while he did feel more liberated but it didn't take him long to realise that he'd fallen into a terrible trap. He'd signed a three-year hire- purchase agreement for the car and would have to continue working all that time to pay it off. The prospect filled his heart with gloom and the time stretching out before him started to seem like an eternity. He'd been kidding himself. What a berk he'd been. He wasn't free at all. Sure, the car had enabled him to get to Chelsea away matches, all around London, down to the South Coast and even up to Scotland. Plus he'd had few near misses with girls on the back seat and although he hadn't yet found one willing enough to agree to the full blown act of which he dreamed he felt the moment of fulfilment couldn't be that far away. But did he really need the car to help him get laid? Women were everywhere in the world yet now he was stuck here because of the car. Every day he dreamed of swimming with the dolphins, visiting ancient sites, exploring the tropics, crossing the equator, meeting exotic people and seeing the new world but he couldn't wait three fucking years until he'd finished paying for the fucking car. All this was going through his mind in the seconds before the crash.

Driving through the crowded rush hour streets of South London on his way to work one morning, Ralph was dreaming of foreign shores and plotting his route to them. He was late as usual and getting later all the time. The traffic was snarled up, zooming forward for ten yards at a time before stopping dead again. Petrol fumes filled the air, the noise of lorries and buses was deafening and, to add insult to injury, the car radio had packed up. It was almost as bad as being on the fucking train. Ralph was pissed off beyond measure and paying no attention at all when the car in front of him stopped abruptly after one of the mad lurches. It all seemed to happen in slow motion. He sensed what was about to occur but couldn't do anything to prevent it. Maybe subconsciously he'd wanted it to happen.

It wasn't a bad accident. Just a bump really. But the effect it had on Ralph's life was immense. During the short moment between realising he wouldn't be able to avoid a collision and the actual impact itself, he had made up his mind. As he sat at the wheel after the bonnet of his car had become inextricably twisted together with the boot of the one in front he chuckled softly to himself and said aloud 'Right, that's it. I'm off.'

Glancing across the street at the scruffy, gloomy shops of Wandsworth High Street a flashing neon sign in one of the windows caught his eye and burnt a glimmer of hope in his mind. It almost shouted at him.

'LOW-COST FARES' it announced. 'LAST MINUTE REDUCTIONS'.

A feeling of liberation welled up inside him and for the first time in his life Ralph felt fully awake. It was one of those special moments.

Nobody seemed to take any notice as he stepped out of the car and wandered slowly into the travel agent. He was oblivious to the ranting of the middle-aged driver of the car he'd collided with who, in between shouting and gesticulating, was crazily attempting to separate the two vehicles with his bare hands.

Half an hour later Ralph re-emerged on to the pavement, hailed a passing cab and instructed the driver to take him straight to the Crown and Sceptre as fast as he could. He needed a fucking drink, and quick. As his cab pulled away, he viewed the scene that continued to attract quite some attention from passers by. The bloke with the bashed-in car was still obviously agitated and upset. He was being interviewed by a policeman whilst another policeman was ineffectively trying to direct the traffic which had jammed up as far as the eye could see. A recovery vehicle was loading up Ralph's car. There was a huge din of blaring car horns and shouting from the many frustrated motorists whose lives had been put on temporary hold while it was all sorted out.

Now travelling in the opposite direction of his original intentions and leaving behind the chaos he had created, Ralph chuckled softly to himself again. The day after tomorrow he'd be out of there.

THE BEAUTIFUL GAME

Play It Simple, Nice 'n' Easy

Football's an easy game if you want it to be. You don't have to make a defence splitting pass every time you get the ball. Or dribble round everyone and try to score every time you get the ball. Play it easy. If there's nothing much on, make something happen. Pass it to someone close by and move into space for a return ball. Tell your team-mates to get their arses moving by running into space, creating options and stopping their daydreaming.

You have to create options for yourself and the team. They need to create options for you. We must all be creative together.

And that's in life by the way. Not just football.

16
Kafka and the Grinning Gigolo

A few more gulps of lager were called for. The regular studio team, that motley collection of clapped-out footballers orchestrated by Dennis the grinning gigolo, cringed quietly in front of the cameras, furiously biting their fingernails and shifting nervously in their seats as they listened to their celebrated guest.

Soon, sweat began to form in their hair and on their brows and before long it streamed profusely down their red faces and soaked into their shirts until large damp patches began to form under their arms. They imagined viewers throughout the country screaming in shock at Ruud's foul-mouthed invective and covering their children's ears lest they be cursed forever upon hearing such beastliness. He can't say that. Where the fuck does he think he is? The Folies fucking Bergerè?

Many viewers worshipped the ground on which their favourite pundits walked even if they realised the old codgers could hardly kick a ball straight on it any more. But this was disappointing. Now the smart-suited soccer icons appeared like startled rabbits caught in the headlights and could only manage to smirk in a laddish sort of way in response to Ruud's public airing of the troublesome 'S' word. Clearly, elements of doubt had crept into their cosy equation. Was their authority being tested? What if people believed these crazy ideas? Would Gullit's popularity rating soar above their own? Or would the viewers join the true experts in disowning this nonsense of trying to link our great game with such a sordid activity as sex? Yes, surely they were bound to agree there was no place for such turgid pornography in sport. But even as they reassured themselves, a terrible vision loomed in their minds – their own credibility slipping quietly round the toilet bend and slowly out to sea. Whoever would have thought that four little letters could create such a fuss?

It reminded Ralph of the time many years ago when Kenneth

Tynan earned himself a place in broadcasting history by being the first person to say 'fuck' on television and the entire nation reeled in shock as if no one had ever heard the word before. But of course, supposedly respectable people always did become childishly bashful at the slightest allusion to sex despite it being as fundamental to our lives as food and drink.

Ralph had often experienced this juvenile attitude in the pub during serious, after-work drinking sessions when any mention of sexual congress would cause fully-grown men to titter like schoolboys caught reading *Tit-Bits* behind the bike-sheds. On occasion he watched in amazement as they burst into uncontrollable mirth at a lewd innuendo that would make even Bernard Manning cringe. They were compensating for their perplexity. Although they might have grown physically to adult size their libidos were stuck in adolescence. Whilst maintaining a pretence of respectability, they had never managed to progress spiritually from the primitive attitudes of childhood and so they behaved like sniggering school kids. Copious amounts of alcohol temporarily removed the inhibition that normally disguised this unfortunate condition and thus, on these beer-fuelled occasions, the true state of their minds in all its juvenile turmoil was revealed to everyone except themselves. They, of course, were far too pissed to realise that the mask was slipping.

But although the silly gits may have joked unashamedly in the pub after a few tongue-loosening drinks with their mates, when it came to offering an opinion on sexual matters in a more formal setting such as a business meeting or dinner party it was a different story. Suddenly they underwent a metamorphosis of Kafkaesque proportions and were highly affronted by any mention of the subject. Adopting a most serious tone, they'd launch into a passionate diatribe against the evils of pornography followed by a load of garbled old nonsense about standards in society. They might even have tried to suggest that it was only out of a deep sense of duty that they themselves had ever performed the rather rude act of sweaty intimacy and naturally they made quite sure they didn't enjoy it. Not even in the slightest. Sexual intercourse for fun? No thanks. We're respectable. According to society, this was the correct attitude to a thorny subject.

The result of all this silliness was an irrational phobia for the essential, basic and most enjoyable function of sexual intercourse. A virtual allergy to the very thing that most people liked doing more than anything else even if they couldn't quite bring themselves to admit it. A ridiculous paradox of which there were many in our deranged society.

Needless to say, these comedians never felt horny or had fantasies or fancied anyone other than their spouses. No sir! They were also a bunch of liars. Some ended up in massage parlours seeking executive release from their pain provided by ambidextrous young ladies whilst others took to the solitary slap. Then there were those who gained solace in food. Great lorry loads of it. Fatty, sweet, creamy or fried. As much as they could stuff in their necks as often as they could get it. Otherwise they might have gone completely mad and done something they would really regret like joining the Conservative Party or becoming a Hereford United supporter.

In the process, sex had become trivialised and the creative energy it produced was channelled into the negative role of maintaining the status quo. Perhaps it was this that set Ralph apart from his fellow beings. He just couldn't accept the way things were and was always on a mission to change them for the better. But most people didn't want to be challenged in this way. They preferred the quiet life. They wanted everything to be better but they didn't want it to change. It followed therefore, that any television personality who displayed an aloof disdain towards sexual matters was held in high esteem by the vast majority of viewers who much preferred not to be bothered by the whole messy activity. Ruud Gullit was clearly not in this category. But what did he really mean by sexy football? Teams playing in the nude? Replica bondage gear? Ralph didn't think so. Along with most other football purists he knew exactly what Ruud meant. He was talking about the beautiful game. The game that turned you on with its skill, beauty and excellence.

17
Foreign Muck

Ralph paid off the cab, entered the pub, strode up to the bar and ordered a large scotch. He swallowed it down in a single gulp and ordered another even before the barman had brought his change. This time he added a little water and went to sit in the usual place by the window. It was early evening before the gang started showing up by which time Ralph was glowing all over in his newly discovered combination of freedom and alcohol. Lots of both.

'You're early,' said Cheesy, 'Got the sack or something?'

'No, left.'

'What just walked out?'

'No, never went in.'

'They won't like that.'

'Too bad.'

'What'll you tell 'em?'

'Nothing.'

'You'll 'ave to tell 'em something when you go back.'

'I'm not going back.'

'What, got another job?'

'Nope.'

Cheesy was mystified.

'What are you going to fucking do then?

'Going abroad.'

They were all flabbergasted by the glib announcement.

Ralph explained what had happened with the car.

'You mean you just left the bastard in the middle of the fucking road?'

'Yep.'

'And you've left your job?'

'Yep.'

'And you're fucking off abroad?'

'Yep.'

'When?'

'Day after tomorrow.'

An awkward silence descended over the group until Darryl Bingham piped up. 'What the fuck do you want to do that for?'

'Observe other cultures, see different ways of life, taste different foods, meet different people.' Ralph scanned the dowdy interior of the Cosh 'n' Helmet. 'I mean, this can hardly be the fucking be all and end all of civilisation can it?'

'Yes it fucking can,' said Wilkie Wilkes. 'This is the best country in the world, every cunt knows that.'

'How the fuck can you say that? You've never been further than twenty miles from your own fucking doorstep.'

'There's no fucking need. What have they got that we haven't?'

'Well you'll never fucking well know if you don't fucking well go and find out. Daft sod.'

'Sounds to me like you're the daft sod. No job, no car and you'll probably get eaten by cannibals. Where are you going anyway?'

'Israel.'

'Oh well that's it.'

'What do you mean that's it?'

'You'll be murdered by Arabs.'

'Wouldn't go abroad myself,' said Chalky White. 'Put money in foreigner's pockets.'

Ralph was getting fed up with this. He'd thought they'd be pleased for him. Impressed that he'd had the courage to break away.

'That's fucking daft,' he said, 'Don't you want to visit the world's great cities? Eat real spaghetti in Italy. Snails in Paris. Paella in Spain?'

'I wouldn't eat that fucking foreign muck,' said Chalkie becoming passionate as he warmed to the subject.

'Why the fuck not,' asked Ralph. 'What's wrong with it.'

'It's fucking rubbish. I don't like it.'

'But you've never tried it. How the fuck do you know you don't like it.'

'Look, I haven't fucking tried it because I don't fucking like it. All right?'

Ralph felt like knocking their heads together. But why should he bother to argue? He had his ticket in his pocket and he was off.

THE BEAUTIFUL GAME
We Must All Work For Each Other

This is one of the things that coaches always say but what does it mean?

It is absolutely no good standing still like a statue and waiting for someone else to make things happen.

It is also useless waving your arms about in a frenzy shouting 'Here, here!' if you've got three markers breathing down your neck.

Neither is there any point in calling for a pass from the farthest possible position away from the bloke with the ball. He just won't be able to get it to you and that will be your fault not his. You know he can't get it that far so don't be silly.

Don't be lazy either. You can only be lazy if you happen to be Gazza or Le Tissier or Zola or Del Piero or someone like that with exceptional skill and a superior talent for the game and if you do possess such ability there is absolutely no need for you to be reading this.

Find some space. Move into a position where it's easy for the player with the ball to get it to you. Run off the ball taking your marker with you and creating space for others to exploit at the same time.

Talk to your mates and let them know where you are but watch out! Don't shout for the ball and then move away because the bloke with the ball is going to pass it to where he heard you shouting isn't he? And you aren't there any more are you? Plonker.

Pick the right moment to call and make it an urgent, loud, insistent request but make sure you're in a good position to receive the ball and do something positive with it.

Don't call just for the sake of calling.

Call because there's a fucking good reason to get the ball to you.

Don't do anything unless there is a fucking good reason for doing it.

And that's in life, by the way. Not just football.

18
Mayhem at the Palace

Not long after Ralph had made his momentous decision to be a footballer the truly great day arrived when he went to his first professional football match. His Dad took him and he would never forget it.

Crystal Palace versus Queens Park Rangers in the Third Division South.

Anyone who loves football remembers their first match as an almost religious event in their lives and Ralph was no exception. On that chilly December afternoon sometime during the mid-fifties, his life changed for good.

It was one of those childhood memories that sparkled in the mind and he sometimes wished he could travel back in time to touch and feel the occasion just for a moment.

The heavily crowded train pulled in to Norwood Junction and Ralph and his Dad squeezed themselves off amongst a massive throng of blokes in big, thick overcoats who were all on the same mission. They made their way out of the dingy station into the drab, terraced streets of South London which, under a gloomy ceiling of winter-grey clouds must surely have been the most depressing environment the world had to offer. Ralph started to feel sorry he'd come. But he needn't have worried. It would all turn out well in the end.

The shivering constituents of a mainly silent multitude all headed in the same direction with what seemed like the most serious intent. It occurred to Ralph that they were like Muslim pilgrims on the road to Mecca. Quiet, determined and on their way to worship at the shrine.

'Which way is it?' he asked.

'Follow the crowd,' his Dad answered.

Sure enough, after a twenty minute walk without having to check the route, they reached Selhurst Park and joined one of the many long queues that snaked their way back from the narrow entrances around the ground. As they slowly shuffled forwards Ralph stared up in awe at the massive floodlighting gantries that seemed like enormous giants peering benignly down on the mayhem below and listened to the heavy metal clang of turnstiles as, one by one, the pilgrims were admitted to the holy compound. He had no idea what to expect. How was he to know? There was hardly any football on TV then and no entire matches except England internationals and the cup final so kids didn't know anywhere near as much about the game as they do today.

The only evidence of affinity amongst the more devoted fans was either a rosette or a club scarf. Many carried those old wooden rattles with which they attempted to encourage their team to greater heights by energetically whirling the awkward contraptions round and round so that they generated a sort of loud, grating sound. Highly inspirational! Ralph eventually acquired one himself and wouldn't have left home without it on a match-day.

Football matches in those days were a predominately working class domain and about the cheapest thing you could do on a Saturday afternoon. Nowadays, of course, attending a match had become a bloody expensive exercise that only the privileged could afford. Whoever would have believed it?

At Palace it was three and six in old money to get in or one and nine if you were a kid but if you arrived with a grown-up he would lift you over the turn-style without paying. This was common practice carried out with the full approval of the man on the gate and the club. Everyone did it. Imagine trying it today. They'd lock you up!

When it came to their turn, Ralph's father had a few words with the steward, handed over a few coins and entered through the turn-style, but Ralph was lifted over by the bloke behind them in the queue. It made him feel slightly inadequate, like a gatecrasher at a party. They entered the ground, found the right entrance to the huge stand and climbed a creaking set of wooden stairs that seemed to groan under the weight of the surge of humanity arriving en masse. It was about ten minutes to kickoff.

As they searched for their places, Ralph and his dad were jostled by grey men (no females to be seen) in grey and brown clothes who all seemed to have brown, nicotine stained roll-ups hanging from their mouths. There were thousands of them hurrying around wearing worried frowns as if they were late for something very important.

Later Ralph realised that they were merely anxious not to miss the kick off and in fact he had become just like that himself. These days he liked to be in his seat, programme in hand, knowing what the teams were and fully prepared for the game long before the players appeared.

Ralph hung on to his dad's hand for dear life. He'd never seen so many people in one place before. The combined smell of urine, stale tobacco and alcohol was almost overwhelming to a young lad. Everything was steeped in it.

They climbed up the stairs from the dark bowels of the stand and emerged into the sudden brightness of the arena causing Ralph to blink and screw up his eyes. When he opened them again and slowly managed to focus on the breathtaking sight spread out before him, his world had changed forever. This, of course, was the moment all football fans remembered best. Your first glimpse of the pitch! It was as if he had arrived on a film set, brighter and more colourful than ordinary life. What a sight! Fantastic! The massive swathe of deep green grass glowed with an energy that drew his gaze like a magnet. It was smooth as a billiard table save for a few brown patches in the goal-mouths and on the centre circle. Bright white lines marking out the playing area were stuck thick and true on the shimmering turf and the goals at each end stood upright and perfectly rectangular unlike the crooked old bits of timber that he was used to in the local park.

The players were already out and warming up. In stark contrast to the dowdy, grey and brown, worn old threads of the crowd, they appeared to have been dressed by a top fashion designer. Meticulously turned out in shiny, brightly coloured strips of claret and royal blue halves versus navy blue and bright white hoops they had obviously all taken the trouble to look at their very best. Hair slicked back with dollops of Brylcream completed the glamorous effect and added an ethereal, shining ambience. Ralph was impressed beyond measure. They looked fantastic. Like gods. Larger than life itself. Smart enough to go to a dinner and dance. They seemed to glide across the ground with the ball at their feet as if it were physically attached to their sparkling, lightweight boots. (Until then, Ralph had assumed that football boots were always covered in mud.) Effortlessly, these fit, muscular athletes controlled and propelled the stitched leather sphere with an amazing speed, skill, strength, and accuracy that was far beyond the capability of normal humans beings. They only seemed to touch the thing and it shot half way across the pitch. They were supermen. That was it. He wanted to be just like them.

Although it was only mid-afternoon, the floodlights had already been switched on to augment the modest illumination offered by a meagre winter sun which, despite its intermittent brightness when it occasionally managed to penetrate the dark grey clouds, failed to spread warmth. But for Ralph there was no need. He felt spiritually heated by the intoxicating atmosphere and the anticipation of a top football match. What a prospect! Talk about colourful! It shone and it was brilliant. He could hardly take it all in.

The infernal dreariness of normal life had been left outside the gates. The boredom of the working grindstone and academic drudgery ceased to exist. The moment they entered the ground everyone in the crowd had begun a new existence together. All their worlds were converted to a communal experience of vibrant colour, top sport and the joy of relaxing outside. For the next one hundred minutes (only ten minutes for half-time then) there was nothing of any pressing importance to worry about except whether their team would win. On that day, Palace was Ralph's team.

As kickoff time approached the excitement mounted. The great Johnny Byrne was playing for Palace and so was Vic Rouse, the Welsh international goalkeeper and Ronnie Allen, a new signing from West Brom. 'It's the Burns and Allen show,' Ralph's Dad joked. Ralph could hardly muster a laugh. He was wide-eyed and breathless. Utterly transfixed by it all.

For two weeks since the last home match only the players and the Manager had occupied the ground, training assiduously to an eerie backdrop created by the huge, empty shell of the main stand and acres of empty terraces. But now the whole place had filled up with tens of thousands of spectators and was brimming over with a great multitude of expectant humanity.

The ref's shrill whistle pierced the air to start the match and a huge roar went up that reverberated throughout the ground and filled the sky. Ralph had never heard such a deafening din. It felt like the pulsating tremor of a volcano erupting. It shook all his senses. Scared him out of his wits. It woke him up with a thrilling rush of elation that had never left him since.

Suddenly, the game was underway and being played at breakneck speed. Great skill, tough tackling, fast running, powerful shooting, thrilling excitement.

The happy crowd of tens of thousands was singing and yelling in cacophonous harmony. They all shouted 'Windy!' when a player hoofed the ball high into the air or made a mistake. Ralph never found out what 'windy' actually meant although he still found himself shouting it at matches much to the amusement of everyone around.

When Palace were on the attack the shouting and rattle waving rose to an ear-splitting crescendo and when they scored half way through the first half the whole place erupted in an huge uproar. People stamped their feet on the wooden floor so that the stand shook crazily as if it might fall down and in a frenzied fervour to cheer their team, the massed crowd on the terraces lost its communal balance and cascaded down towards the pitch. It was frightening, it was magic. The heady atmosphere filled Ralph's whole body as if it had been injected straight into the main artery. Once again, in a moment of stark revelation it only took a moment to decide.

'This is me,' he said quietly to himself as a rush of excitement made its way from the back of his neck right down his spine and tingled his toes. It was another of those moments. Forty odd years later it was still coursing around his system and he was a hopeless addict.

He was to feel that same rush many times since but later in life it was also associated with music, literature, painting and, most of all, sex.

Football has a lot in common with sex as everyone knows.

19
Lust in Utopia

People might say that he went for all the wrong reasons. Not out of ideology or belief or commitment but just to escape. Why did there always have to be a reason for everything? Sometimes you just did things out of instinct and often they turned out to be the best things you ever did. Just like in football.

If Ralph had felt the faint inklings of sympathy with socialist ideals before he went to live on the kibbutz, by the time he returned after that first momentous year he was utterly convinced. To have experienced it at first hand was great. From each according to his ability, to each according to his needs. It actually worked. He saw it actually working. With this simple egalitarian ideal they had made the desert bloom. Created something beautiful out of nothing. A place to be proud of where they wouldn't be exploited nor exploit anyone else. A virtual Utopia filled with the scent of a million rainbow-coloured flowers, where sparkling water flowed freely in the desert, and children flourished and ran free in the warm sun.

It wasn't perfect. No society with people in it would ever be perfect. But it was a bloody sight better than what he was used to. Everyone working together for the good of the community at large. Yes, there were those who took advantage and didn't work that hard but there were others who worked twice as hard as they needed to. It all balanced out in the end. Like most things in life.

But Ralph held his enthusiasm in check. After all, the whole country was surrounded by enemies who had vowed to kill all the Jews. Drive them into the sea.

Hanna Leiberman epitomised everything that was good about the kibbutz. She worked in the orchards from five in the morning driving tractors, organising pickers, liaising with the packing station and even making coffee for everybody.

Ralph was assigned to work there when he first arrived and couldn't keep his eyes off her arse. What a wonderful specimen it was. Tight and beautifully rounded, just waiting to be squeezed like the oranges she grew. Slim and sunburnt with short, dark hair, strong arms and smooth thighs, Hanna wore the skimpiest shorts and the tightest t-shirts. But it was the boots that got him. Robust working boots with heavy duty socks. Very attractive. She was a revelation. So fit, happy and energetic. Ralph had never seen anyone who seemed so completely at one with their environment. It was funny how lust could alter your perception of the truth to the point where you gained such a completely false view of it.

She even caused Ralph's first foreign erection. He was up a ladder picking fruit from the top of a tree and happened to glance down as she drove by on a tractor with the gear stick vibrating between her legs. Her little wave as she passed by seemed to indicate that she reciprocated his interest. He would have to do something about this. But later on at coffee time she rebuffed his approaches with a scathing arrogance that shook him.

'Can I come and see you?'

'No, I'm too busy.'

'You can't be busy all the time.'

'I can be what I want.'

After weeks of rejection, Ralph summoned up the courage to take the bull by the horns. Maybe she was just a little shy. He found out where she lived and set off to visit her. Until then he'd never been to the area where the Members lived and found himself enchanted by the calm and peaceful atmosphere. Water sprinkling on luscious green lawns, fruit trees full of plump, exotic produce, huge flowers ablaze with colour and the pungent scent of herbs and spices wafting on the balmy evening air, seducing the senses into wilful submission.

Like a sort of tropical Milton Keynes.

There was no answer at the first knock but just as he was turning to leave the door opened. He hardly recognised her. She was wearing a floppy, one-piece garment like a large t-shirt that immediately made him wonder if she had anything on underneath. She was rubbing her eyes and looked tired.

'Hello,' Ralph greeted her cheerily. 'I've come to visit.'

'Nobody visits at this time. It's siesta.'

'Oh, sorry, I just wanted to see you.'

'But I don't want to see you.'

'Are you married?'

'That's none of you business.'

There was a short pause.

'You look nice,' he said.

She blushed.

'I think you'd better go.'

'A cup of tea.'

'What?'

'Let's just have one cup of tea and then I promise I'll go and never come back.'

Maybe the look of eagerness and desperation in his eyes influenced her in some way because after a momentary hesitation she relented.

'All right but don't make a noise, my Mother's asleep.'

'You live with your Mother?'

'Is it so strange?'

Hanna's Mother, Esther, had been born in Germany where, as a young woman, she had lived in constant fear of a Nazi jackboot crashing through the front door. But since coming to Israel all that had changed. She now lived in constant fear of Syrian tanks appearing over the hill above the kibbutz. There was always someone who wanted to kill all the Jews.

Hanna was the product of a love affair between Esther and a certain Alf Lewis from Ashby De La Zouche, a British soldier at the time of the British mandate in Palestine. Esther had thought Alf shared her feelings and that they would be married, difficult though that might have been given the political circumstances. The Jews were sworn enemies of the British who seemed to be doing their best to prevent them from establishing their National

Homeland and Esther could easily have been branded a traitor.

Love conquers all. Isn't that what they say? In her romantic naïveté that is certainly what Esther believed and she was overjoyed when she discovered she was pregnant. Perhaps there were good things in the world after all. But the moment she happily informed Alf of her delicate state he ran out of the house and was never seen again.

It all happened a very long time ago but she never spoke about it. Still too painful. What was the point of raking up the pain of the past when there was so much pain in the present?

But of course Hanna made it hard for her to forget. She was the living, breathing link between the past and the present and although Esther loved her daughter as much as any Mother did, she could hardly look at her without sadness in her heart.

Those eyes, that mouth, that look. They were all Alf's.

'Couldn't we be friends?' Ralph asked as Hanna placed two glasses of lemon tea on the table.

'I told you. I'm too busy.'

'Too busy to have friends?'

'I have to look after my Mother.'

'What's wrong with her?'

'She's had a difficult life. Any Jew from Nazi Germany has had a difficult life.'

'Tell me.'

She spoke falteringly often with long pauses between sentences.

'They took them to Auschwitz. My Grandparents were murdered in the gas chambers. Mother managed to escape. I don't know how. She won't say. She was about my age at the time. She walked to Holland, hiding all the time from German patrols and local Nazi sympathisers. But it took many weeks without any real food to eat and she was exhausted and frightened. It was dangerous for Jews in Amsterdam too. Somehow she managed to get to Italy and the Jewish Agency put her on a boat for Palestine but the British didn't let it land and sent it to Cyprus. There were hundreds on her boat and there were many other boats. They were put in camps again. Many were very sick and some died on the way. It was too much. Escaping from one camp and being put in another. I don't think she ever really recovered. She got here eventually but she's been exhausted ever since. Nobody who went through that ever recovered completely. There are others here on the kibbutz and it's the same for all of them. Other things happened. I can't tell you.' She turned away.

It was the first time Ralph had been face to face with the reality of the stories he had been hearing all his life from the safe haven of England's Home Counties and at first he wasn't quite sure how to deal with it. If his own ancestors had made different decisions it could easily have been his own story.

Listening to Hanna, Ralph was assailed by an emotion of such intensity that tears welled up in his eyes. He recalled all those discussions with his Father about Jewish identity which hadn't really meant a great deal to him at the time. But they did now. For the first time since deciding to make football his hobby he felt himself actually starting to believe in something serious.

He took Hanna's hand. 'Look, I'm sorry,' he said, 'I didn't realise.'

'Of course you didn't', she replied snatching her hand away. 'You're on holiday. Why should you be bothered with all this?'

'But I'm Jewish too. Your struggle is my struggle.'

'No it isn't, said Hanna, 'When you've finished here you'll go back to your comfortable life and you'll forget about me and the kibbutz. It's nothing to you.'

But she could hardly fail to have noticed that he was touched by what he'd heard.

Maybe he wasn't as bad as some of those who came here. Don't weaken, it'll end in tears like all the others.

'Please let me see you again.'

'It's no good. Anyway, I know what you really want. The same as any man.'

No one had ever referred to Ralph as a man before. It made him felt quite grown up.

'I need to know more. You can teach me.'

'You don't want a teacher, you want a girlfriend. A Mother perhaps. Well I'm not interested. Sorry.'

'Please, I won't give up on this.'

'Who do you people think you are? You come here for a few months, trick your way into peoples' affections and when you've had enough you disappear without even saying goodbye.'

'No, I'm not like that. Let me see you again. I promise I won't touch you. We can talk, that's all, be friends.'

'I told you already, I'm too busy. Anyway, I'm ten years older than you. Now you must go and please don't come here again without an invitation.'

Of course, the more she turned him down, the more he wanted her.

At dawn the next morning, Ralph arrived for work to find that the roster had been changed and he'd been moved to the late shift in the factory. Hanna must have organised it so that he would be starting work just as she was finishing. When would he see her now?

During the following days Ralph roamed the kibbutz in search of her but to no avail. He scoured the dining room, coffee lounge, members' room, sports hall and swimming pool but Hanna was never anywhere to be seen. Where does she go? Surely she can't be at home all the time. It wasn't worth just going round there and getting knocked back again. She's bound to turn up sooner or later.

The Beautiful Game

Trends always filter down from the top and it used to be the case that if the national team played a negative, defensive type of game, the influence would be felt throughout the country at all levels.

But in the whacky, corporate-controlled world of today, it has come to pass that the top club teams in the best leagues in Europe, which for the uninitiated are Italy, Spain and England, are actually better than the national sides. This is where the standards are made because it is where most of the money is concentrated.

European Club Managers have the cream of players of all nations at their disposal. Available on the open market to be bought by the highest bidder. For this reason the top club teams in Europe are actually more valid footballing yardsticks than the international ones. If we consider it important to try and identify the best that is. Normally, in a competitive activity, that would be the main point of it.

All right, I know, part of the great charm of the game is that the underdog can win occasionally and who would disagree with that. But these days, a match against an obviously weaker footballing nation is regarded as a banana skin waiting to happen. So much so that the underdog almost becomes the favourite.

Now whilst we all love to see a no-hoper succeed from time to time, we also need the giants to display their superior ability and brilliance so that it is clear who is the best and finest. We need to know. We need the standard with which to compare ourselves. Without this we are lost and confused. We can't tell good from bad. Or good from evil.

Of course, international tournaments do appeal to the more nationalistic supporter and very passionate they can be. But most football fans prefer to watch their club sides to their national team which makes you wonder about the purpose of international matches and whether or not that sort of competition will ultimately be able continue in any meaningful way.

20
Hanna's Heartache

It was early summer and getting hotter with each day. Most people went to the pool to relax after work. It was the main recreation area during the seven or eight months of the very warm season. But despite the intense, energy-sapping heat, there was nearly always a hectic game of football in progress on the adjacent grassy area and Ralph usually joined in even though he found it excruciating. Not because of the heat, he could handle that, but because everyone who got the ball just ran forward with it beating anyone they could and trying to shoot. Nobody was interested in passing except him. The problem was that he'd make a pass and then hardly see the ball again. The bastard just never came back.

He left the game covered in sweat, jumped in the pool to cool off and went to sit with Danny, a kibbutznick with whom he'd become quite friendly whilst working together in the factory. It was hot, very hot and the heat made Ralph doze off.

He entered a fitful slumber during which he dreamed of Hanna sitting on her tractor parked up in a secluded part of the orchard after everyone had gone home. She was thinking about him playing football. What a body, see how he moves, such skill, such grace, so beautiful. She stretched out her own lithe form and allowed her bare arms to brush lightly over the nipples that pushed out through the worn fabric of her work t-shirt. It set off a light throbbing in her groin and she let her legs splay out sideways either side of the gear-stick. She moved forward until she felt the familiar feeling of the bulbous plastic handle rubbing against her increasingly excited clitoris that was outlined in the skimpy, tight denim of her shorts.

No, I said I wouldn't do this. But I can't help it when I think about him.

She leaned back and writhed her hips around until it

produced the desired effect. After a short while she was soaked in sweat with the effort. But she liked that. It made everything slippery and sensual. Like being covered in honey or olive oil. Sweat everywhere. Slippery. Over everything. She rubbed it in all over her body. Anything to heighten the pleasure as much as possible.

She positioned herself exactly as she knew would work the best. So that the gear-stick was on the edge of her sweaty, wet pussy that now demanded satisfaction. Slowly the handle that had been touched by countless male orchard workers started to enter the warm, dark, sopping tunnel of her wildly aroused body and she started to climax.

She trembled gently and let out a muffled cry. What did she feel? Pleasure or pain? Who could tell? Only she knew. Ahh! Ahh! And it was over. And her legs ached. And her heart ached. And she needed a man. What she really needed was a real live man to fulfil her properly.

Ralph slipped back into consciousness covered in sweat, his brain clouded by the hot sun that beat down relentlessly. Luckily he had been lying on his stomach otherwise the massive erection he woke up with would have been highly embarrassing.

The dream felt real, as if he could have reached out and touched her. It occurred to him that there was only a very thin dividing line between dreams and reality.

Tenuous, diaphanous and most highly fragile.

'Your back's burning, white man,' Danny informed Ralph. 'Turn over before you start frying like a pig on a spit.'

'What do you know about pigs Jew-boy?'

'You'd be surprised what I know. Turn over. You'll get sick.'

'I'm not quite done yet.'

'Suit yourself.'

Ralph decided to switch subjects as a diversion while he worked desperately on the task of reducing the size of his cock before his skin turned to crackling and the thin layer of fat beneath started to bubble like Welsh rarebit under a grill.

'Why don't you prats ever pass the fucking ball?' he asked Danny.

'You mean just give it to someone else?'

'That's right.'

'Why should anyone want to do that if they don't have to?

'Because it's how the game should be played. I thought you people believed in cooperation.'

'We do. But that's in life, not in football.'

'I think football is a part of life. A very important part.'

'You wouldn't say that if you'd seen your friends dying in wars.'

'Why play football at all then?'

'It's a release. Anyway if you lose the ball there's always someone there to win it back. That's co-operation.'

'But you've got to lose it first. Good tactics.'

'Fighting back is part of our culture.'

'I think the possibilities of people working together are greater than the sum of possibilities of those same people working independently. In life and in football.'

'That's a good one. You sound like my grandfather.'

'Oh thanks.'

'No really, he was a great man. One of the founders of this place. There was nothing here when they first came except rocks and cactus. All you see around you now was built on ideals similar to what you just said.'

'Did he play football?'

'No, but he could dance the hora all night and drive a tractor, how do you say? Like a bastard.'

They laughed.

It had worked. Ralph could now turn over and sit up normally but he couldn't get the dream out of his mind.

Ralph scanned the area for a sight of Hanna but she was still nowhere to be seen.

'Do you know Hanna Leiberman?' he asked Danny.

'Of course, we grew up together.'

'Has she got a boyfriend?'

'I doubt it.'

'Why do you say that?'

'It's a long story.'

'Can you tell me?'

'Ah, so the horny English football maniac is interested in Hanna.'

'I think she's great. Have I got a chance?'

'As much as anyone else.'

'How much is that?'

'Practically none.'

'Why?'

'It's a long story.'

'I wish you'd stop saying that.'

'Look, if I was you I would look for someone else. Hanna's situation is complicated. She's a nice girl but not for you.'

'Thanks.'

'I didn't mean it like that. There's been unhappiness and she finds relationships hard. You're only here for a short time. It's not what she needs.'

'Maybe that's her decision.'

'For sure.'

'Where does she go? I never see her around.'

'She keeps to herself. It's easier.'

'What are you talking about?'

'She was married. It didn't work out. After that she lost interest in a lot of things.'

Once Ralph had got Danny talking the whole story came out.

Hanna had been married to Yossi Barak, another of the group that had grown up together. They were childhood sweethearts which is unusual for kids on a kibbutz. Normally they were more like brothers and sisters and sought romance outside their own settlement. But Hanna and Yossi were inseparable.

Hanna was an intelligent, beautiful, sensual young lady and Yossi was her male counterpart. Clever, handsome, athletic, brave

– a veritable prince among men. The two of them stood out from the bunch and it didn't surprise anyone when they announced that they wanted to marry. It was an occasion of much rejoicing on the kibbutz and a great party was held in celebration. This perfect, loving couple was a symbol of everything the founders had toiled to build. Everything that was good. Born out of the misery of the past they represented new hope for the future. Everyone agreed it was a match made in heaven and waited with huge expectations for the offspring to start arriving. But it all went wrong after the six-day war when Yossi returned home from the front. He never talked about what he had seen but he was a changed man. Suddenly sullen, argumentative and depressed, the flashing smile that had entranced all who met him had been replaced by an anguished, tortured expression. He was in torment. He hardly shaved, hardly ate and couldn't even be bothered to change out of his dirty working clothes. He didn't come home for days on end and when he did he ignored Hanna completely. Before the war they had made love all the time, day and night, whenever there was the slightest opportunity. Now he didn't even touch her and resisted any of her approaches. Hanna was at her wits' end. Even a peck on the cheek would make him snap.

'Don't, leave me alone.'
'What's the matter?'
'Nothing.'
'Let me help you.'
You can't help me. No one can.'
'Why do you keep disappearing?' No answer.

Of course, Hanna was the last to find out what everyone else knew and that was that Yossi had been screwing any other woman who would let him. They were queuing up. Although he had turned into an unkempt, troubled individual, he hadn't lost his rugged good looks or sex appeal. Indeed, maybe his tortured presence made him even more attractive to those women who deluded themselves that a few moments of loving attention would help to cure him of his anguish. A sort of charity fuck. Of course, there were those who didn't need such an excuse. Those who had secretly coveted him for years. Now was their chance to get their hands on the body of this handsome young man without any romantic complications. To taste the mercenary joy of unadorned physical pleasure with no questions asked. To live out a fantasy. To fuck for fuck's sake.

Whatever the motives, those who succumbed to the temptation of this penis-without-a-conscience included other members' wives, female volunteers from different countries who came to help with the harvest, soldier girls seconded to the kibbutz for a week or two, tourists who happened to be passing through and quite a few of Hanna's own friends. Every female of any size, shape or age that he could get hold of.

Except Hanna.

The whole sad, sordid business began to give rise to social problems as complaints about Yossi's indiscretions flooded into the kibbutz secretariat from angry, cuckolded husbands and the parents of lovelorn young girls who had been fucked and then summarily rejected. Many tried unsuccessfully to intercede but Yossi was in self-destruct mode and unreachable. People kept their distance. He gave the impression he could lash out at any moment. At the same time, Hanna started to become aware that many of her friends, even those she'd grown up with and known all her life, were either avoiding her gaze or looking upon her with expressions of pity. The poor girl was confused. Why were they acting like this? She must have been blind. Or maybe she knew but couldn't admit it. Either way, it was some while before her friend, Sonia, found the courage to take Hanna aside and tell her what was going on and it shook the poor girl to the bone.

The very same day, Hanna moved out to live with her mother and started divorce proceedings. She also started to take showers four times a day as if she was trying to wash away the disgrace of Yossi's infidelity and hardly ever went out except to work. On a kibbutz you had to work or you were nothing. This was a lovely young lady who had formerly embodied the life and soul of the community at festivals and social gatherings and been the focus of so many dreams. Now it was her that turned sullen, argumentative and depressed. She spurned all invitations and hardly spoke to a man except for the odd, sordid fling when the hungers of the flesh became too much to bear and even then it was more of an exercise in self-flagellation than love. It was never love. She was still in love with Yossi. The old Yossi.

'And where is this Yossi now?' Ralph asked Danny.

'At this precise moment he is sitting about twenty yards to your right.'

'What?'

'With his wife and kids.'

Ralph ventured a glance.

A tall, swarthy, slightly overweight man sat on the grass drinking a bottle of beer whilst pushing away the two exuberant, blonde children who were trying to jump on him. They were obviously the products of the leggy, blonde woman who lay next to Yossi covered in sun oil.

'She's Swedish,' said Danny. 'He's got his escape now if he needs it.'

'You mean they live here on the kibbutz?'

'Yes.'

'So that's it. No wonder she doesn't go out. She doesn't want to bump into Yossi and his new family. And I thought she was avoiding me.'

'Typical, conceited English,' said Danny 'You think the whole world revolves around you and your fucking empire. But it's not just Yossi she's hiding from. It's life.'

'Don't you fancy Hanna?' Ralph asked.

'She's like a sister to me.'

'Yes but do you fancy her?'

'We all grew up together. Shared bedrooms, saw each other in the shower.'

'Sounds like the perfect opportunity. It must have crossed your mind.'

'It's different on a kibbutz.'

'How different? Do you all have you hormones removed or something?'

'We were like brothers and sisters.'

'But you must have noticed her.'

'All the guys noticed her. Of course we did.'

'I'll bet you all fancied her.'

'Only one was good enough for her.'

'So you do fancy her then?'

'Yes.'

Ralph kept a constant look out for Hanna but only occasionally caught the odd glimpse in passing when she refused to even acknowledge his existence let alone deign to speak to him. If she was with friends she always seemed to be in intense discussion and didn't even say hello. If she was alone she quickened her step and walked in the opposite direction. What on earth could he have done to incur such loathing? But he still fancied her like mad and was determined to strike up a friendship somehow. He was sure they would get on if she would just give him the chance. But time was running out.

It was Shevuot, a sort of harvest festival, and Ralph decided to go along and watch the celebrations. Maybe he would learn something.

As a kid Ralph had often been reluctantly dragged to the synagogue for the various festival services only to be bored out of his mind as the congregation sat in sombre reverence mouthing prayers by rote in an ancient Hebrew dialect that most of them didn't even understand. But this was much more like it. Here they were laughing, dancing, singing and drinking wine in the open air. Tables groaning with food were laid out all over the lawn by the dining room, coloured lanterns were glowing in the trees and three generations of kids, parents and grand-parents all mingled happily together. A band made up of kibbutz members played and sang some of the traditional Jewish melodies he remembered from his childhood whilst others danced the hora barefoot on the grass in huge circles with arms linked, gyrating first one way and then the other.

The atmosphere intoxicated Ralph. Not only had these people worked together to build something from nothing but they also provided their own entertainment.

He was drawn towards the dancers and as he came closer felt the rhythm of the music seeping into his bones. His feet and arms began moving involuntarily and then suddenly he was dancing himself. Dancing in a way he never had before yet somehow knowing the steps as if he he'd been doing it all his life. He was elated and possessed by a spirit that made him want to join in and be part of the celebration. He couldn't help himself. Rushing towards the group, Ralph broke into the circle grabbing the arms of dancers to either side and in a second he was whirling around with the others.

A crowd gathered round to watch the crazy English boy acting the fool. Everyone assumed he was drunk. They'd seen it all before. Young English visitors who drank gallons, didn't wear a hat or cream as a precaution, generally refused to show any respect for the fierce, cruel Middle Eastern sun and usually ended up thoroughly sick as a result. But in fact Ralph hadn't had a single drop. He was merely joyful as he discovered his roots.

The music speeded up and the dancers laughed as they adjusted their own tempo accordingly. Dancing to the right, Ralph was pulled around by Arik, the kibbutz secretary. Stop, the direction changed and his gaze switched to the left. Whoah! It's you! It was her. The person whose hand Ralph had grabbed and was now pulling him around anti-clockwise was Hanna. Once again he hardly recognised her. Her face was shining, her eyes sparkled and she looked happy. But when she caught sight of Ralph her face dropped and she seemed somewhat less than amused. That momentary glance of recognition stopped him dead in his tracks just as the circle changed direction and he was caught unawares. Whoops! The sudden contra tug pulled Ralph off balance and he fell to the floor bringing down Arik with him and then three or four more until there was a pile of bodies in a heap with everyone laughing their heads off. Everyone except Hanna.

'Sorry,' Ralph apologised to everyone around as they all got to their feet. 'Sorry, I think I slipped.' But nobody seemed to mind much. He watched Hanna walk off towards a table on the far edge of the lawn where she sat down next to an elderly lady whom he took to be her Mother. After a short while Ralph followed her over.

'Can I sit here?' he asked Hanna.

'Try it,' she replied.

'Is this your Mother?'

'So many questions.'

The Mother now spoke. 'Hanna please, be polite to the young man.'

'Yes, this is my mother. Her name is Esther.'

The old lady stretched out a scrawny arm in Ralph's direction.

'What is your name young man?' she asked. Her English was perfect like Hanna's.

Ralph stared at the atrophied limb held out towards him and gasped. It leapt out at him. Socked him in the eye. Lights were flashing. Sirens were blaring. He was stunned.

A number consisting of six digits was tattooed on Esther's forearm and the significance of this discovery struck him immediately. For a moment he was speechless. Anyone who bore such an indelible mark could only have been branded with it in horrific circumstances. It was the number they burnt on to each prisoner as they were herded like animals into Nazi concentration camps. What must this diminutive, harmless, charming person have been through for no other reason than she had been born Jewish?

Some hated blacks, some hated Jews. Everyone hated someone. If we didn't hate maybe we couldn't love.

Once again Ralph was shocked to confront the reality of stories he had been told as a child and in his eyes the status of the frail old woman in front of him was suddenly elevated to that of a heroine.

'What is your name?' she asked again.

'I'm sorry. Ralph. My name is Ralph.'

They shook hands.

'I'm honoured to meet you,' said Ralph, bowing his head as if greeting the Queen.

'Oh please,' she said 'I'm just an old woman.'

He had a thousand questions to ask. What was it like? What did they do to you? What did they make you do? How did you escape? But the only question that he could muster was, 'Can I have some wine please?'

'Help yourself young man. You're very welcome.' She waved in the direction of a wine bottle and he poured himself a drink. A very large one.

Hanna went back to dance leaving Ralph with Esther.

'Sometimes I think it's the only thing that makes her happy,' said the old lady.

'Pardon?'

'Hanna. She doesn't have much fun in life except for dancing.'

'Well frankly,' said Ralph, beginning to recover his composure as he soaked up the vino, 'Much as I hate to be rude, I can't say that I am at all surprised.'

'Oh, and why is that?'

'Well, I think your daughter is wonderful, really I do, but since I've been here she's done her best to ignore and insult me. I'm a bit hurt by it actually.'

'I see. You must make allowances. She had an unhappy marriage.'

'I know and I do sympathise but I understand that was some time ago. Surely it's time to live again. Of course that might be difficult if she can't get over her hatred of men.'

'Quite a psychologist aren't you, young mister Ralph from England?'

Ralph was suddenly overcome with embarrassment. The cheap Israeli wine had taken control of his brain and he'd shot his stupid mouth off. As usual, he'd gone too far.

'I'm sorry, It's none of my business,' he apologised. 'I never know when to shut up.'

'It's okay. You may even be right. But you must take into

account that some things take longer to get over and some people take longer to get over them. Look at you for instance.'

'Me?'

'Yes. You've only known Hanna for a short while and already you feel hurt by her. You just said so.'

Ralph hung his head in mock defeat. 'I'm a complete idiot,' he said.

'No, not an idiot. You're young. You don't know yet.'

'Know what?'

'Exactly.'

They watched the dancers for a few minutes until it occurred to Ralph that, despite his Jewish upbringing, he couldn't remember what Shevuot actually commemorated. He thought it must have been one of the minor festivals but all festivals were the same to him as a boy. You went to the synagogue and listened to old men murmuring in a strange, guttural language and occasionally bursting into song for no particular reason that was immediately obvious.

He turned to Esther for an explanation but noticed that the colour had drained out of her cheeks.

'Are you all right?' he asked.

'I'm feeling a little weary. Perhaps you would walk me home.'

'Of course. Shall I get Hanna?'

'No, let her dance.'

Ralph walked Esther home, made sure she was okay and was about to leave when Hanna burst through the door, her eyes blazing with anger.

'Where's my Mother?' she snapped.

'She's went to bed, probably asleep by now. I think she was very tired.'

'Who told you to come here?'

'Well actually she . . .'

'You can go now.'

'I was only trying to help'

'Looking after my mother is my job.'

'Yes, but . . .'

'It won't do you any good.'

'What won't?'

'Helping my mother to try and trick your way into my bed. It won't work. I know what you're up to.'

'Look, your mother felt tired and asked me to walk her home. She didn't want to drag you away from the dancing so she asked me to walk her home. That's it.'

'And I suppose you want a medal for it?'

'No I don't want a fucking medal for it but I don't think I deserve to be treated like a fucking criminal either.' Ralph was starting to get really pissed off. He couldn't hold himself back any longer. 'Look, what the fuck is your problem? Sort it out for fuck's sake. You can't live like this. It isn't living. I was only being friendly but all I've had in return is rudeness and insults. What is the matter with you? I've had enough of this bollocks. I'm off.'

But just as he was opening the door to leave she grabbed his arm.

'No, don't go,' she said, 'You're right. I'm sorry. It was rude.' She seemed to be on the verge of tears. 'Thank you for helping my Mother. Please stay and have a cup of tea.'

Hanna made herself busy with the kettle while Ralph sat on the couch that converted into her bed at night. He was sitting on her bed. Things were looking up.

'I was married once but it broke up,' she explained as she sat next to him. 'My husband was unfaithful. Since then I haven't been comfortable with men. I can't trust them any more. It's not that I don't want relationships but I can't manage it at the moment. Sometimes I think I'm going crazy. I never thought there'd be anyone else but Yossi.'

'But you must have your needs like any woman.'

'I put it aside. You can easily live without romance. I can't have a proper relationship. Not like you want.' Ralph wasn't convinced. He sensed she wasn't convinced herself. It was only what she said, not what she believed. Not what she felt.

She was a woman in her prime. Of course she had needs, achings, cravings, desires, urges. She knew that men looked at her because she could feel them looking. And she knew they wanted her because she could feel that too. And she wanted them. All of them. She wanted to cling tightly to a man's excited body and arrange herself in such a way as to invite the deepest penetration. To feel the ultimate pleasure. The perfect orgasm. But it was impossible. She could hardly even look at a man let alone make love to him. Except for the tawdry occasion when she went on a binge with that drug addict of a playboy she picked up in a bar in Haifa. Ha! Couldn't have been much of a playboy or he'd at least have been prowling the night clubs of Tel Aviv. And that wasn't love anyway. Nothing like it. It was more like the sexual Olympics. You know. He who comes first comes last. The amphetamines kept them going all night which was all that mattered. She refused to even kiss him. But he didn't mind. He wanted to come again and again. That was all. Perhaps it was the only thing they had in common. It made her feel like an animal but she couldn't help it.

Of course, she wasn't about to tell the young English lad all this. Or that in the years since her marriage the only other way she had managed to satisfy herself was with the help of the bulbous wooden handle of her kibbutz issue pruning fork. No wonder she was bitter. There was a great sadness in her eyes.

Hanna handed Ralph a glass of tea but he placed it on the table, stood up and took her in his arms. Their lips met but her mouth remained firmly closed. She drew away.

'No I don't think I . . .'

'Ssshhh . . . It's okay.'

She let Ralph hold her close, cheek to cheek. He could feel the warmth of her body and knew she must have been able to feel his erection against her stomach. His hand slipped up to her breast but she pushed it away.

'No, please, not that.'

'Okay.'

Ralph tried to be gentle realising that one false move would see him out of the door. He started to rub his groin lightly against hers and felt her respond. Yes, only slightly perhaps but there was a definite response. He pulled her slowly down onto the couch and she didn't resist albeit still kept her legs tight together despite his efforts to prise them apart with his right knee. Now they were rubbing their bodies together in the same rhythm, the momentum increasing as they both started to get carried away. Ralph knew he had to stay in control. He'd rarely got this far before and didn't want to do anything silly that would spoil it but he couldn't help himself. He put his hand on Hanna's breast and squeezed it gently. This time she didn't try to stop him but gasped gently and clung on so tightly that he could hardly breathe.

It would have been full-blown sex if it weren't for the fact that they were both fully clothed. Almost identically in fact in jeans and t-shirts. It occurred to him that there were a number of layers of assorted fabrics separating their sexual organs but everything seemed to be working as well as if they had been naked. Still she wouldn't kiss him, much as he tried to make her. Ralph had rarely felt so excited. The tingle in his cock had intensified to the point where he felt it might explode any second and discharge its contents to every corner of the room.

For some strange reason at this point, Ralph started to think about his mates in London. Chalky, Wilkie, Cheesy and Darren. He could see them all sitting in the pub. Fuck off you guys, can't you see I'm busy. Then his mind strayed to Stamford Bridge and he began to recall some of the great goals he had witnessed. Terry Venables, that volley from a corner. Bobby Tambling, after a solo run from his own half. Stanley Mathews for Stoke in his last ever match. A piece of brilliance that won the game.

What the fuck was the matter with him? Had he gone completely mad?

Suddenly she stopped moving. Had he done something wrong? But he didn't stop.

He couldn't. He was almost there. Then, to Ralph's great wonderment, Hanna opened those strong, kibbutznick legs, wrapped them round his thighs and started rubbing her groin against his even harder than before. She was thrusting now. She was almost there too. Her eyes were wide open and there was a frightened look on her face. Suddenly she let out a huge gasp and her body quivered uncontrollably with relief bringing little sobbing yelps of satisfaction from deep within. At the very same moment, Ralph's tingle burst in his pants and huge squirts of dampness filled the area around his groin. They stopped moving, released their grips and slumped sideways on the couch away from each other.

'That was great,' said Ralph after a moment or two, 'Really beautiful.'

But she was crying. Tears streamed uncontrollably down her face and mingled with the sweat that had been generated by their frenzied activity on this warm night.

'You must go now,' she said quietly.

'Will I see you tomorrow?'

'No. I have to go away for a few days but I'll be back on Wednesday. I'll look for you when I get back.'

How could he tell her now? How could he tell her that he had booked his return ticket and was leaving for London on Tuesday?

Ralph opened the door to leave. She kissed him on the cheek.

'Bye then.'

'Bye.'

The Beautiful Game

Why is it that the England team enters every international tournament with such high expectations of winning and why are we so fucking surprised when we get knocked out? After all, we've only won the sodding World Cup once and it had to be held at home in order to do it.

Without any doubt, the reason we consistently fail at the top level is the result of antiquated coaching methods combined with the very limited English perception of how to play the game. These have now fallen way behind practically all other countries that can realistically be regarded as serious contenders for the top honours.

Somewhere along the line, some deranged dimwit at Lancaster Gate decided that if we couldn't match the skill, vision, guile and imagination of foreign teams we would have to substitute these attributes with others that we could muster, namely speed, strength, athleticism and passion. Clearly, the idea behind this defeatist tactic was that if we were fit, fast and tough enough we might manage to physically overcome other teams even if they were much more skilful and tactically aware than we were.

Miss out the midfield altogether. Route one.

The other route of attempting to become as skilful and tactically aware as the more advanced nations must obviously have been dismissed out of hand as unlikely to succeed. Fucking shame.

Unfortunately for us though, this approach proved a total failure. As a result, our confidence is shot and most other countries, even smaller ones without much of a football pedigree, have a good chance of beating us.

Two simple facts emerge from this and they are that:

1. The best football teams in the world are the most skilful.

2. England teams are uncomfortable on the ball.

While this situation is allowed to continue it is unlikely that we will manage to win anything at all because the passion on which we have always relied to get us through is no longer sufficient to match the tremendous skill and vision of other top international teams. Anyway, those other teams can now match us for passion as well.

21
Juicy Jennifer

On the day Ralph returned from his first trip abroad, he said a quick hello to his parents and then made a beeline for the Cosh n' Helmet to see his mates. He had a lot to tell them. There they all were, just as he'd left them almost twelve months earlier, still sitting at the same table with the same drinks in front of them.

'Here he comes,' Chalky said as Ralph entered the hostelry with a wave. 'The wanderer returns'. And they all split their sides laughing at his witty comment.

'Where was it you said?' asked Cheesy, 'France, Spain, fucking Peru?'

'Actually, I've been working on a kibbutz in Israel,' Ralph informed them. But I managed to visit a few other places on the way back.'

'What the fuck's a kibbutz?' asked Wilkie.

'A sort of communal farm where everyone's equal.'

'What do you mean fucking equal? People aren't fucking equal.'

'Except in the eyes of the fucking Lord,' someone chimed in with the exaggerated reverential tone of a vicar. Pause for mighty guffaws of drunken laughter.

'People are equal,' said Darryl in mock reverence before delivering his predetermined punch-line. 'It's just that some are more fucking equal than others.' Another roar of merriment. Clearly they were all completely pissed but Ralph was sober as a judge.

'Well if you're so fucking keen to be equal with us,' said Cheesy 'I suggest you get a fucking round in. You bastard. You haven't fucking bought one in months.'

'That's because I've been away if you hadn't noticed, you pillock. Anyway, I didn't say I wanted to be equal with you bastards. I wouldn't want to sink that low.'

'I thought you said we're all fucking equal.'

'No, I said they have a society in which they are all equal and fucking interesting it is too. But I'll get you a drink in, dickhead. If you think you can handle another one.'

After an unsuccessful hour or so of trying to have a proper conversation, Ralph gave up. He had wanted to tell them all about what he'd seen and learnt while away but they just made silly drunken jokes and burst out laughing at everything he said.

It was Saturday lunch time and Chelsea were away so, tired of their nonsense, Ralph felt it was the ideal time to start getting organised. But before that, he thought he'd just pop in and say hello to Jennifer, the girl at the travel agency who had sold him his ticket to Israel on that fateful day. She'd been very helpful and he'd taken quite a shine to her. What a fucking mistake that was.

'Hello sir. How was Israel?' She remembered him. A promising sign.

'Great thanks, I'm just thinking about my next trip.'

'I do envy you,' she said. 'Being able to go off wherever you like.' Little did she know that he didn't have a pot to piss in.

'I envy you working in a place like this,' said Ralph.

'It's just a job.'

'Yeah, but it's better than working in a factory. I'll bet you travel all over.'

'Where are you thinking of going?' she asked.

'I'm open to suggestions.' He fixed her with the sort of gaze that invited her to take a double meaning from his words.

'I don't know where to start,' she said. 'Greece? Australia? Sweden? America?'

'Actually, I had been thinking of a tour of the great football stadiums of Europe. But America sounds good. Maybe South America. Yes, that's it. South America.'

You'd have thought he was Marco Polo the way he was going on.

'I'll give you some brochures.'

'Look, when you finish why don't we have a drink and you can tell me all about it.'

'Don't know about a drink. But we can have a coffee if you like.'

'Where have you been to then?' Ralph asked Jennifer after they had ensconced themselves at a corner table in the little café and the waitress had taken their order.

'Nowhere,' she said, 'Unless you count three days in Le Touquet.'

'Le Touquet?'

'Not my choice. It was a present from a customer. He'd booked for himself and his wife but she fell ill so he gave me the tickets. I went with my friend Mandy. It was a disaster.'

'What happened?'

'We went on a tiny plane from Croydon and flew through a storm. Very frightening. I was sick all the way. On the first day Mandy went off with some waiter bloke and left me by myself. It was November. Freezing cold. I'd never been so bored in all my life.'

'So how do you know about these places then? You seem very knowledgeable to me.'

'From brochures mostly. And from talking to customers. People like you who've actually been somewhere. I've never been anywhere.'

She looked so sad as she spoke that Ralph thought she was going to start crying.

She lowered her eyes. 'I've never told anyone this before,' she said.

'Come on,' said Ralph, 'You need a drink.'

'No really, I shouldn't.'

'Come on.'

'All right. Just the one though.'

An hour and a half in The Dog and Ferret next door and the best part of a bottle of vodka later, they emerged completely sozzled and stumbled crazily towards Jennifer's flat to where Ralph had gallantly agreed to escort her. Actually, flat was a bit of an exaggeration. It was a tiny bedsit not far from Battersea Park.

Unfortunately though, it was right at the top of a high-ceilinged Victorian, five-storey house and by the time they'd climbed the lengthy staircases to reach Jennifer's door, beads of perspiration were dripping uncontrollably down Ralph's face and soaking into his shirt collar.

'That was worse than climbing fucking Everest,' he spluttered whilst desperately trying to catch his breath.

'Come in and have a rest,' said Jennifer who seemed perfectly composed. He supposed she must have been used to it.

The room was up in the eaves that sloped away to the corners of the tiny room leaving precious little headroom in places. It was so small that there was hardly enough space for both of them in it. The only items of furniture were a single bed and a formica topped kitchen table with matching chair. A piece of electrical flex strung sideways across the room formed an improvised washing line on which a few pairs of panties, stockings and a bra were hung out to dry. On the table, the half-eaten remains of last night's repast, a Bird's Eye dinner for one, lay congealing in its tray.

'I don't usually invite people up here,' she said, 'It's hardly big enough for socialising.'

'Don't worry, we can take turns breathing in.'

Jennifer laughed. She still seemed light-headed but the climb had sobered Ralph up. He took a few steps over to the tiny window which offered a quite stunning view over South London and searched for landmarks.

'The place maybe on the small side,' he started to say turning back to face Jennifer, 'But the view is really terrif . . .'

But he was stopped dead in his tracks by the eye-catching sight that now confronted him in the room. Blimey! Jennifer had stripped down to her underwear and was lying on the bed in a seductive pose.

'Come on,' she said. 'Let's do it.'

'Oh, er, I didn't realise I, er . . .'

Ralph was stupefied and hardly knew where to look but of course he couldn't keep his eyes off her body. The body that he had been imagining with the aid of his x-ray vision for the last couple of hours and which now, for the most part anyway, he needed imagine no longer. She was a large girl, of that there was no doubt, but very fanciable nevertheless with smooth unblemished, olive skin, large breasts and chunky thighs. She reminded Ralph of the American actress Shelley Winters in the film 'Alfie'.

But it was Jennifer's face that had first attracted him and even now he still felt it was her most alluring feature. Gorgeous, smiling, pouting with bright eyes, pearl-white teeth and an expression that seemed to say 'Let's be friends'.

Of course, like a horse trader seeking a decent fetlock, Ralph had already surveyed every aspect of Jennifer's physical features and arrived at his usual, most avowed intention of trying to seduce her at some stage just as he had with every girl he'd been out with. So far though, none of them had seen fit to fully assist him in his lascivious aims. But this was a wholly unexpected turn of events and it caused Ralph to enter a state of extreme paranoia. Maybe it was because of this that the idea of failure crept into his mind. Or perhaps he subconsciously interpreted the removal of her clothes as a blatant challenge to the manhood that was still such a mystery to him.

Whatever the reason and despite the fact that he had always yearned for precisely this kind of situation, he found himself inventing ridiculous excuses not to go through with it. She wasn't his type. What if he didn't come up to her expectations? Perhaps she was perverted and wanted him to perform depraved acts with her. Maybe she wanted paying for it. He might get the pox. She might get pregnant. Her boyfriend might turn up. Her father might turn up. Her mother might be coming up the stairs at this very moment. What if they all came together? Fuck! Suddenly his mind entered a surreal trance in which Jennifer appeared to him as a hirsute gorilla with curly tufts sprouting thickly under her arms, between her toes, out of her ears and, much more disconcertingly, from underneath the pantie elastic between her legs. He even imagined that the area of her inner thighs was covered in a sort of five 'o'clock shadow.

This can't be it. Surely this can't be the first time. He might be traumatised for life.

Now he was in a blind panic that made him desperate to escape from the room but it wasn't going to be easy. Jennifer was between Ralph and the door and would have to move to let him past. What possible reason could he offer for leaving so quickly? How the fuck was he going to get out of there before something terrible happened?

'Oh, er, well I don't know if we should,' he managed to blurt.

'What?' she snapped. This was a turn up for the books.

'Well, we hardly know each other,' he said. But she must have thought he was joking.

'That's a good one.' She held out her arms. 'Come on. Don't tease.'

'No, really . . . I don't . . .' She began to realise he was serious.

'What did you come up here for then?'

'Well, to see you home I suppose. I didn't mean to take advantage. It's only our first date. It's not even a date really.'

'Now I've heard it all.'

'I didn't realise this was what you had in mind.'

'Me? ME? You must be joking.' She was angry now and had started to raise her voice. 'You've been ogling my bits all night. Think I didn't notice? Why do blokes always pretend it's never even crossed their minds? Do you think we're all stupid or something?'

'Well er . . . I er . . .'

'You only took me to the pub 'cos you thought I might get drunk enough to get my kit off. Don't deny it. I wouldn't have come otherwise.'

She was right of course. But now he'd completely gone off the whole idea and didn't really want to discuss it any more. There was an uneasy silence. After her fit of anger Jennifer had become quiet, morose even. The smile she'd worn almost constantly since leaving the pub had vanished and tears now slid down her face gathering mascara on the way and forming long black streaks down her cheeks. Another one crying. Why do they all cry?

'You must think I'm very ugly,' she sobbed.

'No I don't. Really I don't. I think you're very attractive.'

'I feel like a slut. Throwing myself at you like that.' Now she was weeping profusely. She gathered a bedcover round her shoulders. Fucking hell. How did this happen? It was the last thing he'd expected and certainly the last thing he needed. Emotional bollocks. But he did like the girl and felt a bit sorry for her. Ralph sat down next to Jennifer and put his arm around her for comfort. How could he get out of there?

'I do like you. Really.'

'Well you've got a fucking funny way of showing it.'

He toyed with the idea of relenting.

'Oh, all right then. I suppose we could have a quick one if you really insist.'

But he didn't feel like it. That's rich! Every minute of every day he thought about sex and how to get it and now for the first time in his life he could actually have it and what do you know? He didn't feel like it. Great. How the fuck did he reach that conclusion? Well firstly he didn't have a hard on which was a pretty good indication. He'd had one in the café as he gazed down her cleavage and in the pub when she crossed her legs and another coming up the stairs as he looked up her skirt from behind despite the effort of the climb. But now the old chap was as limp as an overcooked spaghetti.

And secondly? There wasn't a secondly.

What the fuck was wrong with him? Why was it that he was always chasing girls for sex but now that it was being offered to him on a plate he didn't want it any more? What kind of fucking pervert was he exactly? His mind was in turmoil. It felt like a Jackson Pollock painting. As if someone had flung different colours of paint all over his head and was cycling around on his brain.

In the end Ralph drew a large breath and decided to say it all in one sentence.

'Look, I-do-like-you-really-very-much-and-I-do-fancy-you-and-I-was-looking-at-you-and-I-did-think-about-it-a-few-times-actually-but-I'm-just-a-bit-surprised-that's-all-you-know-that-you-wanted-to-do-it-just-like-that-and-I-wasn't-sure-how-to-handle-it-but-I-would-like-to-see-you-again-and-have-another-try-and-maybe-it'll-work-out-okay-next-time-because-I'm-not-sure-what's-wrong-with-me-at-the-moment-and-I-didn't-mean-to-upset-you-because-I-know-what-it's-like-believe-me-I-know-what-it's-like-when-you-get-turned-down-and-I-really-must-go-now.'

'What?'

'It's the voices you see.'

'What voices?'

'I hear them all the time.'

'What fucking voices?'

'Since I got kicked in the head playing football.'

'What are you talking about? What voices? What do they say?' Jennifer began to look startled.

'Oh, you know, things like, go up to that man and hit him over the head with an axe.'

'What?'

'They're very insistent.'

'Oh, my God.'

'I can hear them now.'

'What?'

'They're trying to get through but I can't quite make out what they're saying.'

'Jesus, fucking Christ, can't you turn them off?'

'Why should I turn them off? They're my friends. Now, please, I must ask you not to take the name of Our Lord in vain or we shall never enter the kingdom of heaven.'

'God all fucking mighty.'

'There you go again. I'm afraid you may have to be punished.'

'What do you mean, punished?' It was panic stations now.

'It isn't me, It's the voices.'

She tried to stay calm.

'Right, I see. Okay then. Well. Oh my goodness, look at the time. I didn't realise how late it was,' she said, stifling an imaginary yawn. 'Maybe it's time to call it a night.'

'But it's only half past eight.'

'Is that all? Goodness. How time flies when you're enjoying yourself.'

'Actually, I'm a bit tired myself. Maybe I should go. Is there a hospital near here? I think I forgot to bring my pills. I haven't had one since yesterday.'

'Yes, why don't you fuck off, er, sorry, slip of the tongue. I mean thank you very much for walking me home and it was lovely to have met you and perhaps you should rush off to the hospital before they close.' That was his cue.

'Okay,' he said. 'Bye. I'll phone you.' And in a second he had disappeared through the door, down the stairs and was almost at the bottom before just making out the bitter, frightened tone of her reply.

'Don't fucking bother you fucking pervert,' she shouted softly after him.

For years after this episode, Ralph was at a loss to explain how he could possibly have spurned such a gilt-edged chance to indulge in the sort of sexual experience he had always craved. In the end and after a great deal of thought and introspection he put it down to one of two factors. Maybe for him there had to be some romance attached to sex. He couldn't just do it without being in love. Yes, perhaps he was just a romantic fool. But if that wasn't the reason for his abject failure on that fateful night then there could only have been one other possibility. He was a fucking idiot.

A week or so later Ralph happened to pass by the travel agency where Jennifer worked and noticed a flashing neon sign in the window next to the one that had attracted him in the first place. 'SPECIAL TOUR OFFER' it announced. 'THE GREAT FOOTBALL STADIUMS OF EUROPE'.

THE BEAUTIFUL GAME
The No Pass Back Rule

The idea behind this was to prevent teams playing for time by constantly passing back to the 'keeper. But teams playing for time will obviously only do so towards the end of a match. So, if they insist on having this rule, why have it in the first half at all? And if you do have it, how do you decide what is a deliberate back-pass and what is unintentional? A goalkeeper might easily interpret a situation differently to a referee and give away a free kick close to goal.

It all encourages the panic syndrome that causes players to just hoof the ball out of defence for safety's sake. Boring. We wonder why we can't find central defenders who will step out and carry the ball stylishly forward like Franz Beckenbauer or Bobby Moore or any Brazilian centre back you care to mention. Well this rule is one reason. Defenders don't have the security of knowing they can pass back to the 'keeper if necessary and so they take no chances. Therefore it stifles creative defensive play. Any rule that has this effect must surely be entered into the stupid category.

Also, where is the offence committed? By the goalkeeper when he picks up the ball or by the player who passes it back to him?

When this rule first came in and before players and referees had got used to it there was confusion about this which ended up with free kicks being taken a yard or two from the goal with every member of the defending team on the goal-line. Really silly. A nonsense. That's the problem with the prats who make the rules. They put players in situations that made them look completely daft.

22
Gasps of Pleasure

Since returning from Israel it hadn't taken Ralph long to decide that it was time for a change. Time to start living the way he really wanted. The episode with Jennifer had been an unmitigated disaster and not at all the start he had been looking for. But he decided to put it down to experience and vowed that nothing like that would ever happen again. His new life started here and now and he would devote himself exclusively to the cultural and political revolution. Become a man of letters and essays. An authority on literature, art, film, the theatre and, of course, football. He would eat at the finest restaurants, develop a wine cellar and join avant-garde clubs where he would befriend the most outrageous celebrities and intellectuals of the time. Naturally, he would surround himself with a bevy of beautiful, sophisticated women who would fall over themselves to accompany him to book launches, private viewings and film premieres. He would indulge himself in the myriad of artistic wonders that the great city of London had to offer with occasional forays to Paris, Rome, Amsterdam, Berlin and Madrid for special events. And then there was the book of course. He must publish it as soon as possible. The world was waiting. But first he had to find somewhere to live. He needed to be independent and free and as he couldn't afford a car it would have to be somewhere in London. As close to the centre as possible.

Within a week Ralph had moved into a small bedsit in Kilburn and began to wonder if he hadn't moved to the centre of Belfast. On his first night out in a local pub a kindly soul enlightened him. The reason so many Irish were to be found in the area was because they arrived on the ferry in Liverpool, got the train to London and the furthest anyone could walk from Euston carrying two full suitcases was Kilburn High Street.

After a few days considering what kind of work he would be

prepared to undertake, Ralph gave up his pretensions of signing for Chelsea, writing a football column for the *Guardian* or managing a rock band and found himself a job driving a small van which was quite handy in the circumstances as they sometimes let him keep it overnight.

As for women, he'd never had it so good. Available young females of different shapes, sizes, opinions and nationalities roamed free all over the place. In clubs and bars, at meetings and demonstrations, at concerts and galleries. They all seemed much more friendly and cosmopolitan than any of the women he had previously known.

There were even some quite tasty young girls living in his own house. One, Sally Bartholemew from Shrewsbury, rented the room next door to him on the second floor that they shared. Shortly after Ralph had taken up residence she invited him in for a cup of tea and he noticed with glee that her bed was exactly adjacent to the position of his own on the other side of the wall. The tiny rooms left little option. She was only separated from him at night by the wafer thin width of cheap hardboard that divided their two bed-sits. They were practically sleeping together! Now he was sure he had heard her moving in the night. Stifling those little gasps of pleasure as she made herself come. But had she heard Ralph? He hoped so. Although she was too straight and prissy for his taste he had to admit that he did fancy her a bit and thought she would probably be an easy conquest if he put his mind to it not to say his hand on it. So he added her to his reserve list in case all else failed.

The more Ralph discovered about politics the more radical he became. Of course, nowhere was the failure of capitalism more obvious than in the world of football.

Private investors had muscled their way in and upset the balance so that all the money and power was now concentrated at the top end of the game whilst all the smaller clubs were broke and hanging on for dear life. But the fat cats couldn't have cared less. They made no effort to try and understand the deep meaning football had for its genuine supporters. They knew fuck all about it. They thought that a manager pulling a player off at half time was an allusion to hand relief in the dressing room. Or that Chester versus Chesterfield was a local derby. Or that Franco Zola was a French novelist. All the game represented to them was a money-making device and they were quite prepared to sell its soul if they could make a decent profit. Stuff the fans!

All right, Ralph knew. It was called commerce and those who worshipped at the altar of supply and demand would probably have said that it regulated everything perfectly without the need for other controls. But they forgot that football was not a commodity to be bought and sold. Not for those who cared anyway. Football was a living thing with a soul. It belonged to the people. The fans and football lovers who had made it great and given it the value that attracted the parasitic business people in the first place. Why didn't they all just fuck off and leave us alone?

Watch out football fans! They're stealing our game.

Ralph preached this holy sermon whenever he got the chance but he could never seem to get it through to his old mates. Not that he saw them much these days. A distance had grown between them.

'Fuck me Ralph, if you're so keen on fucking communism why don't you fuck off and live in fucking Russia?' Wilkie once asked him after suffering one of his more trenchant diatribes on a rare visits back to the Cosh n' Helmet.

'Look, you prat, it's about fucking time we stood up and claimed our fucking rights. Anyway, I'm not a communist, I'm a revolutionary humanist.' Actually, by this time Ralph's political stance was somewhere to the left of Ché Guevara.

'You'll be supporting Moscow fucking Dynamo next,' said Darryl, always quick to belittle anything Ralph said or did.

'For fuck's sake. The very soul of football is under threat and all you bastards can do is insult the bloke who's trying to save it.'

He was fed up with their silly statements. They just didn't understand the nature of their own oppression. As long as there was a referee to swear at, a dirty magazine to wank over or a pub in which to get drunk beyond oblivion, they were content. They didn't even notice that the beer was watered down.

For their part, although they made light of it, they were shocked by the Bohemian company Ralph kept and horrified by the idea of trying to change the fundamental nature of society by bringing about a redistribution of wealth.

Albeit in this respect, there was one particular point about which Ralph was most adamant. Although he yearned for a glorious revolution, if it was planned to break out on a Saturday afternoon when Chelsea were at home they would have to schedule it for some time after 5:45 p.m. if they wanted him to take part. Fervent though he might have been, there were certain things he was not prepared to sacrifice for the cause.

'What the fuck's a revolutionary fucking whatsit then?' asked Wilkie.

The Beautiful Game

There is a widely held view that there are too many foreign players in the English game taking jobs from locals and hindering the national team's prospects because they keep our players out of club teams. Bollocks!

It is nonsense to think of the introduction of overseas players into most of the top British clubs as some sort of a threat to our game. In fact, they've improved it no end and we should embrace them for that.

Ideally, there would be nothing to stop anybody, whatever their profession, travelling the world to live and work wherever they pleased without hindrance or restriction. Inasmuch as many people from many places would probably relish the opportunity to come here, it also opens up the inviting prospect of us being able to go there. Courage mon brave! Be not afraid. We were only talking about people. They might come in different colours, speak different languages, eat different food or even pray to different gods but they all have mothers who love them and feelings the same as us. Some are even quite nice. As nice as us. Nicer than us. Remember, we are all brothers.

The panache, style and vision that Continental players have brought to our game has added a new and exciting dimension uplifting its quality in the process. They have helped transform the Premiership into perhaps the most exciting sporting spectacle available today even if the skill factor is still somewhat lacking from the home contingent. Many local players have benefited from this and, as any Chelsea fan will tell you, the best example is Dennis Wise who became a highly sophisticated footballer in the presence particularly of Gullit, Di Matteo, Zola and Vialli.

It is easy to blame the failure of the England team and the desperate struggle of every club not in the top half of the Premiership on the influx of foreign players because it removes the spotlight from our own deficiencies in the coaching department.

But is the influx of foreign players not just a convenient excuse for our failures?

Or could it be that the actual reason for bemoaning the influx of foreign players is a dislike of foreigners whether they play football or not?

And is that in life by the way, or just football?

23
Black Hats and Bollocks

Ralph's older brother Nathan had always been much more respectable although you might not have guessed as much from his appearance nowadays.

His unkempt, dark beard and shabby old black suit made him look like a professional assassin who was down on his luck. More of a thrush than a jackal. The scull cap that always sat slightly askew over his rapidly growing bald patch was intended to remind him, as with all good Jews, of God's lingering presence above. But the rather obscene expanse of blubber that hung slightly askew over his trouser waist was a more annoying and insistent reminder to him that he was, in fact, a fat pig. The combined effect was of a man who appeared at least ten years older than he was.

But it hadn't always been like that. In his teens Nathan had been a rather dapper young man about town with a keen eye for the ladies and Ralph had looked up to him as a role model. He had wanted to be just like his big brother. How times change! Now Ralph did everything in his power to be the exact opposite of his neurotic sibling.

The shallow nature of communication between the two of them had become a source of disappointment to Ralph over the years. He found it frustrating that Nathan tended to avoid discussing the great subjects of women and football as brothers usually did and, of course, when it came to politics it always ended in an argument.

'You can't trust the Arabs,' Nathan would say.

'What, none of them?' Ralph would ask.

Somehow, they'd managed to take completely opposite turnings down the highway of life. Whilst Ralph was busting a gut in his efforts to be a bohemian, revolutionary, secular free spirit, Nathan sat back in his favourite armchair with his most comfortable slippers on, quite content in the knowledge that he was a conservative, anal-retentive, religious bigot. It caused Ralph to wonder if some essential element of his brother's being hadn't been surgically extracted while his back was turned. That he'd been reduced to spiritual impotence by a sort of vasectomy of the intellect.

But not everyone felt that way about Nathan. In local religious circles he was revered as a minor saint and afforded the kind of respect usually reserved for holy men, even though he was actually an accountant by trade. But, as we all know, the increasing influence of accountants was such that they would eventually assume spiritual leadership from the Rabbis, Priests and Mullahs and end up ruling the world in every way. Perhaps Nathan had sensed the trend.

Nathan had married Leah Berkovitz, the daughter of a Rabbi and gone to live in Jerusalem where they had managed to raise a brood of devout, self-righteous, moody little prats who lived in total, unquestioning adherence to the Torah. In his typically irreverent fashion Ralph tended to refer to this branch of the family as the 'black hats', a description that infuriated his brother. It was an allusion to the ultra-orthodox religious zealots who were easily recognisable at the Western Wall or in Hatton Garden or the El Al desk at Heathrow as they minced about in their long black coats and huge black hats. They were so extreme in their crazy beliefs that they couldn't even bring themselves to recognise the State of Israel because they claimed it didn't comply with biblical prophesy. But at the same time, of course, they didn't mind taking advantage of the safe haven afforded by a Jewish homeland in an anti-Semitic world full of raving fascists who were out for their blood. Hardly surprising then that Nathan took such exception to the jibe.

Once, on a visit back to England, Nathan overheard Ralph using the derogatory expression in discussion with his own wife, Sophie. A shikse, God forbid.

It was at a family gathering to celebrate Grandpa Goldstein's eightieth birthday during which Ralph and Sophie were making the best of the free booze that no one else seemed much interested in. They had somehow managed to get themselves completely sozzled on the sweet, thick, kosher wine that normally appeared only on festivals and high holidays and hadn't realised that Nathan was within earshot. Not that it would have mattered. Ralph's attitude to formal religion had never been a secret.

'Has it brought world peace?' he would ask. But a huge row ensued.

'Why do you insist on making fun of the way we live?' Nathan shouted.

'Because it's a load of old bollocks,' was Ralph's reply.

Bollocks was his favourite word.

24
Sarah's Secrets

The animosity between them went back some time. Over the years, Ralph's occasional visits to his brother in the land of milk and honey had usually ended unsatisfactorily. Particularly the time when he put the milk back in the meat fridge. According to Jewish dietary laws, milk and meat products must be strictly segregated and many of the better-off, orthodox families had two fridges to carry this out effectively. It was only a silly mistake, but as far as Leah, his sister-in-law, was concerned in was an offence punishable by death or castration or both. Not that she actually said anything. She had a problem communicating with Ralph at the best of times because she considered him completely beyond the pale. A total heathen. She could hardly even look him in the eye.

'Come on, he's not so bad and he is my brother,' Nathan told her but it was no good.

'He fornicates with shikses and he eats pork. How much worse can you get?'

'But he did work on a kibbutz.'

'They're all as bad as he is in those places.'

She refused to allow Ralph any credit for the idealism that had driven him to spend quite some time, albeit a few years before, on a primitive, isolated settlement with no mod cons. Helping to cultivate the homeland with hard labour and by the sweat of his brow. He slept with non-Jewish girls, ate non-kosher food and, for all she knew, was in league with the Devil. As far as Leah was concerned, Ralph was damned.

After the fridge affair, he felt distinctly hostile vibrations emanating from the dumpy, uptight, little woman whenever he was in her vicinity. Leah was like that. Talk about stereotyped. With her hair in a bun, her flowered tabard and the almost permanent scowl on her face, she was straight out of the Shtetl. Although

Ralph tried his best to make allowances, he found it almost impossible to be in the same house even for a short time. It was worse than living with an Arsenal supporter. He was sure his brother would have overlooked his little misdemeanour but not Leah. The moment she discovered Ralph's heinous sin she started frantically grabbing the sullied food out of the fridge and heaving it all into the dustbin, screaming curses as she did so as if whatever punishment was coming their way would be compounded for every second it remained. There was loads of it. They always had a kitchen full of fatty stodge to eat.

It always amused Ralph when his brother's whole family regaled him so bitterly, as they often did, with indignant criticism of his own non-kosher eating habits. As if God had decreed some sort of holy menu. Actually, that's probably what they did think. On the evening of the great fridge incident, they all set about him furiously in response to the little joke he made as they sat down for supper. It was only a casual aside about maybe fancying a plate of lightly grilled seafood (absolutely forbidden) with a green salad in preference to the enormous helping of meat and dumplings in heavy gravy that had just been plonked in front of him. It was the same meal they always had on a Friday night. Traditional Jewish fare developed among the Eastern European communities hundreds of years ago. The idea was that you left it to stew overnight so that you didn't have to cook on the Sabbath which was also forbidden. Whilst they all scoffed it down with relish as if they hadn't eaten for three weeks, Ralph could only manage to prod the globby stuff around on his plate. He could understand that you might have wished to eat that sort of stuff in the depths of an icy Polish winter but surely not during an Israeli summer when it was forty degrees in the fucking shade.

'For Christ's sake,' he said, realising at the same moment that he was dropping another bollock, 'It was only a joke.'

Of course, what didn't help matters was that later that same night, Sabbath eve, Nathan and Leah were rudely awoken from the deep slumber brought on in the aftermath of their monthly (if Nathan was very lucky) sexual liaison by strange noises emanating from the living room. When they gingerly came to investigate, the silly prudes were horrified beyond measure to find Ralph sliding the knickers down over the lithe, brown legs of a young Sabra girl he had picked up earlier that evening in a bar.

Nathan was incensed and acted instantly. At first Ralph thought his brother was actually going to strike him such was the anger in his eyes. But in the end he merely grabbed both youngbloods by the scruff of their necks and shoved them through the front door, locking and barring it behind them. During this procedure he muttered admonishments. 'Disgusting behaviour, how dare you, this is a respectable household, may the wrath of God be upon you' etc, etc. Ralph and his new friend both had a bellyful of Israeli beer sloshing around inside them and thought the whole thing was hilarious. They were almost pissing themselves.

'Don't worry,' shouted Nathan in a serious tone through the heavy metal door, 'I won't tell your father about this.' For some obscure reason there was a tendency in Jewish families to shield parents, particularly fathers, from the truth if it contained unsavoury facts. But Ralph was used to this. Having always been a problem child he was used to the threat of being shopped to his parents or teachers for one thing or another so he was unimpressed by his brother's magnanimity.

'No please,' he shouted back finding it hard to do so without laughing. 'Tell him. Ring him up now. I want him to know.'

It was then that Ralph realised he was out in the street with his trousers round his ankles and love juice dripping off his dick. Sarah, for that was her name, was standing next to him holding her knickers in her hand. They looked at each other and began laughing their heads off again. Tears were streaming down their faces.

'Come on my little English Jew-boy,' she said, 'Let's go where we won't be disturbed.'

They were surprised to notice a passing taxi in Jerusalem on a Friday night, long into the Sabbath but Sarah hailed it and instructed the driver to take them to Tel-Aviv, the less puritanical, cultural centre of the country where night-life still continued relatively normally into the small hours. They sat on the back seat, sweaty with passion and oblivious to the breakneck speed and dozens of near misses as the vehicle careered wildly towards the coast. In their state of horny arousal, neither had the slightest notion that their driver, a swarthy oriental boy, was not only far too young to be driving but also that he was high on speed and had just stolen the cab a few minutes before picking them up. Not much more than half an hour later they were driving along Hayarkon Street on the Tel-Aviv seafront closely pursued by an armed police car. Ralph and Sarah were so entwined with each other that they hadn't noticed the drama unfolding all around them. Young Abu the driver suddenly pulled off the main drag into a side-street, screeched an abrupt halt and shouted hysterically at them to get out. The lad was in a big hurry. They were still laughing and unaware of the amphetamine pumped eyeballs of their smiling fugitive as they clambered out of the car, Ralph with a huge hard on and Sarah holding out a fifty shekel note in payment.

'It's okay, my treat!' shouted Abu jamming the accelerator to the floor and careering off with tyres burning, just as the police car skidded into view around the corner almost knocking down our two love birds and causing them to jump back sharply towards the safety of the kerb. Even if they'd realised what was going on they wouldn't have cared less. Love was in the air and in their minds and filled their hearts and souls.

Ignoring the bright lights of the bars and night-clubs, Ralph and Sarah walked hand in hand towards the wide, sandy beach that was stunningly illuminated by a huge, Middle Eastern moon. They found themselves a sheltered spot beneath the promenade wall and there, in the warm night breeze, with a background symphony of Mediterranean surf booming and crashing over the massive breakwater rocks, they screwed their brains out for an hour or so before finally falling asleep, completely exhausted.

A couple of hours later the sun rose to start spreading its first, gentle warmth across the landscape and early morning swimmers began arriving. Ralph and Sarah awoke with an aching hunger and, brushing the sand from their clothes, ambled their fuzzy-headed way to a small café where they ate humus with pitta bread and drank thick, Israeli coffee. Mud, the locals called it. Sarah went to the bathroom to freshen up. When she hadn't reappeared over half an hour later, it slowly began to dawn on Ralph that he would probably never see her again. But in a sense he was wrong.

Ralph spent the rest of the day walking around Tel-Aviv wondering what to do next.

On the beach he befriended a cosmopolitan group of young folk who seemed to be at the same sort of lose end as he was. There were about a dozen of them altogether. Scandinavians, Australians, Germans, Japanese, an Israeli by the name of Benny who seemed to be a sort of self-appointed local guru and a beautifully manicured young American girl called Becky whom Ralph immediately identified as a JAP. A Jewish, American Princess. That was how they referred to this particular type of bourgeois maiden brought up in what an Israeli would consider the lap of luxury. Their parents often dispatched them to the homeland to try and toughen them up a bit. You could watch them arriving at Ben Gurion airport every day looking demur and slightly scared. Within twenty-four hours, many entered a state of extreme homesickness and wanted to go home. But those who managed to overcome this initial bout of anxiety wouldn't take long to realise that for the first time in their lives they were free of the parental control that had so far prevented them from indulging in their crudest fantasies. Consequently they were prone to turn completely wild. Becky had been in the country a week, way past the threshold, and seemed to take a shine to Ralph. His Levantine features, curly mop of long, dark hair, athletic build and animal eyes must have tickled her fancy. This was much to the chagrin of Benny, the Israeli, who clearly had unrequited designs on Becky having probably ear-marked her as a meal ticket to the States. The group were dossing down on the roof of a block of flats not far away and, on hearing of Ralph's plight, they invited him to join them. Many slept on roofs in Tel-Aviv. It was the coolest place to be when it was thirty degrees in the middle of the night. Benny didn't seem at all pleased with this new arrangement.

They spent the evening chatting, drinking beer, chewing olives and watching television. Becky made a point of being hospitable to Ralph and was obviously creaming her knickers over him. But, although Ralph had made a perusal of her inviting body and given the matter serious consideration, he'd decided that she wasn't really his type and resisted her advances. Even when, as they sat cross-legged in the half-light of a few candles that provided the only illumination, she slipped her hand up his shorts and grabbed his cock. It made Ralph wince because his circumcised, ever-willing and now swiftly growing young organ was still caked with sweat and sand from the previous night. Seeking a diversion, Ralph's attention was drawn to the television on which a newscaster was describing the events at Ben Gurion airport, just a few miles up the road from where they sat. Something special appeared to be happening and everyone in the studio seemed quite excited by whatever it was.

The cameras were recording the arrival of an Egyptian plane on Israeli soil which Ralph immediately realised was an extraordinary event in itself. In fact, a momentous historical event had begun to unfold before the very eyes of the small group most of whom were not really bothering to pay much attention. They were probably more interested in who would be screwing who that night. Certainly Benny was.

In a conscious effort to cut himself off from the hurly-burly of current affairs since embarking on his travels weeks earlier, Ralph hadn't watched television or read a paper at all so he was out of touch with recent political developments. But as he made out what was being broadcast, he became enthralled. He could hardly believe what he was witnessing. It almost gave him another hard-on.

Emerging through the airliner's door to rapturous applause from the disorganised mass of assembled Israeli government officials was the smiling face of the Egyptian President Anwar Sadat. He had come to talk peace. Amazing! One by one the Israeli dignitaries and their wives shook hands with their illustrious visitor. President, Prime-Minister, Foreign Secretary, Finance Secretary, Home Secretary, Military Generals. But who was this? Ralph recognised that face. He screwed up his eyes to focus more accurately on the small screen. A particularly thickset official wearing an impressive dress uniform now stepped forward to greet the Egyptian President. Behind him, a petite, attractive, relatively young woman dressed conservatively in twin set and pearls and with hair piled up high on the top of her head in one of those ridiculously deranged but supposedly respectable styles, waited her turn to be introduced.

'I don't believe it,' breathed Ralph in amazement. He moved closer to the set. 'It can't be. Yes it fucking well is. That's Sarah!'

The others hadn't been taking much notice until now but as Ralph's voice rose to a crescendo, their attention turned to him. What was all the fuss about?

Benny seemed particularly interested.

'Ow you know it Sarah?' he asked in his thick accent.

Ralph started to back away from the television holding his head in his hands.

'I know her. I met her yesterday in Jerusalem. We came up here in a taxi and spent all night screwing on the beach. But she didn't look like that. She was wearing sexy clothes and her hair was all over her face.' He couldn't prevent himself becoming a little whimsical. 'She looked lovely.'

Turning to face Benny he identified the look on the Israeli's face as puzzled cynicism.

'A taxi from Jerusalem,' Benny repeated. 'On a Friday night?'

He was clearly doing his best to discredit Ralph's story.

'It's true,' he insisted. 'She disappeared just before I met you lot.'

'Well if this is so,' said Benny adopting a most serious tone. 'I suggest you leave the country as soon as possible.'

'Why? Do you know her?

'Everybody knows her.'

Who the fuck is she?' Ralph asked with trepidation.

'That is Sarah Levy,' Benny answered.

'Yeah, Sarah,' said Ralph trying to cajole more information from the Israeli. 'But who is she?'

'Wife of Motti Levy, that man in front of her.'

'And who the fuck is he exactly?' Ralph braced himself for the answer.

'Head of the Shin Bet.'

Ralph felt the blood draining from his face and started to feel sick.

Anyone who had spent time in Israel knew that the Shin Bet was the most secretive, powerful and feared section of the Israeli secret service.

'You're fucking joking.'

'I'm not fucking joking as you put it.' Benny informed him. His tone had become smug partly because of the debilitating effect his information was clearly having on Ralph but also because he'd noticed a worried look spreading across Becky's features as she conducted a close examination of the hand she had now withdrawn from Ralph's shorts. Sniffing at thumb and forefinger as she rubbed them together, her expression was gradually turning to horror as she began to identify the pungent, gooey substance that now covered those expensively manicured digits.

'This Sarah that you say you know,' continued Benny with quiet satisfaction, 'Is Mrs Levy, wife of probably the most powerful man in the country next to the Prime Minister, and a ruthless bastard.'

'Pardon?'

'He's known for it.'

Benny related the story that all Israelis knew.

Sarah had tricked Motti into marriage by claiming to be pregnant by him and in his position he couldn't afford the scandal. Motti was a good twenty-five years her senior, his first wife having died in a terrorist incident many years earlier. Sarah had met him in some posh hotel bar, got him drunk and afterwards told him they'd done whatever was necessary to make a baby. The idiot had believed it although some said he was madly in love with her. But he was an idiot either way. After the wedding it turned out there was no baby at all. It was just a trick. She was only interested in his power and position and this was just the opportunity she had been waiting for. Since then she'd had lots of affairs and had become a regular feature in all the papers. She was a horny little tramp and everyone knew it. Her philandering had turned her into a national celebrity and she milked the publicity for all it was worth. There was a standing joke in the country that when she died she'd have to be buried in a 'Y' shaped coffin. But it wasn't funny as far as Motti was concerned. It drove him insane. He couldn't control her lascivious behaviour and he couldn't stand it. Eventually he became bitter with the way Sarah made a laughing stock of him even to the point of sending his henchmen round to kick the crap out of any of her boyfriends that he found out about. Some say he even had Sarah beaten up which was hardly discreet and of course it only added fuel to the fire. There were girlfriends too, so the story went and that only caused Motti to become even more incensed. In fact, the rumour was that Sarah's last lover was injured so badly after a particularly brutal attack that she was lucky to be alive. It was a classic story of sex and violence and guaranteed to sell a few copies.

By the time Benny had finished Ralph had turned as white as a sheet and sat quite still with his mouth open in a state of shock. He had assumed that Sarah was just a local girl out for a bit of fun and he certainly didn't need all this cloak and dagger bollocks. But that was the sort of thing that happened to Ralph. He'd jump in head-first without any regard for the consequences of his actions and end up shitting himself when he'd realised what he'd done. All he could think of was how delectable the liaison with Sarah had been and how sad that it was clearly now over. But it had also been the straw that broke the camel's back of his relationship with his brother, involved him in a high-speed car chase with armed police and now brought him to the verge of a National scandal. Not bad for one day! But that was Ralph for you. Ruled by his heart alone.

Benny now played his trump card. Turning to Ralph he asked, 'The police car that followed you to Tel-Aviv?'

'What about it?'

'Can you be sure it was police and not Shin Bet Special Forces?'

It didn't take long for Ralph to decide. Time to go home. Anyway, the football season was kicking off next weekend. In the morning Ralph went straight to the airport and caught the first available plane back to London. All the flags were still out from the day before and, as they took off, he noticed the Egyptian president's plane parked on the edge of the field surrounded by armed soldiers. He was sorry to leave. He felt at home in Israel. But he wanted to go home. Talk about confused. He was as confused and perplexed as the hedgehog that attempted to seduce a hairbrush.

Ralph didn't relax until he was through customs and on the bus into town, but even then he wasn't sure where to go.

It was at times like this that he thought of Monica, who he'd known on and off for years. A bright, intelligent, free spirit of a girl, happy and glowing when she was in love, depressed and suicidal when she wasn't. Throughout all their respective romantic dalliances they'd always kept in touch, sharing confidences and sometimes a bed, but without strings attached. It was their tacit agreement. No pressure, just fun and friendship. They were too much alike for anything more serious and they both knew it. But they felt good in each other's company. In a way they were soul mates. Safe.

How comforting to know that if all else fails there's at least one person in the world that you can rely on for a little tea and sympathy. Yes, Monica's was the place to be.

She answered the door in her dressing gown.

'Hi handsome, perfect timing.'

What a relief. Friendly face, warm welcome just what he needed.

'How come?'

'Just getting into bed on my own. Feeling a bit lonely. Come in. Must be three months since I've seen you.'

She was all over him as soon as they walked through the door.

'You've got sand in your hair,' she said as she embraced him, pressing her body against his. 'Mmm, three months to make up on.'

As Ralph's cock began to rise to the occasion, he remembered that it was still covered in sand, sweat and God knows what else from two nights ago.

'I'll just have a quick shower'
'Can't wait'
'You'll have to.'

The Beautiful Game

Technological Bollocks

Some say that technology should be employed to help enforce the rules but not me. Not on your fucking nelly.

What we need is a set of simple rules that can easily be enforced by one well-trained referee and two well-trained linesmen. Sorry, referee's assistants. Together with this we also need a change in the way the game is played.

Managers are always complaining about the number of fixtures their teams have to play and that their players get knackered and injured all the time as a result.

You don't need a degree in rocket science to realise that the way to solve this is to slow things down and play a more controlled, cultured type of game. Then there would be fewer injuries, a less frenetic approach and the game would become more beautiful and absorbing.

Of course, this is exactly the opposite of current trends particularly in Britain where, as we are constantly reminded, speed, strength and athleticism are encouraged over skill, vision and imagination. Clearly we are going in the wrong direction.

I said, 'WE ARE GOING THE WRONG WAY ABOUT IT.'

If we want to get to heaven that is.

As for those who espouse the wonders of modern technology, I will ask again. What has this great technology ever actually achieved? Has it created world peace? Or love and understanding between people and nations? Or rival football supporters?

Answers on a postcard please to:

Mahatma Gandhi, The Football Association, Cloud Cuckoo Land, Planet Zog.

If it was up to me we would all break free and fulfil ourselves in any way possible without all these silly rules and regulations which are stifling the game and indeed, life itself.

25
Marcia – The First Football Nymphomaniac

The first time is the best.

In Ralph's search for female companionship he discovered that political meetings offered the best opportunities because you could talk and get to know people without having to be introduced. He could pretend to be vitally interested in the burning issues of the moment whilst really eyeing up the crumpet with a view to a pull. And there wasn't much competition. The other blokes were all so deadly serious that as soon as he bowled in with a few corny jokes the women were all over him. Naturally, his rivals were eaten up with envy but there was nothing they could do about it without admitting they were more interested in sex than social change and that would have been politically incorrect. They all had the impression Ralph was some kind of modern-day Romeo dipping his wick all over the place and he certainly wasn't going to dissuade them from that false illusion. Notwithstanding the truth of the matter which was that, despite his most avid efforts, no female had yet allowed him to actually penetrate her. But the time wasn't far off. It couldn't be surely.

By the way, don't think Ralph wasn't interested in the burning issues of the moment. He most certainly was. But he was equally as interested in the burning feeling in his groin. He couldn't help it. It just seemed to take over at times.

Her name was Marcia Levy and Ralph met her at a political event that he had attended solely for the purpose of meeting someone like her. In those days, although he tried his best to project an image of maturity and experience, Ralph was still just a shy young lad struggling to find ways of approaching girls for sex whilst trying to pretend it was the last thing on his mind. Actually, it was the very first thing on his mind from the moment he woke up and all day long.

She had those typical Jewish good looks. Wild, curly, shoulder-length black hair cascading around her face and half covering her flashing dark eyes which seemed to say 'Here I am but only if you make an effort.'

An ankle length black dress described her lithe body so closely that, with Ralph's imagination, she might as well have been naked and the clearly visible nipples of her palm-sized breasts indicated tantalisingly that she wore no bra. This was quite revolutionary for the times and Ralph was to find out that she was a very revolutionary girl in more ways than one. She was a nymphomaniac. Just what he needed.

He sat behind her at the meeting whilst some intensely boring political speaker droned on about a lot of meaningless old political bollocks but Ralph didn't hear a word.

He couldn't have cared less. He was already in love with Marcia and he hadn't even met her yet. Although the speaker was pathetically dull, Ralph was excited as hell.

He couldn't keep his eyes off her and she must have felt the heat of his passion burning from behind because once or twice she looked round in his direction. But of course, like a prat, he pretended not to notice.

For one short moment, their eyes met and Ralph thought he detected the slight hint of a smile which immediately gave him a big hard on. In those days the sap was rising in the young man's blood to such an extent that he used to go around with an almost permanent erection. He just couldn't control it. A girl only had to hold hands with him and the old chap would jump to attention quicker than a soldier when the sergeant major entered the barracks.

From his carefully chosen vantage point Ralph was able to eye Marcia up and down, lasciviously drinking in every curve and ripple of her divine body and imagining all sorts of utterly disgusting scenarios involving her and him with no clothes on.

Thank fuck they couldn't read your mind!

After the meeting, everyone stood around chatting over tea and biscuits in a serious sort of way with concerned looks on their faces as if they had been entrusted with a terribly important decision on behalf of the whole human race.

Amongst the crowd, Marcia's beauty shone out like a diamond and her smile radiated warmth throughout the gathering. Ralph was desperate to talk to her but couldn't get near. She was obviously the most popular person in the room and everyone was vying for her attention. At one stage she was involved in what seemed to be a very intense and not entirely friendly discussion with the lecturer, an apparently quite eminent African gentleman called Joe Sadhu from the Socialist Party of Ghana. But Ralph wasn't close enough to hear what they were actually saying and anyway he was far too absorbed in staring at her tits. Suddenly, Marcia turned away from the speaker and began walking in Ralph's direction. He had taken up a strategic position by the door so as not to miss her if she left quickly and felt quite pleased that the tactic had worked.

As she approached, her face enraptured him. The dark eyes, full mouth and that black, downy hair that grew by the side of her ears. He was off again! He began to wonder if the same sort of hair grew on the small of her back or on the inside of her thighs or in the crack of her arse.

'Hello,' ventured Ralph. More to avert attention from his lightly throbbing member than because he could think of anything sensible to actually say to her.

'Oh hi,' she replied, 'Have we met?' Her manner was somewhat off-hand and Ralph sensed she was slightly annoyed about something. His spirits dropped. What had he done?

'No, I don't think so,' he said, 'Should we be formally introduced?' He was pleased he'd managed to pull off this cocky approach because he was shaking like a leaf inside.

She seemed to relax. 'Sorry, didn't mean to be rude. It's just that fat bastard Sadhu. He's rubbed me up the wrong way.'

Ralph wanted to rub her up. Any way she would let him.

'Some sort of political disagreement?' he inquired, desperately trying to find something of even slightly interesting or amusing value to utter.

She lightened slightly and smiled. There was a short pause when Ralph somehow knew it would be a mistake to say anything. She seemed to be mulling something over in her mind.

'Would you like a drink?' she asked. 'I think the pubs are still open.'

His heart leaped. Would I? Not fucking many. Bet you're dying for it. What colour knickers you wearing? Let's have a look. Can we go somewhere and fuck afterwards?

'That would be very nice,' he said.

Entering the King's Head, Ralph felt a little nervous because although he was comfortable in the Cosh 'n' Helmet he didn't have much experience of other pubs and wouldn't normally have taken a girl into one. Pubs weren't quite respectable enough for that in those days. Taking Jennifer was okay because it was an impromptu arrangement. Anyway, she'd been in a bit of a state and needed a drink. You could even have called it medicinal. But if it was pre-arranged, most girls would be bound to construe that you wanted to get them drunk so they wouldn't know what they were doing and let you have your wicked way with them. This, of course, was quite correct. Having it away was all most lads had in mind. But, for fear of frightening off their prey, they did all they could to hide their lascivious lustings and pretend that sex was the last thing of interest. Then again, most girls were quite aware of this and consequently always on guard. What strange social conventions we invented for ourselves. Did life really have to be this complicated?

Until then, Ralph had been used to entertaining young ladies in coffee bars, the back row of the cinema or the field behind the housing estate. Neither was he a hardened drinker having mainly been used to shandy. But he couldn't order shandy now, she'd think he was a sissy.

On the way there he had been having a debate with himself about what to drink.

Shandy was definitely out. Wine? Too poncy. Whisky? Couldn't be sure what it would do to him. Vodka? Not after the last time. Rum and coke? Too flash. Cocktail? Don't be a dickhead. He decided on light ale. Not too strong, a bottle is only half a pint but it's quite manly. The sort of tipple that a discerning drinker with great experience in life would have. Right, that's it.

'As they approached the bar Marcia said, 'I'll have a pint of Guinness.'

'Two pints of Guinness please,' Ralph ordered.

They found a table and Ralph took a few huge slurps of the black stuff as if he drank it all day. In fact, he'd never had it before in his life and it was a bloody sight stronger than he expected. The effect took him completely by surprise.

He felt the dark liquid splosh straight down into his stomach and make its way round his body. It shot round his arteries, whizzed through every muscle, galloped to each extremity and lit up his brain. When his eyes had stopped watering he was able to focus on Marcia as she settled into her seat and crossed her legs which, at the time, seemed like the most overt sexual statement he had ever encountered. But then, he hadn't encountered many.

He kept telling himself not to stare at her private parts but the harder he tried the more he couldn't help it. Although she was wearing a one piece, ankle-length dress, the diaphanous nature of the fabric was such that Ralph was able to make out every curve and ripple of her body. He became transfixed for a while on her tummy and belly button that were clearly outlined through the clinging garment. He felt an urgent desire to explore the area just below it. That little triangular bush that he knew must be lurking in between the upper thighs of her crossed legs.

He began to feel that he had known her all his life.

'I feel like I've known you all my life,' he blurted. Who said that? Shut up you prat.

'That's original,' she joked.

'What was the problem with Sadhu?' he inquired. 'He seemed to have upset you, was it about his talk?'

She threw her head back and laughed heartily.

'Not really,' she said, 'He just wanted to fuck me and wouldn't take no for an answer'.

Pardon? What did she say?

He swallowed hard which is fucking difficult with your mouth wide open and almost choked on his beer. Had the alcohol affected his hearing? He'd never heard a female use that word before or mention anything so intensely personal but she was completely unabashed. He felt his eyes glaze over again and was vaguely aware that he had started to say something himself but it was like listening to a third person sitting at the table with them.

'What makes you think I don't?' he heard himself blurt out in a gruff, croaky sort of voice that he didn't recognise as his own. It wasn't his voice. He didn't even think the words were formed in his own brain. What the fuck was he saying? It must have been the alcohol talking. Well that's it. A few minutes was all it had taken him to make a right mess of it. She'd never take him seriously now. Might as well be off. Say goodbye and go home to bed.

'I don't think that at all,' Marcia replied.

Blimey! And she's still here? Things were improving by the second!

The blood positively rushed into Ralph's nether regions swelling his cock to outrageous proportions and pushing the unwieldy member hard up against his metal trouser zip so that it cut in and chaffed quite painfully.

He shifted around in his seat trying to get comfortable and took another demonstrative swig or two of the old Nigerian lager to divert attention from his bulging crutch. How the fuck was he ever going to get up and walk out of that place?

He felt pretty pissed already and was dismayed to notice that there was still at least half a pint still left in his glass.

There was a pregnant pause while Marcia seemed to be waiting for Ralph's reply and he casted around for a witty retort but couldn't think of one. He couldn't think of anything. His mind was in his trousers.

Ralph was just about to utter some other inanity when the cry of 'Time gentlemen please!' blasted through the alcohol fumes and cigarette smoke. Shit. A dark cloud swept over him. Was it that time already? How could he keep this going if they had to leave? Pub staff began to collect empty glasses, almost yanking them from the hands of drinkers who were still trying to finish the dregs. The shouting barman was so menacing that he might as well have been yelling 'Fuck off you bastards!' What a way to treat customers. But was he calling time on Ralph's hopes?

'Come on,' said Marcia. 'I've got some beer at my place'.

Her place! Whoah boy! A girl with her own place scored ten out of ten. Everyone knew that. Particularly in Ralph's case because he'd only just moved out of his parents' house and there'd never been much point in taking a girl back there. No point really, unless they'd wanted to play Monopoly. But there was only one thing on his mind in those days and it certainly wasn't Monopoly. Well, strip Monopoly maybe. He was moving into uncharted territory here and the thought made him slobber at the mouth.

Ralph gulped down the remaining content of his glass in a few huge swigs, stood up, felt dizzy and sat down again.

'Come on dickhead,' he said to himself. 'Don't fuck it up'. He was in a hurry now but only seemed able to move in slow motion.

Marcia uncrossed her legs, stood up and started walking towards the door with Ralph following behind like a faithful sheep dog. His eyes were fixed firmly on the rhythmic rising and falling movements of her firm, rounded bottom and he felt like making a grab for it. But in his efforts to keep up with her he wasn't paying attention to where he was going and bumped into a door post. Silly git. He prayed she hadn't detected the hopeless, alcohol-induced state in which he was trying to function whilst trying to appear at least capable if not entirely normal. Problem was, it seemed to be getting worse. His head was swimming.

Marcia only lived round the corner from the pub which was just as well because his legs were now in such a wobbly state that he wasn't altogether sure how far they would carry him. He wasn't sure about anything. They didn't talk much on the way. It didn't seem necessary.

After what seemed to Ralph like an overland trek of about three weeks, they arrived at the door of a block of flats. Actually, it was only about a hundred yards from the pub and couldn't have taken more than a few minutes but time and space had now taken on new dimensions for him. He was a slobbering wreck.

Marcia magically produced a key from somewhere and let them in through the wooden outside door and then an inside security glass door. She led Ralph to a lift and slid back the heavy metal first door and then the second. They entered the cubicle and she closed the first and then the second door. She pressed the appropriate button and the ancient contraption lurched upwards as they smiled at each other from its opposite sides. Actually, Marcia was smiling. Ralph was leering. How complicated life can be, he mused. They had negotiated six doors already since arriving at the building and they weren't even there yet.

Finally, after what seemed like an age, Marcia entered the apartment with Ralph trotting dutifully behind wondering how on earth he would manage to pull off the masterful seduction he had in mind.

'Take it slowly,' he said to himself. 'Don't rush her. Try and sit next to her and put your arm on the back of the seat just to check how she reacts. Then see if there's a chance to dim the lights. You've only just met this girl and you really like her. Don't frighten her off by being too hasty. She'll think you're a sex maniac.' He had it all worked out.

'But you are a sex maniac,' he was debating with himself now.

'Yes, but you don't want her to know that.' He told himself. Don't forget, it was still only about forty minutes since he'd met her.

Ralph shuffled into the flat closing the door behind him. He assumed Marcia had continued further on inside but as he turned to follow he almost bumped into her. She had stopped and was standing almost to attention right in front of him. They were face to face and just a few inches apart. So close that he could feel her warmth and smell the odours of sweat and scent wafting from her body. There was a pregnant pause while they stood gazing at each other. Marcia seemed to be glowing and her inviting smile made Ralph want to just melt into her. A tingle of heavy-duty magnitude was building up in his groin. Without any further ado the two instinctively made a lunge for each other like all-in wrestlers at the sound of the bell and suddenly their lips were locked together with suction as strong as a sink plunger. They were licking each other's tonsils, feeling each other's bits and thrusting their groins at each other like Brazilian samba dancers. There was a great deal of grappling, groping, clothes ripping, temperatures rising, juices flowing and heavy moaning all at once. It was bloody hectic. It was the first time any girl had let Ralph touch her all over like that with no questions asked. She was totally abandoned.

Previously, Ralph had only had one encounter that might possibly have qualified as the real thing but the nervousness that had accompanied the event had led to a rather dubious conclusion. Inasmuch as the female concerned had willingly removed her knickers rather than Ralph begging her to do so, which had been his primary tactic with any potential prey up until then, matters seemed to have been developing in a decidedly promising fashion. But this was followed by a great deal of fumbling, groping in the dark and general uncertainty. Although the act was completed satisfactorily as far as Ralph was concerned, he was never entirely sure whether he had actually managed to penetrate the young lady in question and felt it would have been churlish to ask. As he went abroad shortly afterwards and never saw her again, a question mark was left hanging over the whole sordid business that was still there to this day.

But Marcia was a different kettle of fish altogether. It was as if he had switched onto autopilot and had been doing it all his life. With a presence of mind that surprised him, he pulled her skirt gradually upwards from behind until he felt the warm, bare flesh of her arse. This is bloody good, he thought. This is going very well indeed. But then he realised she was wearing no knickers and almost shot his bolt. Somehow though, Marcia seemed to sense this and squeezed his love handles so violently that he shouted out in pain. It certainly had the effect of delaying things on his part. Could it be true? Had she been out in public wearing nothing at all underneath?

They fell to the floor rolling around in a state of thrilling, thumping, panting, pulsating passion with Marcia tearing at Ralph's trousers in an attempt to release the old chap into the wild. But it had bulged up so big and hard that it was putting pressure on the zip which refused to open. Impatiently, Marcia pushed Ralph back, took hold of his trouser waist with both hands and ripped the garment asunder so that his swollen willy plopped out like a huge tent pole. She grabbed the hot throbbing item with one hand whilst sliding her skirt up her thighs with the other. Then, in one instinctive, urgent movement, she lay back, drew up her knees, parted her legs wide and guided Ralph's bursting sausage towards her. A moment later they were doing it properly. This is really it, thought Ralph. It wasn't her first time that was for sure. She was a bloody expert.

He was carried away by Marcia's sumptuous, all-embracing attention to the point where he felt no fear or pain. Only love. She seemed as grateful to him as he most certainly was to her. She kept saying 'Thank you' every time he thrust forward.

'Thank you, thank you, thank you, thank you.'

They woke up thoroughly exhausted at about three in the morning, curled up in an intimate embrace. They were still lying on the floor just by the front door seemingly welded together. At first, Ralph couldn't quite work out where her body finished and his started.

Talk about feeling fucked. Now he understood the true meaning of that phrase.

'I'll have that beer now,' he joked.

'You'll do as you're told,' she replied

'Have I taken advantage of you?'

'Yes thank you.'

'Why were you so upset with Sadhu?'

'Didn't fancy him.'

Ralph realised that for her this was almost a crime. But who was the criminal?

He felt warm all over and was about to drift off into dreamland when he felt a probing hand moving up his thigh. Marcia began to massage his sexual member which seemed to have entered a permanent state of erection. She began to clench the muscles of her buttocks and groin in and out as if she was trying to work herself up again. She didn't have to try very hard. A faraway look swept across her face. Half smiling, half serious.

'Bloody hell, not again.'

'Yes again,' she commanded softly as if in a dream.

Ralph was lying on his back and started to roll over towards her but she pushed him back and mounted him by cocking a leg over as if she was getting on a bike.

She held him down by the shoulders, sat upright and leaned back.

'Don't move,' she ordered.

'Okay.'

It was about noon before they woke again, still lying by the front door. Ralph felt a rough, chaffing sensation on his back and pulled the doormat out from under him.

It said 'Welcome' on it.

Now, you may be wondering what this has all got to do with football.

Well quite a lot really because Marcia was actually the first football nymphomaniac or at least the first one Ralph had come across. (Excuse me).

THE BEAUTIFUL GAME
After You – No After You

Whilst unfair gamesmanship has reached new heights on the football pitch, there is a strange practice which displays the most curious desire of players to be good guys.

It is the 'Throw it back to them' scenario. The 'look at us, aren't we nice, we're letting you have the ball' convention. It is bollocks. I refer to the situation when a ball is kicked out of play to allow an injured player to be treated. In the old days, the ref would stop the game and a dropped ball was the method used to get it going again once the injured player had had water squirted over him by the physio or trainer as they used to be called. But now the ball is kicked into touch by a player on whom the mantle of concern for a fellow human being has irrationally descended and then deliberately thrown or kicked to the opposition on the re-start. There is nothing in the rules to cover it. Players have invented it for themselves. It is mad. It is also beyond the control of the referee.

In all other areas of the game, players take whatever advantage they can whether it's fair or not. Have you ever seen a player fling his arm in the air and appeal for 'Their ball ref!' when the ball goes out of play? Most players will try to claim it even if they know for sure it's the other side's ball. What you do see is shirt-tugging, hair-pulling, bollock-squeezing, punching, spitting, racial-taunting, sexual-taunting, throat-grabbing, eye-gauging, scratching, biting, elbowing and, of course, kicking. Sometimes you even see hair-raising tackles that are so frightening they deserve a prison sentence. So what is it about this so-called convention that causes players to end up being polite enough to unilaterally give the ball to the other side? Perhaps they should make a little presentational speech with it. 'In the interests of fair play I felt it was only right I should give you the ball and in doing so I hope you will accept it in the true spirit of sportsmanship with which it is offered.' Very fucking likely. Why the fuck do they do it when they are all cheating bastards in all other respects? It is totally out of character and thoroughly unconvincing.

This convention produced a most extraordinary situation a few years ago in a cup match between Arsenal and Sheffield United. You must remember it. A Sheffield player was injured and the ball was kicked into touch by one of his own team-mates to accommodate the physio. On the restart, the ball was thrown back in by an Arsenal player with the intention of giving it to a Sheffield opponent. But one of the Gunners' foreign players who had only just been signed and was unaware of this fair play convention, (or so he said) intercepted the ball in an advanced position behind the Sheffield defence and passed to a team-mate who easily scored what proved to be the winning goal. This led to wild objections from the Blades' management, players and fans amid the utter disgust and total indignation of everyone in the football world including even the scorer's own team-mates. What happened? After the match Arsenal actually offered to replay the match because they agreed it had been unfair.

Now I would be the very first to advocate fairness and decency in sport but this is plain insanity. There are hundreds of matches every week in which things happen that, with the benefit of television replays, are shown to be unfair such as: The ball clearly crossing the goal line but no goal given: Or vice versa: Clear handball in the penalty area but no penalty awarded: Or vice versa: Penalties awarded for tackles that were perfectly fair: Or vice versa: Goals disallowed for offsides, which weren't: Or vice versa. It happens all the time in match after match and these mistakes often determine the winner so why on earth should they have played this particular match, Arsenal v. Sheffield United, again? But in the event it was replayed and the score was exactly the same as the first time, 2-1 to Arsenal, so no change there but a tidy extra revenue for the Gunners from another sold out home fixture. Of course, the most puzzling aspect of this particular incident is that if Arsenal agreed that the 'unfair' goal was the reason to have a replay, it must then follow that the result of the original match was a 1-1 draw and should really have been replayed at Bramall Lane. But I suppose that as far as Arsenal are concerned, there has to be a limit to this fair play lark.

26
Marcia's Match

When they finally awoke Ralph was completely stiff and thoroughly exhausted but glowing all over. Like a new man. Or perhaps like a real man for the first time. As he lay there, awake but dreaming, the alarm mechanism of his body clock automatically sprung into action and he realised it was Saturday. Now Ralph used to feel that in the football season at three o'clock on a Saturday afternoon if you weren't at a football match something must be wrong. So, after that first, wonderful, delicious, exhausting collision with Marcia, he decided that the ultimate compliment he could bestow on her was to invite her to come along to a match with him.

Of course, he usually went with his mates and he knew they would think it very strange if he turned up with a female. You just didn't invite girlfriends to football matches in those days. They wouldn't have wanted to go anyway. But after the night he'd just been through, he was in the mood for new and exotic experiences and anyway he wanted to show her off. He wondered how he could manage to casually slip into the conversation that he had spent the night at Marcia's place.

Marcia had never been to a football match before. She said she didn't believe in it. Quite naturally, this statement reduced Ralph to a state of chronic bewilderment in which he was unable at first to form a cogent response. It turned out that, being an extreme left-wing political thinker, she had decided to oppose any activities that were competitive. Anyway, she had planned to see a Jean Luc-Godard film at the NFT. But later on, after a chat in which Ralph waxed lyrical about the artistic merits of the game and the benefits it offered to the working classes, she agreed to come.

Chelsea *v.* Cambridge United in the old Second Division. Should be a belter!

They decided to go by tube. It was only a few stops but the

whole train was bursting to the gills with rowdy football fans. Ralph and Marcia were pressed close together and couldn't keep their hands off each other much to the growing fascination of the crowd around them. Naturally, Ralph had his usual hard on. The revolution had not so far affected this most endearing of his qualities. Furthermore, Marcia knew all about it because she was stroking it through his tight jeans and occasionally giving it a little squeeze. Although he felt a bit self-conscious, Ralph had a raging desire to ravish her on the spot and seriously began to wonder whether he could manage to slip it in without anyone noticing. Except Marcia of course. She'd notice all right but he was pretty sure she wouldn't mind and he didn't think their audience would for that matter. Not the Chelsea fans anyway. He wasn't quite so sure about the Cambridge lot albeit most of them were merry with drink and probably wouldn't have minded if he had performed cunnilingus on Marcia whilst she hung from the hand straps.

With a determination usually reserved for those who climb mountains or sail oceans single-handed, Ralph managed to unzip his fly a little and extract just the tip of his helmet through the small opening. Feeling the warm, bare flesh on her finger tips, Marcia's eyes immediately lit up with delight and she began undoing her own zip. They pressed closer together until about an inch of his cock was inside Marcia's jeans touching her pubic hair. To achieve this he had to bend his knees. She squeezed her thighs together and clenched her groin muscles in an effort to manoeuvre the old chap further inside towards the ultimate goal. Ralph thrust forward obligingly holding her arse steady as he did so but it was a struggle. It's not easy when you're standing up. Particularly when you're surrounded by hundreds of people who are becoming more interested by the second. Of course nobody could see what they were up to because of the way they were all packed in like sardines but they must have started to get some idea of what was going on. Nearly there. One more heave and it would be in. Ralph was just about to try and lift Marcia's leg to facilitate a full entry when the train arrived at Fulham Broadway, the doors opened and everyone swarmed off onto the platform. Bugger! Oh well, maybe on the way back. Ralph was thankful for the cover of so many people because now he was left with a huge stiffy and there was nothing he could do to get it down.

They walked hand in hand in the freezing cold along the Fulham Road and, for some reason, maybe because it was Marcia's first time, a brief memory of his own first match at Palace with his Dad flashed into Ralph's mind. My, how grown up he had become! By the time they reached the ground he was relieved that the bulge in his jeans had withered to more manageable proportions because he had started to worry about how he would negotiate the turnstile. They entered at the Shed end. Ralph's spiritual home. He looked around for his mates but it was a bit early. They'd still be in the pub. So he led Marcia towards his usual position behind the goal but half way along the terrace she stopped.

'Not here,' she said. 'Up there,' pointing to the upper tier of the east stand.

'That's the stand,' Ralph informed her. 'We usually stand here.'

'But it's all seats up there,' she said. 'Why do they call it the stand?'

Christ, he thought, this girl doesn't know anything.

But she was so insistent that Ralph couldn't deny her any more than he could last night. He tried not to think about last night. He didn't want old Percy to wake up again.

Marcia pulled Ralph by the hand over to the point where you transferred to the stand. In those days, once you were in the ground, you could go anywhere you liked and just paid the steward if you wanted to transfer to a more expensive area.

'But I like to be near the action,' Ralph pleaded with her.

'It's much nicer up there.' And she was off.

Up they climbed. Up, up, up. Right to the top row of the uppermost section.

'Here's fine,' she said and they took their seats miles up from the pitch.

There was no one else within twenty yards of them. Ralph

sighed. He pulled out his programme and started to explain a few things about football and the match they were about to see but Marcia didn't display much interest. She was only interested in snogging. Her hands were all over Ralph. Oh well. Percy stirred.

Ralph scanned the shed far down below for his buddies but still couldn't see them anywhere. They'd be really surprised he wasn't there. He never missed a home match. And they certainly wouldn't believe he was up in the stand.

The players came out and the game kicked off. It was uneventful at first and much to his surprise Ralph found himself enjoying Marcia's amorous advances as much as the match. Definitely a first. He noticed she seemed to hug him a bit tighter when Kerry Dixon was on the ball.

'Who's that one?' she asked. She was sitting legs apart and her ass was moving around as if she was trying to get more comfortable.

'Which one?'

'The one with the long legs and big strong thighs and that lovely tight bum in those skimpy little shorts.' Ralph felt a tinge of jealousy.

'That's Kerry Dixon, our striker,' he informed her. 'He's one of the best in the country.'

'I'll bet he is,' she said. And slipped her hand into Ralph's coat, down his jeans and grabbed hold of his cock which immediately responded in its usual, reliable fashion. Bloody hell! Not here, surely? Automatically, Ralph reciprocated by slipping his hand through her coat and down her jeans but her own hand was already there. She'd been diddling herself off! He placed his hand over hers. Marcia looked at him and smiled.

'Hello,' she said. And began to manipulate them both at the same time. This must have been what she had in mind when she dragged him up there. Horny little bitch!

A promising move began. David Speedie raced down the wing past three defenders and passed the ball in. Ralph felt Marcia stiffen a little and both her hands moved quicker, seemingly influenced by the momentum of the action on the pitch. Chelsea were in an advanced position on the edge of the Cambridge penalty area. Speedie to Dixon. The ball came closer to their goal. Marcia moaned and slipped her legs over the seats in front. Dixon to Speedie. Gaps appear in the Cambridge defence and her legs open a little wider. Her fingers were working overtime now and she gasped. Speedie to Dixon. He began to take aim. 'Shoot now!' she screamed. The nearest person to them, an elderly man ten rows in front, glanced round, coughed nervously and turned back to the action on the pitch. Dixon shoots. Her hand tightens around Ralph's willy and he's bursting. It's a goal! The crowd roars.

'Ooh, aah,' groans Marcia. She's shaking like a bastard.

'Aarrghh!' yelled Ralph. Exploding all over. 'Up the fucking blues!'

It was half time. The crowd calmed down, Marcia calmed down, Ralph calmed down. They sat up. Ralph glanced over towards the shed and there they were. Cheesy, Wilkie and all the rest. They'd spotted him up there and were waving wildly to attract his attention. When they realised he'd seen them, they all gave him the thumbs up. Ralph took his sweaty, gooey hand out of Marcia's jeans and gave them the thumbs up back. Unknown to him, they weren't at all impressed.

'Look at the cunt. Some fucking revolutionary he is. Up there with the fucking toffs.'

'Who's that scraggy bint with him?'

'Dunno, some old slag he's trying to get his leg over.'

'He'll be fucking lucky.'

'How come, do you recognise her?'

'No but if she's at a football match she must be a fucking lesbo.'

'Yeah.'

THE BEAUTIFUL GAME

The Premiership environment has become a larger than life experience with fabulous, luxury stadiums, instant replay screens, world-class players, celebrity fans, fancy restaurants and even comfortable seats from which you get an uninterrupted view of the pitch including both goals. On television, each game is analysed to a ridiculous degree with computer enhancements, varied camera angles, statistics and endless interviews with managers, pundits and players, some of whom can hardly speak English. The British ones anyway. Nowadays, every so-called expert can spew out a plethora of statistics in depressingly arrogant and authoritative manner and they all go around nodding sagely in agreement with each other. To prove their points they bombard us with minor, irrelevant facts drawn from the mass of information now at everyone's disposal via the papers, Teletext, the Internet and television. Indeed, our minds are saturated with vast banks of useless data that, at the end of the day, mean absolutely nothing. Because one of the great qualities of our beautiful game is that no facts or figures can enable even the biggest Mr Brainy Bollocks to accurately predict the outcome of any match.

Even a top team packed with international megastars that has won its last ten games can't be sure of winning the next one. Even if it was playing against the bottom team that hadn't won for months, was decimated by injuries and had just sacked its manager. Quite obviously, this is one of the most endearing aspects of the game and one reason why we love it so much. Hereford United can beat Newcastle United. Sutton United can beat Coventry City. Wrexham can beat Arsenal. Anyone can beat Manchester United – please.

If it wasn't like this, and everything went according to the form book we'd all win the pools every week.

But we wouldn't win much.

27
Rosenbloom and Humperdink

He had already upset his mother by announcing he was a vegetarian just as she was about to serve up the roast lamb and she wasn't at all impressed by his statement that just the vegetables would be fine.

'You need meat,' she informed him. 'A growing young man needs plenty of protein.'

'Really Mother, it's okay. You can get by quite easily without meat. Anyway, I'm not a kid any more. I'm fully grown already.'

It was a Friday evening and Ralph was visiting his parents for the first time in quite a while. It wasn't going well. The outfit he'd turned up in clearly hadn't met with his father's approval even though the scruffy jeans, 'Ban The Bomb' t-shirt and coloured bead necklaces represented the smartest items in his wardrobe. In fact, he didn't have a wardrobe. Just a crumpled pile of clothing at the end of his bed. Well, mattress actually. But if the clothes weren't bad enough, his beard certainly tipped the balance. A bushy, unkempt foliage stuffed with the congealing remnants of various recent meals. There might even have been a family of starlings nesting in it for all you could tell. Beards like this were all the rage in the hippy circles Ralph frequented these days. His Dad was on his case as soon he arrived.

'Oy vey. What kind of a meshuggener beatnick is this?' he asked, shaking his head in bewilderment as he opened the door. 'Mother, Fidel Castro is here for dinner. Oy vey. And you used to be such a smart young man. What have you turned into?'

'A comfortable young man,' said Ralph.

The older man sat down to read the paper in order to immerse himself in familiar routine and avoid listening to this strange weirdo claiming to be his son. Where had he gone wrong? He'd seen Ralph, spoken to him, it was no good. Let's get back to normal. But it wasn't long before the subject of a job came up. Ralph had gone on the dole. He didn't have time to work. He was a writer and political activist now.

'You can't live on hand-outs,' his Dad shouted with accompanying gesticulations. 'You must work. Get yourself a proper job. I'll talk to Jack Rosenbloom the accountant. He'll take you on as an apprentice if I ask him. The ganef won't pay much but it's honest work and you'd have a secure future.'

It wasn't the first time he'd tried to persuade Ralph to be an accountant but he would've had to hold a gun to his head.

'No thanks Dad. I appreciate you wanting to help but really. I think I'd rather be dead.'

'Nonsense! You can't live without working. Everyone must work.'

'I do work. My own work. Anyway, it's poetic justice. Being financed by the state that I'm trying to bring down.'

'Oy vey.'

After an hour or so of this Ralph was bored beyond belief when it suddenly occurred to him that he hadn't seen the lads for quite a while and being Friday night they were bound to be in the pub. So he made his excuses and walked round to the Crown & Sceptre. Sure enough, there they all were. Except Cheesy of course. No one had seen him for years. Ralph got himself a drink, walked over to the usual table and sat down without saying anything. Everyone stopped talking and glared at this strange creature that had plonked itself down at the table. Their table. The table that was theirs. But it didn't go away. It just sat there. At their table. Said nothing. Just sat there.

Ralph wondered how long it would take them to recognise him through the curly, bushy triffid that covered his entire face.

Wilkie was talking to a rather attractive young female whom Ralph didn't recognise.

'Of course, I could have been a professional footballer,' he was saying.

'Really? Why didn't you then?' she asked.

'Cos he was no fucking good at it,' Ralph interjected.

Wilkie directed his hard bastard glare at Ralph but said nothing in response. He was never one to cause a fuss. But the quizzical look on his face indicated the glimmerings of recognition. A conversation got underway about the England football team.

'There's no easy games any more,' someone was saying.

'There fucking well should be,' said Ralph.

They all looked at him in amazement and then Wilkie piped up. 'Ralph, is that you?'

'Of course it's me you prat. Who the fuck did you think it was? Englebert fucking Humperdink?'

'Fucking hell, look at him. He's a fucking hippy,' observed Chalky.

'I'm just being myself.'

'Oh yeah. Why do you look like all the other fucking hippies then?' asked Darryl who had never managed to overcome his general suspicion of everything Ralph said and did even though they hadn't seen each other for some time.

'I suppose you're on drugs,' commented Chalky.

'I've smoked pot,' Ralph announced haughtily. They were all horrified.

'I don't believe it,' said Wilkie. 'That's terrible. Ralph a drug addict.'

'I'm not a fucking addict.'

'That's what they all say.'

'Smoking a joint doesn't make you a fucking addict.'

'Yeah but it's a slippery slope, all that drugs bollocks.'

'For fuck's sake. I've just smoked pot a few times. I didn't say I was shooting heroin up my fucking eyelids or whatever it is they do with the fucking stuff.'

'Once you start you can't stop.'

'Of course I can.'

'That's what they all say.'

'Look you fatheads. There's all sorts of drugs. I've only had marijuana. Not the hard stuff like heroin or cocaine. Marijuana isn't addictive anyway.'

'Yeah but it leads onto the hard stuff. I've heard all about it. You've had it mate.'

'Don't talk bollocks. That's like saying if you have half a pint of bitter you'll become a fucking alcoholic.'

He'd only been in there five minutes and they were at it already. Just like the old times.

Ralph gestured towards the rather tasty looking girl he didn't recognise and whispered in Wilkie's ear.

'She with you then?'

'Sort of.'

'I thought you were going out with Susan Barnes.'

'I was.'

'What happened to her then?'

'Dumped her.'

Ralph thought this was hilarious. Wilkie had always struggled get girls to go out with him at all without dumping the one who had actually agreed to it.

'Why?'

'Asked her to marry me but she turned me down.'

'And that's a reason to dump her?'

'I want to get married.'

'Why?'

'I'm twenty-six. Don't want to leave it too late.'

'Too late for what?'

'Look, my Dad got married at twenty six and I want to do the same.'

'When did this all happen then?'

'Today.'

'And you're already going out with this other girl. What's her name?'

'Jill Etherington. Well, er, no not really.'

'What's she doing here then? How come I've never seen her before?'

'She's visiting Susan from Brighton. They were mates at college or something. We were all supposed to be meeting up here for a drink but Susan didn't fancy it. Probably too upset. Jill just turned up like we arranged. Couldn't just ignore her could I? Just because I chucked her mate.' He kept alluding to break up as if he was proud of it.

'She's quite nice,' Ralph observed.

'Yeah, actually she's a lot fucking nicer than Susan. Maybe she'll marry me instead.'

'I always thought you were a bit thick, now I know you're a fucking idiot.'

The tables at the Cosh consisted of chunky, rectangular slabs of polished wood surrounded on three sides by leatherette covered benches. Jill and Wilkie were at the top end, hemmed in on the opposite side to Ralph by Darren and Chalky. Next to Chalky was a rather dowdy looking older female who had obviously seen better days.

Ralph's heart skipped a beat. If he wasn't mistaken, it was Martha, the highly promiscuous daughter of their school caretaker and a legend of local folklore. Although now a mature woman, Ralph remembered her as a ravishing young girl who was lusted after by all the lads with good reason. In the half-light of the gym storeroom after school she was known to turn a trick or two for anyone who was prepared to donate his dinner money for the privilege. Full-blown sex or a plate of chips? You choose. They were practically queuing up in the corridor to hand over the few coins clasped tightly in their sweaty palms. Even some of the more elderly teachers, so the story goes, were thought to have succumbed to her modestly-priced charms albeit in darkened studies with the curtains drawn. She did a roaring trade and might even have got away with it if she hadn't been silly enough to start splashing her hard-earned cash around. The odd designer garment was easy enough to pass off, she could have picked it up in a charity shop, and the precious items of jewellery with which she was increasingly adorned could easily have been donated by admirers of whom there were plenty. But it was when she turned up one day in her new Lotus sports car that the game was up. It was quite an acquisition for someone on the dole. Her father was furious. Not because of the way she earned the money. He had no illusions about her chastity. 'Just like her fucking mother,' he used to say.

No, he was pissed off because at the age of only sixteen she had been earning a fortune just for lying on her back and enjoying herself while he had to clean out the filthy, fucking toilets in exchange for a measly pittance.

Eventually the scandal broke but somehow she was never prosecuted even though in those days prostitution was regarded as a far more serious crime than it is now. Some say the headmaster managed to sort something out with the authorities to save the name of the school whilst others suggested that the police superintendent in charge of the case was one of Martha's customers. Either way, she was free to go on to the university of her choice (after all, there were no academic qualifications needed in her profession) and she ended up in Oxford offering a nice line in scholarly relief to the sons of leaders who would one day become leaders themselves. The prestigious institution of higher learning accommodated many budding little lords and masters who could all quite easily afford her special services which they craved with a passion so it was mutually rewarding for all concerned. Indeed, everything went extremely well until one hot and sticky summer's afternoon when Martha broke her cardinal rule by offering a freebee to the aristocratic father of one of her most regular clients. (She called them clients now). Pater had been up on a visit to his horny young offspring who spent most of his time, and his dad's cash, avidly pursuing a line of research into sexual fulfilment in preference to his chosen subject of Mediaeval European history. Hardly surprising really. Martha and the dad were caught unawares by the Dean, of all people, in the men's toilet of the cricket pavilion. She was on her knees with his upper-class prick in her mouth and his superior balls hanging around her chin. Although everyone else was shocked, Martha found it highly amusing because only an hour or two earlier the father, having arrived unannounced, had almost caught her unawares in exactly the same position with his son. All generations catered for! In fact, all it amounted to was the fairly usual sort of university high jinks and there probably wouldn't have been much of a fuss about the incident if the errant dad hadn't been the British Foreign Secretary at the time.

At first, Martha thought the reason the college chief had entered such a state of profuse anger as he burst upon the sordid scene was jealousy for her much admired expertise. She was renowned for her blow-jobs. But as it turned out, it was jealousy of a different kind that had caused the tantrum. Only just the night before the Dean had been reciprocating profuse declarations of undying love from the bisexual politician whose member now threatened to rupture Martha's tonsils. The Dean was a broken-hearted, lovelorn old fool acting mainly out of spite. He simply couldn't live it down and as a result Martha was run out of town. The sum of one thousand pounds plus the earnest threat to spread a rumour that she was irreparably diseased was enough to induce her to leave quietly and so she returned to the only place where she knew she could ply her trade. Back to the green, green grass of home. Or on it mostly.

Martha had changed a great deal from the girl Ralph remembered from the old days.

He still carried the vision of her as a friendly, bright girl who seemed to be liked by everyone but the years had taken their toll. Now her face creased into a million lines when she coughed and she spoke with the deep rasp of a heavy smoker. She also looked older than Ralph would have expected.

He stood up to let Wilkie slide out.

'Okay, my round, what do you want?'

Chalky and Martha ordered pints of lager and Jill a large vodka and tonic. Ralph decided on a second pint of Guinness. It was his drink now.

Wilkie duly trotted off to queue at the crowded bar. He'd be some time yet. Just the chance to get to know more about this Jill person. Ralph slid towards her along the bench and the whiff of scent mixed with her alluring body odour immediately raised his interest. After Marcia, he was entirely confident of his chances with any woman.

He thought he was God's gift.

'Hello,' he said.

'I've heard all about you,' said Jill. 'The anarchist, right?'

'Sort of. It's a long story.'

'I'm in no hurry.'

At first she hadn't seemed like much to write home about but close up Ralph began to find her most alluring. She wore a plain raincoat that gave little away, being tightly buttoned as if she hadn't yet decided if she was staying or going. But the two symmetrical bumps that protruded around chest height indicated that she was very well endowed. As the rest of her was hidden beneath the table, he was unable to discern exactly how well proportioned she was although what he could see gave a most promising impression. Full lips, just the way he liked them, laughing eyes that showed she was up for some fun, straight, white teeth indicating she looked after herself and long fingers which she slid up and down her highball glass, occasionally playing around the rim with her index finger. Ralph imagined those sensuous digits coaxing his prick and, as usual, it sprang to life. Ready for action on demand. Luckily though, he didn't have to hide the growing protrusion because it was tucked away under the table where no one could see it. The more he spoke to Jill, the more he warmed to her. She was obviously intelligent and even liked football but, of course, the two things went together in Ralph's mind anyway.

He craned his neck to see how near Wilkie was to being served.

'He'll be ages yet,' said Jill. 'He's a wimp. That's why Sue dumped him.'

What was that under the table?

'He told me it was the other way round.'

There was something touching Ralph's leg.

'Don't be silly. She was fed up with him begging her to marry him all the time.'

It was moving along his thigh. Was it someone opposite trying to put their feet up on the bench?

'But they've been together for ages.'

Ralph was getting concerned. It was approaching his nether regions. He wriggled in his seat.

'Yes but she's got lots of boyfriends. She doesn't want to get married, She's still having fun.'

Fucking hell, it was touching his cock!

And then he realised what was going on. Jill had slipped her hand under the table and was rubbing it up and down on what had now become his fully erect, rock hard organ which was throbbing violently in response. Blimey! What a turn up for the books! He hadn't taken Jill to be that sort. More the demur type. Not that he was complaining. No sir. But he wasn't quite sure how to react. He'd never been accosted this way in a pub before so he just continued as if nothing special was happening. That he was used to this sort of thing. It wasn't easy.

'The poor bastard would be gutted if he knew,' he said.

Jill squeezed Ralph's old chap so hard that he felt little drops of fluid squeeze out of the tip and soak into his pants. Ooh, nice.

'I know. It's the only reason I came. He was blubbing his eyes out when Sue told him earlier. It was really pathetic She asked me to keep an eye on him in case he did anything silly.'

She was working Ralph into a lather but he still didn't let on he'd noticed. What a git. How could he not have noticed?

'He thinks you'll marry him instead.'

At this, Jill threw her head back and laughed like a drain.

'That'll be the day,' she said and carried on laughing. She was splitting her sides. It seemed like a bit of an over reaction to Ralph but he wasn't really in the mood for amateur psychology. There were other things on his mind. Not only his mind.

Now Ralph responded. He leaned over and whispered in Jill's ear.

'Very handy,' he said, slipping his own hand under the table and sliding it up the inside of her thigh. Bare flesh, no stockings, no tights.

'Oh, so you've noticed then,' she whispered back, opening her legs slightly to accommodate his prying digits.

'Couldn't hardly miss it,' he said slipping his forefinger under her panties to tease her moist, warm clitoris and causing her to emit a soft, breathless gasp.

She leaned over again and whispered 'Talk to me dirty.'

'You're a horny little cunt,' Ralph whispered and felt her groin muscles clench in response.

This is good, he thought. This is bloody good. Out of the corner of his eye Ralph noticed Jill exchange a knowing little smile with Martha who must have sussed what was happening but he still attempted to appear perfectly normal as if nothing untoward was going on. He even tried to continue a normal conversation but it was interspersed with little gulps and coughs influenced by the manual hanky-panky under the table.

'England Managers are, ahhmmmm, always making excuses f-f-for their teeeams, yes, huup,' he said whilst desperately worrying if he was about to ejaculate in public for the first time.

'Mmm, not up to it are they,' replied Jill dreamily.

Just then, Wilkie returned with the drinks.

'Guinness is fucking expensive, he said angrily. Everyone at the table laughed.

'What?' he asked in his most clueless fashion. And they all laughed again.

The diversion had caused Ralph's erection to wilt slightly and he thought there would hardly be a better opportunity to go to the gents. He was bursting. If Jill continued to take him in hand it might be a long time before the chance would arise again and then he might have a crisis on his hands.

'Let me out Wilkes,' he said standing up. ' I need to point Percy at the porcelain.'

'Want a hand?' asked Chalky and he and Martha both laughed. Martha must have told him what was happening under the table. He would never have worked it out for himself. Silly bastard. How did he end up with her anyway?

'I'll manage thanks mate.' And off Ralph went, barging his way through the crowded bar.

As the foam created by the sheer force of liquid gushing out of him frothed up in the urinal Ralph started making plans. Go for a curry, take a few bottles back to his place, make a night of it. He couldn't wait to get back to the table. But as he walked out of the gents, Jill was waiting for him.

'Come on,' she ordered and, grabbing his hand, led him through a small side door into the beer garden. It was cold, damp and dark and, being enclosed by walls on every side, completely secluded. She pulled Ralph over to the darkest corner, unbuttoned her coat, leaned back against the wall and held her arms open in anticipation of his embrace. In seconds they were thrusting at each other in a flurry of passion.

'Brace yourself,' she commanded and, putting her arms round Ralph's neck, took three little jumps and then a larger fourth on which she lifted up her legs and folded them round his waist until she was clinging on to him like a koala bear hugs its mother. He put his hands under her suspended buttocks and heaved them up enough to enable him to open his fly and pull out his todger which he eased into her via the route his fingers had navigated a little earlier under the table.

She seemed lighter than Ralph expected but her weight was still quite a strain on his knees although it didn't bother him much at first. Is it any wonder?

'Talk to me,' she said as he lifted her arse up and down with his hands.

'You're a horny little cunt,' he said.

'No, not that. Talk to me about football.'

'Football?'

'Yes, tell me the team.'

'What team.'

'You know, the team that won the world cup.'

'Brazil?'

'No, not Brazil.'

'Brazil won the fucking world cup,' said Ralph authoritatively.

'No, our team. Tell me our team that won it. Who was in it? You know don't you?'

'Hey, lady, that's my subject.'

'Go on then, tell me the team.'

'You don't know someone called Marcia do you?'

'Tell me the team. Come on, tell me.'

Ralph started reciting the members of England's team from 1966.

'Banks, Cohen.'

'Yes, that's it, come on.' And she started reciting with him. She was getting more and more excited with every name.

'Bobby Charlton, Jack Charlton.' Yes, yes. Ralph's knees started to give out. They were trembling like a weight-lifter's.

'Styles, Ball.' Yes, yes, yes.

Having to hold Jill's weight and with her legs squeezing the breath out of him with every thrust, he wasn't sure if he could keep going until the end even though his instinct told him it wasn't that far off.

'Moore, Peters.' Yes, oh yes, yes.

Ralph didn't have the puff to carry on reciting but it didn't matter because Jill continued by herself.

'Hurst, Hurst, Hurst!' she screamed as they clung to each other in a final, frenetic moment of bliss.

They made their way back into the bar with Ralph struggling to keep up with Jill. His battered knees had lost all feeling and their ability to bend making it almost impossible to walk. He had to hang on to people as he grappled his way back to the table before practically collapsing into his seat. He had intended to make a date with Jill for later but no sooner had they rejoined the others than she announced she was leaving.

'Right, I'm off home, bye all.' And she was gone.

'What have you said to her?' asked Wilkie a few moments later.

'Nothing mate.'

'I know you, you bastard. I'll bet you said something to put her off me.'

'No really I didn't. Fancy a curry? I'm fucking famished.'

The Beautiful Game

Excuses, Excuses

Managers at international level are always saying there are no easy games any more. There bloody well should be.

In fact, it's just a bland statement issued before every match by all international managers to get their excuses in early and cover any awkward or embarrassing defeat if it happens. It was probably dreamt up as a PR tactic at an International Football Managers' Union meeting and written into the International Managers' handbook under the heading, 'Kidding the fans and shafting journalist gits who are asking awkward questions.'

How could a game between England and say Moldova or Luxembourg or the Faroe Islands not be considered easy compared with matches against Brazil, Italy or Germany? Those small countries have few professionals if any and some even have trouble raising any sort of a decent team at all.

In marked contrast, our players are full-time professionals in every sense of the word with top coaches, excellent, hi-tech training facilities, professional advisors and fuck-all else in the whole world to worry about. They're paid extraordinary sums of money to disport their skills. They're all bloody millionaires.

Quite obviously therefore, we should be absolutely miles ahead of Third-World teams who can't even manage to start a training session until their players have finished a hard day's work in the coal mines and then had to catch a bus to the training ground. The ones who can afford the fare that is. Miles ahead? We should be out of bloody sight. There should be no doubt at all about the outcome of these David and Goliath situations. I mean really, what the fuck do they do all week? These highly-strung, overpaid drama queens. It's an excuse, that's all. A universal excuse for international managers so that they won't lose face or their jobs if they get a disappointing result.

28
Spicy Bollocks

Thankfully, the Taj Mahal wasn't busy and they didn't have to wait long to be served. Ralph was so hungry he could have eaten a curried horse. He ordered masses and fell on the food when it arrived at the table as if he hadn't eaten for weeks.

'Bloody hell,' said Wilkie, 'What's made you so hungry?'

'Too much sex,' Ralph answered pushing a rolled up chapati stuffed with rice and curry into his mouth.

'Very funny,' said Wilkie. 'But look, I saw you flirting with Jill and I want you to promise me you'll keep your hands off.'

'Oh yeah, why?'

'Because I love her, she's the girl I want to marry.'

'What?'

'It's true.'

'Don't be fucking ridiculous.'

'What's fucking ridiculous about it?'

'Well first of all it was only today you asked Susan to marry you for fuck's sake.'

'Ah, yes. That's want I wanted to mention. It was only a trick.'

'What?'

'Look, Promise me you'll keep this a secret.'

'Okay.' Truth be told, Ralph was more interested in stuffing his face than Wilkie's fanciful nonsense.

'I knew she'd turn me down. That's why I asked her. It was an excuse to leave her.'

'Why do you need a fucking excuse?'

'I'm not like you Ralph. I couldn't tell her I didn't want her or that I never really fancied her. The only reason I got friendly with her in the first place was so I could meet Jill but I sort of got stuck with her. That was eight years ago. Eight fucking years. It's taken me eight fucking years to get out of it. But I've always been after

Jill. She's the one I really want. Always have done.' Ralph was flabbergasted.

'I'm flabbergasted,' he said

'I'll tell you something else.' Wilkie continued.

'What's that?'

'I think she fancies me too.'

Ralph felt the curry burning his insides as he wondered how to break the news to Wilkie softly.

'Look, Wilkie,' he said, 'You're a mate and I say this with all sincerity . . .' But Wilkie's interjection stopped him in his tracks.

'For fuck's sake Ralph,' he said tersely, 'Don't talk to me as if I was a fucking basket case. I know I haven't been around as much as you but fucking spit it out will you.'

'Okay. All I want to say is don't get your hopes up. I don't think Jill is interested in getting married to you or anyone else.'

'How the fuck do you know that. You've only just fucking met her.'

'Yeah. But somehow I feel I've got to know her quite well.'

'Don't talk bollocks. I've known her for the best part of ten years. That's how long I've been working on this plan. Now, finally, we can be together and you're trying to fuck it up.'

'Look, I don't want to fuck anything up,' said Ralph, spooning more rice onto his plate. 'I'm just trying to get you to face the truth.'

'You always think you know better than everyone else. Well you may have been right about some things but you're making a big fucking mistake this time buddy.'

'All right, have it your own way. Just don't say I didn't fucking warn you.'

What a complete prat Ralph thought. And he's so sure of himself.

The next day Ralph phoned Jill at Susan's. He was dead keen to carry on where they left off. He let the phone ring for ages before anyone answered but eventually it was picked up and he heard Jill's voice. She sounded a little flustered.

'Er, yes, hello.'

'Hi, it's me, Ralph.'

'Yes?'

'I'm phoning you up,' said Ralph. He was in his jolly mood.

'Look, I'm busy just at the moment. What do you want?'

'I should have thought that was obvious. When can we get together?'

'We can't.'

'What? Why not?' His mood was changing rapidly.

'I can't, that's all, ok . . . Bye'

'Hang on a minute, wait. No, not ok, What about last night?'

'Forget it. It never happened.'

'Yes it fucking did and I've still got the wobbly knees to prove it.'

'Look, I can't see you and that's it.'

'But why? There must be a reason.'

'I'm getting married.'

'What? You didn't say anything about that last night?'

'I didn't know last night.'

'Are you trying to tell me that someone asked you to marry them this morning?'

'Yes.'

'Anyone you know? Or was it a total stranger?'

'It was Wilkie. I've got to go.'

'What? And you actually said yes?' Astounded wasn't the word.

'Yes.'

'After all you said about him last night?'

'I didn't mean it. Please don't tell him.'

'Don't worry.'

'I must go. Someone might be listening.'

'Who might be listening? Who cares? What is all this cloak and dagger bollocks?'

'Please, don't do this Ralph.' She was becoming agitated.

'Is he there now?'

'Yes, and Susan. She's a bit upset.'

'Why?'

'She wants him back. She's in bits. Pleading with us not to go through with it. It's all a bit fraught. I didn't think she'd mind. I thought she was finished with him.'

Fuck me, they're all fighting over the silly prat now, Ralph thought to himself.

'But why did you agree to marry him?'

'He asked me.'

'That's a reason?'

'I want to get married'

'Why?'

'Before it's too late.'

'Ha, ha. You two must have been having a right fucking cosy little chat.'

'Look Ralph, do you want to marry me?'

'No.'

'Well that' all right then.'

And she hung up.

THE BEAUTIFUL GAME
Flavour of the Month

Teaching youngsters to play a passing game with free expression will help make the world a more beautiful place. That is the whole point of football and the reason they call it the beautiful game.

If we want our kids to flourish and be happy we must provide them with a healthy stimulus that they themselves consider a cool alternative to all the other nefarious pursuits that attract them like flies round a fanny when there is nothing else on offer.

Football is definitely cool. It is flavour of the fucking month.

Since the advent of the Premiership and all the hype that accompanies it because of live television coverage, football has become an enormous attraction for youngsters of both sexes who make quite a contribution to the huge wealth that now exists at the top end of the game. If there was any logic, reason, decency or sense around then at least some of those big profits would be filtered down to fund better facilities for juniors.

Of course, the highly talented few will always be catered for because they represent a good business proposition. But all kids are entitled to enjoy playing football if they want. Whoever they are and whatever standard they may be. Male and female, rich and poor, able-bodied and disabled, good players and not so good players. To do so, they all need flat, properly tended and marked out pitches, goals with nets and without holes, decent changing facilities with easy access, hot showers, qualified coaching and either flood-lit Astroturf or indoor training halls for the winter months.

They need it, they deserve it and in this supposedly enlightened society of ours it is about fucking time the authorities provided it. Free.

29
The Promise of Fulfilment

The shape of a female thigh outlined by a slinky, seductive garment. The inviting cleavage bulging forth from a low-cut gown. The thin lace of a delicate pantie against the soft skin of the lower stomach. The feel of a young girl's erect nipple between his fingers. The moan of delight as she responds to his touch. The feverish excitement as she allows him to remove the silky-smooth, fabric of her private undergarments. Uncovered flesh. The thrill as she finally submits to the aching need in her groin. Feelings laid bare. The parting of her legs as she willingly opens herself to his engorged member. The promise of fulfilment. The world-stopping tremor that brings unrivalled satisfaction to mind and body. The point where one body cannot be separated from another.

The peace, the quiet, the glow, the love.

Man was born to live alone and that was certainly true. One of the truest things there was. But the closest you could get to another human being was through sex and Ralph lived for it. Yet it would do far more than just engorge his penis. It had a magical and sublime effect that, whilst upon him, would render all other things completely meaningless.

Similarly, when Ralph watched Chelsea play football everything else would disappear from his mind and he would be as lost in a world devoid of boring, everyday reality as when he parted the labia to feast on the succulent fruits of love inside.

When they scored it was like an orgasm. Not of the penis but of the soul. A point at which he lost control of all bodily functions and, just for that fleeting moment, experienced a feeling of pure pleasure. Of calm. Of freedom. A moment when he and team and the rest of the crowd were together, as one.

And it was the same when he played the game himself. If a good move involving all the players produced a goal, everyone in the team was elated and hugged each other. They were a single unit. They had achieved something together. Something they could not have done alone.

At these moments, Ralph was drawn to the conclusion that football was about as close to sex as you could possibly get without actually fucking. Not that he wanted to fuck his team-mates. He was anything but that way inclined. The very idea of it made his skin crawl even though he was quite happy to be tactile with a homosexual on a platonic basis. No, he just wanted to be with people. To work with people. To co-operate with people. To love people. Christ was it hard.

But despite the difficulties brought on by a selfish society and the seemingly avowed intent of most of his mates to shoot his ideals out of the sky, he hung avidly to the one most cherished belief he hoped he would never relinquish. That the possibilities of people working together were far greater than the sum of possibilities of those same people working independently.

In life and in football.

As far as Ralph was concerned people who said that football was just a bunch of overgrown kids chasing around after a ball didn't know what the fuck they were on about. Most of them were so stupid that they weren't even prepared to listen to anyone who did. You just couldn't talk to them.

Unfortunately, they didn't know what they were missing.

To Ralph, the roar of delight when your team scored was an expression of pure joy. There was nothing to rival it – apart from sex. Surely anything that turned on masses of people in this way and created such happiness had to be a force for good in the world.

Yes, there were lots of prats associated with football and the game was not perfect by any means. But we didn't live in a perfect world and if we were going to agree that football was art (yes, that's right) then we would also have to agree on the widely accepted principle that art reflected the state of the society that produced it. Yet the communal expression of togetherness generated on the football terrace was certainly unique and priceless. You couldn't bottle it and take it away.

It was an experience of heightened perception, of elation, of love. Perhaps the only indication many people had of the way they wanted to feel all the time. Of the way they wanted to be in life. Of true fulfilment.

As such, it created for Ralph, at certain times, a similar feeling to that which he experienced when facing one of the world's great paintings or listening to a great musician or reading a fine book. Similar to the warm feeling of satisfaction after eating an exquisite meal prepared by a loving chef or drinking a fine bottle of wine with friends. Similar to the satisfaction he felt after copulating with a girl that he loved. Although he always insisted that he loved every girl he ever copulated with. At least a little. It was beautiful, uplifting, poetic, athletic, and skilful. It was a craft. At its highest level, it was most definitely art. If you wanted it to be.

There was no comparable situation in which so many people found themselves in such a friendly state of complete agreement or where you could hug a complete stranger without fear of being arrested or punched on the nose.

There was simply nothing like it.

Ralph always said that he caught the football bug over forty years ago and there was no sign of a cure yet. That's the way it was if you were a football follower and those who made silly statements about twenty-two prats chasing after a ball simply failed to understand the wonderful, aesthetic qualities of the game or the brotherhood amongst fans which had no parallel in modern life.

You could enter a pub anywhere in the country or even abroad and strike up a conversation about football and there was no other subject that was as eagerly debated or universally accessible. Certainly not politics or religion.

Football transcended politics and religion. That was for sure.

30
Lust at First Sight

Maybe it was a function of ageing or perhaps he was just shagged out after so many years of sexual debauchery but whatever the reason, Ralph began to feel a strong urge to have a regular companion. A female who would share not only his bed but all the other things in his life. Someone who had a similar taste in people, liked the same sort of food, and enjoyed going to concerts, cinemas, galleries and the theatre. This perfect partner would, even in the thick of winter, be willing to accompany him to football matches where they would freeze their bollocks off together or, in her case of course, her tits. That person was going to be hard to find. Ralph worked out that she would have to be a cross between Debbie Harry, Germaine Greer and Rodney Marsh although he hastened to add that he didn't fancy blokes and if Rodney Marsh ever laid a finger on him for any other reason than to get his attention to find out what he wanted to drink, he would punch his fucking lights out. What he was after was beauty, intellect and a passion for football. Together these added up to his dream girl.

But this wasn't your normal settling down mularky. Ralph didn't want a mortgage or a nine-to-five job or a house in the suburbs with an estate car parked outside. He was a revolutionary and always would be. He needed a mate. That was all. A soul mate.

It was about that time that he met Sophie and his fate was sealed.

Ralph remembered the occasion most distinctly as one of those turning points in his life. It was at a Saturday night party somewhere in south-east London. Earlier that day he'd watched Chelsea lose to Liverpool so naturally he was in a foul mood and even a few pints in a pub on the way there didn't help. To cap it all, the moment he arrived, some pillock of a Liverpool supporter he knew from the Sunday leagues came up to him holding out the badge on his replica shirt and taunting him with a chant of, 'Three, one, three, one, three, one, three, one.' He had an arrogant smile on his stupid face as if he'd scored all their fucking goals himself.

Ralph felt in urgent need of a good, stiff drink but all he could find was half a bottle of sweet Martini, two bottles of Pomagne, a small bottle of some dubious nut liqueur from Lebanon and the even more dubious plonk that he had brought himself. There was nothing for it but to slip out in search of an off-licence but it wasn't an area he was conversant with so he would have to investigate. The nearest place was a pub but they didn't do off-sales so Ralph had a quick pint and a double whisky chaser and set off again in the direction advised by a local. It must have been a good twenty minute walk before he came to a High Street and found a late night grocery store where he bought a couple of quarter bottles of whisky and set off back to the party. On the way it had started raining and Ralph was getting soaked to the skin but he decided to treat it as a sort of penance. God knows why he had to be such a martyr. He gulped down mouthfuls of whisky to keep himself warm as he walked. By the time he was passing the pub again he'd already finished the first quarter bottle and felt like another pint to wash it down. So he went back in and before he knew what had happened he'd had another two together with a few more double whiskies. When he finally got back he was sozzled, soaked and starting to shiver wildly with the cold. He felt like he'd just trekked across the Antarctic. A few more gulps of whisky warmed his insides but now he was ravenously hungry. Bloody starving.

Loads more folks had turned up by this time and the house had become quite crowded. Ralph glanced around in search of available females but they all seemed to be with blokes. He was just about to write the evening off as a celibate waste of time when his eyes came to rest on a vision of beauty that immediately set off a klaxon in his libido. Slim with long dark hair and bright eyes, she wore a most alluring outfit consisting of a tight black top, flowing green skirt peppered with silver star-signs and shiny, red boots. She was sitting cross-legged on the floor with a bunch of long-haired blokes who were passing a joint round. Most of the other partygoers were a fairly straight lot whose disapproval of this activity was obvious even though most of them were pretty high themselves on the mind-bending substance of alcohol. From time to time they each cast angry looks at the druggies who had taken over the stereo and were feeding it with weird, avant-garde music to which dancing was impossible.

But the pot-heads had reached another astral plain and were blissfully unaware of the annoyance they were causing the other guests none of whom was bold enough to intervene and get Abba and Slade back on.

Match of the Day was just starting and all the blokes crammed into a small room to watch it on a tiny television. When Chelsea came on Ralph couldn't bear to watch. He'd temporarily forgotten the empty pain in his guts but now his churning, gurgling stomach reminded him that if he didn't eat something soon he might pass out. He went off in a desperate search of food but after scouring the kitchen all he could find was half a sausage, a few soggy crisps and two pieces of stale sponge cake all of which he wolfed down before anyone else could get their mits on it. It tasted like pure ambrosia. When the programme finished all the guys came streaming back in discussing the various matches or, more precisely, the goals from the Premiership.

It had always annoyed Ralph that there was only one programme entrusted each week with informing the nation about the latest developments in our beloved national game and all they could do was show Premiership goals as if nothing else mattered. Well try explaining that to a Hartlepool United fan. The Producers of the programme probably thought the Vauxhall Conference was some new type of people carrier.

We needed the whole story. Not just news of the pampered elite.

Ralph knew he should have avoided it but he couldn't help it.

'Fucking crap programme,' he said to no one in particular. But a rather menacing individual with an XXXXXXL Charlton shirt covering his huge beer belly took him up on his statement.

'What do you mean crap? Don't you like football or something?'

'Like it, I love it,' Ralph replied with a passion. 'But we'll never get anywhere with crap programmes that only show the fucking goals from the top division.'

'But the Premiership's the best league in the world.'

'Who says?'

'It's a fact.'

'Oh really? Have you seen any Italian or Spanish matches recently?'

'Er, no. But why bother when our football's the best?'

'Been abroad at all?'

'Certainly have.'

'Where?'

'Spain and Spain.'

'Sorry?'

'Been twice,' he replied authoritatively. 'Same place. Enjoyed it first time, went back. No point sodding about.'

'Any good?'

'Too fucking hot. Not bad in the end though. Found a place with John Smith's on tap. Did English breakfast all day too. Pity it was so fucking hot though.'

'Didn't you have paella?'

'What's that?'

'You know, famous Spanish rice dish.'

'Never heard of it. Anyway, they did English breakfast. Best food you can get. Did fish and chips in the evenings too. Great. What more could you want?'

'Sounds ideal. Ever thought of living there?'

'No mate. Wouldn't live there if you paid me.'

'Why not if they do English breakfast and everything?'

Using his fingers, he counted off the reasons.

'Too hot. No Premiership. Don't speak English. It's abroad.'

'Why go at all then?'

'Get a tan. Makes you look better. Feel good."

'You could feel good all the time if you lived there.'

'Fuck off mate. No Englishman in his right mind would swap living here to go abroad.'

'See any football over there?'

'Football? No mate. Their tellies didn't have the Premiership. Only Fucking Real Madrid and some other foreign side.'

'Barcelona?'

'Yeah, how did you know?'

'Just a wild guess.'

'Have you been to Torremolinos then?'

'No, but I've been to the Nou Camp.'

'What's that?'

'Barcelona's ground. Saw them against Real. Fantastic stuff.'

'Wouldn't bother myself.'

'Why not?'

'Well it's crap isn't it? Why watch that crap when I can see Charlton every week?'

'Good point.'

'I reckon Charlton would beat that lot every time if they got the chance.'

'But Real are the European Champions.'

'Yeah but it's only Europe isn't it. They only faff and fiddle around with the ball.'

'I think they call that skill.'

'But it'll never get 'em anywhere. They need to put themselves about a bit. Get stuck in. They'll learn one day.'

It was midnight and people started leaving in droves. Ralph was getting tired and thought about making a move himself. Normally he would have risen to the challenge of a contentious discussion about football but he could see where it was going and with the alcohol starting to wear off he wasn't in the mood. Anyway, he was due to play for his Sunday side at ten in the morning and always enjoyed it so much more without a hangover. So he decided to call it a night but the insistent calling of his bubbling, distended bladder required urgent attention. He made his way up to the bathroom on the upstairs landing. The door was open and he was about to enter when he noticed someone in occupation. It was the sexy, little hippy girl humming along to the music while she applied her make up. As she leaned forward over the basin to focus in the mirror her skimpy skirt rode up the back of her legs. Whoah boy! Just a little more and he might get a glimpse of her knickers if she was wearing any. This could be interesting. He leaned against the wall and watched her for a while, drinking in the tightness of her hamstrings and the curve of her thighs. He felt entitled somehow. She had no idea he was there. He felt like approaching her silently from behind, lifting the flimsy fabric of that skirt and slipping his todger in while she leaned over the basin painting her face.

'You should have done,' she told him when he mentioned it a few weeks later after they were already live-in lovers.

She gathered up her various pots, tubes and brushes, threw them all into a plastic bag and turned to leave. It was then that she saw Ralph.

'Oh, sorry,' she said. 'Didn't realise anyone was waiting.' Bright eyes, smiling, friendly, great legs, slim, sexy. Very fucking sexy. His heart leapt. It was lust at first sight.

'No problem.'

'You look like you've just trekked across the Antarctic.'

That was it.

'Can I take you home?' he asked.

'I came with a bloke.'

A cloud swept across his heart.

'Oh, pity.'

Why did he feel like this? He didn't even know her. She looked him up and down.

'But I can tell him to fuck off if you like.'

What? How could she say such a thing? What sort of heartless person was she? Did she have no feelings? How would the other bloke feel if she just disappeared with him? Really, some people had no scruples.

'Yes tell him to fuck off,' said Ralph.

The Beautiful Game
Set Pieces

What is the point of a goalkeeper kicking the ball up in the air as high and as far as he can? In my opinion none. When the thing finally returns to earth there's only a fifty-fifty chance of his own team retaining possession. It's the same story with most set pieces. Too often the ball is just kicked into a crowded goalmouth and it's a lottery who gets on the end of it. This is Sunday League stuff and it is hard to accept that players who are paid a king's ransom are unable to stretch their minds in order to conjure up more innovative ways of going about it. We really need to be more creative about this sort of situation. You see it week in week out in the Premiership. The ball launched hopefully towards goal with nothing else in mind other than someone may be lucky enough to force it past the keeper or a defender may make a mistake and score an own goal.

In marked contrast, the fantastic corners taken by Tosh Chamberlain, the great Fulham winger of a golden former era, were a joy to behold. Whenever the Cottagers were awarded a corner in those days it was almost as good as a penalty. Tosh used to exchange witty banter with the crowd as he placed the ball and prepared to perform his party piece. We loved him. We knew what was coming. Taking a short run up (there was no room for anything else) he'd belt the ball with huge force so that it was propelled like a bullet at about knee height into the goalmouth. It only needed a touch and it would be in. Tosh's corners were lethal and often led to goals. Now, you could say that this was also just hopefully kicking the ball in the direction of the goal but in this case it wasn't. Tosh was completely in control of what he was doing. It was his own invention and it was accurate, skilful, spectacular and successful. Why doesn't anyone do it now? It would be a lot more exciting than watching centre halves trying to head hopeful high balls using only the advantage of height rather than skill as an aid. Free kicks like this are boring. Does this have to be the sum total of inventiveness at set pieces? What do these highly-paid players do all week? Surely they've got time to practice these things. Of course they have. They've got all the fucking time in the world.

# 31
Black Forest Gateau

They ended up at Ralph's place exploring every little nook, cranny and orifice of each other's bodies, having sex in every possible known position and a few others to boot. He could have re-written the Kama Sutra. It was three days before they emerged from the bedroom, totally exhausted and ravenously hungry. Ralph could hardly walk.

He fell into the kitchen in a desperate search for the sustenance he hoped might recharge them enough to jump back into bed and carry on where they'd left off. But the contents of his fridge mirrored those in most bachelor pads. A carton of milk, yellowed with age and covered in grey fluff, a lump of rock-hard cheese with cracks the size of the Grand Canyon, three tubs of yoghurt two years past their sell by date and the remains of a three week old Chinese meal, totally congealed and stuck, maybe forever, to the plate on which it sat.

The stench as Ralph opened the fridge door was so repugnant he almost passed out.

'We'll have to go out,' he shouted through to the bathroom where Sophie was busy in the shower sluicing off the sweat and slime of the last three days.

'Okay,' she shouted back. It occurred to him that she was a very accommodating girl. Very accommodating indeed. Ralph suddenly realised that he had absolutely no idea what time it was. He rummaged around in the stained bedsheets and found his watch. Almost midnight. Fuck. They'd have to get a move on or everything would be closed.

He glanced at the answer machine next to the bed and noticed there were three messages. He pressed the playback button and recognised Chalkie's voice.

Chalkie was the self-appointed manager of the Sunday side which meant he told the lads where to meet and at what time. But he took no part in tactical decisions. There weren't any. However, that didn't stop the prat behaving as if he was Alex Ferguson.

He was shouting.

'Ralph you cunt. Where the fuck are you. Kick-off's in five fucking minutes. Are you there you cunt. Pick up the fucking phone you bastard. You've got to fucking play or we'll have to put Wilkie in. For fuck's sake Ralph. Get your fucking arse down here sharpish you cunt.' Fucking hell, the match. He'd forgotten. Hardly surprising really.

The second message was also Chalkie, still shouting.

'Ralph you cunt. Where the fuck were you? Lost four-three. Had to put Wilkie in. What a cunt. Scored a hatrick. All own goals. What a cunt. No one's talking to him. See you at training Tuesday.'

The third message. Chalkie again. By this time Ralph wondered if he should change his surname by deed poll to 'You Cunt'.

'Ralph you cunt. Where the fuck are you? Why weren't you at training you bastard? Listen you cunt, don't let me down again this weekend you fucking cunt.'

The only establishment still open when they arrived in the Broadway was a steakhouse which normally wouldn't have interested Ralph but there was no choice. They were too involved with each other to care much anyway. But they did need to eat. Everyone needs to eat after three days of nonstop sex.

It was a rather dowdy, badly lit establishment and almost entirely empty save for a rather large couple sitting in a corner eating enormous ice-cream deserts and a bunch of swarthy looking waiters and cooks sitting at the back playing cards. One of them stood up and looked at his watch as they entered.

'You're just in time sir,' he said as he approached them. 'We were about to close.' Why did these people always address only the male member of a couple as if the female didn't exist?

'Oh good. Our lucky day then.'

'This table all right sir?' as if she didn't have a point of view on the subject.

'Yes fine thanks.'

The sweet trolley was parked close by and as they took their seats they both perused its contents with famished expressions. Ralph had taken a fancy to the fresh fruit salad and Sophie was eyeing up the Black Forest Gateau with a glint in her eye.

'I like chocolate when I first get up,' she said. 'Let's have some coffee to wake us up.'

The waiter came to take their orders.

'First we'd like some coffee,' said Ralph. 'We're a bit tired you see.'

'Yes sir.'

'And then I'll have some fruit salad and my friend will have chocolate cake.'

'What, to start?'

'Yes please.'

The waiter glanced towards his card-playing colleagues as if to say 'We've got a right pair here lads.'

'And for main course sir?'

The smell of food had made them hungrier than ever so they ordered the biggest steaks on the menu, baked potatoes with sour cream plus extra portions of onions, mushrooms and tomatoes.

'That should do it,' said Ralph confidently.

'And to finish?' asked the waiter. 'Soup and prawn cocktail maybe?'

'What?'

'Sorry sir. Just my little joke.' And off he went.

They devoured their sweets with great relish, chatting away as they did so.

'Do you er . . .' Ralph was about to ask.

'Do I er, what?'

'I just wondered if you liked football.'

'Football? Er, well I don't dislike it,' she said.

Promising, thought Ralph. Very promising. After all, she could have entered one of those prejudiced diatribes like girls often did about twenty-two grown men running about after a little ball.

'I don't suppose you support any team in particular do you?'

He crossed his fingers and prayed she wasn't going to say Arsenal.

'Who do you support?' she asked.

'Chelsea,' he answered proudly. 'All my life.'

'Well I support Chelsea too then,' she said.

Ralph was glowing all over. What a girl!

The waiter reappeared with two enormous plates piled so full of food it was spilling over the sides.

'Bon apetit.'

'Thanks a lot.'

Ralph and Sophie looked at each other.

'Did we really order all this crap?' asked Sophie.

'Must have done.'

'Why?'

'Don't know. Hungry I suppose.'

Suddenly she burst out laughing.

'What?

'I forgot,' she said 'I'm a vegetarian.'

'Fuck,' Said Ralph. 'So am I.'

'Really?'

'Well two thirds anyway.'

'What?'

'I always eat meat and two veg.'

They both laughed and peered down at the food. The great slabs of steak were sitting in pools of blood that had seeped down their sides. The sight was so gruesome it made them both feel quite sick. They picked at the mushrooms and nibbled a few mouthfuls of potato but neither could manage to get much down. The sweets had sated their appetites completely. They were full. Pushing the plates aside they continued chatting. After a few minutes the waiter came back.

'Everything okay sir?

'Fine thanks. Couldn't be better.'

'You sure sir?'

'Yes really. Everything's great. Could we have the bill please.'

'Er, certainly sir.' He shuffled away again looking puzzled.

Ralph paid up cheerfully and even left a hefty tip. He was in a really good mood. As they walked away from the restaurant Ralph glanced back through the window and saw their food being devoured with enthusiastic gusto by the card players on the back table.

THE BEAUTIFUL GAME

Telly Football

Watching telly highlights of matches you have attended can make you feel as if you had entered some strange sort of time warp. Although the teams and date and venue appear to be the same as the game you thought you had witnessed a few hours earlier the television cameras seem to have recorded an entirely different event. Suddenly, the side which was on top is struggling whilst the poorer lot are now playing better than Real Madrid. In the end, you're left wondering whether you had actually been there at all. It's because they insist on screening mainly just the goals.

In football goals are everything but goals aren't everything. Sounds daft but it isn't. Obviously, in order to win a game you needed to score at least one goal but the simple fact is that the player who actually propels the ball into the opposing net is not necessarily the main contributor to the creation of that goal. When kids watch these match snippets they might see players like Ryan Giggs or Michael Owen or Ronaldo beating three players and cracking the ball into the top corner of the net and that's what they think football is all about. But of course it's only part of the story. What they are being denied is a chance to observe the general contribution to the game of those star players or indeed any other, less illustrious ones. What the kids don't see are players hustling for the ball or making themselves available for a pass or completing hundreds of short passes or running off the ball in all sorts of inventive ways to make space for others.

The way the game is presented on television is based on the short attention span theory in which people, particularly kids, are encouraged to want what they are sold. The good bits are plastic wrapped for convenience in tasty, bite-sized portions just like a TV dinner. But also like a TV dinner, the actual fare is far removed from good wholesome food and there are no fresh vegetables to aid the digestion. However, it's easy and quick to prepare and if you can't be bothered, it'll do. Perhaps it's the convenience to which you become addicted rather than the substance itself. It's easy to get used to something that makes your life easier even if it's not good for you.

You've had five pints of lager, now. You're hungry, now. You want something to eat, preferably fried meat, now. You can't wait so stick a packet in the microwave, now. You've got it, now. It tastes like crap, now. You're not hungry anymore, now. You feel sick, now. Time for more lager, now.

Some people would starve in their armchairs rather than walk to the kitchen to peel and cook a fresh vegetable. But if you ate nothing but processed food all your life your stomach would go out strike and your taste buds would fade away from sheer boredom.

Delicious experiences that can enrich our lives and make us better, more fulfilled human beings are available to us all. Why would anyone want to miss out on any of them? But as a result of the plastic television approach to football, most people, particularly kids, find it easy to accept what they are being fed and can't really be bothered to contemplate a change of diet.

Having scoffed the snacky tit-bits, they are simply not prepared to develop their pallets by concentrating on an entire match involving all the rest of the mouth-watering ingredients that combined to create a succulent football feast. Their diet leaves them full and bloated but not satisfied. As if they had eaten a gargantuan portion of greasy, cold, fish & chips after eight pints of lager and now had trouble getting to sleep.

They are being sold terribly short and this will not help their enjoyment or understanding of this great, uplifting game or, for that matter, any other.

But the nature of television with all its commercial pressures determines that telly highlights will only show the spectacular bits of games and that is what the kids end up trying to emulate.

In most cases, unless they have access to any proper coaching, that is what they will continue to do for the rest of their footballing lives.

32
Blast From the Past

Ralph and Sophie were hardly out of each other's company for the next few years. They did everything together including going to Chelsea. In fact, she became as avid a fan as Ralph if that was possible. That sealed it. They were a couple. An item. Peas in a pod. Soul mates.

One Saturday morning Ralph woke up full of flu. His head was thumping, his nose streaming and he didn't even have the energy to raise himself into a sitting position. He dozed on and off for a few hours until, roundabout lunch-time, Sophie brought him a cup of tea and some aspirin. She was dressed up warmly in her big coat with a woolly Chelsea hat and her Chelsea scarf.

'Going shopping?' he asked.

'Fuck that for a game of soldiers,' she answered. 'I'm going to the match.'

'What, Chelsea?'

'Well I'm not going to Upton Park dressed like this.'

'Yes but, I mean without me?'

'Well you're in no shape to go. Look at you. I bet you couldn't even get it up for me.'

'Oh no?' He grabbed the scarf that was wound round her neck and pulled her backwards onto the bed.

'Let me go you sex maniac,' she ordered.

He nibbled her ear and slipped his hand under the various layers of clothing until his fingers found that favourite spot of hers. Feeling his swiftly growing erection through the bedclothes, she started to moan softly and spread her legs almost by instinct.

Got her, he thought. But suddenly she wrestled herself free and jumped off the bed.

'No you don't,' she said, 'I'm not going to miss the kick off just for the sake of a quick one with a snotty nosed invalid like you.'

Women do have a really special knack of knowing how to dent a bloke's confidence when they want to.

'I'm coming too then.'

'All right but I'm not waiting. If you're coming get up and come now.'

Ralph struggled out of bed, head thumping, body aching and grabbed his jeans that were hanging over a chair. But he still had an erection and had difficulty pulling them on over it.

'Come on,' she ordered impatiently. 'I'll go without you if you're not ready in two minutes.'

'For fuck's sake get down you fucking bastard!' Ralph shouted angrily at the old chap. There was no way she was going to that match without him.

Eventually Sophie led Ralph out of the front door and into a waiting taxi.

'Special treat,' she announced. 'And here's another,' handing him a hip flask full of his favourite brandy. This was the girl for him and no mistake about it.

Ralph loved Saturdays. There was no need to get up and rush out anywhere, you could go to the pub and have a few pints in the morning without anyone accusing you of being a layabout and come the afternoon, joy of joys, there was football.

This particular Saturday morning he woke up feeling relaxed and good. The previous night, he and Sophie had enjoyed a sumptuous Italian meal with lashings of good, strong wine followed by a few hefty slugs of decent brandy at home before going to bed and fornicating their way through most of the night. He was content. Perhaps as content as he ever had been in is life. He had risen with a song in his heart and a spring in his step and wandered down to the bakers to buy fresh croissants for breakfast. On his return the smell of percolated coffee greeted him like a long, lost friend. Life was good.

Ralph set about arranging the table with butter, jam, sugar, milk, everything they needed for their favourite repast. He glanced over at Sophie who was sitting on the sofa flicking through the colourful pages of a book on impressionist art. Her silky, Chinese dressing gown hung loosely open so that her substantial nipples were just visible as they peeped out from the side of the seams. Strong sunlight poured through the window playing in her hair and on her body. Ralph thought she looked exceptionally beautiful that morning and started to become aroused. He walked over behind of the sofa and began massaging the back of her neck.

'Mmm, that's nice.' She closed her eyes as Ralph's probing fingers sent tingles through her body.

He leaned over and kissed her neck. Sophie uncrossed her legs allowing her book to slip to the floor. After her shower she smelled as pure and fresh as a baby. Now Ralph caught sight of the little drops of moisture that nestled, glinting in the sunlight, in her pubic hair.

He leaned forward over her shoulder and slid down her body licking her nipples on the way and then her belly button until his face was buried in between her thighs. By this time he was upside down with his legs in the air and his reproductive tackle hovering enticingly in front of Sophie's face. He felt her unzip his jeans and rummage around until she extracted his cock and slipped her lips around it. Her groin muscles tensed as she responded to the light teasing of his tongue between her legs.

Just then the phone rang. Sophie struggled to say something which only came out as an unintelligible mumble due to the expanded fleshy protrusion that now filled her whole mouth. The phone was on the coffee table just within reach and Ralph thought he'd better answer it in case it was one of the lads calling to arrange where to meet before the match. When Chelsea were at home Ralph met his mates in one of the pubs near the ground while Sophie went shopping in the Kings Road and joined them half an hour before kick off.

'Hello,' he said. 'West Hampstead Fuck Palace.'

'Is that Ralph?' It was a female voice with a foreign accent.

'Er, yes. Sorry, I thought it was someone else.'

'Ralph Goldstein?'

'Er, yes. Who's that?'

'Hanna.'

'Who?'

'Hanna, from the kibbutz. Remember?'

'Oh, er, yes of course I remember.'

'How are you?'

'Er, yes okay thanks.'

'Is this a bad time? You sound busy.'

He could hardly tell her that he had a mouthful of pubic hair and someone was sucking his cock.

'Er yes, er no, I mean where are you?'

'In London. Can I see you?'

'Er, yes. Okay.'

Ralph arranged to meet Hanna in the pub near the ground and hung up. Had he just made a big mistake? He slid down to the floor and in the process there was a soft plopping sound as his cock pulled itself away from the suction of Sophie's lips.

'Sorry,' said Ralph 'were you trying to say something?'

'Yes, I was trying to say don't answer the fucking phone you fucking fuck wad.' She was pissed off. He could tell. He sat next to her, fondled her tits and tried to kiss her. But the moment had gone.

'You've missed your chance,' she said.

'I'll make it up to you later.'

'You'd better.'

'I'm gong to the pub a bit earlier today,' he said.

'Who was that on the phone?'

'Oh just someone I met in Israel.'

THE BEAUTIFUL GAME

The pressure to get a result causes most professional sides to include a number of players of the kind that, in the old days, were called 'stoppers'. You know the type. Workaday players who run all day and all night, tackle hard, harry the opposition, don't 'Let anyone down' and are generally prepared to perform any act short of actual murder to stop the other team playing. Although effective in their limited aims, these players stunt the flow of the passing game and make it utterly boring in terms of the sort of sexy football spectacle that most fans want to see. At the same time, flair players are often not selected on the basis that their work-rate is low or that they aren't fit enough. Well sod that. No one complained about George Best's work-rate and by some accounts he was pissed out of his head most of the time. But that didn't stop him creating moments of magic or being loved by everyone in the game or regarded as one of the all time greats did it?

Whilst it might be true that you can't rely on these highly talented individuals to put in a 100 per cent 'Run-yer-bollocks-off-for-ninety-minutes' type of performance in every match, the fact is that in a moment of inspiration they can turn a game your way and thrill everyone in the process.

Stand up please, Matthew Le Tissier, Paul Gascoigne, Johann Cruyff, Pelé (and most of his team-mates), Gianfranco Zola, Chris Waddle, David Ginola, Roberto Baggio, Georgi Kinkladze. You know the ones.

Actually, my favourite player of all time and without question one of the best ever in this genre was Charlie Cooke formerly of Chelsea and Scotland. Charlie had an amazing ability that sent waves of joy through his audience. He was an artist in the truest sense. Whenever he got hold of the ball a buzz of expectancy went round the crowd because everything he did was beautiful even if it didn't always come off for him. He was just poetry in motion. And that's what we want. Poetry in motion.

All right, you can sit down again now.

33
Hanna's Plans

Ralph arrived at the pub an hour earlier than usual but the lads were already there and, judging by their inebriated state, had been for some time. His first thought as he entered was that perhaps he should have arranged to meet Hanna somewhere else. As usual though, he hadn't been quick-witted enough to spot the potential complications. It was the story of his fucking life. But why was he making such a cloak and dagger issue out of it? Surely there was nothing left between Hanna and him. There wasn't much in the first place. Did he still hold a candle for her? Surely not. It was years ago. He could hardly even remember what she looked like.

'Fuck me, you're early. She kick you out of bed or something?' asked Chalky as Ralph approached the table.

'Yeah, that's right, very funny,' said Ralph. 'Anyone want a pint?

Everyone wanted a pint.

Ralph got a round in and they started chatting about football. What else?

He sat with his back to the door looking round nervously every time it opened.

'Well I'm fucking fed up with them,' said Wilkie Wilkes. 'They're a bunch of cunts. If we don't win today, that's it.'

'What do you mean, that's it?' asked Darryl.

'That's fucking it. I'm never coming again.'

'That's what you always say.'

'Well I mean it this time.'

'You always say that too.'

'Look you bastards, I'm fucking serious.'

'Don't be fucking daft.'

'What's fucking daft about it? Why should I support a bunch of cunts?'

'Because you're a cunt yourself.'

'They let you down every fucking week. They're a bunch of cunts. Why should I waste my fucking money on a bunch of fucking cunts like that?'

'What the fuck else are you going to do on a Saturday afternoon?' asked Darryl.

'Stay at home and wank into a fucking bucket,' suggested Chalky helpfully.

'I'll support a different fucking team.'

'What, another bunch of cunts?'

'Well they couldn't be as big and fucking hairy as Chelsea. Think of all the money I've spent coming here year after year and they just let you down all the time. They're a bunch of big, hairy, fucking cunts.'

'This wouldn't have anything to do with getting turned down for that loan would it?' Darryl wanted to know.

'How the fuck did you know about that?'

'Everyone knows about that.'

'I thought a bloke's bank details were fucking confidential.'

'Not if one of your mates is a bank clerk at the branch where your account is,' said Ralph.

Chalky blushed. 'Er, Customer Services Adviser,' he informed them.

'What?'

'That's what I am. Not a fucking bank clerk.'

'What's the fucking difference?'

'More responsibility.'

'Does that mean they pay you more?'

'No.'

'Why do it then?'

'More job satisfaction.'

'And you're satisfied with your job?'

'No I fucking hate it.'

They all took a hefty slurp of ale whilst trying to decipher the sense in what Chalky had just said. There wasn't any.

'Who the fuck else would you support then?' asked Chalky in

an effort to deflect attention away from himself.

'Dunno. QPR maybe.' They all looked aghast.

'What? Have you gone fucking mad?'

'That confirms it,' said Darryl. 'He's a cunt.'

'Well they've got that Stan Bowles. He's a fucking good player. I like him.'

'So fucking what? Who else have they got?'

Wilkie considered the question for a moment. 'All right then, Fulham,' he said.

'Fucking hell,' said Ralph. 'I'm going to sit at another fucking table in a minute.'

Just then Wilkie's eyes lit up. 'Fuck me. Look at that bird that's just walked in. I'd give it one.' Ralph swivelled round and saw Hanna making her way to the bar.

For once they all agreed with Wilkie. They would all give her one.

She looked as stunning as when he first met her albeit entirely different. The worn, old working clothes had been replaced by tight jeans, high heels, a low-cut blouse and short leather jacket. She would have turned heads wherever she went. Ralph's mind drifted back to those early days in Israel. Driving past him on the tractor, the dream he had had by the pool, the night they danced together, that last night in her house with her Mother asleep in the next room. Suddenly, he was overcome with feelings that he didn't understand. Was it love? How could it be? He was in love with Sophie. Surely you couldn't love two women at the same time. Could you? But wait a minute. Had he gone mad? It was fucking years ago and he didn't know her that well even then.

The lads looked on amazed as Ralph stood up, walked slowly over to the bar and started talking to this beautiful stranger. She was ordering a drink as he approached from behind. 'Shalom Hanna,' he said.

She turned to face him.

'Hello Ralph. I've missed you.'

Her face was as beautiful as he remembered. Shining eyes, olive skin, full mouth. She was almost perfect. He didn't know whether to kiss her or hug her but in the end they shook hands.

'I'm surprised. I thought you would hate me.'

'Why?'

'Well, you know. I left without saying goodbye.'

'It doesn't matter. We're together again now.'

'Oh, right. Good.' Puzzled wasn't the word.

They found a couple of seats which wasn't easy because the place was already filling up with Chelsea supporters. It was only an hour or so to kick off and there was some serious imbibing to be accomplished before the referee blew his whistle to start the game. Again Ralph wondered if he shouldn't have arranged to meet her somewhere else. She seemed completely out of place here.

Why had he run out on her like that? Why hadn't he bothered to write? He'd meant to. Guilt gnawed at him.

'Look, I'm sorry I left like that without telling you. I've been meaning to write but, you know, I mean . . .'

'It's okay.' She stopped his ranting. 'We're together again. That's all that matters.'

'Er, yes. Tell me what brings you to London?'

'You of course.'

'Me? Why me?'

'My mother died. I've left the kibbutz. There was nothing to keep me there any more so I came looking for you.'

'I'm, sorry. I liked your mother.'

'She liked you too. She told me if she'd had a son she would have wanted him to be like you.'

'What? You're kidding. I didn't think she noticed me much.'

'She was fond of you.'

'Tell me, how long are you here for?'

'I've come to stay.'

'What, in London?'

'Why not?'

'When did you arrive then?'

'Yesterday.'

'Yesterday? So I'm the first person you contacted?'

'I don't know anyone else.'

'But what are you going to do? How will you live?'

'I'll get work eventually.'

Ralph thought about this. 'There isn't much for orange growers round here,' he said. They both laughed.

'Don't worry my love. I've got some money for the moment.'

My love? Did she say that? What's going on?

'I thought kibbutz people didn't have money.'

'Normally they don't but my Mother left me some. I didn't know about it. She got reparations money from Germany. According to the rules she should have given it to the kibbutz but she kept it hidden under the bed. She gave it to me the night before she died. I don't know how long it will last.'

'How much is it?'

'About fifty thousand dollars.'

'What?'

'Is that a lot? I don't know. How long do you think it will last?'

'Fucking forever I should think.'

'Is it enough to buy an apartment?'

'It's enough to buy two fucking apartments.'

'Oh. Good. Will you help me buy one?'

'Er, well, I suppose I could.'

'Great. Can we go now?'

'What?'

'I'd like to get one as soon as possible. I thought we could buy one today.'

'What?'

'Can we go now?'

'What, to buy an apartment now you mean?'

'Yes.'

'Er, no I'm sorry I can't.'

'Why not?'

'I'm going to a football match.'

'A football match?'

'Er yes, Chelsea.'

'Look, I know you like football but is it more important than our future?'

'Our future? What are you talking about? What future?'

'We'll be so happy, I know it. You won't have to work. You can write your book. I'll keep you.'

This was starting to get fucking complicated.

'Oh, er, well I see, well, er, I don't know really. It's all a bit of a surprise.'

'Come on, let's go and find a place for us.'

'But you can't just go out and buy an apartment like that.'

'Why not? Don't you believe I've got the money?'

'That's not the point, First of all you . . .'

'Look.' She took a plastic carrier bag out of her small rucksack and handed it to Ralph. He peered inside. It was full of high denomination dollar bills.

'Fucking hell. Is it all in here?'

'Most of it. I've spent a little.'

'But you can't walk about with that much cash on you.'

'Why not? It's mine.'

'Look you idiot, it's asking for trouble. You'll get mugged.' Nervously, he scanned the faces around them. Suddenly they all looked like escaped convicts. Armed robbers. Ralph clutched the bag tighter to him and wondered how he was going to deal with the situation without upsetting Hanna. Tears were already welling up in her eyes. She could snap at any moment.

'I'm sorry,' she sobbed. 'Sorry that I'm such an idiot.'

'Look, I didn't mean to shout but this can be a dangerous city if you don't know what you're doing. Thieves and muggers all over the fucking place.'

'Never mind. Can we go now?'

'What?'

'To buy the apartment. We'll be so happy . . .'

'No, I'm sorry but I can't.'

'Why not?' It was her favourite question.

'Well for a start I'm already living with someone.'

'What another woman?'

'Er, yes. Well, girl. Well I suppose she's a woman really.'

A cloud crossed Hanna's face, her lips started quivering, her face collapsed and tears started streaming down her cheeks.

There was a pause. Ralph wasn't sure what to do or what might happen next.

He was about to put a consoling arm round her but suddenly she grabbed the plastic bag that Ralph was still holding, stuffed it into her rucksack and got up to leave.

'This was such a stupid idea,' she said. 'I'm so stupid.' And made off quickly through the crowded room towards the exit.

'No Hanna wait,' Ralph shouted and ran after her.

His mates, who had been trying to monitor events from the other side of the bar, were agog. What the fuck was going on? What was in that bag? Who the fuck was she? They stared incredulously as he rushed past their table in hot pursuit.

'What are you lot gawping at?' Ralph shouted at them whilst making a grab for the door. But by the time he got through it and into the street she was gone. Thousands of fans mostly in Chelsea blue now thronged the surrounding area. He looked one way and then the other. No sign. She could have been anywhere. He'd never find her now.

'Shit!' he exclaimed under his breath. 'Well handled you cunt. Fucking shit.'

Just then Sophie bounced round the corner.

'Hello mister, you buying?' she joked, but when she saw Ralph her face dropped. 'What's the matter? she asked.

'Oh, er, no, nothing really.'

'What are you doing out here? Where's your friend from Israel?'

'Gone.'

'Shame. I would have liked to meet him.'

'It was a her.'

'Oh. I see. And did she come all the way from Israel just to see you?'

'Yes I think she did.'

'Well I hope you saw her off.'

'Yes,' said Ralph. 'I saw her off all right.'

The Beautiful Game

People always make excuses for the England football team that are usually trotted out just after we've lost a match. They are as follows:

1. The players are knackered because of the number of games they have to play.

2. Foreign players are preventing English players from getting into their club sides.

3. Injuries hamper selection.

4. The team hasn't had enough time to train together before the match.

It's the same old story every time and it is about time we stopped being taken in by all these bollock weak explanations. Whether or not any of it is true is of no consequence. You simply can't continue to make the same excuses time after time. It isn't professional. You have to deal with the problems. Problems are there to be solved. Anyway the problems lie elsewhere.

As a friendly gesture to whomever happens to be the current national manager please allow me to provide some answers to the points raised above which, as we all know, are the time-honoured dilemmas of all our national managers in recent times.

1. All international teams and their players have a rigorous schedule of games and none more so than Brazil, the team currently ranked number one in the world and regarded by most people as the best. Anyway, for fuck's sake, players only have to run around for ninety minutes at a time. They've got no fucking right to be knackered. If they're not fit, leave them out.

2. Foreign players in England have enhanced our game and helped many of the local players around them to progress and improve much more than if they weren't there. In fact, they have helped the national team rather than hindered it.

3. All teams have injuries.

4. The England team now spends much more time together than they used to and it makes no difference.

34
New Horizons

Sophie was always bouncing everywhere in her smiling, enthusiastic way. One day she bounced in through the door, back from what Ralph thought was a shopping trip or perhaps a visit to a friend. Sophie had lots of friends. Everyone liked her. But she'd been to the doctor's.

'Hello my little spring chicken,' he greeted her. Half a bottle of Chilean Cabernet and Ralph was anybody's.

'Hello booboo, we're pregnant,' she answered. Ralph nearly dropped his glass.

They hadn't planned anything. Well Ralph hadn't anyway. Sophie looked at him, wondering how he was going to take it. But he was elated.

'That's great,' he said. 'Wonderful.' Little did he realise just how radically their life was about to change.

Ralph hadn't made a decision to settle down. He didn't want to settle down. But here he was sliding into a situation in which he needed to stay in one place and make a permanent home. Naturally, he wanted the best for his kids as parents always did. But unlike most, there was a limit to what he was prepared to do to get it.

Ralph had always thought that the desire to have kids was some kind of emotional need. To make little beings that looked like you, acted like you, talked like you. The hope was that you could help them to avoid the mistakes you made, but that was easier said than done. Once they had a mind of their own they ended up just as silly as everyone else. A couple of years later he and Sophie had two. Natalie and then Joe. They opened new horizons for Ralph. New horizons in love. A love that didn't need to be explained or analysed or doubted. Love in its purest form. If you could have produced a powdered version you could have sold it for thousands a gram.

During the tides of emotion that swept over Ralph as he settled into his new role as a father, he came to a significant conclusion. It was this. In a changing world that was rapidly becoming more difficult in every sense, love was the only thing that had any meaning or value at all. This had always been the case, it continued to be the case and despite anything that might happen, always would be the case. Love was the answer to everything. There was no substitute for it. In football or in life.

Of course whenever he attempted to explain this philosophy to any of his old mates they just took the view that he was a soppy cunt.

'For fuck's sake Ralph. You never change. Why don't you fucking grow up?'

One day Ralph and Sophie were taking their two little offspring to the park across the road from their second floor flat in north London. They stood by the roadside waiting for a gap in the incessant traffic that spewed exhaust fumes all over them as it raced past. The situation was ugly, horrible and fraught with danger from the speed of the traffic, the pollution it produced and the stress it caused. As they waited feeling frustrated and helpless, Ralph began to wonder what damage his kids might be suffering from this madness and a most cogent question entered his mind. What the fuck were they doing there?

'I'm not sure London is the right place to bring up a family.' He shouted at Sophie straining to raise his voice above the din of lorries and buses.

'Can't hear you above the traffic,' she yelled back.

'I said let's fuck off and live somewhere better.'

She didn't disagree.

'We can always move to my little hometown in Herefordshire.' She said. 'The air's cleaner, there's more space and maybe you'll find the peace and quiet you need to finish your book.'

It seemed like such a good idea at the time, even though Ralph had actually been thinking more along the lines of Hawaii, Antigua or Tuscany when he made the suggestion.

The Beautiful Game

International Inconvenience

It's a paradox. Football managers can't do their jobs properly for fear of losing their jobs. Of course, like everyone else I could pick a better England side than the national manager but, most unfortunately, they didn't give me the job.

Under the full glare of the media spotlight, England bosses are always under extreme pressure and although they all tend to start with upbeat statements and attacking credentials it isn't long before they become worn down and start to feel they can't afford to make a mistake. Eventually, they are functioning under so much stress that it affects their approach to tactics and their choice of players.

As a result, with the entire country breathing down their necks, England managers over the years have put aside their real dreams and aspirations in order to pick sides more in the hope they wouldn't lose rather than in the belief they could win.

It's the fear factor. Selections reflect the manager's fear of losing the match, his reputation and his job rather than the spirit of picking teams to go out and dazzle everyone on their way to great victories.

What the fuck has happened to courage of convictions?

The antithesis to stress in our society can be found in many forms including art, music, literature, entertainment, sex, sport of all kinds and practically everywhere in the so-called civilised world with the notable exception of North America, football.

Another paradox then. That an activity designed to be pleasurable and relaxing can induce so much stress amongst those running it.

But don't worry.
Let me do it.
Go home, relax and put your feet up.
I'll take over as England Manager tomorrow.

35
Humanist Guerrilla

Because Ralph had only ever regarded his present situation as a temporary stop on the way to Utopia he had never managed to fit in properly wherever he was. Over the years, he had become reconciled to being a square peg in a round hole and more or less accepted this as his destiny. But he still sought a perfect existence even though he had long since realised there was no such thing. How naïve could you get?

Most observed his quixotic and seemingly endless mission to reorganise the world around him with great amusement. It took up a great deal of time and energy and was probably the reason for his general under-achievement. Perhaps if he had focused more on developing his own qualities instead of getting himself caught up in every social and political issue that came along he might have got further. Silly git. Certainly he was capable of much more. Everyone said so. But he had always thought of himself as a sort of humanist guerrilla on a permanent mission to change the fundamental nature of society and, as such, he was always on duty.

Therefore, at a time in his life when he should have been organised and settled he found himself languishing in the grey, metaphysical area in which the enthusiast and the nutter meet in mutual appreciation.

Of course, most of those who knew Ralph couldn't be bothered with his fancy ideas.

It had always been the same even in his schooldays. Whenever he launched into one of his heart-felt soliloquies about the state of the world, his mates would all look impatiently at their watches and start making excuses to leave.

'Is that the time?'
'Must get on.'
'Got to make a phone call.'

'Time waits for no man.' That was certainly true.

They couldn't even be bothered to listen to Ralph expounding his theories let alone assist him with his perfidious exploits. They liked things the way they were. Or they thought they did. Perhaps they just didn't want to be challenged.

To them, he was simply a pain in the arse. Loveable but naïve.

Most of Ralph's friends and acquaintances were pre-occupied in the main by money and material possessions. Just like most people everywhere. A better house, car or job. The latest stereo, mobile phone or computer. It was all they ever talked about. When they babbled on with glee about the great choices available to them, that was what they meant and it left him nonplussed. To him it was no choice at all. It wasn't as if they were being offered the option of abolishing the defence budget or altering the school curriculum or changing the voting system or walking down the street naked.

He often tried to explain to anyone who would listen that although they believed they were in control of their lives they were in fact only in control of a tiny and relatively unimportant part of them. But they didn't want to know. It was against the basic tenets of society on which they had come to rely. Their talk bored Ralph. He was interested in elevating the spirit, travelling in the mind, spiritual fulfilment, love and peace. He was an ageing hippy. A nutcase.

In the old days there had always been plenty of others like him who wanted to change the world. He used to meet them all on picket lines, or at demonstrations, or rock music benefits, or film festivals or poetry readings or agit-prop meetings in pub halls. But the days when Ralph could easily find soul-mates who shared his convictions were long gone and those former friends and political allies were now mostly stockbrokers. Or computer operators. Or dead.

However, wacky though he may have seemed to most ordinary folk, you would have to admit that he had his strong points. Certainly, the general knowledge of life that he had gleaned through a most tortuous process of trial and error during his varied and strange career was of immense value and unlikely to have been learned in any other way. Not even at the best university. Nevertheless, few bothered to take Ralph seriously and he struggled to bring his vision to bear on the surrounding environment. Tell you what though. You could rely on Ralph. Trust him with your life. There were not many for whom you could make that claim.

PART TWO

Error

36
Local Hero

When they first moved into the area, Ralph thought he would check out the local club, Kingbury Town, and see if there was anything he could do to help. His own competitive playing days were well over but, loving the game as he did, he still wanted to be involved somehow. So he went along to a meeting and by the time it was over he'd been elected to the committee. He felt like Ron Atkinson coming in to bring success to an ailing team in some unglamorous backwater.

The next Saturday at about midday, some of the other committee members turned up to take Ralph to a first team match. There was Les Cartrwright, a bellicose, self-made local businessman who was the chairman, 'Bulldog' Bevan, plumber, manager of the first team and Harry Hartson, who was a minor official in a bank and officially club secretary. Actually, it seemed to Ralph that Harry was merely a general factotum who got lumbered doing everything that no one else wanted to.

The team didn't have a home venue where they could play in their own town because there were no facilities acceptable to the league they played in so they ground-shared with another club in the Forest of Dean about fifteen miles away.

Ralph had never been there before and was looking forward to it but as they drove up into the forest a sense of foreboding swept over him. A dense fog had begun to drift over from the Bristol Channel and before long they couldn't see a fucking thing. The others were unperturbed by this as they soldiered on albeit slowly.

'We'll be out of it soon,' someone said. Sure enough, as they climbed higher on the narrow track up through the woods the fog began to clear. It was like being in an aircraft climbing above the clouds. Everything was now crystal clear, bright and almost magical but Ralph's mind, still slightly dulled from the after effects of a barrel-full of Spanish wine the night before, began to operate in one of its weird modes. He had been warned that this sort of thing could happen in the forest. Perhaps it was the altitude or the glimmer of sun through the mist in the trees but the whole atmosphere took on a surreal feeling and he began to wonder what on earth he was doing there.

'What the fuck am I doing here?' he said aloud without thinking.

The others laughed but he hadn't really been trying to make a joke.

He didn't know what he was trying to do.

'Don't worry,' said Harry, 'It's not as bad as it seems.' How the fuck did he know?

They passed through a small village and his fellow passengers started making rude gestures and taunting remarks as a sign displaying the name 'Barney Hill Sports and Social Club' flashed past the window.

'What's all that about?' Ralph asked.

'That's who we're playing today,' said Harry.

'So why aren't we stopping?'

'We're at home today, our ground's a few miles further on.'

'What? You mean we're having to travel further to our own home match than the away team?'

''Fraid so. Until we can find a ground in our own town.'

That'd be a bloody good one for Trivial Pursuit he thought.

Every now and again another car would pass in the opposite direction. A Vauxhall Cavalier, a Honda Civic, a Ford Fiesta, a Citroen Xantia, an Austin Montego, a Toyota Corrola, a Volkswagen Scirroco, a Rapier, a Puma, a Jaguar. Where the fuck did they get all these names? Who were they trying to kid with their glossy images? Cars were lumps of metal on rubber wheels not mysterious eastern winds or predatory animals. Jump into my Scirroco and we'll be off like the wind! Farting our way to eternity.

Other possibilities drifted into Ralph's mind that more accurately reflected the state of the world around. The Ford Steak And Kidney Pudding, the Vauxhall Viagra, the Rover Dildo, the Fiat

Cowpat, the Nissan Nipple, the Lancia Lavatory, the Peugeot Plonker.

'Here we are,' a voice announced. He must have dozed off.

They had arrived at a location high up in the Forest of Dean with spectacular views over rolling hills that undulated towards the Severn Estuary, just visible in the far distance, glinting magically in the freezing winter sun.

As soon as Ralph stepped out of the car he started shivering like a blancmange. It must have been at least fifteen degrees colder than down in the valley from where they had come.

'Fuck me it's chilly up here,' he said.

'Arse ole' butt.' The sound came from a weird creature dressed in a peculiar one piece, scruffy, torn, khaki, ex-army outfit that covered him from head to toe including a headpiece that only left a small amount of unshaven face in direct contact with the elements. To Ralph in his recently roused state it was a frightening apparition that could have been the ghost of Shackleton of the Antarctic but it turned out to be George, the groundsman who had been struggling for some hours to get the muddy, threadbare pitch into a playable condition.

Les must have noticed the puzzled look on Ralph's face because he gave him a little nudge and said, 'He means yes mate. He's a Forester. He's talking Forest.'

Apparently it was a form of endearment. So the creature from the black lagoon was just being friendly. Clearly, the city boy had a lot to learn.

They had arrived early ostensibly to prepare things for the match but there was still plenty of time and Len said, 'Let's have a drink before we start.'

It was the best suggestion Ralph had heard all day and he eagerly agreed. How could he possibly have known what was about to happen?

They walked a few yards to the ramshackle clubhouse that resembled a large, rectangular barn and entered the modest, wooden building. Two gaudy fruit machines flashed away on a far wall and a few elderly patrons were scattered about mostly watching the flickering television positioned high on a shelf in the corner. Three of them were hunched over the morning paper perusing the racing form. On the tables in front of them stood glasses of local cider that glistened and bubbled as they caught the glimmering rays of cold winter sun that occasionally filtered through the grubby windows.

Straight ahead was a semi-circular bar to which the Town contingent made a beeline and perched themselves on the stools surrounding it.

'Where's the lovely Marlene then?' asked Harry.

'Ah, Marlene,' replied Les whimsically. 'The day doesn't really begin without a glimpse of the lovely Marlene.'

'Or two,' Bulldog added to the knowing winks, nods and laddish laughter of the others.

Just then, the door behind the bar opened and a vision of earthy beauty appeared. It was the chubby, smiling, ruddy face of Marlene the barmaid, partly obscured by locks of tousled, blonde hair that tumbled uncontrollably down to her shoulders. Her more than ample biceps bulged and strained with the weight of two full crates of beer that she had just heaved up from the cellar and now carried through he door. Ralph at his fittest would have struggled to carry just one of them. But without any shadow of a doubt, the most obvious and outstanding feature of this imposing female unit was her enormous bust. Ralph had never seen anything like it. The pink breasts wobbling precariously over her ridiculously low-cut blouse were so enormous that they would probably have kept a couple of football teams fully nourished for at least a month. They seemed to enter the room a few minutes before the rest of her. Ralph immediately realised what the others had been joking about.

'Hello lads,' she cheerfully greeted them. 'What can I do for you boys?'

'That would be telling, Marlene my little cherub,' answered Les. He was clearly smitten.

'Come on Les,' she goaded him. 'You can tell me. It'll be our little secret.'

'Well there is something you could give me a hand with,' he replied, winking at her. They all laughed.

'You're all the same you men,' chastised Marlene albeit with a playful smile. 'One track minds all of you.' Obviously she was quite used to double entendre repartee of this type and, like all good barmaids, even seemed to encourage it. But, although she dismissed Les's rude come on, Ralph had the impression that she would have quite happily offered her body to all of them for fifty pence and a currant bun. He made a mental note of this in case it came in useful one day.

Marlene pulled each of them a pint whilst they all peered lovingly into the fleshy Grand Canyon of her cleavage. At one stage as she performed this sacred duty she purposely leaned a bit further forward to give them a better eyeful.

'A quick one for yourself?' Les offered.

'I'm not that hard up, thanks,' replied Marlene, 'But I'll have a half with you if you're offering.' It's not what Les really meant but he bought her a drink anyway.

'Give me a shout if you need me,' he said and returned through the door whence she came. As she left, Ralph noticed that her bottom was about as big as her bosom. They all stared intently at her posterior, drinks in hand, until the door closed behind it. Ralph also noticed, although it didn't fully register until some time afterwards, that she seemed to smile almost intimately at Bulldog as she disappeared back into the cellar. They all took a few large gulps of ale and exhaled in unison as hardened drinkers do.

The familiar, moustachioed features of Des, the housewives' favourite, appeared on the television screen with news of the afternoon's team line ups. Arsenal had bought Kanu and Chelsea were fielding a side without a single British player.

The first pint.

'Fucking disgusting,' said Les 'You can't call it the fucking English league any more.'

'Too many fucking foreigners,' agreed Bulldog.

'Fucking mercenaries,' added Harry.

'Yeah, no wonder we haven't got a decent England squad if our lads can't even get into their fucking club teams,' said Les.

'Something should be done about it,' said Harry.

'I haven't got a problem with it,' said Ralph, 'The more the merrier, I say.'

They all glared at him.

'You would say that, you're Chelsea. How can you support them now though?'

'Why not? I've managed it for over forty years. I'm not fucking changing now.'

'But they haven't got a single English bloke in the team.'

'So what? Chelsea's my team. Always has been, always will be. I'd never change. Anyway, it's the quality of the football that interests me. I'm overjoyed these great players have come to the Bridge. They may not be consistent but they've dished up some beautiful football. Different class.' There was a moment of silence.

'But it's ruining the England side,' said Harry.

'No it isn't.'

'Well how come the England team's crap now?'

'That's easy. We don't coach kids to pass the ball. All they learn to do is run forward with it or kick it into the penalty area and hope someone can force the fucking thing into the goal.'

'What's wrong with that?' asked Bulldog a bit sheepishly. 'How the fuck else are you going to play?'

'Passing, running off the ball, building from the back, using flair, skill, working for each other. You know, not doing the bleeding obvious all the time.'

Bulldog seemed perplexed.

'That's not the English game. That's continental.'

'Call it what you like but it's better to watch, more skilful, artistic, beautiful. We can learn a lot from foreigners coming in. They're improving our game, not damaging it.'

There were puzzled looks all around. It didn't take Ralph long once he got going.

A tall, well-dressed young man of about twenty-five with an athletic build and long, confident stride now entered the bar. It was Ivor (the engine) Phillips, Town's centre half and captain. He was the first clean-shaven bloke Ralph had set eyes on all day. He'd obviously caught the last part of the discussion on his way over.

'No fucking foreigner's gonna teach me anything,' he said approaching the group.

'That's right Engine mate,' greeted Les. 'Pint?'

The second pint.

Les got the round in and Bulldog went off with Ivor the Engine to talk tactics or, more probably, about how they could force the ball into their opponents' goal from corners and free kicks. The group was joined by Ray Ashford, Chairman of Elton Athletic, the host club whose ground they shared. Athletic didn't have an away match that Saturday so Ray thought he'd come along and give Town the once over. He pretended it was just to be sociable but the Town directors were under no illusions that his real purpose was to nick any of their players he fancied if he could. It was an open secret that he was keen to sign Ivor Phillips. In fact, rumour had it that he had already offered Town's captain a new tracksuit, a hot meal on training nights, use of a second-hand Ford Capri Ghia and a night with his wife if he'd sign for Athletic but Ivor hadn't gone for it. Not that he felt any need to remain loyal to Town. After all, they'd never done him any fucking favours. But it was the daughter he was after. He'd had the wife already.

'Pints all round here please Marlene,' ordered Ray. 'Put them on my tab darling.'

The third pint.

'Heard about Chelsea?' Ray asked the group.

'Yeah, disgusting,' said Les.

'Mercenaries,' added Harry for the second time.

'Too many foreign bastards over here,' said Ray. They all nodded in agreement.

'This is Ralph our new director, he's a Chelsea man.'

Ralph and Ray shook hands. He was pleased with his new title. Hadn't realised he was a director. Had a nice ring to it. What do you do? I'm a Football Club Director.

'You must be pissed off,' said Ray.

'How do you mean.'

'Chelsea. All fucking foreigners.'

'No, delighted actually.'

'But there isn't a sodding Englishman in the side.'

'So what?'

Ray was flabbergasted.

'This is fucking England,' he said.

'It's a great side though. That's the main thing.'

'Maybe, but it's no fucking good for England. Our lads aren't getting a decent shout. No wonder the England side's crap.'

'Doesn't have to be like that. I think overseas players should play for England while they're here,' said Ralph. 'We'd have some kind of a fucking side if they did.'

There was a dumb-struck silence while they all tried to absorb the statement.

Finally, Harry said, 'But it wouldn't be England would it?'

'Why not? It doesn't really matter what you call it. Nationalities aren't that important. The main thing is the quality of the football.'

'It'd be the end of civilisation as we fucking know it,' pronounced Les.

'No it wouldn't,' said Ralph, 'Just a reorganisation of priorities, that's all. After all, the top club teams in Europe have got players from all over and they're better than the national sides now.'

Mistakenly thinking that they might be impressed with the concept he was putting forward, Ralph continued. He was in his element now and thought they'd be impressed with his revolutionary ideas. Wasn't that why they made him a director? Looking back, it amazed Ralph how he could have lost the plot so completely.

'Anyway, in the future there'll probably only be five teams playing internationals. Europe, America, Australasia, Asia and Africa.'

'Oh yeah, and what are we?' asked Les, 'Fucking Europe I suppose.'

'Of course.'

'Fuck that,' said Harry, 'I'm fucking English mate. I'm not in favour of joining fucking Europe.'

'What do you mean joining Europe? We're in it. It's not some strange place somewhere else. We're part of it whether you like it or not.'

'You might be,' said Ray, 'But I don't agree with it. They'll have us all eating fucking croissants for breakfast next.'

'Who says?' Harry seemed worried.

'European rules,' said Les. 'It's all decided in Brussels.' There was a hush whilst they all gulped noisily at their beer. 'But I'll tell you what,' he continued in a voice quivering with emotion. 'I'll never give up my fucking English sausages. Over my dead body. Fuck that.' It was uttered with all the intensity of Churchill's 'We will fight them on the beaches' oration.

'Well said, Les mate,' said Harry.

'Wait a fucking minute,' said Ralph. 'We won't stop being English by co-operating with our European neighbours. We won't lose our national character if we join a common currency. We won't forget how to play fucking cricket.'

'Can't be too careful,' said Ray. 'They might get us playing that game they have over there. You know, like big marbles.'

'Boules,' said Harry.

'Same to you,' said Les. They all laughed. The beer was taking over.

'Look,' Ralph insisted. He hated this anti Johnny Foreigner attitude. 'France and Germany are completely different from each other. The people, the way of life.'

'They're all fucking foreigners though. Anyway, so what?'

Blank expressions surrounded Ralph.

'They're the most avid Europeans. They've adopted the Euro, they're right next door to each other.'

'Er, so?'

'Well they haven't become like each other. They don't speak the same language. You'd have to go a long way to find bratwurst for lunch in Paris and you don't hear much French spoken in

Berlin.' He thought he'd try to put it on a more readily acceptable level. 'French footballing style is different from German footballing style.'

'Don't mind a bit of bratwurst,' commented Les whistfully. 'With chips and mayonnaise. It's mayonnaise on chips over there you know.' He added knowledgeably.

'In fact, it's just the same as in football,' Ralph continued. 'We can learn a lot from the continent but the problem is that although others have overtaken us we still think we're the best.'

'We are the fucking best,' said Les.

'Course we fucking are,' said Ray.

'We won't be if we go into fucking Europe,' said Harry.

'Can't risk letting those foreign bastards ruin our way of life,' said Les.

'But life is a darn site better in most other European countries,' said Ralph.

'How the fuck can it be?' asked Harry. He turned to face Ralph. 'You Europe lovers are all the fucking same. You're all so fucking keen on the fucking place but I don't see any of you living over there.'

The others all nodded in agreement and took another communal slurp of beer.

Fuck me it's like being in the Cosh 'n' Helmet with those other nit-wits, thought Ralph remembering old times.

'Anyway lads, let's not get political,' Les said.

Ralph agreed. Politics was a mug's game.

But he couldn't help it. Someone had to say something.

THE BEAUTIFUL GAME

Of all the negative conventions that have surreptitiously crept into the modern game in recent times, the worst must be the way that defenders are allowed to 'shepherd' the ball over the by-line.

This is when a ball is being chased by a forward and the defender barges and pushes his way in between the two using his body strength to hold off the attacker and keep him away from the ball until it rolls to safety.

If it happened in any other area of the pitch it would be penalised as obstruction with good reason.

It is obstruction.

It relies on brute force to triumph over skill and should be stamped out immediately.

Skill should be preferred over brute force in all circumstances.

And that's in life by the way, not just football.

37
Crazy Kevin

Ralph realised he was bursting for a slash. It was urgent.

'Where's the bog?' he asked.

'You mean the fucking pissoire?' enquired Les to great guffaws of laughter from the entire group.

'Damen or fucking Herren?' Harry joked. They all laughed again.

'You better tell me quick before I piss my fucking pantaloons.' More laughter.

'Through that door, into the hall and right up the other end on the right, or should I say fucking gauche.'

'Merci.'

He had to hurry. He wasn't used to drinking before lunch and he'd had three pints interspersed with a quite a few shorts of whisky that had magically appeared in front of him at regular intervals during the preceding hour or so.

As he descended from the barstool Ralph realised he was actually quite sozzled. His head was muzzy, his knees felt weak and he wasn't sure he could walk in a straight line. But he mustered his energy and made off in the way he'd been directed. He needed that piss. He managed to walk through the swing door but it sprang back in a surprisingly sharp fashion bashing him up the backside and pushing him a few feet into the room. Gathering his senses, he found himself standing in a long, narrow, dimly lit function hall where he could just make out a small bar to one side and tables arranged in a line along the full length of the other. Right, where's that pisser? Ralph was having to think very carefully about everything he did now. Which foot to move first for instance. But just as he he'd focused on the avenue of his intentions and was about to move off he heard strained breathing interspersed with a rhythmic grunting coming from somewhere in the hall. It was the unmistakable sound of human copulation.

He took a few steps forward and then he saw them. It was Marlene and Bulldog, hard at it. Well, he was anyway. She was sitting on one of the tables leaning back on her muscle-bound arms for support with her legs dangling wide open over the sides and her substantial fanny perched conveniently just on the edge. Bulldog was standing upright facing her and away from Ralph with his trousers round his ankles. Marlene's skimpy top together with her enormous brassiere, a magnificent feat of engineering by anyone's standards, had been pushed up to expose her gigantic mammories that flopped sideways and wobbled furiously as bulldog, knees trembling violently, thrust into her with mounting insistence.

Marlene seemed singularly unimpressed with the whole business. She looked at her watch and yawned.

'Hurry up Bulldog, mate, I've got to get back to the bar.'

'All right, all right, but you ain't going nowhere 'till I've had me fucking tenners' worth.'

Ralph was in two minds. To get to the gents he'd have to walk right past them. Should he be discreet and leave or should he carry on? No, he wasn't going back. He had to empty his bladder before the fucking thing exploded. As his made his way forward Marlene caught his eye, smiled and winked as if to say 'I'll be finished here in a minute if you fancy a go on me after.' She was totally unabashed. It was as if he'd come across her making a cup of tea or carrying out some other such menial task. As for Bulldog, he had no idea there was anyone else in the room.

Finally, Ralph reached the urinal and as the heavy stream of hot liquid splashed against the porcelain urinal sending clouds of steam upwards to mingle with the condensation on the walls, he remembered the saying he had once been told they had in Sweden. A good piss is like half a fuck. Better than some of the fucks I've had, he thought as a wave of relief filled the space created by the fluid draining out of him.

Ralph had taken quite a liking to Bulldog even though he was a fairly uncultured individual. Although not exceptionally tall you would have to say that he was a big man. Big-boned and muscular with big hands, big feet and generally big features altogether. He gave the impression that he needed a lot of everything. Ralph guessed that he probably ate loads, imbibed gallons, excreted huge faeces and fucked a lot.

He was a product of his environment. No doubt you needed someone like that to keep the lads in check. They were mostly products of the same environment.

When Ralph returned to the bar, the place had become quite crowded. The visiting team and its entourage had turned up and Athletic club members and spectators were also arriving in numbers. Usually, Town only had about fifty supporters at home matches but as they were playing Barney Hill from just down the road they were expecting at least twice that number today. Les was rubbing his hands at the prospect because they had an agreement to share the bar takings with Athletic. Ray Ashford was keeping a close eye on him.

Bulldog was back in his seat at the bar as if nothing had happened chatting with a small, mousy individual. Pinned to his worn suit were a number of badges that mostly seemed to have a connection with football associations. Some were awards.

'This is Bill Watkins, said Bulldog as Ralph approached. 'Today's referee.'

'Oh, right, hello,' Ralph greeted him.

'Good afternoon,' said Bill.

'That's an impressive array of badges,' commented Ralph trying to focus on them.

'Yes they do draw admiration.'

'What are they?'

Bill pointed to them in turn. 'Referees' Association, County Referees' Association, FA, County FA, Accrington Stanley Supporters' Association, Keep Sport Clean, Viewers' and Listeners' Association, Caravan Club, Rosemary Clooney Appreciation Society, Good Listening Club, Scouts' Instructor, Health and Efficiency Readership Award.

'Health and fucking Efficiency?'

'It was a long time ago.'

'And are you applying the new directives regarding forward play?' Ralph enquired.

'What fucking directives?'

'You know, encouraging forward play. Giving the benefit of the doubt to forwards in off-side decisions. Not being too harsh. Keeping play moving. That sort of thing.'

'Look,' said Bill. 'If the linesman flags it's offside. If they fuck me about it's a yellow card and if they do it again they're off.'

'And that's it?'

'That's it.'

'Always know where you stand with Bill,' said Bulldog.

'Yeah,' said Bill turning to Bulldog. 'And if your lads give me any sort of hassle this week the price will be double next time.'

Bulldog coughed nervously. 'I'll tell 'em,' he said.

'Right, I'll be off,' said Bill.

Ralph was puzzled and a bit worried. He waited until Bill was out of earshot before turning to Bulldog.

'Do I take it that the little weasel's open to bribery?' he asked.

'I wouldn't really call it bribery.'

'Look, either it's fucking bribery or it's fucking not.'

'It is but it isn't.'

'I don't understand.'

'Know where he's gone?' asked Bulldog 'To see the fucking opposition. He'll get the same amount out of them as he did from me. Cheating bastard. You can't win. If you don't pay him he'll make it difficult for you on the field but if you do it only equals things up.'

'Two bribes are better than one?'

'You got it. Same again?'

'I don't think I should.' Ralph was only just re-entering reality after the last one.

Bulldog thought that was very funny.

'Don't think you should. That's a good one,' he said laughing. 'Same again Marlene.'

'You'll be fucking lucky,' she said emerging from under the bar where she'd been connecting up a new barrel. 'Oh, sorry Ralph. Didn't see you there.'

The fourth pint.

There was quite a crowd around the bar now with many waiting for drinks. George the groundsman had come to help Marlene who, Ralph had now discovered, was actually his wife.

As more people pushed up to be served Ralph got squeezed along into the midst of another group of folk who were involved in what seemed like a familiar discussion.

'Too fucking many of 'em over here,' said a middle aged, portly individual who looked like an extra from a Mad Max film. He wore mostly black leather, had a shaved head and tattoos of naked women on both his bare arms.

By this time Ralph had consumed enough alcohol to feel quite confident about entering other people's conversations even if they did look like escaped convicts.

'I suppose you're going to say that it's ruining the English football team,' he said.

'What you on about mate?' asked his new friend but not in a particularly friendly way.

'You know, too many foreign footballers keeping our players out of club teams. Not giving our own youngsters a shout. I don't agree actually. I think that . . .'

'I wasn't talking about fucking footballers.'

'Weren't you?'

'No'

'What then?'

'Darkies'

'Darkies?'

'Yeah.'

'You mean . . . black men?'

'Yeah, niggers. Asians too for that matter. We've let in too fucking many.'

'But most of them were born here. They're as English as you and me.'

'I don't fucking think so mate.'

'I assure you they fucking are.'

'Look, some of 'em may have an English passport but they'll never be fucking English.'

'British.'

'What?'

'We have British passports.'

'Whatever. But they're not.

'Not what?'

'Fucking English.'

'You mean fucking British.'

'Fucking British then.'

'Why not?'

'They're a totally different fucking colour for a start.'

'So what?'

'They're different, any bastard can see that.'

Ralph was starting to lose his cool.

'Some people might say that was a racist point of view,' he said.

'Racist? I'm no fucking racist. I just think we should send 'em all back where they fucking came from.'

Ralph felt his hackles rising. He began to wonder if he hadn't accidentally stumbled on the headquarters of Ku Klux Klan, Forest of Dean section. He was getting intensely annoyed with this mad, tattooed git but having entered a fearless state of bravado brought on by copious amounts of alcohol he was warming to the debate and oblivious to the potential danger of the situation.

'And what about the Jews?' Ralph asked.

'The yids? They can fuck off too. But they'll have to leave all the fucking money they stole from us.'

'Fuck off? Where to?'

'Any fucking place that'll 'ave 'em.'

'Why not the fucking gas chamber? Come on you bastard. I'm Jewish. Why don't you march me off to the fucking gas chamber? That's what you'd fucking like to do isn't it? You fat cunt.'

People were looking on and listening in total amazement. There was going to be a brutal killing. Any moment now.

'What did you call me?'

'You heard.'

Little did Ralph realise that if the mad, tattooed bastard hadn't been taking handfuls of the strong tranquillisers prescribed by his doctor to protect the local population from the vagaries of his temper, his Jewish guts would have been decorating the walls of the establishment by now. He was about to ask if the cretin had finalised his plans for the final solution when Bulldog grabbed his arm and pulled him over to the other side of the room.

'You don't want to start getting into an argument with him,' he said. 'He's a fucking maniac.'

'I'd say he was a fucking Nazi.'

'Look, call him what you like, that's Crazy Kevin from Barney Hill and he'll tear your fucking head off soon as look at you. Come on, drink up, there's just time for another round before kick off.'

'Oh, I think I'll pass if you don't mi . . .' But Bulldog was already on his way back to the bar. Les and Harry had found themselves a table so Ralph went to sit with them while Bulldog got the drinks.

'Enjoying yourself?' asked Harry.

'Great thanks.'

Bulldog returned with a tray loaded with four pints and four large whiskeys.

The fifth pint.

'Where did you play your football then?' asked Len.

'Home counties mostly,' answered Ralph. 'Abroad a bit. Played for Palace as a lad but . . .'

'What, Crystal Palace?'

'Yeah, but only for the jun . . .'

'Fuck me, didn't realise you were a professional. And abroad. An international too.'

'I just happened to . . .'

'That'll impress the lads. Palace eh,' said Bulldog.

'Yes but only for a season, and just in the jun . . .'

'You'll have to watch from the bench with me. I could use your advice. The Barney Hill boys'll shit a brick when they find out.'

'Really, I don't think I can be of much help, I . . .'

'Don't be so modest. A professional and an international,' said Les. 'That's fucking impressive.'

'No, you see, I just happened to be in certain places and . . .'

'This'll teach the bastards,' said Bulldog.

Ralph had played in Germany, France, Israel, Barbados and even Brazil. But he hadn't been involved in international transfers as they assumed. Wherever he happened to be on his travels he'd just turned up at the local club and asked for a game. Usually he ended up in the second or third team. But they didn't want to know that. They preferred to believe that an element of glamour had touched their lives and they didn't want to let it go.

38
Trial and Error

The conversation caused Ralph's mind to drift back to his schooldays and one day in particular. It was a Saturday morning after a school football match when Willie Williams called him out of the changing room and summoned him to his study.

'What the fuck 'ave you done now?' Chalkie asked Ralph as he started to gather his things and make his way reluctantly over to the master's office.

'Dunno. Maybe I stepped out of my fucking box again.' But it was good news.

'I've been approached by a scout from Crystal Palace. He wants you to go for a trial at the club next Thursday afternoon. Don't know why. You can't even hold your position properly. You'll have to get your parents approval. Interested?'

He didn't need asking twice. An afternoon off school to play football was acceptable in any circumstances. He was to turn up at two 'o'clock sharp in the car park outside the ground at Selhurst Park. Ralph almost floated home. His mind was a blur. This was his big chance and Thursday just couldn't come quick enough. Although he now supported Chelsea and had done for some years, he began to dream of playing on the sacred turf of the famous football ground where he had seen his first match. He wondered which of the first team players might be there. He didn't mind playing for Palace for a while. Just until Chelsea came in for him of course.

By Thursday afternoon it was tipping down. Ralph arrived at the ground exactly on time to see a bunch of other boys all about his own age already waiting. The small group of expectant adolescents stood around getting soggier by the minute and not saying very much until a minibus pulled into the car park and the driver ambled over towards them. He was a tall, athletic, muscular man with short, ginger hair and was wearing a full Palace kit including shorts despite the weather.

'Right,' he said in loud, sergeant major fashion. 'I'm Tom Birtles. It was me that invited you here and I'm conducting today's trial. Let me make it quite clear from the start, I don't like time wasters so anyone who wants to piss about can fuck off now.'

There were no takers. They were all shit scared of the big git already.

'Okay let's see who's here. Answer when I call your name. Atherton, Barton, Brice, Donald, Finch, Goldstein – that's a funny name.'

'It's the only one I've got.'

'Yids aren't much good at this game,' he said. 'Oh well, you're here now I suppose. Johnson, Mannion, Peters, Sissons . . .'

They all boarded the bus as directed and Tom Birtles drove to Sydenham Park a short distance away where the trial was to take place. Not at the ground itself as Ralph had hoped and there were no first team players around. Only Tom Birtles.

He first made them run ten times round the park to get warmed up before starting any ball work. Ralph was disappointed. It was almost as bad as being at school with Willie Williams. He just wanted to play football. After the run, they all collapsed in a big heap panting their lungs out.

'You lads need to get fit,' said Tom. 'Three years in the fucking army, that's what you need.' No answer. They were all shagged out and trying to catch their breath.

'Now then. I'm a scout. Know what that is?'

'You know how to tie knots?' Came an unwise reply from the lad called Peters who was just trying to be clever.

'A football scout you numskull.'

'You know how to tie knots in football boot laces?' The even more unwise reply this time from Finch brought a ripple of laughter from the group.

'Clever lot we've got here haven't we. Right, my job is to find young football talent for the club. It's my sole responsibility and they only take lads on my say so. There's thousands of lads to take your place if you give me any shit so my advice to you is to keep on my good side because I can kick you out at any time I like and I don't even have to give you a reason. Got it?' They all nodded.

'Right, Peters, in goal that end and Finch at the other.' The two boys moaned. Neither was a 'keeper but they had no choice.

'What position do you play Cohen?'

'Goldstein.'

'Whatever.'

'Inside left. Number ten.'

'Left-footed?'

'No.'

'Why do you play there then?'

'Always have done. I feel comfortable there.'

'But you're right-footed.'

'I told you that.'

'So why do you play on the left?'

'Well it isn't always strictly left is it? It's a creative position. You can go anywhere.'

'Don't know what you're talking about. Left is fucking left. Why would they call it inside left if it didn't mean play on the fucking left?'

'Johnny Haynes doesn't stick to the left. Or Bryan Douglas.'

Haynes, of Fulham and England was captain at both club and international level and generally thought to be one of the finest passers of a ball in the game. He and Bryan Douglas of Blackburn and England, both number tens, were Ralph's favourite players.

'What the fuck have they got to do with it?'

'Well, they're both number tens.'

'You should be number eight.'

Ralph was already fed up with this. He got the picture.

'If you say so.'

'Right, Finkelstein. Inside right,' said Birtles. And just to underline it, 'Number eight.'

After the group had been split into two teams they played for about an hour with Tom Birtles acting as both referee and coach.

'You're too far forward Levi, get back to your position,' he shouted on one occasion.

Fucking hell, thought Ralph, not this bollocks again. But he was unwilling to jeopardise his chances so he did what he was told and stayed deeper spraying long passes out to the wingers and through the middle for the centre forward. He pretended he was Johnny Haynes as he had seen him many times playing for Fulham at Craven Cottage. Actually, Haynes had just become the first British player ever to receive the gargantuan salary of one hundred pounds per week. Fuck me! thought Ralph when he heard about it, how the fuck was he ever going to spend it all.

He was just warming to the occasion when the whistle blew and it was all over. Was that it? They all boarded the mini-bus and in no time at all Tom had dropped them back at the ground, the others had gone and Ralph stood there on his own wondering what time the next bus home would be. He'd never felt so alone in all his life.

For weeks afterwards, the moment he opened his eyes in the morning he raced downstairs to check the post with the final words of Tom Birtles ringing in his ears.

'Well done lads, we'll be in touch if we need you.' But day after day there was nothing from the club and he became more and more dejected. He thought he'd done all right at the trial but had he managed to overcome the anti-Semitism of that Nazi, Birtles?

'Fucking Jew hater,' he muttered to himself as he finished sifting that day's mail without joy. The world was a rotten place.

'What's the matter son?' Ralph's dad was standing at the bottom of the stairs and had noticed the look of utter dejection on his son's face.

'Still no news.'

'Look, don't get your hopes up. Not many get in.'

'But I did well. It's only because of being Jewish he hasn't selected me.'

'You can't be sure of that.'

'You weren't there. You didn't hear what he said.'

'He's not the first and he won't be the last. Don't you think I know what it's like?'

'Well why aren't you angry? How can you just lie down and accept it? We've got to do something about it. Claim our rights.'

'Angry? Of course I'm angry. How could I not be angry? I've had it all my life. Lost half my family to anti-Semitism before you were even born. But it's better not to make a fuss. It only makes matters worse.'

That day Ralph went off to school with a heavy heart. Life just wasn't worth living. At lunch break, he was half-heartedly kicking a ball around with the others when Willie Williams sought him out.

'Goldstein, my study, ten minutes.' What the fuck did that prat want now? More fucking heartache for sure. But it was good news. Great news.

'Mr Birtles has been in touch. Much to my surprise he was impressed with you at the trial. Says your use of the long pass was excellent. You've been selected to play for Crystal Palace Juniors on Saturday. Of course that means you won't be able to play for the school but we'll manage without you if necessary. Interested?'

He could hardly speak. His head was swimming. He was suddenly full of love for everyone and everything. He loved his mum and dad, his brother, the Rabbi who'd taught him Hebrew for his Bar Mitzvah, Bully Bullock, Barking Barton and even the Jew-hater Tom Birtles. Particularly him. It was all Ralph could do to prevent himself from leaping across the desk and giving silly Willie a big kiss.

'Yes,' he said quietly.

'Pardon boy? Speak up lad.'

'I said yes Sir. I am interested.'

39
Jed, Smudger and the Moron

'Come on mate. Almost time for kick off.'

Ralph returned from his time travelling to realise that Bulldog was tugging him through the crowded bar towards the door. When they stepped outside the cold air hit him as if he'd been slapped in the face with a wet fish. It sobered him up a little in the head but his body was far slower to respond. By now Ralph had so much alcohol inside him, far more than he'd been used to for years, that it was all he could do to keep up with Bulldog who now strode with great purpose like a soldier, high on speed, bursting for action at the front. To reach the home bench they had to pass the visitors' end to the jeers and drunken ribaldry of their opponents which Bulldog countered with vigorous double handed 'V' signs. These in turn encouraged the Town fans to raise their level of disgusting taunts and counter insults. The crowd was larger than expected and the small stand was packed. Altogether there must have been nearly a hundred and fifty spectators around the ground split equally in affinity between the two teams.

When they finally reached the dugout Ralph was relieved to find that it took the form of a small hut with a bench inside. Somewhere nice and cosy to hide he thought.

'I'll just slip in here,' he said to Bulldog. Ralph sat down, leant back against the wall of the hut and closed his eyes. What he really would have liked was just to lie down and go to sleep preferably somewhere nice and warm. After a few moments he caught the whiff of cigarette smoke and sensed he wasn't alone. Blinking open his eyelids he saw a diminutive, relaxed looking figure with whispy, light hair leaning nonchalantly against the other side of the hut and observing him with some interest. As he managed to focus more clearly he noticed that this person wore a ragged track suit with holes in the knees and was taking occasional drags on a

Benson & Hedges in between large gulps of special brew from a can. There were a number of freshly stubbed out dog ends on the ground in front of him.

'Hello mate,' he said when he realised Ralph had noticed him.
'Hello.'
'Played for Palace I hear.'
'Fuck me word travels fast round here.'
'International too eh?'
'Look, I only played for Palace jun . . .'
'Good to meet you mate, my name's Jed.' He slid across the bench and shook hands with Ralph.
'Hi Jed. What are you, physio or something?'
'You must be joking mate. Physio, that's a fucking laugh. This is bucket and sponge country here. It's a fucking comedy show. Bulldog sploshes it about if anyone's daft enough to let him. We don't have the hi-tec stuff you guys are used to. I'm the sub.'
'Oh.'
'Should be playing really but I was a bit fragile when I got here.'
'What, injured?'
'No, hung over.' He stubbed out his cigarette and lit another.
'Oh.'

Ralph managed to stand up and walk the few yards to where Bulldog was issuing his final battle instructions.

'Listen you bastards,' yelled Bulldog, 'Don't play like a bunch of fucking poofs like last week. Get in there and fucking kill 'em.'

Rousing stuff albeit not the most sophisticated approach.

'Do you mind if I ask something?'
'Not at all mate.'
'Do you allow that sort of thing?' Ralph gestured towards the dug out.'
'What sort of thing?'
'Chain smoking on the fucking bench.'
'What, you mean Jed? No he's alright. Anyway, it's fuck-all if you consider he had sixteen pints last night. I'm surprised he's even here. Fucking good effort.'

The whistle went and the game started. Town were on the back foot right from the kick off as wave after wave of attacks forced them to defend very deep. Mostly on the goal line. More fog had swept in and enveloped the far side of the pitch so that when play drifted in that direction the players disappeared for a while and then reappeared a few moments later like Dr Who travelling in between time zones. On one occasion, as the players re-emerged like ghostly apparitions through the mist two of them were grappling and trying to kick bits off each other. The other players all rushed over and separated them allowing the ref to step in between the warring factions.

Adopting a defiant pose with back straight, head facing at forty-five degrees and arms held out with palms vertical, he resembled a continental policeman attempting to stop traffic from opposite directions. It was a stance he had perfected from hours of practise in front of the mirror.

'Fuck, it's Jocky Wilson again,' Bulldog shouted to Jed who until that moment had displayed little interest in the match but now came rushing to the sideline to check on the action.

'Daft cunt,' said Jed.

'Steady Jock,' shouted Bulldog. But it was too late.

Jocky Wilson, Town's centre forward, had been dragged up in the Gorbals and spent most of his early years fist-fighting his way through life. They were all like that where he came from. He was brought up in a violent society and wasn't going to be fucked about by anyone. He'd already been sent off three times that season and now he was being yellow-carded.

'He'll be fucking off again in a minute,' said Bulldog.

'Daft cunt,' Jed repeated.

The game restarted and Barney Hill were soon on the attack again. The opponent who had squared up to Jockey Wilson broke through into the area with a great deal of determination and was about to shoot. Jockey, clearly on a mission of unmitigated revenge, had run back through the lines of defence and was bearing down on him fast.

'No, you bastard!' shouted Bulldog. 'Don't fucking do it!'

He could see what was about to happen. The shot was sliced and bounced harmlessly out of play behind the goal but Jockey, having launched himself feet first, was now airborne and out of control. Even if he had wanted to, there was nothing he could do to reverse the momentum that took him crashing into his hapless foe in an unadorned and clearly pre-meditated act of pure violence long after the ball had gone. There was a bloodthirsty cry of pain as the player went down clutching at his groin. Pandemonium ensued. Within seconds, Jockey was surrounded by almost the entire Barney Hill team all trying to get a swing at him. They remembered him from old and wanted their own back. In an effort to calm things down, the ref, who now feared a full-scale riot, was furiously waving a red card at Jockey whilst blowing his whistle and pointing to the penalty spot at the same time. Then, in an act of what Ralph thought was quite impressive bravery, the official dived into the crowd of players, grabbed hold of the stroppy Scot and pulled him from the melee with blood now streaming from his face. Holding the red card further aloft, he pointed to the sideline. Meanwhile, Jed had taken matters up with the opposing bench.

'It was a fucking dive, you cheating fucking bastards!' he screamed.

'I'll fucking dive on you in a minute you fat fucking bastard,' came the reply from Barney Hill's manager, a large, menacing looking individual. Jed let the matter drop.

'Get off you cunt.' Bulldog shouted at Jockey, 'Before you cause any more fucking trouble.'

But he didn't want to go. Shrugging his shoulders and shaking his head as if he had become the victim of some sort of terrible injustice, he resisted the tugging of his team mates who were trying to pull him over to the side and squared up to the ref. The two of them seemed to be having a furious argument.

'What the fuck's he said this time?' asked Bulldog rhetorically.

'He's a fucking liability,' said Jed. 'Why don't you drop him?'

'Oh yeah. And who's gonna tell the mad bastard, you?'

'All right, all right, I take the fucking point.'

The fucking point was that anyone who told Jockey Wilson he was dropped ran the serious risk of being summarily executed by the Scottish Assassin as they called him.

He didn't take lightly to criticism.

Cutting a sad picture, Jockey finally but reluctantly agreed to leave the field. Head bowed, he trooped off towards the far side of the pitch and disappeared into the fog.

The Barney Hill player entrusted with the task of taking the penalty paced out a run-up equivalent to that of a West Indian fast bowler. Facing him was Town's keeper, Barry 'The Moron' Moor who was also a complete nutcase. Tall and skinny with shoulder-length, frizzy hair and a full, curly beard, his appearance was not entirely dissimilar to Rasputin on a bad hair day. Moron held the dubious distinction of being the only player in the history of the game to have been sent off twice in the same match. The first time it was for being drunk on the pitch although no one would have noticed if he hadn't asked the ref to lend him a bottle opener. He'd left his own in the changing room and was becoming increasingly desperate to get into the bottles of extra strength lager he had neatly lined up behind each of his goal posts.

Even then he might have got away with it if he hadn't lost his temper and called the official a useless cunt when he couldn't oblige. The game had only been going about ten minutes and The Moron was most upset that his Saturday afternoon enjoyment had been curtailed in such summary fashion. As he left the pitch he was already plotting to get his own back on the man in black and if he hadn't been such a dickhead the plan might not have backfired so terribly.

He went straight to the changing room and shaved his entire head. Hair, beard, sideburns, the lot. A short time later he appeared on the touch-line looking for all the world like Yul Brynner in a Kingbury Town football strip. Nobody recognised him at all. Everyone assumed he was a new player who'd just been signed up. All they saw was this gangly, bald weirdo whispering into Bulldog's ear and the two of them laughing their heads off.

When a town player got injured, Bulldog sent The Moron on as an outfield player in place of a sub who hadn't turned up. But it didn't last long. The first time a high ball came near him he leaped up like Gordon Banks to catch it and was immediately penalised for handball. The idiot had only ever played in goal before and couldn't adjust. A short while later, he dived at the feet of the opposing centre forward somewhere in the vicinity of the centre circle and grabbed the ball with both hands. That was it. He was off again. He'd only been on three and a half minutes. The whole plan was a disaster.

'Why can't you handle the fucking ball like that when you're in fucking goal you fucking idiot,' Bulldog shouted at him as he returned to the dug out. He'd stopped laughing by that time.

The Moron now prepared himself to defend the penalty. Here was his chance to show his worth by doing something heroic for the team. They'd never taken him seriously even though he turned up every week and placed himself in positions of extreme danger for the club's sake. But he always got the blame when things went wrong. That was his lot as 'keeper. Every goal against was his fault and he was always the laughing stock. Now he'd show them.

He mustered all his powers of concentration and focused himself on the job at hand.

The penalty taker, having sensibly dismissed the fanciful notion of delicate placement, charged in like a maniac and swung back his foot with the intention of striking the ball with all the strength of which he was capable.

The Moron, using every last ounce of his own skill and experience, took off like a leaping gazelle towards the top right hand corner of his goal, flying majestically through the air with all the grace of a Bolshoi ballet dancer. It was a most wondrous and spectacular sight. An athlete straining every sinew as he pushed himself to the very limits of commitment and ability.

Unfortunately however, the ball was heading in the opposite

direction. The penalty taker had scuffed the shot and sent it bobbling slowly and painfully along the sodden turf to creep inside the post to the goalie's left. Glancing back whilst in mid air, Moron saw the ball trickle over the line.

'Shit,' he uttered quietly to himself before landing with a heavy splat in a particularly gooey part of the goal-mouth. Ivor Phillips wasn't quite so mealy-mouthed.

'Fucking idiot,' he screamed at Moron as he picked the ball out of the net. 'Why the fuck don't you keep your fucking eye on the fucking ball you fucking cunt.'

One nil. But the situation didn't last long due to a gigantic stroke of luck for Town. Or was it luck? Nobody ever found out.

Shortly after the penalty, Town had a goal kick which Moron in his own inimitable style sliced out towards touch at the far side of the pitch. Everyone assumed the ball had gone out of play even though it had vanished into the fog.

The Barney Hill defence pushed up to the halfway line and their 'keeper went to the edge of his area anticipating he might get a pass from the throw in. But all of a sudden out of the murk and the mist the ball came flying into view like a space capsule re-entering the earth's atmosphere.

Unnoticed at first, it soared high over the Barney Hill defence on a trajectory that would carry it to a point somewhere between their 'keeper and his unguarded goal.

Smudger Thompson, Town's left-winger, was the first to spot the ball coming back in and, realising no one else had seen it, started to sidle over towards where he thought it might land whilst trying not to alert his opponents to his fortuitous discovery. In order to maintain the deception he even struck up a casual conversation with the Barney Hill centre half, Tim Masters, who was kneeling on one leg tying his boot-lace. Actually, the two men were brothers-in-law.

'Kid's okay?' Smudger enquired edging backwards.

'Kid's? Yeah, they're okay thanks.'

Funny, he thought. Smudger didn't usually give a toss for the kids. Where is the little toe rag anyway? Shouts of alarm began to go up from some of the Barney Hill boys on whom the awful truth was just dawning. Tim Masters turned round to see Smudger, who had quickened his step with each stride, now break into a sprint in an effort to get to the ball first and grab some of the glory that had eluded him all his life. The ball splashed down in a puddle and stopped dead in the mud roughly in the area of the penalty spot just a few tantalising yards from the goal. If only Smudger could get there first. One simple little side-foot and it would be in. The goal yawned invitingly as he struggled forward as fast as his unfit body would carry him. Now he wished he hadn't had that third pint before kickoff. He'd worked out that even though he was way behind the opposing defence he couldn't have been offside because he was in his own half when he first saw the ball and that must have been after it was last kicked because it was in midair. Anyway, how the fuck could anyone know when it was last kicked? No one even saw who kicked it.

'You bastard!' cried Tim Masters leaping to his feet and chasing after Smudger. Being altogether much fitter and faster, he soon began closing in on his cheating brother-in-law. The Barnie Hill goalie, who now realised with horror what was happening, was also on his way at full speed to try and save the situation. In the event, they all slid in from different directions and reached the ball at the same time which gave Smudger a distinct advantage. As he was a drunken, fat-bastard couch potato he was by far the heaviest and his weight on the slide carried all three over the line so that they finished in a crumpled heap at the back of the goal with the ball underneath them.

One-all.

But the question on everyone's lips was where the fuck did that ball come from and who kicked it over? Suspicion centred around Jockey Wilson who was lurking in the fog at the far side of the pitch after having been sent off. But the linesman on that side claimed he didn't see anything.

'I'm sorry, I didn't see a fucking thing,' he said glancing awkwardly at Jockey who had fixed him with a menacing glare.

The ref blew for half-time. The players, referee and linesmen argued furiously with each other as they left the pitch and discussions ensued amongst the crowd as to the validity of Town's goal. A scuffle or two even broke out.

Bulldog turned to Ralph. 'Come on,' he said. 'Let's sort 'em out. You can talk to 'em.'

'No, really I don't think I can hel . . .' But Bulldog wasn't listening. He was already on his way.

THE BEAUTIFUL GAME
Pigs in Shit

The only justifiable reason for sending a player off the field of play is violent conduct or dangerous play. Of course, even this is becoming difficult to judge nowadays because of the high degree of diving, play-acting and cheating that is deliberately perpetrated to try and get opponents sent off. It has almost become an art in itself. Instead of 'Goal of the Month' maybe there should be a 'Football Oscar' awarded for the best dramatic performance on a football field. It would certainly be a lot more fun. The winners would get a staring role in 'Casualty'.

But if we want to stop this sort of thing, and I'm sure most football fans do, then managers have to be brought into it. It is absolutely no good them looking pissed off when one of their stars is dismissed as if they had nothing to do with it. The player who commits an act of aggression, such as an elbow in the face, is responsible for letting his side down but he is not alone in his guilt. The truth of the matter is that managers are just as much to blame because the behaviour of players reflects their attitude and it is about bloody time they started sharing the responsibility when things go wrong. Why are they never held responsible for violence or play-acting on the field? After all, they spend all week with the players. What the fuck do they do all the time?

If managers were penalised in some way for petulance on the field we'd see an end to it all tomorrow and that's for sure.

It is also something of a mystery that, with the huge wealth and expertise available today, sports psychologists are not more widely employed to work with those players who are prone to this kind of dodgy behaviour.

Of course, there's nothing wrong with hard, tough play but only up to the point where it crosses the red line into violence, unfairness and bad sportsmanship. Players guilty of misdemeanours in this category should remember: It's a game, not a fucking war.

Although, why blokes who are paid a fortune just to play football should have such a tetchy attitude is beyond me. They have the world at their feet.

They should be happy as pigs in shit.

40
Jockey Wilson and the Referee's Wife

As soon as they entered the changing room Bulldog made a bee-line for Jockey Wilson.

'What the fuck did you say to the fucking bastard then?'

'What fucking bastard?'

'The fucking referee. He sent you off, remember?'

'Oh, yeah. Not much.'

'Come on.'

'Might have said something about his wife.'

'What about his wife?'

'That I knew her quite well.'

'You told him you'd fucked his wife?'

'Something like that.'

'And?'

'And what?'

'And what fucking else? Why was he so fucking pissed off? I need to know what the fuck you said so I can work out what the fuck it'll cost us to fucking sort it out.'

How could Jockey be such a bashful young man off the pitch when he was such an animal on it? Life did not provide the answer to such questions.

'I think I said she enjoyed it.'

'Enjoyed it?'

'Yes, you know.'

'You mean she had an orgasm?'

'What?'

'A climax.'

'What?'

'She came in her pants.'

'Yeah. Like a fucking train, actually.'

'Spare me the fucking details. And?'

'She said he couldn't fucking do it.'

'Right, let me see if I've got this right. You told him you'd fucked his wife, made her come in her pants and she told you that he'd never managed it.'

'Yeah, I think that's it.'

'I think this is going to be very fucking expensive.'

'Yeah, but I bet he doesn't put it in the fucking match report.'

'Right,' said Bulldog putting that matter aside for the moment. 'This is Ralph our new Director. He's played for Palace and been transferred all over the world so he knows what he's fucking talking about and he's going to tell you why you're all a bunch of fucking plonkers and what we've got to do to fucking well fix it. Okay Ralph?'

'Er, yes, right.'

Ralph looked around. They were all staring at him. Some of the lads had a cup of tea but most were drinking lager from cans. What the fuck was he going to say? There hadn't been any particular pattern to the game so it wasn't just a question of fine-tuning. Anyway he hadn't even seen half of it because of the fog. They all looked at him expectantly waiting for pearls of wisdom to drop from his mouth. But there was no magic formula. They were a bunch of unfit fatties who didn't know much about the game and he doubted that even Johann Cruyff could make them play any better.

'Funny game, football,' he said.

There were a few coughs and murmurs. No one laughed. His mind was a complete blank and there he was at centre stage with the audience waiting for him to pronounce. But it wasn't as if the side needed a little tweak or two. That he could tell a player to tuck in here or drop off there. Tucking in meant supper and dropping off was what they did afterwards in front of the telly. It was much more fundamental than that. Ralph felt like telling them all to go away and learn how to play the game properly.

'Look,' he said in the end. 'You've got to get behind them.' He stared back into a sea of expressionless faces. He felt like Captain Mainwaring from 'Dad's Army' entrusted with bringing order and discipline to a sagging bunch of idiotic soldiers but it gave him an idea. 'Remember, they don't like it up 'em.'

There was a bit of a pregnant pause during which Ralph felt most uncomfortable and was on the verge of total panic when suddenly they all burst out laughing like drains. Guffawing their heads off. For some inexplicable reason Ralph's improvised statement seemed to have tickled their fancy and they were practically wetting themselves. They just couldn't help it. 'Don't like it up 'em. Ha, ha, ha.'

They started taking it in turns to say it over and over to each other, each time sparking off more great roars of merriment. After a while, most of them were laughing so much they were clutching their sides and tears were running down their cheeks. Some could hardly stand up and held on to each other in an effort to gain some equilibrium.

'Don't like it up 'em. That's a good one. Stop it, please. I can't take any more.'

It was infectious. The laughter would die down for a moment then one would start up again and in a second they'd all be chortling in unison like nuns in a brothel.

As they took to the field for the second half they were still pissing themselves and still repeating the phrase to each other. It had become a sort of catch phrase.

'Very impressive,' Bulldog said as Ralph walked back with him to the dug out. 'I think the lads will benefit from that enormously.'

Ralph didn't know what he was talking about but he wasn't going to spurn the compliment.

'My pleasure,' he replied.

'I've never seen them so, well . . . sort of . . . happy,' said Bulldog in a puzzled way.

The second half was a different game altogether. Town played with vigour and purpose and the players were actually passing to each other. Bulldog couldn't believe it. They were like Inter Milan. They popped in one goal, then another. They were scoring for fun. It finished five-one. But there was no doubt who the hero was.

'I don't know what you said to them at half time but you

professionals certainly know a trick or two,' Les said to Ralph in the bar afterwards. 'Pint?'

'Can't we go home now?'

'Home? Not yet mate. We've got to celebrate our great win.'

A pint and a large scotch appeared on the bar in front of Ralph. They were all queuing up to buy him a drink and toast his health. The players, now showered, changed and on their way to their usual Saturday night state of drunken oblivion, were still going around saying 'Don't like it up 'em' to each other and bursting out laughing.

It was three hours later before they climbed into the car to return to Kingbury. By that time, Ralph was completely rat-arsed, weary as hell and with the motion of the car, he started to nod off. But a few miles down the road his senses were rudely assaulted by the unmistakable sound of a police siren. The local bobby and his sidekick flagged them down, got out of their patrol car and sauntered over with their specially rehearsed 'Miami Vice' gait.

Les, who was driving, wound down his window.

'What'sh the problem Occifer? he asked in the most polite drunkese he could muster.

'This your car sir?'

'Shertainly ish.' He was grinning madly.

'Where are you going?'

'Going? Er, going Home.'

'Where the fuck's home?'

'Kingbury. We've been at the match. We're Town Directorsh.'

'Been drinking have we sir?'

'Good heavensh no ociffer.'

'Are you quite sure sir?'

'Well we might have had a shwift half after the match. Jusht to be shoshable you know.'

'That was a fucking lucky win you had today mate,' growled the sidekick.

Les sensed his aggressive tone and didn't want to aggravate it.

'Yesh, very lucky. Very lucky indeed.'

'Using professionals is a bit unfair isn't it?'

'What profeshionalsh?'

'The new coach who played for Spurs.'

'What new coach?'

'The Jewish poof who insulted my brother.'

Oh fuck.

'Craz . . . er Kevin's your brother?'

'That's right mate.'

'Palash,' Les corrected him.

'What?'

'He played for Palash, not Shpurs.'

'Whatever, this is my patch and we don't want any southern poofter yids coming in and trying to take over.'

'No, of courshe not.'

'It's fucking unfair using professionals,' repeated the sidekick.

'Unfair, yesh,' agreed Les willingly.

'Fucking cheating I'd call it, Laddie.'

Ralph was getting distinctly worried at this turn of events and was shivering wildly with fright on the back seat. They'd started by addressing Les as Sir, demoted him to Mate and now he was Laddie. Credibility was plummeting rapidly. He started to envisage a night in the cells being gang raped by desperate criminals.

But Les took the heat out of the situation. Head bowed, he apologised like a sullen schoolboy caught lifting a girl's skirt in the playground.

'Shorry,' he said.

'You're pissed,' announced the first copper, obviously the senior. 'Can you give me any reason why I shouldn't arrest you?'

Les handed him a twenty pound note.

'Bribery is a serious offence you know.'

Les handed him another one.

'Very serious.'

And another.

'All right, fuck off back to your crap little town but if this happens again it'll be fucking handcuffs.'

They started back to the police car.

'Fucking cheats,' said the sidekick as they went.

The police car roared off down a side-street and when it was out of sight they all gesticulated in its direction with 'V' signs and shouted insults at the policemen who were now miles beyond earshot.

'Bashtardsh!'

'Fat cunts!'

'Fucking pigs!'

'Fascists!'

The last was Ralph.

'That was a fucking close one,' said Harry as they drove gingerly off.

'And fucking exshpenshive,' agreed Les. 'But we made enough on the bar to cover it quite eashily.'

When they finally got back to Kingbury, Ralph asked to be let out in town rather than at home. As he was about to close the car door Les said, 'It's the dinner and dance on Friday night. Fancy coming? Tommy Doc'll be there. Mucky Duck. Kick off's at eight.'

And off they went.

Ralph took stock of the situation. There he was standing in Kingbury High Street feeling totally shagged out and ravenously hungry. He looked around. Somewhere there had to be a king prawn tikka masala with his name on it.

The Beautiful Game

The truth is that, to a real football lover, even at its most modest level in a park on a Sunday morning the game is an all-embracing experience and quite perfect as it is. As perfect as anything needs to be. Just happening to pass by when there's a game in progress between Beer-gut Rovers and Fat Gorilla Albion in the Zenith, Athenian, Isthmian, Olympic, Corinthian, Kebab & Chips, Barry's Carpets of Penge League, you become totally involved in the personalities, the referee's decisions and the tactics, such as they are. After just a few short minutes, you care passionately about the game and who wins it even though ten minutes earlier you had never even heard of the teams involved. Suddenly, you're yelling your head off at the players, arguing with a linesman (sorry, referee's assistant), advising the coach on tactics and telling him to get his subs warmed up. Actually, at this level you are considered extremely fortunate if a sub has bothered to turn up. You're having illuminated discussions with everyone about football in general and they all know at least as much about it as the highly paid pundits on telly. This is about a bunch of ordinary folk who love the game playing purely for pleasure. Although, on a freezing cold day in the middle of January on a remote cow-field of a pitch with no discernable comfort for miles around this might be a difficult concept for the layman to comprehend.

But the simple fact is that the game itself has not been improved one iota by the introduction of huge amounts of money at the top level.

World-class players from every continent now adorn practically every Premiership team and have, most certainly, contributed a high level of craft, competence and ability to the game. In the process they have helped create a wonderful spectacle that is breathtaking at times. Maybe the best we've ever seen in this country. They are all most welcome. But the game itself is so simple and beautiful that it is as wonderful to watch or participate in whether it is played by top flight professionals at Wembley Stadium or fat drunks on Hackney Marshes. There is nothing wrong with the actual game itself and there never has been. All you need is a ball.

41
The Annual Bash

Ralph turned up a little late but with great anticipation for the annual dinner and dance which was being held at the poshest venue in town, the Black Swan Hotel. He was looking forward to a slap-up do and the opportunity of talking football all night with the other club members but when he entered the function room it was like the Marie Celeste. All the tables were laid with white cloths, cutlery, place names and a huge silver tureen sat in the middle of each one but there wasn't a soul in sight. He walked over to one of the large, round tables and peered into the tureen. It was half full of a warm liquid that he took to be soup although the puzzling aroma it produced was not such that he could accurately discern its flavour. Ralph looked at his watch. It was already twenty past eight and he was sure they'd told him it started at eight. Had he made a mistake? Was this the right day?

The door to the kitchen opened and two waiters appeared. One pushed a trolley on which a massive hot water urn steamed and bubbled whilst the other held the end of a hose that was attached to it. Ralph watched as they went from table to table filling up the tureens. One of the waiters looked up in his direction.

'Are you lost sir?' he asked.

'Isn't everybody?' Ralph had had a few glasses of wine before leaving home and was in his philosophical mood but the waiters didn't seem to get the joke.

'I thought it was supposed to start at eight.'

'That's right sir. It did. Actually, most of them have been here since well before that.'

He must have looked puzzled.

The other waiter chimed in. 'They're all in the stable bar sir. Keeps them out of the way while we get set here. Out of the door, turn right, down the steps and follow the path. You can't miss it.'

Ralph walked outside. In the distance he could just make out the babble of a crowd that increased as he followed the waiter's directions. It occurred to him that it must have been something like coming down the tunnel at Wembley to play in the cup final with the roar of the crowd getting louder as you approached the pitch.

It was quite a bit further than he'd expected and he was starting to wonder if he hadn't taken a wrong turn when, in the gathering gloom, two shadowy figures came into view rolling around on a grassy patch at the side of the path. At first Ralph thought it was two blokes having a fight but the panting that drifted on the light evening breeze towards him didn't seem aggressive. Not at all. Maybe it was a couple of kids having a rough and tumble. But then he just made out a giggle followed by a woman's voice saying 'Stop it Barry you filthy bastard, put it away, someone might see us.'

'Who cares?' came the reply. It must have been Barry. 'Come on Cathy you horny bitch, we've just got time. You know you want it.'

'Not here, you bastard, what if my old man catches us?'

'What's that prat going to do? He'll be too pissed to notice you've gone. Never could hold his drink that one.'

'No, we can't. Ooh, don't. He'll kill you if he finds out.'

'I'll bet he hasn't seen to you properly for years.'

'That's what you think. Ooh, don't I said.'

'Yeah, that's what I think. I think you're gaggin' for it. I think your knickers are sopping wet. It's like the fucking Niagara Falls down there. Come on, let me slip it in and take you out of your misery.'

'No, no, oooh, Barry don't. You dirty bastard, Ooh, ooh. I said no you dirty bastard. Aah, yes, yes, harder. You dirty bastard.'

Ralph quickened his step. This was fucking embarrassing.

Finally reaching the bar, he opened the door and was almost overwhelmed by a great cloud of alcohol and tobacco fumes that billowed out over him. At the same time his ears were assaulted by the deafening cacophony of hundreds of chattering voices. He peered through the fuggy atmosphere at the throng of revellers inside and halfway across the room he caught sight of Les Cartwright, Bulldog Bevan and Harry Hartson. They beckoned him over with a cheery wave and, with some difficulty, he squeezed himself through the crowd towards them. Everyone was in high spirits. Gales of laughter went up from the different groups of people in turn and every other phrase was a sexual innuendo. The women were all wearing low-cut gowns that barely contained their bouncing bosoms. They all seemed to be in a gay and flirtatious mood and many of the blokes were taking advantage of this good-natured atmosphere to make lewd advances and feel their asses.

'Good bash last year,' one bloke said to another as Ralph passed by.

'Don't remember, was it?'

'Yeah, you fell asleep in the fucking soup.'

'Did I?'

'They found you drunk in the gutter next day. I had to bail you out.'

'Well I must have had a fucking good time.'

'Hello,' Les greeted Ralph, 'Welcome to the dive. Better late than never I suppose. This is my wife Paula and this is Bulldog's better half Christine. Don't know where Harry's lady is. Where's Cathy gone Harry?'

'Get some fresh air.'

She was getting something fresh all right, thought Ralph. But it wasn't air.

'Right, my round,' said Bulldog. 'What do you fancy Ralph?'

'Oh, glass of red wine please.'

They all laughed heartily until Les realised he was serious.

'It's only beer, lager or shorts here,' he said. 'It's not the fucking Savoy you know.'

They all laughed again.

'Pint of bitter then please,' he said. He didn't like mixing the grape and the grain. It had a funny effect on him these days. He fumbled around in his pockets to make sure he'd brought his emergency Alka-Seltzer with him. He sensed he might need it.

Everyone else was already completely pissed and the evening had hardly started.

'I thought you said eight.'

'I said kick off's at eight. This is the pre-match warm up,' said Les. 'It's traditional.'

'You need to build up a fucking big appetite to stomach the muck they serve up here,' offered Harry. He was more outspoken than he had seemed on previous occasions and Ralph thought he was slurring his speech slightly.

They all agreed the food was rubbish.

'Fucking disgusting,' said Les.

'Language,' warned Paula.

'Sorry love,' Les apologised.

Ralph scanned the room to see if there was anyone else he knew, and recognised some of the team members who had been so impressed with his tactical adroitness the previous weekend. They all seemed to be togged up in ill-fitting old suits and posing like film stars. Some of the younger lads were even wearing sunglasses. That was what a suit did for some people. Made them feel important. They pretended it was their normal attire but you could tell it wasn't because of a sleeve too long, a trouser too short, a tie miles from a collar or a shirt hanging out at the side. In many cases all that was needed to complete the look of a total moron was a cock dangling out of a trouser zip. Many of the blokes seemed totally oblivious to the large urine stains that had built up on their saggy crotches during the course of the evening. Ralph wouldn't have minded betting they all had raggedy, soiled underpants on underneath too. Not that he was conversant with their underpants you understand. He was just guessing. But it was a qualified guess having observed the messy shreds hanging in the changing room last Saturday.

This manic, strict insistence on a dress code at certain events like annual dinner and dances or sportsman's evenings was the height of inverted snobbery as far as Ralph was concerned. The attendees were hardly the mandarins of taste but by some dint of twisted logic they thought a suit transformed their normally shabby demeanour into a shining presence when, truth be told, they'd actually turned up looking like prats.

He started to wonder why he had agreed to come. He'd never enjoyed this sort of formal occasion. It was the tie thing that really got him. For some daft reason you weren't considered respectable without one. Many clubs through the divisions insisted their players wore suits and ties on match days even though many of them were complete yobos who wouldn't normally have dreamed of wearing such an outfit in real life. But Ralph had always considered that ties were particularly useless items of apparel and, in a relatively permissive world, it was baffling why they carried so much social significance. There must have been millions of workers in tie factories around the world who relied on these funny little scraps of coloured cloth for a livelihood and he wished them all well. But at the same time he believed they were employed in a virtually useless occupation just as those employed in the manufacture of guns, tanks and warplanes were engaged in similarly futile endeavours. Working their guts out all their lives in an industry bent solely on destruction.

Who the hell wanted to waste their energy every day making something that was designed to kill people? You didn't even know who might be killed with it. Maybe some really nice bloke from Baghdad with a wife and kids.

But people found it easier not to think about these things. It was just a job, that's all. Main thing is it pays well so don't upset the boss. Never mind about the end product. If you couldn't see it, it didn't exist. Problem was that most workers didn't understand the nature of their oppression. They thought they had to carry on regardless of everything and that they had no choice in the matter of being accomplices to mass murder.

All right, perhaps ties weren't quite as bad as tanks. But they also contributed to a deranged way of life that people just accepted without thinking and from which they couldn't seem to break free. Drawn into the trap of not challenging the way things were for the sake of an easy life. For this reason people believed in God and the Royal Family and Manchester United.

Really though, how could you judge a person by whether he was wearing a tie or not? Why should you want to anyway? Of course, there was nothing wrong with wearing a tie if you liked them but there was something fucking strange about having to. Even in today's supposedly liberal society there were still plenty of upmarket establishments run by ostensibly intelligent people where they wouldn't even let you through the door if you happened to arrive without a bit of cloth flapping around your neck.

A posh restaurant or the House of Lords may be one thing if the bastards really insist on standing on ceremony but a football match? Don't be daft.

Ralph didn't notice them insisting females wore ties. What about sexual equality?

A nudge in the side brought him round from his dreamy state.

'Here's your drink.'

'Oh thanks.' Ralph casted around for an interesting topic of conversation. 'They're watering down the soup you know,' he announced. Everyone looked puzzled except Les who pulled Ralph quickly aside and lowered his voice.

'That's right,' he whispered. 'Cuts down on cost. Anyway, by the time we get over there the bastards won't know any difference. They'll have a gallon of soup and a few loaves of bread down them in two minutes flat and most of them won't even bother with the main course. They'll be straight onto shorts.' He gave Ralph a knowing wink.

Just then, Cathy walked up to the group adjusting a bra strap. A couple of leaves had affixed themselves to the back of her skimpy dress and there were grass marks on her knees. Ralph wondered if Harry had noticed these blemishes or if he had any idea how they might have come about. At the same time he was struck by Cathy's fulsome good looks. Full lips, full face, full figure. Buxom but not fat. Large but not too big. She looked as if she ate well, slept well, had loads of orgasms and enjoyed life.

'Hello Cath love,' greeted Harry. 'Enjoy your walk?'

'Lovely thanks.'

'This is Ralph, our new Director.'

'Oh good, a fresh face. Hello Ralph.' He felt himself being sized up by her gaze.

'Hello,' he answered. He was about to utter something flirtatious but before he could get the words out a sudden, violent explosion shook the shit out of him and shock waves came crashing through the building.

'Sorry folks,' came a cheery voice over the PA accompanied by ear-splitting feedback.

'What the fuck was that?' Ralph asked nobody in particular. His eardrums were erupting.

'Watch out!' said Bulldog. 'Dinner gong!'

In fact, the sound in question was a recording of a Korean ceremonial gong that the proprietor of the hotel, Max Bainbridge, had brought back from a visit to the Far East.

He used it to herald announcements over the many loudspeakers throughout the complex and regarded it as one of the specially endearing features of the establishment. However, on this particular occasion, no one had checked the controls on the ex-professional, 5,000 watt amplifier before switching it on and for some reason it was set on full volume. Some cunt must have been fiddling with it. The resultant boom would have registered significantly on seismic measuring equipment. As it was, the buildings of the hotel were still vibrating for a good few minutes after the blast.

There was a mad scramble for the exit. Most of the attendees had been drinking for a couple of hours and were famished. There was absolute chaos for a while as two hundred people crazed with hunger all tried to get through one small door at the same time in a desperate rush to get to the food. After the pandemonium had subsided Ralph strolled slowly after them. He was the last one.

As soon as he entered the function room he realised the madness had followed them. The tureens had already been emptied and their contents devoured. Great splodges of soup and the crusty remnants of bread rolls littered all the tables and the babble of discussion was even worse than before. Ralph searched for a spare seat and eventually ensconced himself with three other people who were already seated at a table right at the back in a secluded corner. He was about to introduce himself to his fellow diners when a team of young waitresses of school age streamed out through the kitchen door each carrying an armful of plates which they started distributing to the rabble. As Ralph's portion was unceremoniously plonked down in front of him he asked the waitress what it was.

'Boiled chicken, boiled potatoes and boiled cauliflower,' she informed him.

'And what was the soup.'

'Chicken.'

Ralph knew there was a chicken factory in the area. A huge concern with enormous sheds where thousands of the poor birds were bred and then murdered in horrible circumstances before being turned into various products for sale in supermarkets. Chicken Delight was the biggest employer in the area and many of the club's players and officials worked there. He'd heard all the gruesome stories. They said it was like Belsen. Apparently, Les had done some kind of deal, the details of which were a bit sketchy, to persuade the company to sponsor the first team.

Ralph pushed a fork into the lump of specially formed chicken substitute sitting on his plate but something restricted his efforts. He tore the partly synthetic item of so-called food apart to reveal a piece of plastic printed with yellow and red writing. 'Chicken Delight' it said. 'Your guarantee of quality.' He sighed and pushed the plate away.

'And what's for pudding? he asked the young waitress who had been observing his actions with great interest. 'Chicken blancmange?'

'No pudding today sir,' she answered in robotic fashion without spotting Ralph's cynicism before adding, 'Any complaints should be directed to Mr Les Cartwright from the club.' She spouted by rote as if she had been rehearsing the statement in order to get it word perfect before meeting her public. But without waiting for a response she turned on her heels and walked hurriedly away. The noise of drunken burbling had died down to be replaced by a flurry of slurping and chewing which gave Ralph the chance to engage the three other people at the table.

To his left was a very slim women of about forty called Stephanie who had obviously seen better days. Ralph thought she looked tired and sad even though she giggled a lot. He put this down to the half empty bottle of champagne she had been drinking her way through since he had arrived at the table. It looked a better bet than any of the other drinks on offer.

'Where did you get that?' he asked.

'Brought it with me,' she replied.

It turned out she'd been married to one of the players, Andy Morris, who was a lot younger than her. But he'd left her a few months previously for a lass who was a lot younger than him. Andy and his new friend were sitting just a few tables away and Stephanie pointed them out. Ralph craned his neck to get a view.

'Fuck me!' he said. 'She should be in a fucking crèche'

'Bastard cradle snatcher, fucking bastard,' Stephanie shouted.

Obviously she wasn't fully over it.

She had only come to the do because she'd bought tickets for herself and her own new boyfriend in an effort to make Andy jealous by showing him she could make it alone. But it wasn't working for three reasons. First, Andy obviously didn't give a toss. Second, her new friend had disappeared some time ago to get some fresh air. Third, she couldn't make it alone.

'Er, what's his name, your new bloke,' Ralph asked.

'Barry,' she said and burst into tears. People started looking over and wondering what all the fuss was about.

'Look,' said Ralph, 'I'm not sure this Barry is any good for you.'

Stephanie shot him a bitter glance.

'What the fuck do you know about it?' she snapped in a highly agitated tone, her voice rising in intensity with every word. 'It's none of your fucking business anyway.'

Ralph tried to calm her down. How the fuck did he get himself involved in this?

'I'm sorry,' he apologised, 'I didn't mean to interfere, but it's not very considerate to leave you here alone like this is it?'

'He'll be back in a minute,' she said, 'He's just getting some fresh air.'

She went quiet for a moment as if pondering what Ralph had said. Then she looked him intently in the face and said, 'Would you like to fuck me?'

'Pardon?'

'You can fuck me if you like. I'm a good fuck. We can go to my place. You can fuck my ass off if you want.'

'Er, well, thank you very much,' said Ralph, sensing a crisis looming. 'I appreciate the offer, really I do, but I'm afraid I can't.'

'Yes you can,' she said. 'Come on. Come back to my place and fuck my ass off.' She could crack at any moment.

'No, really, thanks a lot and everything but I mustn't,' Ralph insisted. 'I'm with someone you see.'

'Well I won't tell her.'

'Oh yeah, where is she then?'

'At home.'

'Well that's alright. She'll never know. I won't tell her.'

'No, that's not it. We've got kids. Actually. We . . . we . . .' he had to be careful here. He sensed she was right on the edge. 'Well, we love each other I suppose.' Wrong.

Suddenly, Stephanie stood up, let out a wail of grief, poured the remains of her bottle over Ralph's head and stormed out of the room.

People stopped talking, the waitresses stood still, silence hung over the proceedings and everyone was looking at Ralph.

After a short while, the hubbub slowly returned and Ralph noticed that Les had left his place at the top table and was threading his way over. It took some time because he was at the far end of the room.

'There's a few complaints about the noise from this table,' he said when he finally arrived.

'You must be fucking joking,' Ralph answered dabbing his hair dry with a napkin.

'No need for that sort of language,' said Les. 'What have you said to that poor girl to upset her like that?'

'Come on,' he said. 'You must know she's a nutcase. I didn't say anything. She's quite capable of upsetting herself.'

'Have you been propositioning her?'

'That's a fucking good one.'

'People are very fond of Steph, particularly since Andy dump ... er, left her like that so they don't want anyone making it worse for her.'

Ralph detected an element of personal interest in the statement.

'And what about you?' he asked.

'What do you mean?'

'Are you fond of her too?'

Les reddened.

'What do you mean?'

'How fond of her are you exactly?'

From Les's embarrassed reaction Ralph realised he was on to something here.

'Look, I'm just marking your card son. Just advising you to watch your step so you don't get off on the wrong fucking foot.'

Les made his way back to the top table. Had he covered his tracks? He wasn't sure.

Ralph turned his attention to the others on his table. To his right, an elderly gentleman in an ancient, threadbare dinner suit had been snoozing soundly since he'd arrived but now stirred himself and screwed up his eyes to focus on Ralph.

'Hello,' Ralph greeted him.

'What?'

'I said hello.'

'What did you say?

'HELLO!' Ralph shouted.

'You'll have to speak up, son, I'm ninety three.'

'Really, well done, that's quite an age.'

'That's quite a fucking age you know, son.'

'Yes, I know'

'What?'

Oh fuck it, thought Ralph. What was the point of being ninety-three if you didn't know what the fuck was going on?

Just then a rather portly, middle-aged man in a dark suit adorned with a huge flower in the buttonhole walked briskly up to the table. It was the manager of the establishment. He made an attempt to converse with the fourth member of the happy troupe, a tanned, slight man of about sixty-five, but it was hard going because he didn't seem to speak English and just sat there with a bemused expression. After a while the manager took his guest by the arm and led him slowly out of the room in what appeared to be a thoroughly bewildered state.

What was going on? Was he being asked to leave? What had he done? Who the fuck was he? Those were the questions on everyone's lips. Certainly, thought Ralph, this was the fucking table to be on. Perhaps he could charge for providing the cabaret.

But who exactly was this shadowy foreign figure? Was he wanted by Interpol? Was he an arms dealer? A drugs runner? Was he involved in white slavery? Had he come to steal the daughters of the town and corrupt them in some terrible way? No, nothing like that. In fact, the man who had been led away was Señor Quilles, a tax inspector from Alicante, who had just arrived that evening and was staying as a regular guest in the hotel. He'd come to visit his elderly sister who had been married to a local man but, since being widowed, now lived in a nursing home in the area. It was Señor Quilles' first trip abroad and had started off remarkably badly when he accidentally boarded the wrong plane and flew to Moscow by mistake. How this could have happened was a complete mystery to all concerned but after some confusion at Russian immigration an airline official led him onto an aircraft bound for London and he eventually arrived fifteen hours late. It didn't help much when his bus from Gatwick broke down leading to a further delay of four hours. When he finally arrived he was so tired and hungry that he just dumped his bags in his room and went immediately in search of a bite to eat. He had wandered into the function room thinking it was the main dining room, saw the soup tureens, sat down and waited to be served. But by that time the waiters had prepared everything for the function and gone for their break before the fun started.

Poor Señor Quilles waited for the best part of an hour all on his own in the huge room feeling very hungry but not knowing how to attract any attention. After a while he started to doze off but a fucking huge bang on a gong suddenly frightened him out of his wits. Then a hoard of crazy maniacs crashed through the doors and started devouring all the soup. They were even sitting at his table. Fuck knows what he made of it all. He must have thought it was a convention of soccer hooligans. Everyone had heard of English soccer hooligans. Even in Alicante.

Ralph could certainly clear a table. There was only one bloke left now and he didn't look as if he'd last much longer either. So he sat back to enjoy the entertainment.

A booming fanfare over the PA system alerted everyone's attention and a door at the opposite end of the room opened to admit the jaunty figure of Tommy Docherty the great football manager from the seventies who was the guest speaker. He entered to great applause not least from Ralph who still loved him dearly from his days at Chelsea. Of course, most of the others couldn't give a stuff about that, they only knew him as an ex-Man U manager. Silly bastards.

Tommy walked to the top table, picked up the microphone and started talking but the mike wasn't working and no one at the back could hear a thing save for the muffled Scottish lilt of the odd word when there was a lull amongst the audience.

Every minute or so the people at the front few tables burst out laughing. They were having a wonderful time. But those at the back had no idea what the great man was saying. At one stage, Ralph just caught the word Bader floating across the room and realised that Tommy Doc must have been telling the old joke about Tony Hately being like Douglas Bader. Terrific in the air but useless on the ground. Every football speaker he had ever heard told that joke. It was so old it had grown a beard.

After the speech there were questions and they all seemed to be about Man U.

Ralph raised his hand and Tommy pointed to him.

'The young gentleman at the back,' he said and everyone laughed.

'Where do you rate Charlie Cooke in your list of all-time greats?' He almost had to shout the question. Unanimous groans of displeasure from all around the room drowned out the answer but just as Ralph was about to ask the Doc to repeat it the disco fired up with a great boom from two massive speakers. Question time was over.

Village People is standard fare on these occasions and within minutes the dance floor was packed with writhing bodies cavorting their arms into positions that spelt out the letters YMCA in time to the music.

Ralph wandered slowly over to the top table. Tommy Docherty was in conversation with Les but seemed bored. Obviously, Les had been doing all the talking. As he approached, Ralph was sure he saw the Doc stifle a large yawn.

'Excuse me Mr Docherty.'

'Hello son. Autograph?'

'Thank you,' he said. He'd give it to Joe to add to his collection. It would be an excuse to talk about the old days.

'You the one who asked about Charlie Cooke?'

'Yes, I am.'

'One of the best, son. One of the very best.'

'Thank you Mr Docherty. Thank you very much.'

At that point Ralph felt it was time to go. Better not drive, he thought. I'll leave the car and pick it up in the morning. It was only a mile or so to where he lived and he could use the fresh air. Setting off down the path that led through the hotel gardens to the front gate he heard a rustling sound in the bushes. What the fuck was that?

'No Richard, you dirty bastard, don't.'

It was a voice he instantly recognised.

'Come on Cath, don't be a spoilsport.'

It must have been Richard.

'No, don't. Ooh, don't I said. What if my old man finds out?'

'Fuck him.'

'I do. Ooh, ooh, Richard. I said no you dirty bastard. Ooh, harder, you bastard. Aah.'

'Call me Dick.'

THE BEAUTIFUL GAME

We Are All Brothers

There is a brotherhood of sports people to which we all belong and which we must respect. This is a difficult concept for kids who basically just want to win and are often upset when they don't. But every effort must be made to help them understand this important aspect that relates to all sport, not just football.

They must be taught to be fair. Hard yes, but fair and sportsmanlike at all times.

You often come across kids who refuse to shake hands with their opponents after a game they have lost. This is silly. Whatever has happened in a game, players must shake hands afterwards.

It's as important as learning how to kick a ball.

If they won't, drop them to the bench next time or don't even select them at all.

Sometimes they must learn the hard way.

And that's in life by the way, not just football.

42
Teaching the Tots

Not long after Ralph became involved with Town, his lad Joe, who was nearly seven at the time, announced that he wanted to play football. There wasn't a team for kids his age in the area and Ralph didn't want him to have to go through the misery of his own early playing days so he decided to start one. He'd always fancied himself as a football manager and saw it as the perfect opportunity to make his own contribution to Ruud Gullit's sexy football revolution.

It was in the middle of winter and all the local playing fields were sodden so Ralph hired the local youth club hall and told Joe to put the word around his mates. He was expecting about a dozen but the grapevine was so effective that about forty boys turned up. It must have been almost the entire population of six and seven year olds in the town. He stood by the door and watched as a procession of cars zoomed into the car park and screeched to a halt, doors opened, kids pushed out and the cars screeched off again. Nobody stopped to inquire who was in charge or if it was safe or what was planned for them. He could have taken them all free-fall parachuting and none of those parents would have known any difference. It was an hour and a half of cheap baby sitting as far as most of them were concerned.

On that first occasion the kids were making the most almighty racket inside the hall and it was impossible to keep them quiet. There must have been an acoustic fault in the building because it was deafening.

Ralph's mate Geoff, an avid Villa fan, had agreed to help out and they both rushed from their respective places of work to be there. But neither had managed to find the time to prepare anything and arrived only with a fervent desire to pass on to their own knowledge and love of the game and to somehow try and teach the kids how to play it.

There they both stood after a ball-aching day at work, surrounded by a hoard of noisy, overactive seven year old boys all letting off steam because they hadn't been allowed to play outside all day due to continuous, heavy rain.

They would really much rather have been in the pub with a decent pint of ale to hand but they'd promised the lads and they couldn't go back on it now.

Ralph and Geoff pretended to have a serious conversation about how to organise the forty little bastards who just wouldn't shut up. The two smiled and nodded at each other but neither could hear properly what the other was saying.

Ralph felt that an opening speech was called for but, clearly, it wasn't going to be easy.

'I think I'll just start with a few words,' he told Geoff.

'Be my guest,' answered Geoff who had heard a few of Ralph's words before.

Ralph adopted his most genial, avuncular tone and welcomed all the kids.

'We all love football and we're going to try and teach you how to play it. But there's a thing or two you need to know.' He'd already had to raise his voice to a shout.

'Football is a game of options but before you can start to explore all the possibilities you must first have possession of the ball.' By now he was almost having to scream above the din. 'Let's assume for the moment that we have got the ball. The first thing to remember is that you are not alone. Football is a team game. You've got your mates around you and the object of the exercise is for everyone to co-operate and achieve something together.'

By now, four of the lads seemed to be involved in a wrestling match, two or three were bouncing balls on the floor, three were involved in an argument about Pokomon cards and six had gone to the toilet from where loud banging noises and the alarming sound of unusually fast-running water could be heard.

The rest were all staring at Ralph and Geoff with vacant expressions. This wasn't like school at all.

Ralph soldiered on. 'If you're in control of the game you can begin to create the options that will help you win it. Be patient. Be smart. Hoofing the ball into your opponent's box and hoping someone will force it into the net is a mug's game. Let's be creative. Let's try and be sure about what we are doing.'

He had just wanted to get them started on the right track but he might as well have been speaking Swahili for all the attention they were paying.

'Right, any questions before we get going?'

A skinny young lad with red hair and freckles put up his hand.

'Please sir, who was George Best?'

'You don't have to call me sir. My name is Ralph. He was a player for Manchester United and Northern Ireland – right, if there's no more . . .'

'Please sir, was he the best?'

'Some say he was.'

'Please sir, do you think he was?'

'Don't call me sir. I don't really believe in the idea of choosing the best.'

This was getting complicated. He began to wish he hadn't bothered.

'Please sir, my dad says George Best is the best.'

'Right, well I'm sure your dad believes that's right.'

'You don't then sir?'

'I haven't got a best.'

'Please sir, why did they call him Best if he wasn't the best?'

'That was just his name.'

'Please sir, why was Best his name if he wasn't the best?'

Christ almighty. He was getting fucking bored with this.

At this point Geoff leaned over 'Tell him your lot have got a player called Wise.'

'What's the point of that?'

'Well, he doesn't exactly live up to his name does he? I mean he's hardly the fucking brain of Britain is he?'

'Yes he fucking is,' Ralph most emphatically responded.

'Right,' he continued, addressing any of the boys that were still listening, 'If you guys want to be the best you'd better start learning something. What we want is some sexy football.'

'Sir, what's sexy?'

'Ask your mother. OK lads, line up against the wall.'

The hall wasn't that big so they decided to split the lads into groups with some playing while the others watched and then change round every five minutes. Ralph and Geoff each took a team and gave each boy a position carefully explaining their individual roles and roughly which part of the playing area they should occupy.

But straight at the kick-off the little sods all hared off after the ball like a shoal of fish chasing a tasty lump of flotsam in the Atlantic ocean moving in unison as if magnetically attracted to the ball.

'Spread out!' they shouted at the tops of their voices but the lads weren't listening. They couldn't hear anyway. Ralph was eventually to learn that 'spread out' was the most over-used expression in junior football.

There was a door at the end of the hall which led to the toilets and at one stage the ball headed in that direction with the entire bunch of little twerps hurtling down after it. They were kicking bits off each other and not taking much notice where they were going when they suddenly reached the end of the hall and, having built up quite a momentum, crashed through the toilet door and disappeared out of sight. When Ralph arrived to sort them out they were still furiously intent on kicking the ball around the urinals and wouldn't stop even though he was red in the face with the effort of blowing his whistle.

'The ball's out,' he was screaming 'Goal-kick for Christ's-sake!' But they wouldn't take any notice. They had yet to learn the significance of the referee's whistle.

THE BEAUTIFUL GAME

Don't try to dribble out from deep positions, it's suicide.

If you get caught and dispossessed on the edge of the box your opponents will be in.

You see it all the time. No one to pass to in a deep position, no one moving into space, no options for the player with the ball so he starts running across the edge of the box with opposing forwards trying to tackle or close him down. It's simply asking for trouble. If that's you and they get the ball off you in that position and go on to score, it's your fault.

Don't say you haven't been told.

I've just fucking told you.

If there are no options and your mates are not creating options to make things easy for you then you must clear it. There is no choice so don't try to be clever. If they score because you made a basic mistake that I have just warned you about, you won't look so fucking clever then, will you?

And that's in life by the way, not just football.

43
Dingbats, Wildebeest and Bulging Canines

Ralph soon discovered that the reason so many boys had turned up was because it was their only real opportunity to play football at all. Chatting to the lads he discovered that forty years on, after a succession of uninterested teachers had tried their utmost to drain him of all enthusiasm for the game he loved, the same problems still existed in school sport. There wasn't enough of it and what there was depended to a large extent on the goodwill of unqualified staff to stay late and work at weekends without pay. If anything the situation was even worse now than in Ralph's schooldays. There's progress for you.

Of course not everyone agreed with this. Some of the teachers were insulted by Ralph's harsh deduction and some of the parents were unwilling to admit that they were failing their offspring in any way.

But Ralph had his answer for anyone challenging this conclusion. 'Ask the kids,' he always said. He knew they'd all say sport in state schools was a mickey-mouse affair. They weren't stupid and they knew.

The only worthwhile instruction available to fledgling footballers was extra-curricular and usually provided by volunteer parents who were far from proficient in the task.

Their main qualification was a desire to give their kids a chance to play the game rather than any ability to coach it properly. How were those youngsters going to learn from people who didn't know? But the parents didn't deserve to be criticised. They were only doing their best with limited resources. In fact, they were hampered just as much by appalling facilities as by the cavernous gaps in their own knowledge.

At many public pitches changing facilities were decrepit, foul or non-existent. Lines were incorrectly marked out, there were no goal nets and grass was not cut well or often enough to allow proper movement of the ball.

To cap it all, every overfed, bulging canine clearly regarded the large, grassy expanse of a football pitch as the most enjoyable place on which to squeeze out a massive great turd with the enthusiastic encouragement of its overfed, bulging owner. Inconsiderate bastards! How would they like it if they fell over in a pile of dog shit?

Once when Ralph was coaching his lads, the grass had been left untended for so long that he almost lost three of the little buggers in the overgrowth. He had warned them beforehand, 'Be careful, and if you spot a wildebeest, run for it!'

He found them still passing the ball to each other about half an hour after the session ended. Kids have little perception of time and they hadn't heard the whistle. It was like discovering Japanese soldiers in the jungle who hadn't heard the war was over. It might have been funny if it hadn't been so fucking tragic.

But it wasn't just the football authorities that were falling short of the mark. In discussions with people involved with other sports clubs in the town Ralph soon realised that all British sporting bodies were run by committees of daft old dingbats who were completely out of touch with modern developments in the sports that provided them with an excellent living. Consequently it was hardly surprising that we British were unable to compete internationally on any sort of decent level even at sports we invented. Indeed, expectation levels were now so low that it was a matter for great rejoicing if any of our sportspeople managed to get past the first round of anything. A depressing scenario although, to be perfectly fair to all concerned, Ralph did concede that if 'Going to the Pub' was ever included as an Olympic event we would probably do quite well at it.

The Beautiful Game

Football provides the perfect example of how youngsters are denied an opportunity to progress and live their dreams because of the Grand Canyon-sized gap that has been allowed to develop between the haves and the have-nots. It works roughly as follows.

At the top end, Premiership players squeeze vast amounts of cash out of the game to finance their fabulous lifestyles. This consists of training for a couple of hours in the morning if they can manage to get up and then watching TV and eating chocolates all afternoon until it's time to get in their Maseratis and go to the pub. Obviously this only applies to those that don't already own their own pub.

But at the other end of the scale conditions for ordinary folk are deplorable. Kids, poor little blighters, are made to change in freezing cold, tin shacks and then sent out to play on council-owned, bumpy mud-heaps without really knowing what they're supposed to do. How on earth will this generate any enthusiasm? It's more likely to put them off the game altogether. Yet despite the gargantuan amounts of tax we all pay, the authorities won't provide even the most rudimentary facilities for them to learn a sport properly either in school or out of it.

It is not as if we are talking about decadent luxuries that are way above our means. Only what is absolutely essential to a happy and healthy lifestyle. But in the end it is parents who have to do everything and you have to ask what the fuck we pay taxes for. They'll have us sweeping the fucking streets next!

However, lest anyone misunderstand, this diatribe has nothing to do with envy. It concerns only the quality of life that by now should be assured for everyone in these modern times. Unfortunately though, after spending great wads of hard-earned cash blasting our foreign brothers and sisters out of Baghdad, Belgrade and the Falklands there isn't much of left over for basics. No wonder everything else is under-funded. No wonder we can't produce any world class sportspeople. In a society that always insists on describing itself as civilised, it's a fucking disgrace. On behalf every tax paying person in the country I now pose the question to which I believe we would all appreciate an answer. Where the fuck does all our fucking money go?

44
Horny Harold and the Mayor's Knickers

They'd been going for a couple of months and, much to Ralph's gratification, a semblance of football know-how had started to become evident amongst the lads. But one week, the normal Wednesday evening slot for footy training coincided with parents' evening at the school most of them attended so he switched it to the Thursday instead.

Ralph knew there was a free slot in the hall on Thursdays but despite a number of attempts, he couldn't get hold of Harold the caretaker on the phone to confirm the change. But he had his own key so he decided to just get on with it and let handyman Harold, as he called him, know later. He made a point of arriving a little early that evening because some of the balls needed pumping up and he wanted to prepare a circuit for ball skill training. Letting himself in Ralph went to the storeroom to get the equipment out but as soon as he opened the door an extraordinary sight stopped him dead in his tracks. He found himself face to face with a spotty, fat, wobbly ass heaving up and down on top of the unmistakable form of a rather large female who was being mounted from behind. The female, who was about the size and shape of a smallish whale, was lying on a pile of rubber mats with her feet pushing down on the floor for leverage. The intrepid rider was standing behind her, knees bent and supported by his grubby hands that were desperately clutching the folds of fat surrounding the area where her waist must once have been. The two were so passionately involved they didn't notice Ralph even though he had switched the light on. In fact, they were grunting and farting so much he didn't think they'd have noticed if he'd started a motorbike up in the room. Ralph leaned against the doorframe and watched them for a while. He could hardly believe it. It was Harold, the podgy, unkempt, mostly drunk, 63 year-old caretaker caught in flagrante! Now he knew there was hope for us all. The old sod was totally starkers except for his thick, woolly socks and sweat streamed down his back to form a little pool on the floor in between his feet. His friend (Ralph assumed she was a friend of his) had hiked her skirt up around her waist to accommodate him. Her very ample thermal knickers which seemed to consist of enough material for at least two double duvets billowed around her ankles like a parachute that had come to rest after landing. It occurred to Ralph that he wouldn't mind knowing who she was. Theirs was a small town and he'd be likely to know her if she was local, but of course she was facing the other way. The huge amounts of sweat-covered cellulite that bubbled all over her massive, shaking, jerking thighs indicated that she must have been about the same age as Harold. There was something slightly familiar about her voice even though the rather high-pitched squeals emanating loudly and rhythmically from her well-endowed person sounded more like a hamster being violently rogered by Arnold Schwarzenegger than any human utterance. The whole room was filled with a strangely pungent odour that must have been similar to the inside of a Mongolian wrestler's jock strap. Ralph was just about to leave when Harold's movements intensified and his friend began to make a hell of a row not unlike a constipated elephant taking its first crap for three weeks. He decided it was worth hanging around to witness the conclusion of matters although he was a little apprehensive about what might happen if the kids arrived because they were clearly not expected.

As the actions of the carousing couple became more rapid their skins took on an increasingly crimson, blotchy hue. They were juddering and heaving and shaking and straining and moaning and then suddenly the female participant of this passion play began to scream in rhythm with their movements 'For or AGAINST! For or AGAINST! For or AGAINST!' She was about to explode all over the place. Ralph could see the headline now 'Three drown in love tryst!' Harold stopped moving and just for a moment or two his face went blank as if his brain had just been removed and suddenly his friend, fat ass, shuddered like a maniac and began to yell 'ABSTAIN! ABSTAIN!' It was then that Ralph recognised the desperate sound emanating from the quivering mass of blancmange before him as belonging to none other than the Lady Mayor of the town. 'Blimey' he thought quietly to himself and slipped out of the door.

Now this was a woman who embodied the absolute essence of respectability, virtue and good taste as far as anyone knew. She was respected as the firmest and most reliable pillar of local society but ever since that day Ralph had tended to think of her more as possessing the firmest and most reliable pair of tits in local society.

She was a regular churchgoer, a tireless worker for various charities and an avid campaigner for less sex and violence on television. 'Because it influences the kids in a bad way and they can't control themselves.'

Now Ralph had absolutely no objection to this formidable lady obtaining whatever gratification she needed in whatever way she needed it but it never failed to surprise him that the more ostensibly respectable the person, the more grubby and basic their secret habits and practices. We tended to revere these figures of authority as if they possessed some kind of higher moral integrity and knew what was best for us mere mortals beneath them but Ralph was quite sure they bloody well didn't. As for Harold, well he was just a horny, drunk old bugger but he never made a secret of it.

Ralph left them to their gruesome grappling because he could hear the boys arriving and it would have been most embarrassing for everybody if they had invaded the storeroom just at that moment looking for the footballs.

About fifteen minutes after they'd started the session, the storeroom door opened and out stepped her ladyship looking slightly flushed but immaculate and without a hair out of place. Her make-up wasn't at all smeared as it had been a little earlier and the mayoral chain now hung proudly around her neck to indicate to everybody the true level of importance and respect to which she was entitled.

Harold followed her out in nonchalant fashion with one hand in his pocket and the other holding his usual cigarette. His shirttail was poking out through his trouser fly. They shook hands as if she was just concluding an official visit and with a deft jerk of the wrist that suggested she was quite familiar with the procedure, swung open the rear exit door which led into a side alley and disappeared into the night.

The Beautiful Game

Creating Space

Drawing defenders out of position is a vital part of the game and in many cases just as valuable as actually scoring because by pulling the other team out of shape you create space for the striker to get his chance. You must create space for each other. You can't play without space to play in.

In junior football, whenever it comes round to picking a player of the season the prize is nearly always awarded to the highest goal-scorer in the team and for weeks afterwards the bighead ponces around thinking he's a hero. This is completely wrong and junior teams should desist from the practice of making such awards. Not that a defender or the goalkeeper should get the awards instead. No, these awards should not be made at all. They contradict the most basic purpose of the game which is that it is, and always was, for a team of players working together.

Those involved in the vital task of coaching juniors should encourage them to understand that everybody's contribution is equally important including the subs who turn out week after week without even getting on the pitch let alone a special award. Actually, it is also wrong to make players turn up week after week without getting on at all. It happens all the time in the junior game but it won't help the poor buggers to improve or learn and might even put them off the game altogether. It won't help the team either because when these sometimes-hardly-but-not-very-often players do get their chance they will probably be too nervous to play well.

This also goes for the left back and left winger too.

All right, I know. If it is a most sacred tenet that every member of the team is equally as important as every other, why mention these two positions in particular?

Because some so-called football coaches incorrectly regard them as less important. The reason for this is that there are relatively few left-footed players around and nobody wants to play there.

Often, a weaker player selected as a makeweight for the team will be dispatched to the left wing where it is considered he won't do much damage if he makes a mistake. The weedier, skinnier type of nonentity is most likely to draw this particular short straw.

At left back it's the same story with the exception that it is more usually the beefier type of not-so-good player who gets shoved into this role with the idea that even if he is useless he might just manage to get a tackle in.

This is a wholly mistaken attitude and just sticking youngsters in without advice or instruction does neither the player, nor the team or the game any good at all. It is far more logical to shift better players to the left even if they are right-footed and let the weaker players play where they feel most comfortable and confident. Good players always seem to get their own way far too much. Bastards!

I'm right-footed but when I was young I used to turn up and offer to play left wing in senior matches just to get a game. It nearly always worked and of course, once you're on you can go anywhere.

It is up to the coach in junior football to work with the weaker players and help them discover their abilities rather than just tolerating them because they want to play football and there's no one else available.

If you take the trouble to work with players who want to play but have no obvious talent for the game you will find positive attributes that can be developed enough to allow them to fulfil a useful function in the team. But if, as coach of a junior side, you are unwilling to exert a little energy in this respect and prefer to adopt the 'He's no good to me' attitude that is so very prevalent then it is probably better if you don't bother with football.

Take up crochet or cookery or origami instead. Anything where you can be on your own and not interfering with kids who want to learn how to play football.

Everyone, even the most useless player ever, has the right to play and to enjoy playing and to be respected and helped by the coach and the rest of his team-mates.

Bear in mind that junior players develop at different times so those who may appear weaker at first may come stronger later. And vice-versa.

And that's in life by the way, not just football.

45
Larry, Gary, Barry and Carrie

In the end they stole that team from Ralph. It was daylight robbery.

There was a bloke called Larry who used to bring his two boys down to the session right from the beginning. Their names were Gary and Barry but he used to call them Ga' and Ba' for short. This always made Ralph laugh and he once said to Larry, 'I bet you're dying to have another and call it Harry, even if it's a girl.' But he could tell Larry didn't see the funny side of it. Of course, he didn't know the whole story then.

Larry's wife, the boys' mother, had apparently walked out on them overnight and gone to live with Larry's best friend. Ralph couldn't quite understand this when he first heard about it. How could any mother do that? But he did now.

From the day she left, the boys never saw their mother again. She just seemed to lose interest altogether so Larry was left to bring them up by himself. He was bitter about it. Every time the subject came up his eyes spat venomous looks all around. The friend who had gone off with the wife was a lot better off than Larry. But Larry did have the great advantage of having almost paid off his mortgage so when the split first occurred he felt fairly secure about continuing to provide a comfortable home for his lads. However, true to form in these situations, things took a decidedly nasty turn for the worse when the wife, Carrie (yes, really) tryed to force Larry to sell the house. She was claiming half the equity through the divorce proceedings seemingly with no regard to where her own boys would live in the future. Larry was gutted. He was a fairly simple bloke and had no idea how to deal with the situation. But he insisted on shouldering all the responsibility himself and the kids never wanted for anything. Ralph admired his stoic attitude. After all, it would have been easy enough for Larry to leave the boys with his mother while he went out looking for a new wife or at least got his leg over from time to time.

Ralph couldn't help but sympathise and did what he could to help. He even wrote letters of reference on Larry's behalf. He thought Larry was a genuinely nice bloke, albeit a bit limited in outlook, who was grateful for the friendship and encouragement he offered. Little could he have predicted how Larry would eventually shaft him so ruthlessly and painfully right up the arse.

Of the boys, Gary, was the right age but Barry was a bit too young for the session so he used to sit with his dad on a bench at the side of the hall watching the other boys play. But he looked so forlorn that Ralph eventually took pity and let him join in. Then it was Larry who was left to sit by himself on the sidelines looking utterly glum so Ralph took pity on him too and asked him if he fancied helping out. He thought Larry would jump at the chance to be involved and he was right. Geoff had long since taken to the comfort of the pub on training nights so Ralph was on his own and grateful for any help he could get. Larry's assistance, even though he had never played the game at any decent level and didn't really know much about it, was very welcome.

As the weeks and months rolled by, Larry became more and more involved and even took the group by himself on the odd occasion when Ralph couldn't make it for one reason or another. He knew all the parents much better than Ralph because he had grown up with a lot of them whereas Ralph had only lived in the area for about nine years. Not enough to qualify for full human rights around those parts of deepest rural England. He often used to joke that he was surprised they didn't stamp a visa in your passport when you entered Herefordshire. But his sense of humour didn't cut any ice with the locals. They stared at him as if he had horns growing out of his head. It didn't even help much that he'd married a local girl. Ralph found out later in a discussion with a Town Council member that this was because Sophie wasn't 'really local'. She hadn't been born in the area. She had only lived there since the age of six.

But by the time Ralph had realised the true extent of local suspicion towards outsiders, it was all over. A huge row had raged out of control, Larry had surreptitiously transferred the entire team to another club and Ralph was out. He had been too daft in the three years since starting, coaching and funding the lads to see what was coming. He had thought it was all about passing his knowledge and love of the great game of football on to the next generation but in the end it was all about local politics and jealousies.

THE BEAUTIFUL GAME

All for One and One for All

Criticism by a player of either a team-mate or the coach is definitely out and if it happens in a game or in training the player committing this offence should either be subbed or sent from the field immediately.

People trying their best don't deserve criticism even if they make a mistake. Everybody makes mistakes and no one deliberately tries to make a mistake so if someone makes a mistake it's just a mistake. You can't turn the clock back, you just have to get over it and get on with it.

Once the moment is gone you can't change what has already happened but with the right attitude you may be able to exert a positive influence on what happens next.

Of course, the chances of this are greatly diminished if you're in a strop and feeling angry with a team-mate or sorry for yourself.

Castigating the poor lad who has scored an own goal or missed a golden opportunity to score at the right end will only make him anxious and deplete his confidence and if you have a go at him the chances are he will make another mistake. You can be quite sure that he already feels terrible about it. Much worse than you do. Kids need to be encouraged when they make mistakes, not treated like idiots.

After all, they're just learning the game.

Actually, any football professional will tell you that you never stop learning no matter how old or experienced you might be.

So don't be bigheaded. Learn something!

Let's learn together.

46
The Boys From Brazil

This was how it happened.

After a few months of training the team began to play cracking good football.

Like Brazil at times Ralph thought. He had managed to get the boys passing and running off the ball which you don't often see at this age. Everyone remarked on the intelligent football they played.

In their first two seasons Ralph had organised a few friendlies all of which they won fairly easily even including a few against older opposition. Then they entered the local 10 and under league under the banner of Town and had every reason to look forward to their first experience of proper competitive football.

For the first part of the season the lads played well and didn't lose a match even against clubs from much larger places with many more players to choose from and a long tradition of coaching junior players through to senior football.

The spirit amongst them was excellent and, in one match against just such an established club, they displayed a perfect example of the sort of teamwork and camaraderie that Ralph was striving to bring about. It was a close fought encounter against a well-organised side that was also used to winning.

Approaching half-time there was no score. Town were on the attack but they lost the ball and it was hoofed unceremoniously out of defence towards their opponents' number nine who was the only player in a forward position at the time. In fact, he was a good twenty yards or so into Town's half and at least ten yards offside. The linesman, who was actually one of the opponents lad's parents, flagged quite furiously but the ref waved play on much to the amazement of everyone watching. Even the boy with the ball pulled up in the expectation of being penalised but still had enough time to gather his wits and go on to score. Ralph's lads were furious and so was Ralph. He'd spent hours teaching them how to deal with the offside rule and they had combined perfectly to bring about an offside situation but were now being penalised for it. Ralph remonstrated with the ref who threatened to report him to the local FA if he didn't shut up and when he continued to press, threatened to send him from the touchline altogether. Mind you, how the official might actually have achieved this was open to conjecture, as they were playing in a public park.

At half-time the boys were complaining about the offside goal which had completely pissed them off. Ralph adopted his philosophical tone.

'Put it out of your minds,' he told them, 'It's in the past. Gone. It doesn't matter any more. Forget it. You're playing well enough to win so just go out and show them who's the best team here.'

'They're just a bunch of cheats,' someone said and they all nodded in agreement.

'No,' Ralph insisted, 'Put it behind you, it's just a rotten decision. It happens in football sometimes. You just have to accept it and get on with it.'

But he could tell they didn't want to let it go and began to wonder if they knew more about it than he did. They certainly knew he didn't like them to argue with him but they were obviously bursting to say more on the subject.

The dressing room went quiet for a minute until Ralph's son Joe took it upon himself and piped up.

'It wasn't a mistake Dad,' he announced with an authority and maturity that impressed Ralph. 'It was deliberate.' Such a way of expression for an eight year old! These boys were growing up before his very eyes.

'How can you be so sure?' asked Ralph, fairly certain in a pompous sort of way that his question would end the dialogue.

'Cos it's his son,' answered Ralph's son.

'What are you talking about? Who is whose son?'

'The boy who scored,' Larry interjected. 'The ref's his Dad.'

'What?'

'It's true.'

'Is it?'

'They do it all the time,' Larry continued. 'All the other teams are fed up with 'em. That kid's the league's top scorer.'

Ralph was taken aback. He wasn't having this.

'The cheating bastards,' he pronounced. 'It's a bloody disgrace' He was bloody annoyed. He had the urge to write to FIFA about it.

'Well you're not going to let them get away with it are you?' Ralph felt his voice rising. He began gesticulating like an Israeli politician and knew his face must be turning as red as the beetroots in the fields around them. Deliberate cheating was against everything he stood for and it made his blood boil. There was absolutely no merit whatsoever in winning by cheating and he had always tried to impress this on the boys. In a voice now quivering with passion he gave them their orders.

'Get out there and show them how to bloody well play football will you. They must be really desperate if they think that's the only way they can win. But you can beat them even if they do cheat!'

A communal cheer went up. They were together on it.

The lads of Town took to the field for the second half with a new spirit of belief and Ralph knew it would carry them through. He was right, they won. Now they knew that if you wanted to succeed you needed self-belief and he felt they were really getting somewhere.

The Beautiful Game

Clever Trousers

Take up unusual positions to confuse your marker, make him afraid to go with you into strange places that are uncharted territory for him.

Don't do the obvious thing all the time. Why not?

Because it's obvious and everybody's got it sussed, nitwit.

You've got to be clever if you want to play football.

Bloody clever.

Johann Cruyff said that football is a game you play with your brain.

Let's face it, he should know.

Make it easy for each other, you'll enjoy it much more.

You need to be brighter, sharper, keener, faster and smarter than the other side, in other words, more alive.

It is absolutely certain that the possibilities created by people co-operating together are far greater than the total sum of possibilities created by those same people working independently.

And that's in life, by the way, not just in football.

47
Tactics and the Beano

Over the months Larry had taken on certain duties which Ralph found a great help.

He had only started the team in order to teach the lads how to play the game which was quite a commitment in itself. But running a side involved a lot of other stuff like getting the lads signed on, being in touch with the league secretary about fixtures, contacting the players about this that and the other, learning first aid. Stuff that he didn't really have time for. He had to make a living whilst Larry was unemployed and relished the chance to make himself useful. Anyway, Ralph was also spending a great deal of time in meetings with club officials, council officers and consultants trying to get some funding to build a proper stadium with decent training facilities which they needed terribly. Consequently, there was a limit to how much time he could spend on the kids although he still provided them with two training sessions a week which was one more than all the other teams had. Larry got to know the league officials, took a course in first aid, organised the laundry rota for the kit, put the nets up before matches and kept in touch with the lads in the squad. This wasn't too difficult because most of them lived on the same housing estate as he did so he saw them all the time anyway. Many of the parents were his personal friends. Old school chums or drinking partners. But Ralph didn't know that then and wouldn't have thought it sinister or particularly significant if he had. He must have been bloody naïve.

By this time Town had become the side to beat and all the parents were calculating how many points they might get and how many would be enough to win the league.

They all started to get far too involved in the whole thing for Ralph's taste. Making suggestions about team selection, tactics and, worst of all, wanting to have a player of the match and a player of the season. All the nonsense Ralph didn't want or believe in.

He'd always coached the boys to play as a team and not for personal glory and certainly didn't want to place any of them on a pedestal of merit higher than the others. It was always goal-scorers who won these bloody things anyway.

It wasn't as if any of the parents knew anything about the game and Ralph resented their intrusion. He was the one who'd had the idea for the team and found the time and money to get it going. Now they were making out that they knew better than he did.

In the beginning, coaching sessions had been an hour of cheap baby-sitting for most of them and just a bit of a lark for the kids but now that it was showing signs of success they all wanted a piece of it. They had started to dream of championships and cups and awards. Ralph wondered if it was some kind of vicarious urge to fulfil a missing element of their own lives through their kids. He even found out that one of the dads had offered his son a fiver for every goal he scored and twenty quid if he scored a hat trick! It was almost criminal as far as Ralph was concerned but the bloke in question refused to listen when he asked him very nicely to please stop doing it.

There Ralph was, freezing his bollocks off for an hour and a half, twice a week trying to instil in those lads the great merit of working as a team and one of them was being encouraged to ignore him and score goals for himself. No wonder the little bastard had stopped passing the ball.

But although Ralph also wanted the team to win every time they played, that wasn't the main issue for him. How they played was just as important. After all, they were just kids, learning the game.

At a meeting called by a couple of the parents to discuss these things, Ralph said 'Look, don't put pressure on these boys. The main thing is that they enjoy it and learn to work together as a team. If they win something, that will be great but don't push them to feel that they have to win just to please you lot. I've always believed that the possibilities created by people working together are far greater than the sum of possibilities of those same people working independently. And that's in life, by the way, not just in football.'

But they didn't get it. They looked at him with blank expressions. One of them coughed nervously, someone else said, 'That's all bollocks' and they started to drift away.

Obviously they didn't understand a thing he'd said. Of course, afterwards Ralph realised they all thought the playing success was down to Larry.

He'd noticed that Larry had taken to wearing a new Man U stadium coat just like Alex Ferguson. Incidentally, Larry was another Man U fan. Almost everyone on his entire estate was. They should have called it Moss Side, Herefordshire.

He had a brand new first-aid kit that he had made himself. A shiny, polished wooden box with lots of compartments in it. He also had a milk bottle carrier in which he carried a dozen Umbro drinking flasks that he used to throw to the lads when they came off the pitch. He did look very professional.

Ralph used to let Larry warm the kids up before the match and never minded if he gave the impression he was the manager of the side. Ralph wasn't in it for personal glory or status. Later, too late really, he realised that this was taken as a sign of weakness.

During the matches Ralph would pass his instructions on to Larry who would relay them to the team. If he wanted a substitution to be made, Larry would signal to the ref and call off the lad he was withdrawing. If a player got injured, Larry would race on with his wooden box and squirt water all over the poor sod who would quickly get to his feet to prevent himself getting double pneumonia.

The parents all got the mistaken idea that Larry was running things and Ralph was just along for the ride. At the time Ralph didn't realise this and so did nothing to counter the false assumption. But it was he who coached the boys, picked the team, devised the tactics and motivated them with his witty, philosophical speeches. He'd paid for all the fucking kit as well.

Most of the other teams they faced played a sort of 5-3-2. But none of them kept their shape very well and often drifted haplessly to a 9-1 when they all stopped thinking and just ran around after the ball like headless chickens. To Ralph, the majority of teams were very badly organised and, once the game had started, whatever happened, happened. Sort of trial and error. But he'd taught his boys to be sure of what they were doing at all times or as much as possible anyway, given their age. He'd devised different formations specially for players of their experience and ability and changed things around according to circumstances unlike the other sides, most of which had the single instruction to kick the ball upfield and run after it. He also invented some innovative set pieces that brought the team a fair amount of success. Ralph could read a game but Larry had difficulty reading the Beano. Of course, the more it went on the more Larry got the credit for everything but Ralph wasn't paying attention to that.

'Come on lads,' he'd shout from time to time, 'Let's have some sexy football.'

The Beautiful Game
Psycho-Tactics

With kids, 95 per cent is about confidence. Poor body language gives away far too much if they let it. A goal goes against them, heads go down, their opponents pick up on it and push on for the second. It's hard for juniors to muster the psychic energy to come back from two down. So an altogether different type of coaching is required along with the ball skills, fitness and tactics. I call it psycho-tactics. It starts from the kick off.

In a professional match at the whistle you often see the centre forward tap the ball sideways to another front player who passes it back to a midfielder outside the centre circle who then plays a simple square ball as the team starts to build from the back. When coaching young kids, advise them against doing this. They don't yet have the knowledge to build a move in this way and what they need is confidence. What can happen when kids follow this standard opening manoeuvre is that while they are passing the ball back the opposition are pushing forward. This results in having to pass it back even further and before you know it, you're in a deep defensive position having lost the advantage of the possession you started with. The psychological edge has been handed to the other side who are now in an attacking position straight from your kick off. With junior football often resembling a war of attrition, it can take some time to recover from this. Particularly if the other lot are able to take full advantage of the gift you handed them and score straight away. Of course, we don't want it to be war of attrition but a flowing, passing exercise that allows everyone involved to express themselves in such a way that we will all be enriched by the experience.

Now there's a thought!

We must try and retain the psychological advantage at all times. Heads up. Fully focussed. Energetic and workmanlike. Looking confident even if we feel like shit. If we're losing it's only a temporary state of affairs and we know how to change it. Don't we? Yes we do. Courage and confidence lads. Let's go forward! Let's be positive!

An excellent tactic if you have the kickoff in junior games is for player 1 to tap the ball sideways to player 2 who lays it back but only a very short distance to player 3 who is prepared and ready to kick the ball deep into the opponents' half. At the same time our whole team, even the goalkeeper, moves forward swiftly. By the time the ball lands somewhere near their penalty area our forwards and midfield are in a forward position with the defence pushed up to the halfway line and the goalkeeper on the edge of his area. The effect is to put the opposition on the back foot right at the start and this psychological advantage can be crucial to the pattern of the game particularly if you can get that early goal. Kids always play much better when they're ahead. They are much more relaxed. Let's be clear about this though. It isn't a tactic I recommend for the whole game but only at the kick-off to try and gain a quick advantage. The kick and rush style (or kick and hope as it is sometimes called) is a boring way to play and we want to be more creative than that. Don't we? Of course we do.

If the other side have the kick off we have to go about things another way which brings us back to my earlier statement about possession. It may sound silly but you simply cannot play football if you haven't got the ball and if you haven't got it you have to go and get it. It can't be stated too often. If you've got the ball you're in control of the game.

In junior games, players don't always seem to accept the kickoff whistle as the actual start of proceedings. They wander about for a while, half-asleep, waiting for something to happen. But they are the ones who must make it happen. They don't want to be reacting to what the other side does. They must force their opponents to react to them. So then, let your opponents know they're in a match right from the start. When the whistle goes (or a split second earlier if they're sharp enough) get after them. Move in fast and hard and show them you mean business. Don't even let them draw breath. Harry them mercilessly until you get the ball. If we want to win we must put in a challenge. We must be bright, alert, determined and right on top of the situation from the first moment of the game. The opponents will be thinking, 'Blimey, this lot are up for it.' And when we do get the ball, we must keep it.

That's our ball and they can't fucking well have it.

48
Baldy and Gargantua

As the season progressed, the atmosphere at matches was becoming increasingly intense albeit more amongst the parents than the players. During one needle match that was taking place on a desolate cow patch in a godforsaken backwater somewhere in the back of beyond Ralph thought there was going to be a riot. How grown up people could manage this in the middle of nowhere was beyond his comprehension but in the event it turned quite nasty. As a rule, Town had what they considered quite a good following with many of the boys' parents, siblings and grandparents regularly coming to support the lads. It was usually about a couple of dozen at away matches, more than most teams. But as they turned up at the opponents' ground in the small village that was the venue for this particular match, they were amazed to find a crowd of hundreds of people gathered around the pitch all eagerly awaiting the start of proceedings. It must have been almost the entire population. Looking around, Ralph noticed that the locals seemed to be treating the occasion like a carnival. There was a barbecue going and a bouncy castle, a few cake stalls and a beer tent. But nobody offered them so much as a cup of tea. There wasn't even anywhere for the boys to get changed. They had to find a quiet corner and change out in the open which is very embarrassing for young lads just on the edge of puberty. Ralph tried to complain about it but couldn't find anyone prepared to admit to any responsibility in the matter.

The home players were already out on the pitch and warming up. Apparently, they used a pub hall just up the road to get changed but they hadn't invited Town to join them as football etiquette would normally require.

As soon as the match started, so did the trouble or so it seemed to Ralph. The home team was very physical right from the start and some of their tackles made him wince. But then a challenge went in from one of Town's players that ended up with a home player on the ground crying his eyes out. Their manager, a podgy, balding forty-something wearing a Man U carcoat (standard issue for Herefordshire Junior Football League coaches), immediately ran on to the pitch waving his arms and shouting at Ralph's boys until the ref ushered him back to the sideline. He carried on muttering things like 'disgusting' and 'foul play' and 'never seen anything like it' and so on and seemed to be directing this invective at the Town contingent. Ralph couldn't see what all the fuss was about. He didn't even think it was a foul. But when the ref gave Baldy's lot a free kick the fat git shut up and they carried on. Baldy then took to deliberately walking up and down in front of Ralph and Larry and the Town supporters. He was accompanied by a great amazon of a woman with a red face and wild blonde hair who Ralph assumed was his wife because she was wearing a Man U tracksuit top. As she lurched along behind him, ranting and screaming, the garment rode right up over her massive posterior which wobbled about inside a pair of lycra leggings that struggled to contain it. The over-tight, over-stretched fabric outlined every ripple of fat on her gargantuan thighs. On the frequent occasions she stooped to extract a packet of cigarettes from the Man U kit bag that lay near the touchline she displayed a pronounced builder's crack much to the great amusement of the watching world.

The hideous couple smoked incessantly as they lurched around scowling angrily and screaming their heads off with white nicotine clouds billowing crazily out of their mouths. Afterwards Ralph found out that they ran the pub where their boys had got changed. The two of them were an absolute nightmare, shouting at Town's parents, shouting at the boys, shouting at the ref, blowing smoke over everyone and running onto the pitch to protest almost every decision except those in their favour. Neither Ralph nor any of his merry band had ever encountered such churlish behaviour.

'Ignore it, humour them,' Ralph advised his entourage.

So they smiled at each other and tried not to react but Ralph had a feeling it wouldn't last.

'Look at them,' screamed Gargantua, 'They're laughing at us.' And aggressive waves of hate started to drift over from the body of home supporters.

Every time the terrible two shouted or ran on to the pitch they drew a loud surge of response from the substantial home crowd most of whom were now deliberately attempting to intimidate the relatively small visiting contingent with a constant stream of bellowed insults.

Baldy and Gargantua then became quite openly menacing and started to bump and jostle Ralph and Larry each time they passed by. It was getting ridiculous. Worse than being at Millwall. Eventually, some of Town's parents couldn't prevent themselves from reacting with aggressive comments like 'Act your age,' or 'Idiots,' or 'Don't be silly, they're only eight year olds.' One or two began to square up in a serious sort of way.

'I'll knock his fucking head off in minute,' said John, the normally mild-mannered father of Town's mild-mannered centre half. Bunched with the rest he obviously felt very macho but Ralph didn't think he would have said such a thing if he'd been on his own. Normally he wouldn't have said boo to a goose.

'Come on lads!' Ralph shouted. 'Let's have some sexy football!'

Just before half time, two of their players and one of Town's were challenging for the ball and it ended up with the three of them in a heap on the ground. The home players were in tears with one clutching his leg and the other his face. Baldy and Fatso immediately ran on to the pitch and started shouting at the ref, wagging their fingers at Town's lad who was clearly mystified by it all and waving their arms in such a way as to indicate that they wanted him sent off. But Ralph had seen quite clearly what had happened and it had nothing to do with his player. As they'd approached the bouncing ball, one of the opposing players had managed to trip up his own team-mate and Ralph thought they were crying more out of embarrassment than because they were hurt. But by now it was obvious that their lads all seemed to dissolve in tears at the slightest provocation. The whole place was in an uproar over the incident. The ref sent Baldy away and he made a beeline for Ralph.

'That's it,' he said with an angry scowl. 'I'm taking my players off. Someone's going to get injured with this sort of dirty play. It's too dangerous.'

'Don't be so fucking silly,' Ralph told him. He'd had enough.

Baldy stiffened and walked right up to him.

'What did you say?' he asked.

They were eyeball to eyeball now.

'You heard'

'Right, I'm reporting you,' he announced, and turned to shout at the distant figure of the ref about fifty yards away. 'He swore at me ref, take his name.'

By his dismissive response it was obvious that the ref had also had enough of the moron.

Baldy was dragged away by some of his parents muttering things like 'Hooligans, cheats, thugs, don't know how to play fair.'

'Come on lads,' Ralph shouted. 'Sexy football now.'

Baldy and his mate looked back at Ralph as if he were some kind of pervert.

On the restart, Town were awarded a free kick much to Baldy and Fatso's disgust. They were practically apoplectic by this time. Ralph was sure one of them would burst a blood vessel if they carried on like this.

In the circumstances he was pleased that his own lads had resisted the temptation to retaliate. Despite the provocation, they hadn't argued with the ref and certainly weren't deliberately fouling or playing dirty. They wouldn't have known how to anyway. It was against everything they had been taught. 'Hard but fair' Ralph always told them.

Town took the free kick and the ball was lobbed high into the middle of the penalty area. It wasn't cleared properly and pinged around for a while, bouncing off players like a pin ball machine. Finally, their goalkeeper gave it a great heaving wallop with the intention of clearing the bloody thing once and for all but it shot straight in the direction of his own centre half who instinctively turned his back to avoid getting it in the face. The poor lad couldn't have known much about what happened but he certainly must have felt the ball rebound off the back of his head and zoom upwards. It seemed to be in the air forever. Everyone watched open mouthed as it looped back over the goalie and came to rest in the back of the goal. Town had scored! Wild cheers and clapping suddenly broke out from the away brigade whilst the home supporters, having made a great noise up until now, went eerily silent. Baldy and Gargantua were absolutely livid. Naturally, they tried to claim it was offside but that was a little farfetched considering that at least six of their players had been standing on the goal line at the time and none of Town's players was the last to touch it anyway.

It was half-time. When the game restarted, a curious incident occurred that Ralph still couldn't quite believe to this day. One of Town's lads had a brother called Chris who was afflicted with cerebral palsy. He loved his football and always enjoyed coming to matches when he was well enough. His grandad, Len, used to bring him along in his wheelchair and Chris was there that day wearing his beloved Man U shirt as usual.

Just after half time Len said, 'He's a bit restless, I think I'll take him for a walk round the pitch.'

And off they went fairly slowly because it was muddy and quite hard going if you were pushing a wheelchair. They reached a point behind one of the goals where Len stopped to roll himself a cigarette. Chris was having a great time. Whenever the home crowd reacted to things on the field with their raucous shouting he waved his arms about and shouted back. Ralph thought he would have taken them all on by himself if necessary. All of a sudden, Baldy was on the field again talking to the referee and pointing at Len and Chris behind the goal.

'What the fuck is it this time?' Ralph asked one of the parents.

'Dunno,' came the response. 'Talk about throwing toys out of the fucking pram.'

The ref waved Baldy away and ran over to talk to Len and

Chris. They seemed to be chatting for some time. Then the ref ran back to restart the game for the umpteenth time and Len began pushing Chris back from whence they came.

'What was that all about then?' Ralph asked Len when they arrived back.

''He said we were putting their goalkeeper off and we had to move.'

'You're fucking joking'

'I'm fucking not,' said Len. 'I'll tell you something else, he's reporting Chris to the FA.'

'What?' exclaimed Ralph, 'Why the fuck does he want to do that?'

'He said Chris was making fun of him,' said Len.

'I've never heard of anything so fucking ridiculous in all my life,' said Ralph.

'Try this,' said Len. 'He says Chris should be banned from matches. Says he's a bad influence.' Chris started banging the arms of his chair furiously.

Turning his face up to the sky, Chris mustered all the energy of which he was capable and issued a plaintive cry. 'Fucking thtupid!'

Ralph and Len to peered down at him in total disbelief. They were the first coherent words the lad had uttered in over six months.

But there was worse to come. One of Town's lads, Jaspal, was an Asian lad and his dad, Raj, who wore a turban, always came to watch his son play. At one stage Jaspal was on the ball when a derogatory remark could be heard most distinctly during a lull in the hubbub of the crowd. A little later the word towel-head came wafting on the breeze in Raj's direction. The home fans now seemed to be doing their best to create a racist incident.

Ralph heard the insults and was incensed. Mindless prejudice really pissed him off. He braced himself to walk over and remonstrate with the numbskulls who had initiated this unsavoury development, but Raj realised what he was about to do and held him back. 'Don't,' he said.

'But we can't have this Raj,' he said. ' We just cannot have it'.

'Please don't,' Raj pleaded. 'We know all about it. We're used to it. Please don't cause any bother on our behalf.'

'Look Raj,' said Ralph. 'If we don't do something about this they'll all get their pointy hats out and start burning crosses in their fucking gardens.'

'I beg you,' said Raj. 'Think of the boy.'

Ralph saw what he meant. It might turn into an embarrassing situation for Jaspal. Here was a real dilemma. How could he just let it pass without doing anything about it?

However, any decision on the matter was put in abeyance because, just at that moment, with only a minute or two of the game left, the whole situation changed dramatically. Ralph didn't see exactly what happened because he was talking to Raj at the time but suddenly the whole place erupted. He turned towards the pitch to see the ref pointing to the centre circle and his boys looking pretty glum and immediately realised that the others had scored an equaliser. With kids, body language usually gives you a pretty accurate picture of the state of things.

It was bedlam. The entire home crowd had invaded the playing area and were all dancing madly around like dervishes. Baldy was hugging Gargantua and everyone seemed to be cheering and doing high fives. The boys in their team had embarked on an elaborate celebration, including jumping and crawling and wiggling their asses. They had obviously spent more time practising this nonsense than actual football. What a bunch of absolute prats! Ralph could hardly believe it.

The scene reminded Ralph of that early Cup Final when the crowd swarmed onto the pitch and were dispersed by a policeman on a white horse. He looked around but the nearest to a white horse he could see was a moth-eaten old donkey tethered in the adjacent field and the only thing it was dispersing in a steaming mass on the grass was the gruesome content of its bowels.

THE BEAUTIFUL GAME

Scenario One

The game has started and you're the man on the ball on the left-hand side of the pitch about halfway into your opponents half and ten yards in from the touch-line.

There are two opposing defenders in front of you.

None of your team-mates are within ten yards of the ball. Your left winger has pushed on behind the defenders facing you and is marked by another defender but is frantically shouting for a pass. The centre forward has run into the middle of the penalty box and is also screaming for a cross even though he is marked by two defenders who are right up his arse. Your left back is standing next to you and is almost treading on your toes in a total dither. Obviously, he's wondering what's for tea.

The only other team-mate you can see is your centre half who is loping forward from the centre circle with a tentative expression and an unsure rhythm as if suddenly afflicted with an attack of piles.

What do you do?

You can't pass forward through the opposing players in front of you. There is no one behind you, the centre forward is too far away and to add to your problems, a square ball to the centre half is fraught with danger. Why? Because if it is intercepted by the other side they will be on the break very quickly and if fatty cocks it up they'll be on the break even bloody quicker.

In modern soccer parlance a player facing this sort of unfortunate dilemma is technically referred to as being 'completely buggered'.

49
Who Ate All the Pies?

There was a short break in the season around Christmas time but when training resumed after the festivities Ralph felt the boys weren't responding to him in the same way as before and they certainly weren't playing as well. For some reason their hearts just weren't in it. They were ignoring him and finding petty issues to argue about yet they seemed to be falling over themselves to pander to Larry's slightest whim.

Larry had started to suggest that other clubs had been head-hunting him and that he might be leaving soon. Big fucking deal. By the way he announced it, you would have thought he was Kenny fucking Dalglish.

The parents were also giving Ralph a hard time, avoiding his gaze and hardly bothering to greet him in passing. They obviously had it in for him about something but he had no idea what. Nobody said anything directly and if they didn't mention it why the fuck should he? Ralph couldn't be bothered to ask any of them even though a feeling in his gut told him something serious was brewing. He asked Joe if he'd heard anything at school but the answer was negative. Oh well, it would all blow over in time. In the meantime, Ralph felt about as popular as a bloke who'd farted in a sauna.

Some of the parents used to hang around to watch the training sessions and their disapproval of Ralph was particularly obvious whenever he shouted 'Sexy football lads!' or used any sort of expletive, however mild. But Ralph knew that if you wanted the attention of eight and nine year-olds you had to work bloody hard for it and a grown-up uttering a supposedly forbidden word was an excellent way to go about it.

The kids all used those parent-sensitive words quite copiously anyway. Although not when the old codgers were around of course. If any of the little angels got kicked in the bollocks during a game they were hardly likely to say 'Ooh I say, that was rather painful. Please be more careful next time.' They were much more likely to shout 'Fucking hell you fucking bastard! I'll kick your fucking head off if you try that again you fucking cunt!' It was a purely natural reaction and although Ralph was no psychologist he thought it was probably unhealthy to suppress it. Anyway, he knew what happened when you told your kids not to swear. The more you told them, the more they did it. Good luck to them. By the way, if you were really that concerned about your kids swearing, all you had to do was tell them old people thought swearing was cool. That would shut them up straight away. Ralph and Sophie said fuck in front of their own children and hadn't noticed they'd become irreparably depraved or corrupt as a result. Let's get our priorities right for fuck's sake. It was hardly a threat to civilisation was it? In a world full of murder, killing, fighting, stealing, cheating, lying, rape, racism, war, violence, genocide and fascism surely there was enough to worry about without bursting a blood vessel over a little cussing amongst kids. After all, how bad could a swear word be? Fuck and cunt were the worst and everyone knew them so who were they trying to protect with their nonsense? No, in Ralph's book swearing was cool. Oops, he'd gone and said it.

If the parents were uptight with him it was too bad. If he didn't coach the little buggers they'd have to do it themselves and none of them knew diddly-point-shit about the game. Anyway, he was the team sponsor and he'd bought all the kit. Without him there wouldn't have been a team in the first place.

Why were they finding reasons to denigrate him? Was it really his colourful language that intimidated them or were they more worried by the way his eyes blazed with passion while trying to express an element of sporting philosophy to the lads? Not that they needed a reason. They'd made their minds up already. They just hadn't told him yet. Being honest and looking people in the eye didn't come easy to them.

Who ate all the pies?
Who ate all the pies?
You fat bastard!
You fat bastard!
You ate all the pies.
You cunt.

Ralph had noticed that it was the less well-off parents who objected most intensely to swearing and it made him mad. How dare they deny their own culture in this way? Didn't they realise swearing was a precious part of industrial working-class culture?

In their desire for some kind of prissy respectability were they now prepared to reject their own heritage and destroy this joyful form of communication born out of the factories, mines and farms where their forbears toiled?

The same parents also castigated their kids for farting and burping which they similarly regarded as beyond the pale even though it provided an endless source of joy and amusement for the little bastards. Perhaps it was all an effort to be accepted in the higher echelons of society. Big deal! Did they really believe they could elevate their social status by keeping their kids swear-free and stink-proof? If so they were making a big mistake. If you were rich you were accepted by other rich folk and if you weren't, you weren't. That was it. End of story. Fact of life. In the end, by gagging their kids and sticking large corks up their asses they tried to define respectability by being more respectable than the ostensibly respectable respectables.

Unknown to them however, the truth of the matter was that around every upper-class dinner table the air was as blue and smelly as the stilton with cussing, risqué humour and explosive farting. Fashionable behaviour in that sort of company. So if you didn't let out a few expletives or shake the building with the odd, reverberating poot every now and again you might just as well have got your coat and left. Bad luck! It was a paradox. In the respectable world nobody gave a toss about being respectable. They didn't need to because they had the money and they made the rules. Actually there was only one rule. The more money you had the more respectable you were.

Ralph believed that social status was purely in the mind. Imaginary bollocks. We should all be accepted for who we were and entirely free to behave exactly as we wished as long as we didn't interfere with anyone else. He had a speech ready for whenever someone might broach him on the subject. It went something like this.

'Take no notice of daft social rules.'

Fuck the nouveau riche! Fuck the aristocracy!

We are all equal! We are all brothers!

Let's free ourselves from all this nonsense.

Let's express the way we really feel.

Let's be free.'

But he never got the chance to use it. There was no doubt if any of those parents had got wind of his crazy ideas he would have been frog marched out of town in five minutes. In the event it took a little longer. Ralph knew nothing about small town politics. There was an ambush at the pass and he was walking straight into it. As far as his detractors were concerned he shouldn't have used that word with the kids. He was corrupting them with his sexy football.

The Beautiful Game

Scenario Two

The game has started and again you have the ball on the left, halfway into you opponents half. This time however, the left back has taken up a position seven to eight yards square of you and is unmarked, the centre forward is running diagonally at the far post taking his markers with him and leaving a huge space which the right-sided midfielder is running into. The right winger is running diagonally at the near post, the centre half has moved over behind you and the right full back has covered his position.

Now there is movement all over the place and plenty of options and the opposing defence is going spare wondering what the fuck is going to happen next.

You can play a simple square ball, or long into the box for one of the runners or, God forbid and say three Hail Marys, back to the centre half.

If you felt confident enough, you could even try lifting the ball over the player in front of you to the left-sided midfielder who has managed to get behind his marker and is heading for the by-line in space.

That's working as a team and for each other.

Football is a game of options and the more options you create the easier and more beautiful it is.

There are always plenty of options available to be created if you are interested.

And that's in life, by the way, not just football.

50
Crime of the Century

Then came the bombshell. It all blew up one Saturday morning as they gathered for a home cup semi-final against a team from another small town like Kingbury who had given them a hard game earlier in the season. Ralph knew his lads would be up for it. You could always tell. The prize was to play the cup final at Edgar Street, the famous home of Hereford United then of the Football League Third Division and it was a great motivation for the boys of both teams.

Ralph pulled up next to one of the other dads who was parking at the same time and their two boys ran off together towards the changing rooms. It was Mel, who Ralph got on with quite well and considered one of his few allies. Actually, Mel's brother was a professional player so he knew a bit about the game even though Ralph didn't think Mel had played much himself. But he always offered to run the line which no one else ever did and was generally quite supportive so he was glad to see him.

'Hello,' Ralph offered in a cheery fashion, 'And how are you today?'

At this point he had no idea what was about to unfold.

'Morning, lovely day,' Mel replied.

'Certainly is,' Ralph agreed.

'Didn't see you at the meeting,' Mel commented.

'No, too busy'.

At first, Ralph had thought Mel was referring to the monthly junior managers meeting that had been held a few days earlier. He had stopped going to them having reached the conclusion that they were a complete waste of time. Town didn't have any premises of their own so any meetings were held in the pub which was always a fatal mistake if you wanted to discuss anything seriously.

Matters would get underway fairly sensibly but then things

would deteriorate very rapidly due to the frequent breaks while people got rounds in. As a result, it always took bloody ages to get through the agenda. By the fourth pint there was never a sensible word to be had from anyone anyway. They would all be slurring their speech and talking about Manchester United and every statement was turned into a sexual innuendo that was greeted by gales of laughter.

Anything Ralph wanted to talk about would always come up in any other business right at the end and by that time everyone was either reeling about in a drunken stupor, chatting up the barmaid or fast asleep.

At one meeting, Gerry, chairman of the club's junior section, had gone round the table asking for nominations for players of the year. All the other teams made these awards towards the end of the season. Players' player of the year and manager's player of the year but Ralph was totally against them.

'No thanks very much,' he said when it came to his turn.

'What do you mean, no thanks?' asked Gerry.

'I don't want to single players out,' he replied. 'It's a team game. I'm trying to get them to play as a team. I couldn't say who's the best and I don't want to try. I certainly don't want the lads to think that I've got a favourite. Anyway, how do you compare a goalkeeper with a striker? I say we abolish the whole idea.'

You could have split the atmosphere with a knife.

Ralph could see that Larry was getting agitated. They had discussed the issue many times before. He knew Larry was in favour of these awards and had already made his own choice of player. But Ralph didn't want any of it. The lad Larry had in mind was too much of a bighead anyway and Ralph wouldn't have thought it at all healthy for the team or for him if he got a prize and his ego was inflated even further. It wouldn't have fitted inside him any more.

Ralph was already aware that it was a contentious issue because Larry and the other parents of his team had made it quite clear they were annoyed with him for refusing to have a sponsor's player of the match every week.

'I'm the fucking sponsor and I don't fucking want it,' he had told them.

All the teams had their own separate sponsors which were mostly small businesses in the town. For them it was a device to get their names in the papers. But Ralph wasn't interested in the slightest. He hadn't become the sponsor to get his name in the papers. There were plenty of other ways of doing that. Ralph sponsored the lads so that they could have a football team and a smart kit they would feel proud to run out in and so that they could learn to play the game properly. It cost a small fortune and involved a lot of work. You couldn't exactly say there was anyone queuing up to take over. What a muggins he must have been!

'But the other teams 'ave always done it,' said Larry.

Ralph could sense the groundswell of opinion against him and realised that Larry was exploiting it to say things in a situation where he had support from others because he never got anywhere in the private conversations they had.

'That doesn't mean to say that we have to do it or that they have to continue doing it,' Ralph replied.

That was one of the problems with small town life. They did things because they'd always done them. When some smart Alec outsider came along with a newfangled idea, they didn't want to listen because it was just some newfangled idea from a smart Alec outsider. Whether it was better or worse than what they had before didn't come into it.

Ralph was touching a raw nerve here and knew he was out on a limb but he'd always been one to stand up for what he believed in or in this case, what he didn't believe in.

'Look,' he said, 'I don't believe in this sort of thing and I can't think of one positive element in its favour.'

'But the lads need an incentive. Everyone does.' It was Vic 'Vicco' Morley, manager of the thirteens.

'An incentive for what?' Ralph asked incredulously.

'Well,' answered Vicco rather slowly and unconvincingly as if he was making it up on the spot. 'To play better and do well.'

'What?' asked Ralph. 'What kid needs an incentive to play

football? They'd all go out knee deep in sulphuric acid to play and you wouldn't be able to stop them. I never needed an incentive to play football when I was a kid. I was out there whenever possible until it was too dark to see the fucking ball and I didn't want any prizes for it. I played because I loved it and so do they. They don't need a fucking incentive. What they need is to be taught how to play the game properly and according to the highest level of sportsmanship.' But there were no takers.

At that point Gerry cut in, 'Well, as we've already placed an order for the cups we'll have to go ahead but as one of our managers seems to be so adamant about it we can leave his team out for now.'

It was hopeless. Ralph could see Larry seething but didn't think it was serious.

At another of these meetings Ralph had been daft enough to bring up the subject of starting a ladies team. He knew from his daughter, Natalie, that there were quite few girls who fancied playing and he also knew that the ladies game was about the fastest growing sport in the country at the time. In the end he wished he hadn't mentioned it.

After all the usual silly jokes about scoring and sharing changing rooms and rubbing liniment in and so on, he said, 'Look, though, really, there are a lots of girls who want to play and I think we should help them.'

It was as if he had placed a large bowl of porridge in the middle of the table and slapped his hand on it so that bits of the gooey mixture splattered everywhere and stuck to everyone in the room. Ralph's proposal was greeted by a deafening silence.

Perhaps they hadn't thought he was serious. Or perhaps they had.

Then Derek Jones, manager of the fifteens, tried to stand up to say something. They didn't normally stand up to speak at these meetings but for some reason, Del Boy as they called him, obviously felt that the importance of what he was about to utter was such that he had to dignify it from an upright position.

However, his attempts to achieve this were not quite so dignified. Twice he rose shakily with liquid sploshing wildly from the cider glass in his hand as he waved his arms about in an effort to steady himself. Twice he didn't make it and found himself sitting down again. His third try was more successful and he was up on his feet but weaving about in the same way as a skittle that had been dealt a glancing blow by a bowling ball and you couldn't tell if it was going to stand or fall.

Derek opened his mouth to speak and tried to point at Ralph, but unfortunately once again, he was using the hand in which he was holding his glass, tipping it forward in the process. Cider poured all over the table and cascaded off the sides into everyone's laps and they all collapsed with laughter.

'For fuck's sake Del Boy,' someone said. 'Fucking get on with it so we can all vote against and fuck off home.'

Derek mustered all his energy and brain power which even in the best circumstances shouldn't really have taken him too long.

'That'sh fuckin' shilly,' he informed Ralph in his broad Hereford accent soaked liberally with local rough cider.

'What is?' Ralph asked.

'Ladeesh fuckin' football,' said Derek.

'Why is it?' Ralph asked. He realised it would be pointless using long sentences or words with more than three letters.

'Cosh it's a fuckin' man'sh fuckin' game? announced Del boy. 'It'sh fuckin' not for the fuckin' likes of fuckin' wimin.'

And, so saying, he collapsed unconscious into the pools of stale cider on the table amid howls of uncontrollable mirth from the entire ensemble.

Ralph never bothered going again after that.

The Beautiful Game

Expletive Deleted

There is a peculiar sort of inverted respectability surrounding football, particularly in the junior game, which seems to have the dubious aim of obliterating swearing not only from the sports field but from the English language altogether. But anyone who has been around the block even once knows that there is no such thing as a serious sportsperson of any kind who doesn't swear their bollocks off constantly whilst competing at the sports field, court, track or pool. Come to think of it, there aren't many who don't swear their bollocks off most of the time whether they're playing sport or not.

Swearing is a valid form of expression in sport and in life and in many cases the only accurate way of expressing certain feelings. For anyone wishing to remain sane in this highly stressful world, swearing is a most vital activity. Indeed, the notion that respectable people don't swear is about as ridiculous as the idea harboured by some that the Queen doesn't go to the toilet.

Those who are offended by what Gazza once most eloquently referred to as 'industrial language' are just being silly. Don't they have more pressing matters to consider? Third-World debt for instance. Or the destruction of the ozone layer? Sometimes there is just no other way to accurately express what you really mean.

Expletive deleted. (Just a phrase I like).

My advice to everyone is to swear as much as you want.

So swear already! Help yourself. No charge. Enjoy it. Say what you mean and don't worry if your children copy you. Encourage them to swear too. Everyone does it. Even those who pretend to be respectable. Except they say 'sugar' when they really mean 'shit'. Or 'Frigging this that or the other' when they really meant 'Fucking this that or the other'.

Feel free, come on, all together now – 'Fuck off you cunt!'

Come on, louder – 'FUCK OFF YOU CUNT!' That's better.

51
Best For the Boys

Ralph and Mel decided to walk over and check the state of the pitch.

Wait a minute, thought Ralph, Mel's not a manager, he wouldn't have been at that meeting.

'What meeting's that then?'

'Over at United,' Mel answered. 'Didn't you know about it?'

He seemed guarded and Ralph wasn't sure if he was being straight up.

There were two clubs in the town, United and Town, they were Town. They had a first team and reserves and nine junior teams through all the age groups and Ralph was trying to start a ladies team.

United had three ropey senior teams which all played in the cloggers' leagues and no juniors at all. Town's first team played quite a few leagues higher than United's and, despite their general unfitness, only five promotions away from the football league itself. In fact, even Town's reserves played a couple of leagues above United's firsts. But United did have a small clubhouse and bar which Town didn't and this proved to be very significant. It was the only decent sports facility in the area. Neither club had an all-weather surface or floodlights or hot showers. In winter, training consisted of flailing about in the mud before it got too dark or trying to play in the carpark by the light of a 60-watt bulb straining to spread a little light through the window of the ladies toilet. It was a hopeless situation yet hundreds of lads were so keen to play that they still turned up despite the decrepit conditions.

Since getting involved with the club Ralph had spent a great deal of time and energy on a plan to obtain the finance to build a new stadium with good training and social facilities for all sports people in the town. He had also attempted to promote the idea that the two clubs should amalgamate to achieve this but eventually had to admit that it was an impossible task. There was an intense and historic rivalry between the two clubs that couldn't be forgotten or overcome. Members of the different factions obstinately refused to set aside their ancient disputes that had even split families in half. Fathers, sons and brothers would cross the road to avoid each other. Some of the people involved couldn't even bring themselves to mention the names of those on the other side let alone socialise together and belong to the same club. They just would not co-operate. It was useless to even hint at reconciliation and Ralph found it utterly depressing.

What a berk. Why hadn't he seen it coming?

They walked around pressing their toes into the pitch to test its firmness.

'No,' said Ralph, 'What was it about?'

'They want the team to go over there,' Mel said.

'What!' he exclaimed, ' To United? Why hasn't anyone asked me about it?'

'Don't know mate'

'Who was there?'

'Everybody'.

'What do you mean, everybody?'

'All the parents, the kids, their chairman, Larry, Nigel. Everybody.'

Ralph started to feel physically sick and extremely annoyed.

'They can't do that,' he said. 'This is my team. I started it, I coach it, I fund it. Christ, I've even just bought them new training tops.'

'The parents have voted to take the team over there,' said Mel.

Ralph was bloody livid.

Turning to face Mel he said, 'But you're one of the parents.'

'I just want what's best for the boys,' replied Mel avoiding his gaze. It was a phrase that Ralph was to hear repeated quite often over the ensuing period.

It turned out that United had invited all the parents and

players except Ralph, Sophie and Joe to a meeting with a view to the team changing clubs. They'd all been treated to a slap up do at United's clubhouse and bar. They'd been seduced.

Of course, the parents hadn't bothered to take into consideration the higher standard of football and coaching their kids had access to at Town. They wanted access to that bar on training nights and match days. They were like lambs to the slaughter and immediately fell prey to the deviously contrived invitation. By the end of the evening, bellies full and heads swimming in alcohol, they all decided to make sure their kids signed for United the following season. Ralph hadn't suspected a thing.

Nobody even bothered to ask him. They didn't care whether he agreed to it or not.

'What the fuck has Nigel got to do with it?' Ralph asked Mel.

'He was running the whole show.'

It all started to fall into place. Nigel Tilley (Silly Tilley as he was often referred to) was the spanner in the works and Ralph couldn't say he was surprised.

Nigel was the manager of one of Town's junior teams but he also played for United in their second team. Actually, he was United's club captain. A capricious man, the one steady element of his character was a deep suspicion of anybody he deemed an outsider and Ralph was most certainly in that category. He was top of the fucking list.

Ralph had long ago sensed that Tilley was unhappy about him, a 'newcomer' to the area, being on Town's committee when Nigel himself wasn't. But that wasn't Ralph's fault. The general feeling in the club was that Nigel could hardly expect to be on the committee at Town while he was on the committee at United. Nobody trusted him and the treachery he had engineered was clear proof of an appropriate judgement.

It was a betrayal.

There were only enough boys in the town for one team in each age group so even Tilley's kid, Adam, was in Ralph's squad. When the row broke out, it rankled with Ralph that after starting, coaching and funding a team that had enabled Adam Tilley to enjoy three years of football, that was all the fucking thanks he got.

Not that he wanted thanks. But he didn't think he deserved a knife in the back either.

But Ralph wasn't local so that didn't come into it.

THE BEAUTIFUL GAME

One and the Same

If you want to be a good team, everyone in it must think the world of each other. Under no circumstances should any player be considered on a higher level than any other.

All must be equal, even strikers. No matter how many goals any player might have scored, he can't have done it on his own.

He can't have run down the wing and crossed the ball to himself or passed it through to himself from midfield. Someone must have passed the ball to him to give him chance to score and that other person is just as important as he is.

Furthermore, while he is mincing about up front waiting for those defence-splitting passes that make it possible for him to nick all the glory and get his name in the papers he is not doing any of the other things that are just as essential to the team's success. Like making the tackle which prevents the other side getting forward or flinging himself through the air to make a daring save which denies the other side a scoring chance. Others are doing those things and they are just as important as he is.

Football is a team game and leaving the field of play with your mates after a hard game knowing that you have achieved something together is the best feeling possible and perhaps even the entire purpose of the exercise.

Lauding individual players is therefore most detrimental to the whole idea.

Even Ronaldo can't play by himself.

52
Santana and Kissinger

Ralph made his way back to the car park and noticed Larry just arriving. He ran over to where the Judas was parking and even before the car had stopped moving rapped on the window and shouted 'What's all this about a fucking meeting?'

Larry pulled on the hand-brake, wound down the window and said 'What?'

'What's all this about a fucking meeting?' Ralph repeated.

'What meeting?' Larry asked. He seemed a bit sheepish.

'The meeting at United,' Ralph shouted.

'It's nothing to do with me.'

'But you were there.'

'I was invited to a meeting, yeah.'

'And you didn't think of telling me about it?'

'It's nothing to do with me,' said Larry. 'I just want what's best for the boys.'

His own boys were in the back of the car. Gary and Barry. They could see Ralph was in a state and were laughing at him. He felt like slapping them round the face.

'You want to teach them some fucking manners,' he said.

'It's nothing to do with me.'

Just then Ralph watched as another car drove up quite fast, skidded a few yards and came to an abrupt halt in a cloud of dust right in the middle of the car park without parking properly. It was Gerry, chairman of the club's junior section. He leaped out of the car leaving the door open and walked hurriedly towards Ralph.

'There's been a fucking meeting,' he announced breathlessly as he approached.

'I know there fucking has.'

'United want to nick all our fucking juniors'.

'I know they fucking do.'

'I've spoken to Les and Bulldog and we've agreed to kick Larry and Nigel out of the fucking club,' said Gerry. 'It's the only way.'

It occurred to Ralph that Club Chairman Les Cartwright and First team Manager 'Bulldog' Bevan took it upon themselves to make a number of democratic decisions on behalf of the club that members never knew about.

Ralph remembered an evening at the Railway Tavern shortly after he had been elected to the committee. It had turned into a sort of initiation ceremony. They had talked about football, women and the relative merits of various alcoholic beverages until way into the small hours. About an hour or so after the beer had been discarded in favour of the single malt, Les had set out his primary philosophy of life to Ralph after gaining his assurance of the strictest secrecy.

'The thing ish,' he confided in a slow drawl as his knees started to buckle. 'If you want shomthing done properly.' He was tottering. 'Do it your fucking shelf.' And fell drunk on the floor.

'Les and Bully are on their way here now,' said Gerry.

'What for?'

'A meeting'

'Oh great,' said Ralph, 'What's the point of a fucking meeting if you've already decided?'

'It's got to be fucking democratic,' said Gerry, 'You've got to have your say.'

'But if you've already made a decision it won't make any fucking difference. You all out-vote me anyway.'

'I know,' answered Gerry. 'But it must be fucking democratic.'

A fairly large cavalcade of cars now approached. Ralph wondered if it was Henry Kissinger on his way to negotiate a settlement but it was the opposition team.

To the rear he also noticed Les's car. He had Bulldog Bevan with him. They both looked grim faced as they pulled in. Les and Bulldog parked and walked over to Ralph.

'United are trying to nick our fucking teams,' said Les.

'Really.'

Although it had been quite bright and sunny when they

arrived it was now turning quite windy, gloomy and cold and there was snow in the air. It occurred to Ralph that it was god sympathising with his ever-darkening mood. 'Don't be silly,' he told himself.

By this time, the parents of the team were huddled at the other end of the car park with Larry and they all seemed to be in deep discussion.

'Right,' said Les to Gerry, Bulldog and Ralph. 'We all know the fucking position, I move we expel Larry and Nigel from the club.'

'What?' said Ralph, 'Just like that without considering other possibilities?'

Les turned to Gerry, 'I thought you said we were all in agreement.'

'I didn't have time to get everyone's agreement,' said Gerry.

'I don't agree,' said Ralph.

'Well it don't make no fucking difference,' Bulldog chimed in. 'You're outvoted anyway.'

'But I thought it had to be democratic.'

'It is,' said Les. 'We're just going to vote on it.'

'But without a discussion?' Ralph queried.

'But it don't make no fucking difference if we've decided and you're outvoted,' said Gerry.

'I think it's too hasty,' said Ralph. 'Can't we talk to them. Try and sort something out?'

'You can't talk to them, they're fucking pathetic,' said Bulldog. 'Why do you think Larry couldn't hold a wife? He's a long streak of piss. The best part of him ran down his old man's leg.'

Of course, what Ralph hadn't known at the time was that Larry's ex-wife was actually Bulldog's sister.

'Well I want it recorded that I've taken no part in this decision,' Ralph insisted.

'Look,' said Les, 'I understand how you feel but you must accept the facts. Approaching players from another club in the middle of a season without permission is a clear breach of FA rules.'

'Has anyone seen the local paper this week?' asked Bulldog.

'Larry's got a fucking ad in there advertising for players for United.'

Ralph was shocked. He'd helped Larry. He thought they were mates.

'Well that's another breach of rules,' said Les. 'Right, that's it, he's got to go.'

'I'll go and tell the others,' said Gerry and he made his way over to the other corner of the car park. A few minutes later he was back.

'The parents won't let the boys play the match if Larry's kicked out of the club.'

'And deny them the chance to get to the final?' asked Les.

'It's parent power over there at the moment.'

'What do the boys say?' Ralph asked Gerry.

'Dunno, haven't asked them. The parents 'ave shooed 'em off somewhere.'

'Okay, look,' said Ralph. 'I resign. I resign as manager of the team, and as a director and as a member of the club. I can really do without all this bollocks.'

'You don't want to let those assholes push you out,' said Bulldog.

'I only got involved to help the lads learn how to play the game. Obviously they don't want me so there's no point in continuing.'

'I thought you were made of tougher stuff.'

'I can do without it.'

'Who's going to take the team out then?' asked Gerry.

'There's no time to get anyone else now,' said Les.

'Let Larry take them,' said Ralph. 'Sort it out later. The boys don't deserve to lose out because of all this fucking nonsense.'

'And let the bastards get away with it?' asked Bulldog.

'No one will get away with anything,' Ralph answered. 'It's the boys that are important. They'll be gutted if they don't play the match.'

Les was on strict orders to get home in time to take his wife shopping and drove off.

Bulldog had the unenviable task of rounding up his first team players which meant dragging them all out of bed and filling them up with coffee to ward off the alcoholic excesses of the night before so off he went too.

All of a sudden Ralph was left alone wondering what the fuck had happened.

Forty minutes earlier he had been as excited as the lads as he prepared for the match. Since he'd woken that morning his head had been full of nothing else. Who to pick, which tactics to use, composing his dressing room speech in which he always attempted to motivate the boys with a mixture of humour and sporting philosophy. Now he felt drained and empty and the day before him offered a prospect as bleak as the weather had now become. In fact, it had turned extremely chilly and the rain was becoming heavier. It matched his mood exactly.

Ralph walked over to his car. In the far corner of the car park there seemed to be an uproar going on with parents shouting, Larry gesticulating and Gerry shrugging his shoulders as if to say 'Well, it's not my fault.'

He placed a Santana cassette in the tape player and tried to cheer himself up. Sitting in the driver's seat, Ralph gazed out over the rain-swept pitches feeling pretty depressed.

But Santana did it every time for him. In the bigger scheme of things this didn't matter at all he told himself.

Just then the passenger door opened and his son Joe slid into the seat next to him.

'What's going on Dad?' he asked in a worried tone of voice.

'I don't really know. I think it's just grown ups being silly.'

'They say you got Larry kicked out of the club.'

'No, that's wrong.'

'But why do they want the team to go over to United then?'

'I don't know,' answered Ralph. 'It's nothing to do with me.'

The Beautiful Game

Whistle Blowers

Play to the whistle. Even if the flag is up, don't assume a ball is out until that whistle goes. Don't assume it's offside, whether you're attacking or defending, until the ref blows up. Continue playing at full pace until you know for sure that play has been stopped.

You see it all the time. Defenders stopped with their hands in the air, like kids in the classroom who want to go to the toilet, appealing for offside.

The ref waves play on, the opposing forward is already behind you and goes on to score. That's your fault even if the ref made a mistake. You stopped and let them through because you assumed too much.

Don't stop until you hear that fucking whistle.

Don't just assume something has happened. Be sure about it.

And that's in life by the way. Not just football.

53
Playing for Laughs

Ralph never went back to coaching youngsters but he still played in a kickabout game on Astroturf once a week throughout the year although he sometimes wondered why the fuck he bothered because the churlish behaviour of some of the other players never failed to make him angry and frustrated.

Most of them were either professional people, business owners or clever-trousers students who, to all intents and purposes, seemed quite normal. In the pub afterwards with a pint of ale to hand they could be amusing, interesting and clearly not without some intelligence. But as soon as any of them stepped onto a football pitch they appeared to undergo a strange and dramatic metamorphosis from decent, socially aware gentlefolk into idiotic selfish, egotistic fiends. All of a sudden they were involved in some sort of personal agenda. A game of their own.

Anyone who has played on Astroturf knows that it is a flat, true, fast surface which, whatever the weather, is absolutely perfect for the passing game. But these tactically-challenged morons refused to pass the ball unless they were absolutely forced to do so and that was only when they found themselves in trouble after making an almighty cock-up of some sort. In that situation, the only sort of pass Ralph got was a hurried, crap lay-off which only had the effect of putting him trouble too. Whenever this happened, the dickhead whose stupidity caused it would invariably make some sort of impatient gesture, such as throwing his arms in the air or sighing heavily or raising his eyebrows as if to suggest that it was Ralph's fault they'd lost the ball.

Bloody infuriating.

It was almost as if they were saying 'Why do I bother to pass to this idiot when he can't play?' Big-headed bastards. Ralph sometimes wondered if they adopted the same approach in their relationships with womenfolk: 'Just lie still while I have a fuck. It won't take long. I'll let you know if I need you to do anything.'

The concept of combining their energies to achieve something beautiful together was completely lost on these ignorant troglodytes. The very idea of passing and teamwork was anathema to them. If they took a word association test they would probably link the word 'pass' with the words 'failure' or 'last resort' or 'impotence' or 'homosexual'.

Whenever they got the ball they just ran forward and attempted to dribble round anyone who attempted to tackle them. Their only other 'tactic', but only after running down a blind alley and getting stuck, was a speculative shot at the tiny, five-a-side goal from absolutely miles out. Of course, there were always loads of better options staring them right in the fucking face but these usually involved a simple pass, the idea of which seemed to fill the mad bastards with absolute horror. Somehow, it just wouldn't compute properly in their minds that their mates were all around them and that a pass, even a short square one, was not some sort of disgrace but an honour. The proper way to play. Why the fuck did they think there were eleven players in a team? What the fuck were the others there for? But no, they wanted to win the game all by their fucking selves. Once they got themselves into a position where the only way out was to pass, it was as if they had a mental seizure or a piece of their brain had gone missing. Lights flashed in their brain, sirens whined in their head and messages began to flash in their eyes like a computer when it went on the blink. 'Disk full!' or 'This command is unavailable at present'.

Automatically a strange, blank expression flooded their faces and they became possessed by dark, satanic forces that sucked all decency and common sense from their beings. They were in league with the devil!

They knew they should have passed and deep down they may have wanted to pass. But they just could not bring themselves to unilaterally slip the ball to another player because it was too much of a challenge to their manhood to admit that they couldn't hang on to it without help.

Ralph found it quite insulting not to say extremely boring if he was unlucky enough to find himself on the same side as any of these loner, self-styled, selfish, individualist, superstar, think-I-can-do-it-all-by-myself types. The problem was that most of the players were like this.

Ralph would be going spare for the team as usual. Running off the ball, finding space, tracking back to help out in defence, making himself available for a pass. Yet all the bigheaded gits would do is shout at him when he didn't pass to them even though they consistently refused to lay the ball off to anyone else. As if a ghastly, incurable sickness was driving them to achieve some sort of personal, glorious gratification. Wankers!

Ralph wanted to knock their heads together. It was like trying to communicate with his mates in the Adelphi all those years ago. Were we never going to discover the delights of simple, joyful teamwork? Would we never understand that the possibilities of people working together were far greater than the sum of possibilities of those same people working independently?

Of course, anyone who really understood the game knew that there was nothing more gratifying to the team as a whole than one of its members, anyone, scoring a goal as a result of a passing move that involved everyone running off the ball, finding space and working together as a single unit for the common good.

Actually, it occurred to Ralph that there was one thing more gratifying but you couldn't really do it as a team. Well, maybe you could but that was the subject for another book.

THE BEAUTIFUL GAME

*Open Letter to the Person in Charge,
The Football Association, London.*

Dear Sir or Madam,

I wish to apply for the post of England Manager.

I have played and watched football for over forty years and coached a junior side for three and a half years before being booted out in wholly unfair circumstances similar to those in which Gianluca Vialli was given the old Spanish archer from Chelsea by Ken Bates. (El Bow. Geddit?)

I realise that my limited international experience and the fact that I haven't actually played or managed in a professional capacity is likely to put me at a slight disadvantage when compared with people like Bobby Robson or Terry Venables for example. However, as the great Italian international coach Arrigo Saachi once said, 'You don't have to have been a horse to be a good jockey.'

Anyway, it is not on this aspect of my qualifications that I wish my application to be considered but rather on the revolutionary style of play that I have devised for future England teams. Accordingly, I propose that the selection procedure should adopt the following guidelines:

Goalkeeper: No problem. We have always had many excellent goalies so we pick the most in form player at any particular time.

Defenders: Only two players with sole responsibility for defending are required. These should be in the stylish, ball carrying mould of Bobby Moore, Franz Beckenbaur, Franco Baresi or Socrates who can not only tackle hard and read the game expertly enough to work a zonal system but also posses sufficient skill to be able to carry the ball forward and pass accurately.

Centre Forward: We will select the current most prolific goal-scorer at any particular time with the second most prolific on the bench.

The Rest: All the other players will be the most skilful and talented ball players at our disposal. They will take to the pitch with no particular instructions other than to combine together, apply their football instincts, express themselves, enjoy it, and use all their talent and skill to the limits of their ability.

That's it.

An example of such a team might be as follows:

Goalkeeper: Peter Shilton.

Defenders: Bobby Moore, Rio Ferdinand.

Centre Forward: Jimmy Greaves.

The Rest: Paul Gascoigne, Glen Hoddle, Johny Haynes, Matt Le Tissier, John Barnes, Rodney Marsh, David Beckham.

Bench: Gordon Banks, Peter Beardsley, Chris Waddle, Michael Owen, Joe Cole, Steve McManaman, Darren Anderton, Tony Adams, Bobby Charlton, Bryan Douglas.

I submit that the psychological effect on the opponents of such a team would be similar to that of facing any of the great Brazil sides of the past.

'Jairzinho's got the ball. Fuck it. Oh fuck, he's passed to Rivelino, this is worse. Fuck, he's laid it to Tostao. What the fuck shall we do? Fucking hell, Pelé's got it. Help!'

I am convinced this method will enable us to play free, beautiful, fantastic football on the same level as the best teams that have ever existed which were of course those wonderful Brazil sides of the sixties and seventies and the 'Total Football' teams of Johann Cruyff and his Dutch team-mates in the seventies.

In this way we can start to balance the speed, strength and athleticism of our current team with the skill, vision and imagination that is sorely lacking not only in football but in life generally. What we need is some sexy football. I am sure we all agree about that.

There is much work to do and I suggest we get cracking as soon as possible.

I am available immediately and will work for nothing although I will need some out-of-pocket expenses.

In the circumstances I would appreciate a response at your very earliest convenience so that I can start making arrangements for an international scouting recognisance mission starting with Brazil when they are next at home in Rio De Janeiro.

Yours etc.

Ralph Goldstein